continued . . .

Riding Wild

"Hot, sexy romantic suspense at its best."

—Lora Leigh, *New York Times* bestselling author

"Forget about a cool glass of water; break out the ice! Each page will leave you panting for more." —*Romantic Times* (Top Pick)

"A wild ride is exactly what you will get with this steamy romantic caper. This sexy and sizzling-hot story will leave you breathless and wanting more." —*Fresh Fiction*

"A nonstop thrill ride from the first page to the last! Grab a copy of *Riding Wild* and take your own ride on the wild side of life!"

—*Romance Junkies*

"What an exciting and wonderful book!" —*The Romance Studio*

"*Riding Wild* is a must-read for anyone who loves sexy romances filled with plenty of action and suspense." —*Kwips and Kritiques*

Further praise for the work of

Jaci Burton

"Burton delivers it all in this hot story—strong characters, an exhilarating plot and scorching sex—and it all moves at a breakneck pace . . . You'll be drawn so fully into her characters' world that you won't want to return to your own." —*Romantic Times*

"Realistic dialogue, spicy bedroom scenes and a spitfire heroine make this one to pick up and savor." —*Publishers Weekly*

"Jaci Burton delivers."

—Cherry Adair, *New York Times* bestselling author

"Lively and funny . . . The sex is both intense and loving; you can feel the connection that both the hero and heroine want to deny in every word and touch between them. I cannot say enough good things about this book."
—*The Road to Romance*

"Exciting, intense. A ride you don't want to miss. [It] will leave you breathless."
—Lora Leigh, *New York Times* bestselling author

"A fabulous read. [Burton] delivers in every possible way."
—*A Romance Review*

"Sizzling-hot sex that will have you panting. I highly recommend this story to anyone looking for a hot read."   —*The Romance Studio*

"One hot novel that I could not put down until the last word. This story has it all: mind-boggling sex, unique and unforgettable characters and a wonderful plot that will grip your heart . . . Raw, dynamic, explosive. Wow!"
—*Just Erotic Romance Reviews*

bound, branded, & brazen

Jaci Burton

heat | new york

THE BERKLEY PUBLISHING GROUP
Published by the Penguin Group
Penguin Group (USA) Inc.
375 Hudson Street, New York, New York 10014, USA
Penguin Group (Canada), 90 Eglinton Avenue East, Suite 700, Toronto, Ontario M4P 2Y3, Canada
(a division of Pearson Penguin Canada Inc.)
Penguin Books Ltd., 80 Strand, London WC2R 0RL, England
Penguin Group Ireland, 25 St. Stephen's Green, Dublin 2, Ireland (a division of Penguin Books Ltd.)
Penguin Group (Australia), 250 Camberwell Road, Camberwell, Victoria 3124, Australia
(a division of Pearson Australia Group Pty. Ltd.)
Penguin Books India Pvt. Ltd., 11 Community Centre, Panchsheel Park, New Delhi—110 017, India
Penguin Group (NZ), 67 Apollo Drive, Rosedale, North Shore 0632, New Zealand
(a division of Pearson New Zealand Ltd.)
Penguin Books (South Africa) (Pty.) Ltd., 24 Sturdee Avenue, Rosebank, Johannesburg 2196,
South Africa

Penguin Books Ltd., Registered Offices: 80 Strand, London WC2R 0RL, England

This book is an original publication of The Berkley Publishing Group.

This is a work of fiction. Names, characters, places, and incidents either are the product of the author's imagination or are used fictitiously, and any resemblance to actual persons, living or dead, business establishments, events, or locales is entirely coincidental. The publisher does not have any control over and does not assume any responsibility for author or third-party websites or their content.

BOUND, BRANDED, & BRAZEN

PRINTING HISTORY
Heat trade paperback edition / March 2010

Library of Congress Cataloging-in-Publication Data

Burton, Jaci.
Bound, branded, & brazen / Jaci Burton.—1st ed.
   p.   cm.
   ISBN 978-0-425-23269-9
   I. Sisters—Fiction. II. Women ranchers—Fiction. III. Ranchers—Fiction. IV. Title.
   PS3602.U776B68 2010
   813'.6—dc22
                2009041103

PRINTED IN THE UNITED STATES OF AMERICA

10 9 8 7 6 5 4 3 2 1

To my husband, Charlie,
the roughest, toughest cowboy a woman
ever had the luck to fall in love with.
You are and always have been my hero.

acknowledgments

To my editor, Kate Seaver—thank you for the time you spent brainstorming this book. Your ideas and insights are so helpful and I always enjoy plotting books with you.

To my agent, Kimberly Whalen—thank you for all that you do to keep me sane, even when I'm a giant pain in the butt. Which I know is often.

To the Writeminded Readers—you are all heroines in so many ways. Thank you for always being there when I need a smile, a laugh and a pick-me-up.

To some very amazing women who have done some very special things for me: Fatin, Jamie and Azteclady—"thank you" just never seems like enough.

To Maya Banks, who talks me down off the ledge more than anyone I know. You have no idea how much I appreciate your always being there to listen.

bound

one

valerie mcmasters didn't know if the old adage "you can't go home again" was true or not, but as far as she was concerned, the thought of home made her want to turn tail and run like hell. Yet here she was, pulling into the Bar M Ranch, a place she swore she'd never come back to again.

She parked her car under the giant blackjack oak tree, several steps back from the sprawling, two-story white frame house where she'd lived since she was born. It had been two long years since she'd last been here. She wanted to get a full-on view of the place, to take it in like a picture.

The late afternoon sun rained down on the gray-shingled roof, highlighting the three gabled windows arranged in neat order along the second story. Her, Brea's and Jolene's bedrooms. When they were kids, all three of them had climbed out those windows at night and sat on the slanted roof to watch the stars and talk.

Shaking off the memories, Valerie grabbed her suitcases out of the trunk, walked through the front door, set her bags down in the gleaming, polished hall and realized that it wouldn't have mattered how long she'd been gone.

Nothing would ever change at the Bar M Ranch. Not the layout of the house, the dusty ride up the long road, the mooing cows greeting her as she took the winding drive along the property line or the barking dogs that wound through her legs as she maneuvered her way to the front door.

The only thing different today was that her uncle Ronald was dead. She wouldn't have to deal with his disapproving looks and his condemnation, or hear his lectures about how she should have stayed on the ranch and how disappointed her parents would have been in her for leaving.

Not that his opinion on things had ever mattered to her anyway. He'd always been full of shit and she'd been old enough to know better. Her parents had loved her. They would have wanted what was best for her, would have understood why she left. Uncle Ronald never knew her at all, never understood how hard it was for her to be here. No one understood.

His funeral was tomorrow. Not that she'd shed a tear for the old bastard, even if he was her father's brother. She'd cried enough when her parents had died, when she and her sisters had to have a double funeral and put both their mother and father in the ground on the same day.

That was the last time she had cried. She hadn't even shed a tear when she packed up and left her husband, left this ranch, left her sisters behind.

She hadn't looked back. Hadn't come back. Not in two long years.

Until now. The only reason she was here was because Jolene had called her, told her she was now one third owner of the Bar M, and she'd better get her ass here for the funeral and help figure out what they were going to do about the ranch once and for all. Jolene had demanded Brea and Valerie give her a month to figure things out.

A month! Like Valerie had that kind of time. But Jolene could be relentless, and yes, she and Brea had kind of abandoned their baby sister to deal with the house, the land, the cattle and everything else. They'd even left Jolene to deal with Uncle Ronald, so they kind of owed her. So Valerie had agreed. Not because she wanted to come back here. Not because she had a stake in the Bar M. As far as Valerie was concerned, the ranch and all it contained belonged to Jolene now. That was going to be her decision and nothing was going to change that.

She had a good life in Dallas and a career that was just about to take off. None of her old life here on the ranch mattered anymore. She'd kissed it all good-bye the day she'd told Mason she wanted a divorce. Then she'd run like hell and hadn't looked back. Hadn't come back.

Until now.

She took a deep breath, unable to hold back a smile at the smell of furniture polish and Pine-Sol. Old memories, old scents. Something was in the oven in the kitchen, the fresh smell making her stomach rumble. She hadn't eaten this morning when she left Dallas, had just grabbed a latte as she drove through Starbucks on her way out of town.

She climbed the long staircase with her bags in hand, walked down the hall to her bedroom and opened the door.

Yeah, some things never changed. The room was exactly as she'd left it, the bronze lace curtains billowing in the breeze from the open windows, the hope chest that had belonged to her mother sitting just underneath the window. The top of the old, scarred chest was always adorned with fresh flowers thanks to Lila, their housekeeper—"manager" was more appropriate, since Lila took care of everything related to the house. The dresser and nightstand gleamed as if freshly polished.

Valerie stared down at the queen-sized bed that Mason had always complained wasn't long enough, that his feet hung over the edge. Though they'd had plenty of room to make love. She stared at the patchwork quilt, remembered how she and Mason would kick it down to the end of the bed every night during their tussles together.

There had been so many things wrong with their marriage, but the sex? That had been oh so right. She still remembered the feel of his unshaven jaw rubbing against the skin of her face. She used to love his scratchy beard, would slide her palm across his jaw because it made her tingle all over.

And his kisses—good Lord the man could kiss. Even now, years later, she had vivid memories of his mouth on hers, the fullness of his lips, the taste of sweat and outdoors and the earthy scent of him whenever he came in from working cattle. He was such a . . . man. He felt like one and smelled like one and God he could turn her knees to jelly.

He was so masterful at what he did, as if he'd been born to pleasure a woman. And even when she'd been young and inexperienced and asked him to take it slow, she'd felt the fires of passion barely banked inside him, and knew how explosive his desires were.

His touch on her breasts, between her legs, the way he could coax her to orgasm faster than a brushfire in the hot, dry summer . . .

She shuddered. Two long years of drought, without a man, without Mason. And just thinking about him could light that flame again.

There were a lot of reasons she'd divorced Mason Parks, but sex definitely hadn't been one of them. If there'd been a way she could still jump that man's bones, without the ties of marriage, she'd have been on him in a heartbeat.

But somehow walking out on your husband and serving him with divorce papers didn't make that man look kindly on his ex-wife or in any way make him want to swoop her up and give her an orgasm.

"I heard you were coming in today."

She pivoted, her heart in her throat as she faced the man she'd just been reminiscing about, and reminiscing in a decidedly sexual way, too.

Two years hadn't changed him much. Still tall, still with that unshaven look, still wearing dusty blue jeans, cowboy boots and a work shirt with the sleeves rolled up, showing off impossibly muscled forearms. He took off his cowboy hat and ran his fingers through his hair. Yeah, everything was still the same. His hair was still brown, his eyes the same color as his hair, and he still goddamned took her breath away.

"Hi, Mason."

"Val."

He swaggered into the room—because he didn't even walk like a normal man. More like a man who commanded a woman to look at him. And really, what woman wouldn't?

She stood frozen to the spot as he circled the bed and moved toward her. Her first thought—run. Run like hell. Her heart started pounding as he stopped in front of her.

"Jolene said she'd asked you to come."

"Yes."

He cocked his head to the side. "Didn't think you would."

"Why not?"

"Because you couldn't wait to get away from here. And when you left you said you'd never be back."

Damn him for remembering. "I'm here for the funeral."

"You hated Ronald."

"I'm here for Jolene."

He arched a brow. "Seems to me that Jolene asked you plenty of times to come. And you didn't. Why now?"

She shrugged, clasping her hands together so he wouldn't see them shake. "It's time Jolene and Brea and I settle a few things about the ranch."

"You could do that by phone and mail."

She circled around him, moved toward the window, needing

some air to clear her head. Being near Mason jumbled her brain cells, made her think of the past, of what she'd missed. She finally turned to face him. "I didn't come back here to argue with you, Mason."

"No, you never liked doing that, did you? God forbid you should say what was on your mind."

He moved in on her again, trapping her between him and the window.

She lifted her gaze to him. "I'm not going to do this with you."

He didn't say anything for a few seconds, then, "So you're finally a doctor. It's been a long time for you."

"Yes it has."

"You worked hard for it. I guess you'll get exactly what you wanted, won't you?"

Not everything. "Yes, I will."

They used to be married. She used to throw her arms around him whenever she saw him, kiss his neck, feel the beat of his heart as he pressed against her. She loved when he held her. It made her feel safe.

She'd never have that feeling anymore, would never feel his body slide against hers in the darkness, would never see his naked silhouette walk across the bedroom at night.

Funny that she never had to think about those things, never had to miss them—until now. Which was why she avoided coming home. Too many memories. Too much pain here. Too much Mason. She inhaled, the scent of leather and horses and him filling her, reminding her of what she'd walked away from.

She shouldn't have come. She was weak where Mason was concerned, always was. And the way he looked at her. She knew he hated her for what she'd done, for walking away, and yet passion raged in his eyes as he bore down on her.

"Valerie."

He took another step closer. She laid her palm on his chest. The contact was electric and her knees went to jelly. "Mason. Don't."

He slid his arm around her and jerked her against his chest. "Don't what? Don't hate you for leaving me? Don't hate myself for still wanting you? You swore you'd never come back, but here you are, and I see the look in your eyes. You want this as much as I do."

His mouth came crashing down on hers and she whimpered, didn't so much as offer up a weak resistance. Her hand curled around the nape of his neck as she fell against him, opened her lips to him, found his tongue and nearly wept with the joy of it. Every single damn reason for how wrong this was fled, replaced by need and rampant desire for the man she'd hungered for these long two years.

His hand found her breast and latched onto it, tweaking her nipple through her shirt and bra. She damned her clothing and moaned against his lips, arching against his hand, aching for his touch. His erection, hard and insistent, pressed against her hip. She slid her hand between them, palming his cock until he groaned and slid his hand under her shirt, under her bra. And when his fingers found her nipple she cried out against his mouth.

"Yes," she whispered. "Yes." She wanted them both naked. She wanted him hard and heavy and thick and pounding inside her right now.

"Goddammit, Valerie." He was panting as he dragged her over to the bed and threw her on it. She'd always loved his passion and his driving, can't-wait-for-it need for her. She pulled off her T-shirt and swallowed as he reached for his belt buckle.

A door slammed downstairs, and like a cold bucket of water thrown over her, it slapped her back into reality.

And he knew it. His hand stilled. She scooted back on the bed, put her shirt on.

"No. I can't do this."

Mason's eyes drifted shut for a fraction of a second, and when he opened them again, fury blasted her.

"Did you do this on purpose?"

Her eyes widened and shock spread through her. "Are you serious? Why would I do that?"

He grabbed his hat and took a deep breath. "I don't know, Val. I've never been able to figure out why the hell you do anything. But it wouldn't surprise me for you to throw yourself at me, fire me up, then douse the fire just like that." He snapped his fingers.

"Oh! Are you out of your friggin' mind? Or possibly just plain stupid? Couldn't you feel my reaction?"

He shrugged as he reached the door to her room. "Hell, for all I know you always faked it."

Fury made her blood boil. She grabbed a pillow from her bed and threw it at him. "You son of a bitch."

His lips curled. "That's more like it. Welcome home, Val."

After he left, she stared in shock at the closed door, unable to fathom what had just happened.

Passion had always flared hot and heavy between them. But so had anger. And now she was riled up, horny and felt wretchedly guilty for having stirred up the hornet's nest.

Shit.

She knew she should have never come home. This was going to be a disaster.

mason parks let the screen door bang shut behind him, the sound echoing in his ears as he hopped on his horse and rode the pasture, letting the cool spring breeze clear his head.

Stupid move.

He'd been riding near the fence line, had seen the car pull up. His horse just found its way to the front of the house. He should have known better than to go in, to walk up those stairs, to go into her room—what had once been *their* room.

To see her standing beside that bed was like tumbling back to the past. Time had frozen.

She'd lost some weight. She was still beautiful, her golden brown hair teasing her chin, her green eyes still wary. Valerie had always had secrets. The one thing that had kept them apart was her inability to tell him what was really on her mind, to open up about how she felt—about anything—but especially about him. In the end he couldn't live with that silence, figured he deserved better.

And yet there he stood in her room, welcoming her back with his mouth and his hands. He'd been all over her like a goddamned dog in heat. Thinking what, that maybe she'd changed? Not fucking likely. He knew better. She was incapable.

Maybe he'd expected that after two years he wouldn't care anymore, that seeing her wouldn't be a gut punch of emotion and need. That time would have healed his desire for her, his love for her.

For Christ's sake, he was a man. Nothing weakened him. He hadn't cried since he'd broken his arm when he was four years old. He was the toughest son of a bitch on the Bar M. Nothing brought him to his knees.

Except this one woman. The one woman he'd loved since he was sixteen years old.

The one woman who could never manage to love him back.

"miss valerie!"

It had taken her a good half hour to pull herself together after that visit from Mason, to feel like she could face her family. Determined not to spend the day hiding in her room, she'd washed her face and firmly pushed Mason out of her mind. Valerie stepped off the bottom stair and ran toward Lila, the family housekeeper, the matriarch of this place. The pain in her stomach dissolved, replaced by pure joy.

Lila had been here . . . forever, had taken over caring for Valerie and her sisters after their parents died. Lila ran this house, kept the men in line, cooked, cleaned, and had become her substitute mother when, at age fifteen, Valerie's world had shattered.

She threw her arms around Lila's wide frame and hugged her tight. She inhaled Lila's scent, always a mixture of cleaning products and baking flour.

"Lila. It's so good to see you."

Lila squeezed her hard. "Girl, you're like a stranger."

Lila was right. She felt like a stranger in her own home. It had been twelve years since she left for college, and two years since she and Mason had divorced. And in between those times she'd barely been here. Even when she and Mason . . .

Well, no sense in dwelling on that.

Lila pulled back. "Let me look at you."

Used to the woman's examinations, she stood still and waited.

"You don't eat enough."

She was used to hearing that, too. According to Lila, if you didn't consume at least an entire cow a day, you weren't eating enough. "I eat just fine. I exercise. I drink a lot of water."

"Bah." Lila waved her hand in the air, dismissing Valerie's claims of health. "Come with me. I just made biscuits."

Already imagining the five pounds about to be added to her butt, Valerie went willingly to the kitchen, which was, as always, spotlessly clean despite all the mud and dirt dragged in by cowboys several times a day. Lila was a godsend, though she was getting on in years. Valerie wondered if Jolene had given any thought to bringing in help for Lila. Lila had to be in her late sixties by now, and the kitchen was enormous, the size of many home's entire first levels. The wood floor gleamed like it had just been polished, the granite countertop sparkled from end to end, and Valerie was certain she could see herself in the chrome sinks.

"Go help yourself to some juice," Lila said as she scooped out two biscuits from the platter on the center island.

Valerie opened the oversized refrigerator—stocked to overflowing as always—poured a glass of orange juice and took a seat at the trestle table that had been in her father's family for generations. She smoothed her hand over the scarred surface, each groove reminding her of times spent with her parents and sisters. She still remembered eating at one of the smaller tables when she was a child, wishing she could be at the "big table" with the grown-ups, where sounds of raucous laughter could be heard as the cowboys traded stories from their days.

Now she was one of the grown-ups and she longed for the simpler times of her youth. Times when her father would pull up a chair at her table, play with her pigtails and kiss her cheek. Or her mother would eat her meal with the girls and leave the men to their stories.

But you could never go back, and remembering just hurt.

"Here," Lila said, setting down a plate of two homemade biscuits, butter and jelly that no doubt Lila had also made herself.

Valerie's stomach rumbled. As a doctor, she was used to going a long time without food. During her internship and residency, she'd gotten used to grabbing a quick energy bar or chocolate milk on the run. To actually sit down and eat was a luxury. Though now that she was about to go into private practice with a group of general practitioners in Dallas, she was going to be able to have more regular hours again. She looked forward to it.

She bit into the buttered and jellied biscuit and let out a soft moan while she chewed. "Oh, Lila. This is heaven."

Lila's weathered face brightened when she grinned. "Thank you, honey. You know how much I used to love cookin' for you girls. Jolene eats her fair share though."

Valerie waved a biscuit in Lila's direction. "Yeah, and she works off every calorie wrestling those cows." Damn Jolene's skinny little ass anyway.

"That she does. The girl gets in there and does as much as the men do. Sometimes I think she's going to work herself to death."

"I doubt that. Jolene's always been a bundle of energy, and she's been working the ranch since Daddy set her on her first horse as soon as she could stand upright."

Lila laughed. "Well, you know that's the rancher's way. Put your kids out there among the horses and cattle as soon as they're old enough to sit a horse."

"I remember." Valerie had ridden her own horse at age four, though under close supervision from her father. Each of the girls had followed in succession. Living on a working cattle ranch meant as soon as you were old enough, you were taught to get in there and work. Fun when you were young, and not as much work, but you had to live the life. She'd loved it.

Until the accident.

Which she didn't want to dwell on. "Where is Jolene, anyway?"

"Out riding the north pasture today. They're bringing in some of the pairs."

"Ah. How many mamas had babies this year?"

Lila shrugged. "No tellin' until they bring 'em in."

"Guess I'm here at the right time, then."

"The right time for what?"

Valerie looked up to see her younger sister, Brea, standing in the doorway. At least she thought it was Brea. Valerie hardly recognized her.

Brea sure looked different than she had the last time Valerie had seen her. As a child, Brea had always worn her hair short. Now it was long, stringy, her bangs so overgrown they hid her eyes. And her ankle-length skirt and equally shapeless blouse covered her body completely. It was almost as if she was trying to hide herself.

Valerie rose from the table and went over and hugged her sister. "Brea."

Brea hugged her back. "Val. You smell like grape jelly."

Valerie laughed. "Lila made me eat a biscuit."

Now it was Brea's turn to laugh. "Of course she did. It's required before you can unpack your bags, isn't it?"

"You bet it is." Lila stepped in to envelop Brea in a bear hug, then held her out at arm's length. "Let me look at you. Too thin. You don't eat enough."

Brea's gaze shifted to Valerie and they exchanged knowing looks.

"Guess I need a biscuit," Brea said, then went to the cupboard, retrieved a glass and poured juice while Lila fixed her a plate.

Valerie watched Brea with some amusement. Funny how easy it was to slide into old habits once you got home.

Home. No, this wasn't home anymore. Home was Dallas, and that's where her new life had begun. She had to remember that. She was excited about her new job. She'd worked her ass off in medical school. The new partnership was her payoff. She was just feeling melancholy and wistful about being back at the ranch again. As soon as she got the hell out of here and back in Dallas she'd be her old, cheerful self.

"When did you get in?" Brea asked in between mouthfuls of thick biscuit.

"Maybe twenty minutes before you. How's Tulsa?"

"Good."

"And how's life as a freelance programmer?"

Brea smiled and said, "Fine."

At least Valerie could see Brea's mouth, which was about the only part of her that wasn't covered up by hair and clothes. "Staying busy?"

"Always."

Valerie shook her head. Had it always been this difficult to talk to her sister? Then again, how long had it been since they'd all lived under one roof? Valerie had moved out at eighteen to attend college. That was twelve years ago. Other than visits home in the summer, she hadn't really lived here full-time since then. She and her sisters had been like ships passing in the night.

And even when Valerie had still lived here, she'd been with Mason a lot. He'd stolen much of her time through college and med school—what little time she'd been willing to give to him. Which in all honesty, hadn't been all that much beyond their first summer together. But oh, what a summer that had been. Would she have married him if not for that hot, sexy summer?

She'd been so impulsive back then.

Ha. Back then? What about now? What about a half hour ago when she'd so easily fallen into Mason's arms, almost eradicating every vow she'd made two years ago to distance herself from Mason. Yeah, that had been more than a little impulsive. And stupid. But she could still taste him on her lips. How could regret taste so good?

"What put the smile on your face?"

Her head shot up. "What?"

"You've got this wistful smile on your face," Brea said. "What are you thinking about?"

Mason. "Nothing."

"No, really, what were you thinking about?"

This part she didn't miss at all. Her sisters always prying into her every thought. "I told you, nothing."

"Liar."

"Bite me, Brea."

"Screw you, Val."

"Ah, the harmonic tones of my sisters, home again. Picking up where you left off, I see."

Valerie swiveled around to face Jolene, their baby sister, leaning against the back door. She wore jeans, boots and a long-sleeved work shirt. Her hair was twisted in dark blond braided pigtails, and her entire body, including her face, was covered in dust from a day out working the ranch. And she looked just as beautiful as always.

Valerie took an affected sniff of the air. "I thought I picked up the distinct odor of cattle."

Jolene snorted. "Nice to see you, too, Valerie."

"Shut the door, Jo. You're letting flies in."

"Yes ma'am," Jolene said to Lila. She closed the door and sauntered into the kitchen, opened the refrigerator to grab a can of soda, popped the top off and took several long and loud gulps. Then she burped.

"Such a lady," Brea said.

Jolene burped again.

"Jolene! Mind your manners."

Jolene giggled. "Sorry, Lila. Couldn't help myself."

"Born in a barn, Mama would always say," Valerie said with an upraised brow.

"Please," Jolene said. "If I recall correctly, you were the one who always won the burping contests."

Valerie raised her chin. "I was ten years old at the time."

Jolene shrugged. "And I live with twenty-five guys."

"Lucky you," Brea mumbled with an arched brow.

Or at least Valerie thought Brea arched a brow. Hard to tell under that thick mop of hair.

"It has its advantages," Jolene said.

"How many pairs did you bring in?" Valerie asked.

"Haven't hit all the pastures yet, but we've gotten about fifty from the northeast."

"Great. Can't wait to go look at the babies."

"You can do more than that. Now that you're here, you can help process them."

Valerie rolled her eyes. "Oh, joy."

"It's your ranch as much as it is mine, Valerie. And yours, too,

Brea. Climb into your old boots, put on your jeans and get to work."

Valerie took a sip of juice and studied her sister. "Is that why we're really here, Jolene? Need a couple extra hands for spring cattle work?"

"I think you know me better than that. I never have trouble hiring hands. But this *is* your ranch. Those who own it work it. So yeah, that's part of why you're here. We also have a funeral to attend tomorrow."

"Uncle Ronald was a prick," Brea said. "It's not like we need to pay our respects to a man we could barely tolerate."

"Brea Louise." Lila narrowed her eyes at Brea.

"Sorry, Lila. But you can't tell me that you had any respect for that bast— For that man."

Lila turned her back to them and ran water in the sink. "What I thought of Mr. McMasters doesn't matter. You speak respectfully of the dead."

Valerie rolled her eyes. "Or don't speak of him at all if you can't think of anything nice to say."

"Then I guess his funeral will be a silent one," Jolene added.

Brea snorted.

Lila turned and gave them all a pointed look.

"That's our cue to head upstairs," Valerie said to Brea.

"Your rooms are ready," Lila said, grabbing a towel to dry her hands. "Supper will be at six thirty."

"That's in an hour," Valerie said. "I just ate two huge biscuits." Which was more than she usually ate in a day.

"Supper is at six thirty," Lila said again.

"Have you forgotten that no one misses supper around here?" Jolene whispered over her shoulder. "Better get unpacked in a hurry."

"I heard that. And you, missy, had better go wash your hands and face before you sit your butt down at my table."

"Yes, ma'am," Jolene said, then winked at her sisters. "Guess I'd better get my butt upstairs to my room, then."

Jolene sauntered off, leaving Brea to lug her suitcases up the stairs.

"Thanks for the help, sis," Brea yelled after Jolene.

"Quit whining. It builds muscles," Jolene hollered over her shoulder as she took the stairs two at a time, her boots leaving a trail of dust behind her.

"She thinks we're lightweight city girls now. Little does she know how hard I worked during my internship and residency. You build muscles rolling bodies and running down hallways, always on your feet." Valerie grabbed one of Brea's bags.

Brea started up the stairs behind her. "I have an awesome gym membership and I work out two hours a day. Pool, weight room, running track. I'll show her ass who's not in shape."

Valerie grinned. Wasn't this month just going to be oh so much fun?

two

as soon as the obligations of supper and conversation were over, Valerie went up to her room to get away, until Jolene knocked on her door and told her Lila wanted them in the family room. Valerie blew out a sigh of frustration. She'd really hoped to hide in here for the rest of the night, but Lila obviously wanted to talk to them. And if there was one thing she'd learned over the years, it was that you didn't tell Lila no.

She made her way downstairs and into the oversized family room complete with three sofas, five lounge chairs and a huge plasma television that hadn't been there the last time Valerie had been home.

"Who bought the television?" Valerie asked when she walked in.

"I did," Jolene said. "We have movie night every now and then when the weather's too bad to go to Dirk's bar in town. Anyone who's around comes. Beer and snacks."

"Fun." Brea kicked off her grotesque sandals and pulled her feet up onto the sofa, tucking them under her skirt.

"What's with those hideous flip-flops?" Jolene asked.

Brea looked over the sofa at her shoes. "What? They're comfortable."

Jolene scrunched her nose. "They're horrible. Are you freakin' homeless or something?"

"You could use a pedicure, too, Brea," Valerie added, grimacing at the state of Brea's feet.

"You guys are so funny. Just because I don't dress straight out of the pages of a fashion magazine like Valerie, or as a cowgirl like you, Jolene, doesn't mean I don't have it going on."

"Oh, you certainly have something going on, Brea," Jolene said. "I just have no idea what *it* is."

Brea shot a pleading look to Valerie, who shrugged. "I don't like the shoes, either. And you need to do something with your hair."

Brea frowned. "Who decided it was pick-on-Brea night?" She shot a glare to Jolene. "You dress like a man."

Jolene rolled her eyes. "It's my job, moron. You want me to wear a miniskirt to wrestle calves?"

"The guys would probably enjoy seeing that," Valerie teased.

"Yeah, I'll just bet they would. And having dust up my coochie would be oh so pleasant."

Right now Jolene wore nearly coochie-baring shorts and a tank top that hugged her generous breasts. She'd taken the pigtails out and brushed her hair so the long blond strands lay in soft waves over her shoulders. Really, her sister was naturally gorgeous, even without a bit of makeup on. It was so unfair. Heart-shaped face, full lips, peachy complexion and hazel eyes with long lashes. She didn't need to do a damn thing to look beautiful. She was country girl personified, and had the face and body to match.

"What are you staring at?" Jolene asked.

"I was just thinking how naturally beautiful you are."

Jolene's lashes swept down, then back up again. "Stop teasing me."

"She's right, Jo. You've always been gorgeous without trying."

Jolene looked to Brea. "You could be beautiful, too, if you'd cut that mop of hair so people could see your pretty face. And put on some clothes that accentuate your body. Honestly, Brea, what are you hiding from?"

Brea shook her head. "I'm not hiding from anything." She picked up a book and shoved her face in it.

Jolene looked over at Valerie. "Not hiding. Right. Have you ever known this girl to not have a book glued to her nose?"

"Never," Valerie said. "Brea. Are you dating anyone?"

"No."

"When was the last time you did?"

"Don't remember."

"Do you even like guys?" Jolene asked.

Brea dropped the book in her lap. "Of course I do. I've had sex before. I'm not a virgin. For God's sake, I'm twenty-eight."

Jolene shrugged. "Just wanted to know if maybe your tastes ran elsewhere."

"You're such a bitch, Jo."

Valerie laughed. "No, I'd say she definitely likes guys. Didn't you see the drool on her chin at supper tonight every time she looked at Gage Reilly?"

Brea's eyes widened. "I was not drooling over Gage."

"Yes, you were. You couldn't take your eyes off him. Not that I blame you. He's gorgeous. All that lean muscle, and his face is gorgeous with his short brown hair and ocean blue eyes. That's one hell of a sexy package. Any woman would drop at his feet. You might try to hide behind your hair, but I saw who you were looking at."

Brea picked up her book. "I'm not even going to dignify this ridiculous conversation by participating in it. It's juvenile."

"Coward," Jolene said. "Always hiding on your computer and in your books. Some things never change." She poked Brea's shoulder. "Real life is out here, Brea. You should try living it."

"Fuck off, Jolene."

In so many ways, this was just like their childhood together. Petty bickering, never seeing eye to eye on anything. Two of them would always gang up on one, and which two would always change—sometimes hourly—depending on which sister needed picking on.

"I see you and Mason still get along well," Jolene said, turning her attention from Brea to Valerie. "You two hardly said a word to each other over supper. And you did your best to avoid eye contact."

Brea peeked over the top of her book.

"Let's not go there, Jo."

"Oh, I see. It's okay to take jabs at me and my nonexistent love life. But yours is off limits," Brea said, picking up the gauntlet.

"I'm not going to talk about Mason. It's ancient history."

"Is it?" Jolene asked with an arch of her brow. "Didn't look or feel that way to me over supper. The tension in the kitchen was thick as morning fog."

"I mean it, Jolene. What is all this animosity about? You invited us here." Valerie felt the pressure building in the room and knew she had to do something to try and diffuse it before things got out of hand.

"And it's about damn time you two slackers showed up. This is your ranch and I'm tired of making all the decisions about it while the two of you sit on your asses and do nothing."

"Hey!" Brea said. "You need us, we're here. All you have to do is ask."

"I've asked plenty. And you told me no at least five times in the past year."

Brea looked down at her lap. "I've had projects. I've been busy."

"Bullshit. You avoided coming here, just like Valerie." Jolene turned her gaze to Valerie. "You and your I'm-such-a-busy-doctor routine are just as bad."

"Oh, come on, Jolene," Brea said, standing. "Valerie was doing her residency."

"And she never had time off? Just like you. Everything is more important than coming home."

"I've had about all I'm going to take from you, Jolene," Brea said, her fingers curling into fists.

Valerie had reached the end of her rope, too. "You must be itching for a fight tonight, baby sister. You need to take a step back and knock this off."

"Or what? You'll punch me out? You'll hurl insults at me? Please. I can kick your ass."

"In your dreams."

Brea crossed her arms and moved up next to Valerie. "Are you going to take us both?"

Jolene tilted her head back and offered up a smug smile. "Bring it on."

"Okay, you three. Enough. You're acting like children." Lila walked in cradling a huge cardboard box.

Their squabble instantly forgotten, Valerie moved to the other side of the room to help her. "That looks heavy. Let me help you."

Lila ignored her and dropped the box on the floor, then swept her hands together and placed them on her ample hips. "Now, you three quit bickering with each other and go through this."

"What is it?" Brea asked.

"It belonged to your mother."

"What's in it?" Jolene asked.

Lila gave her a pointed stare. "If you go through it, you'll find out. There's wine and glasses in the bar. Go have a few drinks and remember why you love each other. You're family. Not enemies."

Valerie felt thoroughly chastised. "Would you like to stay and hang out with us?"

Lila shook her head. "Some things need to be shared privately among sisters." With a wink, she turned and walked through the double doors leading out of the family room. "Night, girls." She closed the doors behind her.

Valerie turned and stared at the dusty box, then up at her sisters. "What the hell is that?"

Jolene shrugged. "I have no idea. I'll go open the wine." She went behind the bar, opened a bottle of Chardonnay and poured three glasses, then brought the glasses to them.

They stood contemplating the box while they drank their wine.

"Are we just going to stare at it, or are we going to open it up and look inside?" Brea asked.

Valerie stared down at the box, then again up at her sisters, who looked back at her expectantly. "What?"

"You're the oldest. You do it," Brea said.

Valerie rolled her eyes. "What are you so afraid of? Do you think there might be live snakes in here?"

"Well, no," Jolene said. "But I still think you should open it."

"Oh, for heaven's sake." She dropped to her knees in front of the box and laid her glass of wine on the floor, then tore open the strip of tape and pulled the flap, staring down into the darkness inside. She frowned, then reached into the box and pulled out a pile of . . . paper.

"What is that stuff?" Jolene asked, coming closer.

"I'm not sure." She handed the first pile to Jolene, who sat crosslegged on the floor on the other side of the box. Then she dove in and grabbed another pile and handed it off to Brea, who had appeared on her other side. By the time she'd dug in and pulled a pile out for herself, Brea and Jolene were chattering among themselves.

"What?" Valerie asked.

"This must be our stuff Mom had kept," Brea whispered, her voice reverent.

Jolene looked up at her, tears in her eyes. "These are our things. From when we were kids."

"Really?" Valerie went through the pile in her lap, unfolding yellowed pages of drawings they'd made, school papers, report cards, notes they'd written to one another.

"It's her box of memories," Valerie said. "Memories of us." Valerie's heart squeezed as she gently unfolded every piece of paper, looking at Brea's, Jolene's and her own name scrawled in their childhood handwriting. The box was full of all these treasures.

"I never knew Mom kept these." Jolene sniffed and held a piece of yellowed paper. "It's a Mother's Day picture I drew for her. I even wrote my age. It's a backwards five."

"I remember her telling me once that she saved everything we ever did. But I thought that was just her being kind. I guess she really meant it." Valerie was elated to find the treasures of these memories, but ached at how bittersweet it was to know her mother had kept them all. It was times like these she missed her mother so much it hurt.

"What's this?" Jolene pulled out a weathered black notebook and flipped through the pages, her wistful smile transforming into a wide grin. She lifted her head and looked at both of them. "It's my M.A.S.H. notebook."

"No."

"Are you kidding me?" Brea asked.

"I'm so not kidding. Look." Jolene handed the notebook to Brea, who flipped through the pages and started laughing.

"It *is* M.A.S.H." Brea handed the book to Valerie, who took it and flipped to the first page.

Sure enough, it was Jolene's M.A.S.H. notebook. Valerie was stunned. "Mansion, apartment, shack, house. Oh, God, how many times—how many years—did we play this game?"

"Look at these pages. I remember so many of these," Jolene said, flipping through the notebook. She glanced up at Valerie and Brea. "Are yours in there, too?"

"I don't know." Valerie rose and dug through the box, pulling out all the notebooks she could find. Six of them in total, two for each of the sisters. "They're all here!" Her pulse raced with the thrill of discovering her old notebooks. She handed the others their books and sat down to page through hers, smiling at her childish handwriting and what she'd written there. They'd started these notebooks when Jolene was eight, Brea was ten and Valerie was twelve. And they'd kept them up until Valerie was—what?—seventeen?

"Dave Exton?" Valerie wrinkled her nose at the circled name under the "Guy I'll Marry" category. "What was I thinking?"

"You were thinking you had a thing for red hair and freckles when you were twelve years old," Jolene said.

"And lanky, gawky guys," Brea added. "Oh, God, Brett Stanton? Gag. What was *I* thinking?"

"Brea and Brett," Valerie said. "I remember we teased you mercilessly about that name combination."

"Funny how one's tastes in guys could change over the years, isn't it?" Jolene said. "And of course, we all chose the mansion."

"And we wanted to live in Paris and drive the Lamborghini," Brea added.

"And have two kids, and be schoolteachers. Those were all the popular wants. But none of us managed to reach those lofty goals, did we?" Jolene said, going quiet as she studied her pages with her lips pressed together.

"We used to have such fun playing this game," Valerie said, smoothing her hand over the yellowed pages of her notebook.

"We played it a lot," Brea said.

"Especially whenever a new boy caught our eye. We wanted to make sure we would end up with him," Jolene added.

Wineglasses were refilled and the room went quiet. Valerie lifted her gaze from the pages of her notebook now and then to watch her sisters, knowing they were lost in their own memories, just as she was, back in a time when it was such a thrill to be in love. How long had it been since she'd felt that way about a guy?

Not since Mason. And not again after him.

"Oh, I have the best idea ever," Jolene said, her lips lifting in a wide grin.

"What?" Brea asked.

"You're going to love this."

"What's your idea?" Jolene always had wacky ideas that usually got them all into trouble, Valerie thought. But they were usually the most fun ideas, too.

Jolene lifted her glass to her lips and took a sip.

"Jolene."

She giggled.

"Jolene!" Brea repeated. "What?"

She put her wineglass down.

"Let's play the M.A.S.H. game again. Right now."

Valerie

WHAT KIND OF HOUSE?

Mansion
Apartment
Shack
House

CAR?

Porsche
Lamborghini
Corvette
SUV

WHERE TO LIVE?

Paris
London
Dallas
On the Ranch

NUMBER OF KIDS

5
3
1
2

GUY

Mason
John
Fred
Bill

OCCUPATION

Teacher
Doctor
Fashion Designer
Actress

three

"play the game?" valerie gaped at jolene. "are you nuts? We're not kids anymore."

Jolene took a long swallow of wine, then went to the bar and refilled her glass, bringing the bottle over to refill her sisters' glasses, too. "Oh, come on. What's the harm in having a little fun? How long has it been since we played this game?"

"Ten, twelve years or so, at least," Brea said.

"Exactly. So let's do it."

Jolene looked so eager and excited. Even Brea was digging in her bag for a pen.

Valerie didn't want to be the one to spoil their fun, and even she had to admit she was eager to take pen to paper and play again.

"Fine. We'll play."

They swept their notebooks to the first blank page and grabbed their pens. Valerie stared down at the blank page for a long time. She wasn't a kid anymore, with childlike dreams of fame and fortune and big houses, expensive cars and the man of her dreams. Real life didn't work that way. But oh, to dream . . .

She put her pen to paper and started filling out the dwellings, the cars, the occupations, where to live and even the number of kids she wanted to have. Jolene was right. It was fun getting into the game again, imagining all the what-ifs. But when it came time to fill in the guys—men she wanted to marry—she drew a blank.

"You stopped again," Jo said.

"What are you, my warden?"

"You paused at the guys, didn't you?"

"What makes you think that?"

"Because Brea did the same thing."

"Hey," Brea said, tilting her notebook away from Jolene's prying eyes. "Quit peeking."

"It's not like I'm going to copy the guys you write down. I already know who I want."

Valerie's brows perked up. "Really. That confident, are you?"

"About who and what I want? Hell yes. Now if I could just get him to see it my way . . ."

"And which guy would this be?" Valerie still found it hard to believe her baby sister was old enough to date, let alone fall in love or have sex. But Jolene was twenty-six, and more than capable of running a ranch by herself. She could certainly fall in love. Get married. Raise a family. Time had passed too quickly. And Valerie had missed a ton of it.

"Walker Morgan."

"Ahh, I thought I saw you making eyes at him over supper," Brea said, a knowing smile spreading across her face. "He's hot, with that coal dark hair and stormy eyes. Yummy."

Jolene licked her lips and scribbled in her notebook. "That he is. And what about you, Brea?"

Brea shrugged, tapping her pen against the paper. "I don't know. I don't really . . . get out much."

"If you'd quit spending all your time falling in love with fictional characters in those books you read and experience real life, maybe you'd have some names to write down," Jolene suggested.

Brea lifted her chin. "There's nothing wrong with reading."

"There is if that's all you do. There's a big ol' life out there just waiting to be lived. Why don't you try it?"

Brea glared at Jolene, then turned her gaze on Valerie. "What about you, Val? Any new guys in Dallas spark your interest enough to put them on paper?"

There had only been one man in her entire adult life, and that had been Mason. He was past, not future. Yet she didn't have anyone else to list there; she didn't date, wasn't interested in it, really. Her life had been about work, twenty-four hours a day, seven days a week, for as long as she could remember. And the only thing that had disrupted her goal had been Mason.

"Val. Val!"

She jerked her head up and looked at Jolene. "What?"

"You done yet?"

She slid her gaze back to her paper. "No. I'm still thinking."

"It never used to take that long," Brea said. "What's the holdup?"

"Give me a minute." She wrote Mason's name . . . then nothing, realizing he was the only man she'd ever wanted. Since she was a teenager, he'd been the only man in her life. How pathetic was that? After Mason's name she listed the names of men who didn't exist. "Okay, done." They switched notebooks to prevent cheating.

"All right, then," Jolene said. "Time to draw a number."

"I'll start the spiral," Brea said. "Valerie, you tell me when to stop."

"Fine."

Brea started a spiral in her notebook, drawing a continuous, gradually outgoing circle. The rule was that you couldn't look at the person drawing the circle so you couldn't guess at how many rows of circles there would be, thereby guessing the outcome. So instead Valerie looked at Jolene, who smirked at her.

"Did you write Mason's name down, Val?" Jolene asked.

"Of course not." She turned to Brea. "Stop."

Brea lifted her pen from the paper. "Okay, time to count." Brea counted the numbers of swirls. "There are seven. Start crossing off your list."

They crossed through the list every time they got to the seventh item, until each category only had one item left. Then they handed the notebooks back. Valerie noticed a few familiar names in Jolene's notebook—ranch hands—and a few unfamiliar names, too. But she'd definitely seen Walker Morgan's name on the list, the man who'd eaten supper with them, the man Jolene couldn't seem to take her eyes off of.

"So," Valerie said, ignoring her own list. "Looks like you and Walker Morgan are going to be very happy together in your mansion in Paris with your two children."

Jolene snorted. "Yeah. You could see me in Paris in a mansion, couldn't you?" Jo shifted her gaze to Brea. "And who were the guys on your list? Didn't see anyone I know except our own Gage."

Brea shrugged. "I just tossed him on there for fun."

"Uh huh," Jolene said. "He looks like he'd be fun. And dangerous. That man is wicked sexy. Think you can handle him?"

Brea blushed. "This is just fantasy."

"Gage is some fantasy, isn't he?" Valerie teased.

Brea lifted her chin. "What about you, Valerie? Who were the guys you had on your list?"

No one real except Mason. She put the notebook aside. "This game was a lot more fun when we were kids."

"And guys were just a wish list instead of reality?" Jolene asked.

"Something like that."

"You wrote Mason's name down, didn't you?"

Valerie nodded, unable to meet her sister's eyes.

"Did something happen between you two today?" Brea asked. "Supper was damned uncomfortable."

Valerie inhaled, then let it out. "He came to see me in my room when I arrived."

"Uh oh. Did you two argue?" Jolene frowned. "I'll kick his ass if he was mean to you."

"He wasn't mean to me. We were talking, and then all of a sudden we were kissing."

"Whoa." Brea's eyes widened.

"Yeah. I didn't mean for it to happen. We're divorced. He and I are history."

"Apparently not," Jolene said, her lips lifting. "You two have always had combustible chemistry."

Valerie pushed herself into a standing position and paced the room. "I shouldn't have come home. I need the distance between him and me."

Jolene reached for her hand. "Hiding isn't going to solve what's wrong between you and Mason."

"It's been working just fine the past two years."

"Has it? Five minutes together and you're tearing each other's clothes off."

She pinned Jolene with a glare. "Nothing happened. I stopped it."

"Dumbass," Brea mumbled. "You two are meant for each other. You have been since the first day you laid eyes on each other."

Valerie shook her head. "I don't think so. His life is here. Mine is in Dallas. We want different things."

"Only because you think you can't live here."

She turned her gaze to Jolene, swept her hand across her baby sister's cheek. "I can't live here. I tried."

Jolene hugged her. "Then I guess you'll have to figure out a way to bury the past and your feelings for Mason. And we'll be here to help you pick up the pieces."

Brea moved in and hugged her, too. "We'll always be here for you."

Shit. Tears pricked her eyes and she forced them back. She threw her arms around her sisters. It had always been her job to take care of them, and now they were shouldering her burdens.

"You know, as much as I hated the thought of coming here, I'm so damn glad to be with you two again. Bickering and all."

Jolene pulled away and grinned. "That's not bickering. That's just sisterhood."

they sat and went through their mother's box of memorabilia for a while longer, drinking wine and reminiscing about their childhood until Jolene and Brea decided to go up to bed.

Valerie wasn't ready for sleep yet. She needed some air, so she pulled the doors open, went straight for the front door and down the porch steps, out into the chilly spring night. By the time she made it all the way to the barn, she wished she'd put on warmer clothes and a jacket; she'd forgotten how cold the nights could get out here in the spring. Goose bumps pricked her skin, making her shiver all over.

She should head back to the house, but too many memories clung there. Instead, she opened the barn doors, and was enveloped in the warmth from the horses.

"Hey, babies," she said in a soft, gentle voice as she closed the door, letting the darkness surround her. She inhaled the scent of hay and horses and smiled. Such familiar smells. Sometimes the things of home just felt right. This felt right. She moved in, careful not to make too much noise in the dark. "It's just me." She wanted to assure them she wasn't some stranger there to harm them.

She heard the movement of hooves, the occasional wuffling of their breathing, but otherwise all was quiet. She moved along each stall, refamiliarizing herself with horses she'd ridden before, and meeting some of the new ones. The smell reminded her of being in here with her father. He'd loved the horses. He'd loved everything about this ranch, about this life. She had, too, until her parents had been abruptly taken away from her. Then she'd hated everything about the Bar M.

Except Mason. But he hadn't been enough to keep her here.

"You could turn some light on in here."

She pivoted, her heart crashing against her chest at the sound of another voice. Mason's. "You scared the hell out of me. *You* could have turned a light on so you wouldn't frighten me half to death."

He flipped on the overhead lights and headed toward her. "I was in the tack room. Heard someone come in. Since I wasn't sure who'd be in the barn this late at night, I figured I'd come out to investigate before I announced I was here. Just in case it was an intruder who wasn't supposed to be in here."

Her goose bumps returned and she wrapped her arms around her chest to hide her upraised nipples. Mason's gaze strayed to her chest, his lips lifted, then he looked at her face again.

"What are you doing out here? And why are you half-naked? You should know it's cold outside."

"I needed some air, I'm hardly half-naked, and I forgot it was so cold until I was already at the barn."

He shook his head. "You never had a lick of common sense, woman." He pulled off his jacket and moved so close she felt his body heat. "Come on. Slide into this."

Irritated at his attitude, she wanted to say no, but that would be childish, so she put his jacket on. It was warm from his body. It smelled like Mason. She pulled it tighter around her, the smell of leather and male almost overpowering to her senses. "Thanks."

"No problem."

They stood that way for too long, Valerie staring up into Mason's so familiar face. He didn't seem to be in a hurry to move away, and he smelled so damn good. And that's exactly what had gotten her into trouble earlier today. She stepped back and turned around. "So you got some new horses?"

"Yeah. Gage is doing a great job training. He's gotten us some beauties."

She walked along the stalls, stopping at a few to lay her hands on some of the new mares. "I can see that." There were so many parts of ranch life she missed. The horses, the cattle. Riding alongside Mason.

She missed Mason.

No, she didn't. She missed sex with Mason. That part had been incredible. Everything else between them had been a disaster.

She reached up to pet a mare, doing her best to ignore Mason's presence. "I guess you stay busy. Not much time for any . . . social life or anything."

"I haven't gotten married again, if that's what you're asking."

She jumped when she realized he was right behind her. She turned to face him. "I assume you wouldn't have been all over me in my room today if you were married to someone else."

"I was all over you?"

"Yes."

"I think you threw yourself at me because you're starved for sex."

If there had been a shovel nearby he'd have been a dead man by now. "You are so full of shit."

"So you've often told me." He didn't seem at all irritated; in fact he looked downright amused. Which just pissed her off even more.

But she refused to let him get to her. "And anyway, that wasn't what I was asking. I was just . . . concerned about you."

He crooked a smile around a piece of straw resting in the corner of his mouth. "Sure you were, darlin'." He turned and walked away.

She followed. "Don't you 'darlin'' me, Mason. I'm not at all interested in your sex life."

He stopped and pivoted, then pushed his hat back and arched his brows. "Oh, so now we're talking about my sex life?"

Her entire body heated, from the tips of her painted toenails to the roots of her hair. "No. We are most definitely not talking about your sex life."

"Okay. Let's talk about yours, then. Gotten any lately?"

Her eyes widened. "Dear God. You haven't changed a bit." She spun on her heel and headed for the barn door.

"Val."

"What?" She wasn't about to stop.

"I'll come by and pick up my jacket . . . later."

"Asshole," she muttered, shrugging out of his jacket and letting it drop to the barn floor. If the cosmos smiled on her, maybe it would fall into a pile of horse shit.

There was no refuge anywhere—at the house or in the barn. But at least the house only contained her sisters. She went through the front door and up the stairs directly to her room.

Unfortunately, Jolene was at the top of the stairs waiting for her.

"What?" Valerie asked.

"What are you running from?"

Valerie rolled her eyes. "Nothing." She brushed past Jolene and went into her bedroom. Jolene caught the door before Valerie could shut it.

Her sister made herself comfortable on Valerie's bed, flopping stomach-first onto it.

"Ran into Mason outside, didn't you?"

Damn Jolene for being so perceptive. "Yes."

"He still has the ability to make your heart hurt, doesn't he?"

When had her sister grown up and become so wise? She started to deny it, but what was the use? "Yes."

"That's why you don't come back here."

Valerie sat on the edge of the bed and blew out a breath of defeat, feeling like she'd failed at running away from the one thing she didn't want to talk about. "Not all of it, but that's part of the reason."

Jo rolled over onto her back and leaned against the pillows. "What's the other?"

That she wouldn't get into. Instead, she lifted her shoulders. "I just needed to move on, to find a life outside the Bar M. I wasn't meant to be a rancher, Jo."

Jo cocked her head to the side and studied Valerie. "I'm not sure I buy that. You were as good at ranching as I was."

"I just didn't love ranching like you do. I was good at it, yes, but you love it. I don't."

"Being good at something doesn't mean you have to love it."

She felt the squeeze in her heart. "Loving something doesn't mean you won't destroy it."

"Ah," Jolene said. "So we're not really talking about the ranch now. You're talking about your marriage to Mason."

She lifted her gaze to her sister. "What?"

"Mason. You're talking about loving Mason."

"No. I'm not."

"You're talking about loving and destroying. That's not the ranch you're talking about, Valerie."

Dammit. Why did everything get turned around to talk of Mason? "There's a damn good reason we're not married anymore. And I'd appreciate if you and Brea would keep your matchmaking fingers out of our relationship."

Jo raised her hands. "Whoa. Okay. Hands off. I get it."

"Good."

Jolene swung her legs over the side of the bed and headed for the door. "But, Val?"

"Yes."

"I think you still love him. And he's not destroyed, so maybe there's still hope."

"Goddammit, Jo!"

But Jolene had already pulled the door shut and hadn't heard Valerie scream at her.

Somehow Valerie didn't think that topic was closed.

four

the funeral was surprisingly well attended considering how much everyone had hated their uncle Ronald. But Valerie supposed most people were better bred than she was and would willingly pay their respects to the mean son of a bitch even if he'd never had a kind word to say to a single soul.

Lila said people attended out of respect for the family. Maybe so. Valerie's parents' funeral had been standing room only. There'd been weeping. Then again, her parents had been kind people. Maybe someone had left Uncle Ronald in a basket on her grandparents' doorstep, and they'd taken pity on him and raised him as their own. Because no way in hell would Valerie ever believe Uncle Ronald and her father were of the same blood. Ronald had been mean as a rattlesnake, always coiled and ready to strike out at whatever innocent victim was foolish enough to get close. And every eye at the church and cemetery that day was bone dry. No one cried over his death. What did that say about a man's character?

They held a luncheon at the ranch after, and lots of folks

attended, which gave Valerie a chance to catch up with people she hadn't seen since she'd left town two years ago. That was both a good and a bad thing. She loved catching up, but hated fielding the same old questions about where she'd been, why she left the ranch, and what was going on with her and Mason.

In that her sisters were her lifesavers, especially Jolene, who steered people away with talk of cattle and horses and the exorbitant price of feed. And Lila, who stuffed everyone's faces with enough food their mouths were too full to talk. Fortunately, Mason had begged off attending the luncheon, claiming he had ranch work to do, so she didn't have to face him along with the questioning stares of everyone from town.

According to them, you didn't leave ranch life. You were born and bred to it, you married into it and you died doing it.

Why in hell weren't they badgering Brea with questions? Probably because she knew how to hang out in a corner and resemble a potted plant. No doubt not a single soul even recognized her behind her scraggly hair and boho outfit. If only Valerie could be obscure. As the oldest, she was the best known other than Jolene.

By the time the crowds had left, Valerie was exhausted. Tension had drilled her shoulders into hard knots. She was glad this day was over, and she wanted nothing more than to hide in her room. Brea and Jolene were in the kitchen with Lila. Valerie stayed in the great room, searching for leftover cups and spoons and the like.

"Rough day?"

Her shoulders tensed at Mason's voice. She turned and managed a smile. "It wasn't too bad."

"Sorry I wasn't here. Bet you had to field a lot of questions about us."

"I managed."

Dirt smudged his face and rained off his jeans as he moved into the room, his boots tapping on the wood floor. God he looked good enough to . . . eat.

It had been a long, long dry spell. The last man she'd been with had been . . . him.

"You look tense."

She lifted her chin and dropped her shoulders. "I'm fine, really."

"I used to know you better than you knew yourself. You're not fine. There are dark circles under your eyes. When was the last time you slept?"

Years ago. "Don't worry about me."

His lips quirked. "Old habits die hard."

He moved in, his fingertips brushing hers. The contact was electric, surprising.

What they had was in the past. It should be dead, buried, along with any feeling she'd had for him. But the *whoa* of chemistry was still there, undeniably roaring to the forefront with the simple touch of fingers.

It wasn't fair that this was happening.

His gaze shot to hers and she was lost in the darkness of his eyes. Memories swirled around her. Their first touch, first kiss, and so many moments after that, mingling together like a movie in fast forward. Despite the self-preserving need to run, her feet stayed rooted to the floor, curiosity and need swirling like a tornado inside her, around her.

"Leave me alone, Mason." She finally found the strength to take a step back.

"Is that what you really want?"

She'd taken his heart and stomped all over it. Why didn't he hate her? Hadn't he moved on? Why did he look at her with the same kind of heat he used to, the all-consuming kind that threatened to drop her to her knees?

She knew she shouldn't have come, that she wouldn't be able to handle this. Handle him.

Shuddering an inhale, she backed up another few steps, breaking the spell. "It's exactly what I want."

The smile never left his face. "I don't believe you."

She skirted around him, unable to meet his knowing look. He'd always known her better than anyone. "Start believing it."

But as she walked away on shaky legs, needing to grip the railing as she made her way up the stairs, even she didn't believe it.

The evidence was in her pounding heart, her trembling legs, her hard nipples. One look, one touch, and she was turned on, wanting him, needing him just as much now as she always had.

She might have divorced him and walked away, but she'd never really left him.

She could talk a good game, but when faced with the man she'd loved and left, she was toast.

She couldn't even convince herself she didn't want him anymore. How was she going to convince Mason?

mason tossed his gloves on the worn table in the main room of his small place just down the road from the main house. Only a few rooms and one bedroom, it suited him just fine. It gave him privacy, away from the hands after a long day.

He left the lights off, needing the cool afternoon darkness of the house to quell the heat raging inside him. He grabbed a beer from the fridge and settled in on one of the old comfortable chairs in front of the fireplace, stretching out his legs so he could just breathe for a few minutes.

How could touching Valerie spark such an inferno inside him? He'd have to get a handle on this and quick.

Then again, he'd seen the fire light up in her eyes, the desire flame instant and hot just like it had been for him. It hadn't been one-sided.

He'd teased her last night in the barn, wanted to irritate her—anything to get some kind of reaction from her other than her usual polite, say-nothing conversation that drove him crazy. And earlier in her room . . . God, he hadn't expected that wildcat, the woman she used to be. But she'd only given him a glimpse, and then as usual, she'd pulled back, locked herself up tight and wouldn't let him in.

So he'd done what he normally did when she drew back from him—he'd pissed her off. She'd always had spirit, but she banked it. He'd seen plenty of that spirit, that lust for life, when they were together, when things had been hot and heavy and good between them.

He hadn't been the one to give up, to run. That had been all her doing. And maybe he should man up and walk away, just let this thing between them die once and for all. But he was also old enough and smart enough to read a cry for help, and Val was screaming loud inside.

He knew Valerie better than anyone ever had. He knew her pain, knew her fear. What he'd told her today was true—he knew her better than she knew herself.

Maybe he'd let go too easily before. Maybe he hadn't given her what she'd been really been asking for two years ago.

Maybe it was time he did.

"so what's going on tonight, guys?"

Twenty pairs of shocked eyes gaped up at her. Valerie stared the cowboys down, having marched to the bunkhouse in an effort to prove once and for all that she did not, in fact, need Mason in her life anymore. She figured the best way to do that was to actually get a life.

"Uh, we're headin' into town for some pool and beer, Miss Valerie."

Bobby, one of the younger hands, nearly knocked over the chair at the long table where a bunch of the guys had been playing poker.

"That sounds like fun. Can I catch a ride with you?"

They all looked at one another. Not at her—at one another.

"Um. We'll check in with Mason first, see if that's all right with him."

Her blood pressure ticked up a notch, but she kept the smile plastered to her face. "Oh, you don't need to do that."

"Uh, yes, ma'am, we sure do. You're his wife."

"Ex-wife."

"Don't matter. We wouldn't dare take you anywhere without askin' him first."

They had all started to back away from her as if she was some kind of pariah with leprosy.

What a bunch of pussies. Could they take a piss without Mason's permission?

"Fine," she said, clenching her jaw. "I'll just take the truck into town."

Imbeciles. Were they children or grown men? She stormed back into the house and stomped up the stairs, threw open her closet and glared at her clothes.

"What bug crawled up your ass?"

She ignored Jolene. Which, of course, meant Jolene came in and threw herself on Valerie's bed.

"Got a date?"

"Hardly."

"Where are you going?"

"Into town. Some of the hands are hitting the bar for drinks and pool."

"Sounds great. I'm in."

"In for what?" Brea had come in, too. Of course. God forbid her sisters stay out of her business.

"Town. Bar. Drinks. Pool."

"Ooh," Brea said. "Awesome. Let me go change."

"Wait for us," Jo said, sliding off the bed and hurrying out the door.

She was about to object, but it would actually be fun to unwind a bit with her sisters. She needed something—anything—to get her mind off Mason. A little drinking and dancing should do the trick.

An hour and a half later they pulled up in front of Dirk's Downtown Dive, a misnomer since downtown was pretty much the actual town itself. The small municipality about forty minutes south of the ranch was the only town around other than Tulsa. And it was the only place to go if you didn't want to take the two-hour drive into the city. So Dirk's it was. And it was hopping tonight. The parking lot was full and the sometimes-worked-sometimes-didn't neon sign was actually working tonight. A cloud of dust flew up as Jolene slid the truck into one of the last available spots in the dirt and gravel parking lot. Which meant the next customer would be parking on the grass.

They climbed out of the truck and Valerie smoothed her shirt down over her jeans, getting used to the feel of cowboy boots again.

Even Brea had changed out of those hideous gypsy skirts and put on a pair of jeans and boots tonight. Jolene had convinced Brea to pull her hair back in a ponytail, which had done wonders for her appearance. At least Valerie could see Brea's face now.

"You look like a different person," Valerie said. "Beautiful."

Brea looked down at the ground. "Thanks. Maybe I've been neglecting myself a bit. I need to do something about that."

"A bit?" Jolene said, a look of shock on her face. "Christ, Brea, you look like you've been living in a fucking cave or something. Tomorrow's Saturday and I'm taking you into Tulsa for a makeover. Hair, nails, pedicure, the works."

Brea grinned. "That might be fun."

Valerie elbowed Brea. "You just want to look hot for Gage."

Her sister blushed under the neon lights. "Dear God, Val. I do not."

"Liar," Jolene said, pulling the heavy wooden door open. "Now, let's party."

The bar was noisy, smoky, and crowded as hell. With lots of cow-boys and very few women.

Perfect.

Of course Jolene knew everyone and shouted out greetings as they wound their way to the bar. She ordered beers while Valerie rustled up a table, which wasn't difficult since most of the guys were off playing pool or standing around talking to one another. A few were dancing with some of the women, but so far the small dance floor remained sadly uncrowded.

Valerie aimed to change that. There were a lot of men present, and she intended to dance with as many of them as she could.

They took seats at the table and Valerie surveyed the scene. Not much had changed at Dirk's since she'd last been here. The scarred wood floor was still covered in sawdust and discarded pea-nut shells. The long bar was littered with beer bottles, some filled, some empty. Raucous country music played—no, that wasn't quite right—it *blared* loud and hard, the heavy bass thumping with a wham wham wham she felt in her chest. The thwack of pool balls could be heard above the noise since several games were going on, followed by either a loud groan or a hoop and a holler when some-one sank a shot.

And it was still early. The real action wouldn't happen before ten P.M.

"This place is hoppin' already." Jolene scooted her butt onto a stool and slid the beers onto the table. "Great idea, Val."

Valerie took a long drink and nodded. "I figured we could all stand to get out of that house." Or at least she could. Two days and she was already suffocating in there. Being at Dirk's was easy. She could blend in, wasn't the center of attention.

Not until the door opened and Mason walked in with a bunch of the guys from the ranch. And everyone in the place smiled and waved at him.

Then all eyes turned to her.

In an instant, whether she liked it or not, they'd all made the connection.

In their eyes, she still belonged with Mason. *To* Mason.

She'd see about that, would show them she belonged to no man. She downed the first bottle of beer in three swallows, slid off the stool and, ignoring Mason, marched her way to the bar and ordered another round.

"You'd better keep them coming," she told Sandy, the bartender. "It's going to be a long night."

Beers in hand, she went back to the table, keeping her focus on her sisters, who both gazed at her with much amusement.

"Fuck off," she said as she took her seat.

"The whole place is looking at you," Jolene said with a smirk as she continued to sip from her first bottle of beer.

Valerie shrugged. "Let them. Nothing to see here." And she still hadn't looked at Mason, had no idea where he even was. Hopefully he'd spotted her and left.

No such luck. As soon as she scanned the pool area, there he was, shooting a game of eight ball with Gage, Walker and Sporty. He wasn't watching her.

Good. Because she had every intention of pretending he wasn't there. He had his life, and she had hers. The two of them were completely separate now. And it was about damn time everyone came to grips with that fact.

"You know, for someone who claims to have no interest in Mason, you sure are watching him a lot."

Valerie's gaze shot to Brea. "I am not. I just want to make sure he doesn't come over here."

"Uh huh."

Valerie downed her second beer. Just in time, too, because Sandy sent over another one. Valerie unscrewed the top and began to drink.

"You keep guzzling them like that and we'll have to pour you into the truck," Jolene said.

Valerie rolled her eyes. "Please. I can drink both of you under the table."

"Is that right?" Jolene signaled for Sandy and held up three fingers. In short order, the bartender appeared with a tray and three shot glasses filled to the rim with amber liquid.

Valerie glared at Jolene. "You did not."

"Let's see you drink me under the table with beer and shooters."

"Bitch."

Jolene laughed. "Quit whining and knock it down."

She did. An hour, two more shots and four beers later, she was feeling free and giddy and ready to dance. The bar was packed solid and she was damn sure there'd be at least one if not a dozen cowboys eager to take her up on her offer to sweat some of this alcohol out of her system on the dance floor.

"I'm off to pick up a man."

"You sure you're gonna make it?" Jolene asked.

"Please. I'm barely warmed up." She hitched herself off the bar stool and made a slow trek through the throng of hot bodies now crowding the dance floor, though she didn't do it in a straight line. Damn whiskey.

When she reached the other side, she kept herself from licking her lips at the slabs of male flesh occupying the game area.

Was there anything sexier than hot cowboys in Stetsons, boots, T-shirts and blue jeans? She didn't think so. Now she just had to zero in on one available guy, grab him and take a twirl.

Deciding steering clear of the guys from the Bar M would be the wisest choice, she chose one leaning against the far wall. He wasn't playing pool, just drinking a beer and watching the action. He watched her approach with definite interest in his eyes.

Oh yeah. He would definitely do. She made sure to use her sexiest saunter to keep that interest. His smile lit up when she stopped in front of him.

"Hey," she said.

"Hey yourself, darlin'. What are you up to tonight?"

She hooked her thumbs in her belt hoops, realizing how rusty she was at this flirting thing. "Just kicking back and relaxing. How about you?"

"Same." He laid his beer on a nearby table and held out his hand. "I'm Cody."

"Valerie. Nice to meet you, Cody."

"You're not from around here, are you?"

"No," she lied. "I have family here that I'm visiting. I live in Dallas."

He nodded. "The big city."

She laughed. He was gorgeous. Broad shoulders, killer dimples. "So, Cody, would you like to dance?"

Before he had a chance to answer, some guy came up and whispered in his ear. Cody went pale, turned back to Valerie and tipped his hat.

"Some other time, ma'am."

He backed away from her as if she had some kind of communicable disease.

What the hell was that about? Did the guy remind Cody he had a wife back home or something? If so, then it was a good thing he'd declined, because if she found out he was married she just might have to kill him.

Fine. He wasn't the only guy in the place. She turned and hit on another, who politely declined. So did another. And another. And she saw a round of hands cupped to ears and whispers and fingers pointing to her.

Irritation set her foot tapping, and it wasn't in time to the hard-driving beat of the music.

She faced all the guys leaning against the wall, her hands on her hips. "Okay, look. I'm a reasonably attractive woman who can hold a decent conversation. And trust me, I'm a great dancer. So what the hell is so wrong with me that has you all running in the opposite direction whenever I come near?"

"They think you belong to me."

Oh. Now it all made sense.

She turned to face her ex-husband with murder on her mind.

five

mason fought a smile as valerie leveled a murderous expression in his direction. Oh yeah, she was pissed. He'd seen it coming as one guy after another shot her down.

But hey, it wasn't his fault that nearly every cowboy in town still thought of her as his wife. And to the cowboy code of honor, that meant hands off. They weren't going to step in his territory.

"You did this on purpose."

He shook his head. "I had nothing to do with it."

"Tell them it's not true."

"What's not true?"

"I'm not your wife anymore. We don't have a connection."

"Don't we?"

Her gaze narrowed. "Mason."

"Valerie."

She poked his chest. "Now you're deliberately trying to piss me off."

"Would I do that?" He turned and walked away, and even over

the deafening noise and music he heard her squeal of outrage.
He grinned and picked up a pool cue, leaned over the table and
took his shot, then grabbed his bottle of beer and took a long
swallow

"She's pissed at you."

Mason slanted his gaze to Walker Morgan, one of his best
friends. "Yeah."

"You intending to do something about it?"

"Nope."

"Man, that's a hornet's nest you're stepping into."

"Maybe."

"Speaking of hornets," Walker said, motioning behind Mason.

Someone tapped Mason on the shoulder. He turned, already
knowing who it was. Valerie never was one to back down.

"If none of these other guys have the balls"—and she'd said
"balls" loud enough for every person in Dirk's to hear it—"to dance
with me, then you're going to have to do it."

Mason laid his cue across the table, turned and grabbed her
hand, dragging her onto the dance floor. "Fine. Let's dance."

valerie's eyes widened as mason wrapped his arms
around her and drew her against him. The heat from his body soaked
into her. Disoriented, she missed a step, while he stayed steady.

What the hell? She'd thrown that out as a challenge, knowing he
wouldn't take her up on it. Mason didn't dance. Not once during all
the years she'd known him had he ever danced with her, including
their wedding day.

But as he held firm to the small of her back, he was relaxed and
moved against her with an easy rhythm.

She cocked a brow. "You son of a bitch. You can dance."

"Never said I couldn't. Just don't like to."

"So what the hell are you doing dancing with me now?"

He gazed down at her and smiled. "I feel kind of bad that no one else will."

She tried to pull away from him, away from the butterflies flitting in her stomach. She wasn't used to being this close to him. It threw her off balance and she didn't like it one bit. Distance gave her clarity, but Mason didn't let go. "I don't need a pity dance."

He laughed. "You think I pity you?" He laughed, then shocked the hell out of her when he bent her over, dipped her and planted his lips on hers.

Her entire body combusted into flames as Mason slid his lips over hers right there in front of God and her sisters and practically the entire town. Their past, all the arguments and hurts, disappeared, and she was once again the sixteen-year-old girl madly in love with the hot cowboy. She was the eighteen-year-old girl who wanted to marry the man of her dreams. She was in her bedroom, getting naked with Mason, his mouth and hands all over her body, awakening her desires, taking her to screaming heights she'd never known before, or since.

When he lifted her upright again, she was panting, her nipples tight points of need throbbing against her bra. Her panties, moist with desire, clung to her skin.

But most of all, she was confused.

"Why don't you hate me?" she asked.

"I don't hate you, darlin'. I don't feel anything at all for you."

That was a downright lie, because as he continued to lead her around the dance floor, the hard ridge of his cock rode against her hip. She glanced down between them, then back up at him with a smile. "I beg to differ."

"You make me hard. Doesn't mean I still love you. Or even that I want you."

She laughed. "That makes no damn sense. Of course you still want me."

"First you don't want to have anything to do with me. Now you're trying to get me to admit that I want you? What do *you* want, Val?"

At the moment, she had no idea. As always, being with Mason confused her, made her feel things she didn't want to feel—things she shouldn't feel.

The song ended, and Mason took a step back, tipped his hat. "Thanks for the dance."

He headed back to his friends and grabbed his beer, took a long swill and didn't even bother looking back at her. He'd just left her standing there like she'd been dumped.

Asshole.

She went back to the table where both her sisters smirked at her.

"Guess he was the one who walked away this time," Jolene said, looking way too amused.

"Bite me." Valerie grabbed the shot in front of her and downed it in one swallow, then chugged her beer. Dancing with Mason had gotten her hot in more ways than one.

"You should just jump him and get it over with."

Valerie's gaze shot to Jolene. "That would be the worst thing in the world. I've been gone two years. Things between us are finally settled."

Brea snorted. "Yeah, things looked real settled between you."

"Uh huh. You totally behaved like a divorced couple out there on the dance floor," Jolene added.

"It was one dance. It didn't mean anything."

"You kissed him," Jolene said.

"I did not. He kissed me. It didn't mean anything. It was just for fun."

"Are you trying to convince us, or yourself?" Brea asked. "Because it looked meaningful as hell from where I'm sitting."

Her sisters could be so irritating at times. "Look. Nothing's going to happen between us. I don't want to give Mason false encouragement, or let him believe there could ever be anything resurrected between us. It wouldn't be right. It would hurt him, and I've hurt him enough."

"Right, because he's just pining away without you. One word from you and he might just curl up and die." Jolene motioned with her head toward the other side of the bar.

Valerie followed Jolene's head motion. Mason had his arm around a gorgeous blonde dressed in skintight skinny jeans that showed off one fine ass, and a body-forming, belly-hugging top that surrounded enormous tits. They were laughing, their heads bowed together. The scene was obviously intimate. The woman had her arm around Mason and rubbed his back in a very familiar way.

Maybe the hard-on he'd sprouted on the dance floor was for the blonde with big boobs, and not for her at all.

Goddammit. She would not be jealous. She'd expected Mason to move on with his life, and he obviously had. Good for him.

At least that's what she was supposed to think. But her stomach churned and her hands formed into fists. She wanted to march over there and rip that blonde away from Mason. She wanted to scream that he was hers and no other woman was allowed to touch him. Ever.

What the hell was wrong with her? Isn't this exactly what she wanted? Mason with another woman represented freedom—closure to that chapter in her life. Did she expect him to hide out on the ranch and pine away for her forever? How stupid could she be?

Yet she couldn't get past the blonde's hands all over her man— correction—all over Mason.

She had to stop looking. It wasn't her business what he did or with whom. It shouldn't hurt.

But it did. She hated that it did.

"Who the hell is that woman?" she asked.

"Candy? She's some bar slut who's been trying to get her hands in Mason's pants for a year or so," Jolene offered.

"And? Has she succeeded?"

Jolene snorted. "Mason isn't interested in her. Doesn't stop Candy from trying every time he steps foot inside Dirk's."

He didn't look like he was trying all that hard to extricate himself from Candy's clutches. "I need another drink."

"Don't you think you've had enough?" Brea asked.

Valerie gathered up a few of the empties. "Oh, honey, I haven't had nearly enough. I'm just getting started."

mason's ex-wife was rip-roaring, on-her-ass drunk as a skunk, which was pretty damned amusing since she usually didn't drink much at all. She was clinging to the bar stool, one arm hung over the back, her ass cheeks barely registering on the seat. Her heels dug into the floor as if they were the only thing keeping her from slithering to the ground and passing the hell out.

He gave her about five more minutes and she'd be on the ground facedown in the discarded peanut shells.

Brea and Jolene were trying to pull her upright onto the seat. No luck, there, especially since Valerie was belligerent and uncooperative, swatting them away like annoying flies in hot August.

"I fine. I kin get home jus fine wishout y'all pishing me off."

He snickered at the slurring. The bar had closed about ten minutes ago, was practically empty. Sandy, who was wiping down the counter, caught his eye and shook her head. He smiled at her and headed toward the McMasters sisters.

"Mason, help. She's a giant pain in the ass," Jolene said, holding Valerie up by the back of her shirt.

"I'll get her home. You two go on."

"Bless you," Brea said, extricating herself from under her sister's arm.

Valerie pushed at Brea. "See, told ya I could drive."

Jolene shook her head. "Girl never had any sense about drinking." She patted Mason on the arm as she walked past. "Hope she doesn't puke in your truck."

Great. He scooped Valerie up into his arms and her head fell against his chest. She tilted her head back and opened two bloodshot eyes to stare up at him.

"Why aren't you with your girlfriend? Jush leave me here and I'll drive myshelf."

He didn't answer, just nodded to Sandy and pushed open the front door. The night was cool. Maybe it would help clear Valerie's head.

"Oh my God, who put me on a roller coaster?" she whined as he walked to his truck.

"You did." He stopped and leaned her against the side of the truck long enough to dig for his keys.

She slumped against him. "I don't feel so hot."

"Imagine that."

He picked her up again and put her on the passenger side, clicked her seat belt into place, then got in and started up the truck, making sure he drove slow and straight, though the mean streak in him wanted to hit every goddamn bump in the road. But he didn't. Not that it mattered, since even in the dark he saw her face grow pale.

"I really don't feel good, Mason."

He punched the button and rolled her window partway down. "Suck in some fresh air."

She did, inhaling and exhaling. And grew white as a sheet.

"Pull over."

He turned down a gravel side road, threw it into park, raced around to her side and jerked her out of the car just in time. She dropped to her knees and he held her hair while she vomited up the contents of her wild party tonight. When it seemed like there was nothing left to give up, he grabbed a bottled water he had stashed in the side pocket of the truck and washed her face, then told her to take a sip. He put her back in the truck and drove back to the ranch, then carried her inside and up to her room.

She was quiet now. Her eyes were closed, and she was limp as a dishrag and soaked through with sweat.

He laid her on the bed, her hair a tangled mess around her face. She looked like shit.

He walked out into the hallway. Brea's and Jolene's rooms were both dark. As a matter of fact, Jolene's truck hadn't been out front. Maybe they'd stopped at the all-night diner in town for breakfast. He supposed he could wake Lila . . .

Well, hell. It wasn't like Valerie had anything he hadn't seen before. He went back into her room, watched her chest rise and fall with deep, even breaths. He pulled off her boots and socks, then undid her belt buckle and unfastened her jeans. He pulled down the zipper and tugged the jeans over her hips and down her thighs, revealing purple silk panties, tiny strings holding them up on her hips.

Christ. His cock twitched to life as he drew the jeans down her legs, his knuckles brushing the softness of her skin. He felt like a pervert undressing an unconscious woman. A woman whose body he knew all too well.

Sucking in a breath, he took the hem of her shirt and pulled it up, baring her flat stomach, her ribs, and over her breasts. Her purple bra matched her panties. She sighed, inhaled deeply, her breasts rising with that breath.

He was fully hard now, mentally cursing this really stupid idea. He lifted the shirt over her head and threw it on the floor, then slid his hands under her back and undid the hooks of her bra in about two seconds flat. Hell, he'd always been good at undressing her, especially when they'd been frantic about getting naked and getting skin-to-skin with each other.

Thoughts like that weren't going to settle his dick down soon.

He pulled her bra off, stood there looking at her dusky pink nipples that hardened to tight points in the cool bedroom, and wished he were anywhere but here. He was no freakin' Boy Scout. He was hard as a fence post and his balls were throbbing. This was the woman he'd spent half his life thinking about sinking his cock into. And here she was, lying in the bed they used to make love in together, nearly naked, her legs softly parted, her nipples hard, just like his dick.

Shit.

"Come on, darlin', let's get you under the covers." He scooped her up long enough to jerk the covers down. She moaned, softly, while he repositioned her, pulled the covers over her. Then she rolled to her side and shoved her nose in the pillow.

He turned off the light and pulled the door handle.

"Thank you, Mason," she mumbled from under the covers.

He closed the door and tiptoed downstairs and out the front door, slamming into his truck and peeling off down the road. He rolled the window down, hoping the cold breeze would chill the heat roaring through his body.

He still wanted her. Even worse, he was leveled by how much he still cared for her, still wanted to care for her. She was still as vulnerable now as she was when her life had been shattered all those years ago after the death of her parents. He'd always thought she'd leaned on him then because of that. Maybe she had. And maybe it had been something more than that. Something that couldn't separate them no matter what.

She'd walked out on him, had made it clear she wanted no part of his way of life. And yet he knew that they were still bonded. He felt it. So did she, even if she tried to deny it.

Maybe they always would be.

And maybe he was just a damn fool.

six

there wasn't enough coffee and acetaminophen on earth to obliterate the hangover Valerie had woken up with. But after a shower, nearly half a pot of coffee and some of Lila's heavy-on-the-carbs breakfast, she decided she might live through the day.

What an epic idiot she was. Thinking she could down all those beers and shots of whiskey when she normally didn't even drink was a lesson in stupidity. Even worse, she hadn't been nearly drunk enough to forget Mason driving her home, or her throwing up on the side of the road, or Mason putting her to bed.

He'd taken care of her when she'd gotten sick. He'd held her hair and kept her from falling on her face in a sick, drunken stupor. Then he'd tenderly washed her face, driven her home and carried her up to her room. He'd undressed her and pulled the covers over her. She didn't deserve such treatment after the way she'd unceremoniously dumped him, divorced him and left him. Why couldn't he be an ass-hole like so many guys she knew? Most men would have left her in the parking lot of the bar and told her she was on her own.

Then again, Mason wasn't most men and never had been. That was one of the reasons she'd fallen in love with him in the first place.

Jolene and Brea had gone to Tulsa for the morning, which meant she couldn't avoid her ex-husband, unless she wanted to spend the day hiding in the house. And it was a warm spring day, and she was no coward.

She slid on a pair of the darkest sunglasses she had, put on her cowboy hat to shield her devastated head from the sun and found Mason out at the cattle pens, roping the calves for branding. She swung over the fence and walked toward him.

"Hey," she said, squatting down and ignoring the smell of burning calf flesh as one was branded with the Bar M mark. Branding calves was as much a part of her life as breakfast.

"Kind of busy here, Val," he said, holding a branding iron to a squalling calf.

"I need to talk to you."

He let the iron up, and the two hands holding the calf's legs let go. The calf sprung up and sauntered off, and was let out of the pen and into the pasture, while the next calf was brought in, roped—or wrestled—into lying down.

"If you're going to insist on being in my way, put on some gloves and get to work."

She sighed, looked around and found a pair of work gloves, then took her place at the front end of a calf, replacing one of the cowboys, who went off to perform another task. She held tight to the calf's forelegs while Mason applied the brand.

They worked silently for a while, her, Mason and Bobby, one of the hands. Valerie found the rhythm relaxing. It had been a long time since she'd done any ranch work. She'd always found it enjoyable, a distraction that required a lot of physical effort, but didn't overtax her mind. And after eight years of having her brain cells filled to bursting with medical school, this was a slice of heaven.

"Thank you for last night," she finally slipped in between brandings.

"Don't worry about it."

His tone was gruff. Probably because he was busy, concentrating on what he was doing.

"Well I do worry about it. I didn't set out to get stinking drunk. Or to have you take care of me."

His gaze lifted to hers while they waited for Bobby to bring the next calf over. "Someone had to, since you were in no shape to take care of yourself."

She leaned back on her heels. "You're not responsible for me."

His gaze was direct. Unnerving. "I'll always be responsible for you, darlin'. You may have walked out on our marriage, but I never walked out on you."

And just like that, the floodgates opened. Tears welled in her eyes and threatened to spill over. She pushed off her feet and stood, jerking the gloves off as she walked away in such a hurry she had no idea where she was going, only that she knew she had to get away from him. Away from here.

She climbed over the fence and kept walking, no destination in mind. She could walk for hours, days, and not reach the end of the Bar M's land. It didn't matter. She only needed space and distance, away from the knot of emotion Mason's words had caused.

But no matter how far she walked, she couldn't escape what he'd said.

She hadn't wanted to come home, hadn't wanted to see Mason. Coward that she was, she'd known what would be waiting for her here. The old feelings, the emotions she'd tried to tell herself were long gone, but weren't. They hadn't died, even if she'd tried her best to kill them.

She still loved him. She'd never stopped. She'd just run away from what she felt, too afraid to stick it out, to see if she could handle loving someone so intensely it made her heart hurt.

She'd loved her parents like that, and had lost them. It had left a hole in her heart so deep she'd never recovered from it. And when she'd fallen in love with Mason, the depth of her feelings for him had scared her to death. Because if she ever lost him, she wasn't sure she'd survive it. So instead, she'd walked away.

Better to have lost than ever to have loved. It hurt a hell of a lot less in the long run. And you win your sanity that way.

Two years later, she didn't feel like she had won a damn thing. Her victory was hollow.

valerie avoided mason and the family the rest of the day. Fortunately Jolene and Brea stayed busy and didn't bother her except when Brea showed off her new look, which was spectacular, as Valerie had known it would be.

Valerie stayed in her room, didn't come down to supper; instead she ate alone upstairs.

Yeah, she was brooding and avoiding, but it worked for her. Better to avoid than to face the truth. She was really good at avoiding truths, had been doing it for years now.

But by night she was bored and restless. She tried a bubble bath and a book, but that didn't help at all. She was tired of staring at the four walls. Some air might help.

Wearing only the clingy short nightgown she'd tossed on after her bath, she figured she was safe since it was late enough that everyone would be in bed. She snuck downstairs and brewed a pot of steaming-hot coffee, knowing the caffeine wouldn't keep her awake. Years of medical school had taught her to sleep when it was time to sleep, no matter what was buzzing around in her system.

She grabbed a blanket off the back of one of the sofas, stepped out onto the back porch with coffee in hand and took a seat on one of the cushioned, wicker love seats. She pulled her legs underneath her, wrapped the blanket over her and sipped her coffee, staring out at the stars. Now this she had missed. The night was clear and quiet, the sky clear of clouds and the stars so close it seemed she could reach out and grab one. She couldn't see the stars like this in Dallas. Too much congestion, too many city lights and buildings, got in the way. Out here there was nothing but her and the endless sky.

Until she heard the crunch of boots on gravel. The good thing about a quiet night in the country was that no one could sneak up on you.

And okay, maybe she'd expected to see him. She knew his patterns, knew he was often the last out at night, roaming the pens, checking the cattle. But if she delved too deeply into why she was out here, she might not like what she discovered.

He stepped up on the porch and took a seat next to her, stretched his long legs out, tipped his hat back and didn't say a word. She liked that he didn't hit her with questions about why she'd disappeared earlier today, or where she'd been.

"I'd forgotten how peaceful it is here at night."

He nodded. "The quiet at the end of the day is one of the things I like best. Gives me time to settle my mind, organize my plans, go back over what I did today and all that needs to be done tomorrow."

"Being a ranch foreman is a big job. You're doing great at it."

She caught the hint of a smile curling the corners of his mouth. "Thanks. Jolene does a lot of the work, too. She's a one-woman tornado."

Valerie laughed. "Always has been. She was born with excess energy."

"And she uses every bit of it running herd on all the cowboys and the cattle. She was born to run this ranch."

"I know. Dad would have been so proud of her."

"Of you, too. Look at you, a doctor now. He'd have busted his suspenders sticking his chest out with pride."

Valerie pushed back the melancholy and settled for a smile as she pictured her dad doing just that. "Thank you."

"So tell me about this new job in Dallas."

"It's a four-physician general practice. One of the docs is moving to Atlanta, so that left an open slot. I worked with all three of the others doing my residency rotation, got along with them well, and they offered me a position when Dr. Greene decided to pull out and move."

"Sounds like a good spot for you."

She took a swallow of coffee. "It is. I lucked into it."

"I don't think luck had anything to do with it." Mason rose, grabbed her cup. "Want a refill?"

"Sure."

He went inside, came back out a couple minutes later with two steaming cups and handed one to her.

"Thanks."

He resumed his seat next to hers and took a couple swallows of coffee, staring out into the darkness. "Seems to me you worked your ass off in school and during residency. I'd say if you got a good offer it's because you're a damn fine doctor. It's that practice you're going to work for that lucked out."

She didn't know what to say to that, was still surprised he was even speaking to her, much less complimenting her. "Thank you. I am very excited about the opportunity. It's nice to finally *be* a doctor instead of a student."

"You've always been a doctor, Val. You've been taking care of everyone around here for as long as I can remember. You put everyone else's needs above your own."

She snorted. "I'm hardly the self-sacrificing sort, Mason. You give me too much credit." She'd always thought herself selfish, putting what she wanted above what was best for the ranch, for her family. For her marriage.

"Aren't you? You put off a semester of college when Brea came down with pneumonia. You nursed her back to health, stayed by her side, then fought like hell to catch up when you went back to school."

"She's my sister. She needed me." Valerie had become the de facto parent after theirs had died. Sure there'd been Lila, but Valerie had always felt that because she was the oldest sister, Brea and Jo were her responsibility.

"She had Lila. And Jolene. And just about everyone else here who could have seen to her. And what about when Jolene fell off the horse and broke her arm? You were the one to splint it right so we could take her into town to get it set and cast."

"That's basic first aid."

"You were fourteen at the time."

She smiled, remembering the curse words streaming out of a then ten-year-old Jolene's mouth when she'd fallen off that horse. And even then Valerie had been immersed in wanting to help the sick and hurt, had rushed to her sister, quieted her tears, had wrapped and splinted her arm against her side. "I love medicine."

"Like I said, you always take care of everyone. When are you going to start seeing to your own needs?"

Her gaze snapped to Mason's. "What are you talking about?"

He laid his coffee cup on the table, took hers and put it there, too, then stood. He pulled her up, held his hands in hers. The blanket tangled between them, the only barrier to keep her naked legs from brushing the denim of his jeans.

"I'm talking about having someone in your life, Val. Companionship, sex, a man to lie down next to you at night."

All those things she'd had and walked away from—with him. The chill of the night evaporated and she was suddenly consumed by heat. Mason's hands, his body so close, his words evoking just what she needed but hadn't had in far too long. "I don't . . . I haven't . . ."

His brows knitted in a tight frown. "How long?"

She tilted her head back and looked him square in the eye. "Since you."

"Goddammit."

He let go of her hands and pulled her against him. The blanket fell to the ground, and her breasts were crushed against his chest. His mouth came down on hers, obliterating thought, objection, anything that was in her mind but the feel of his lips on hers.

On a gasp she accepted the kiss, parted her lips, wound her arms around him. He groaned, one arm sliding down her back to draw her even closer.

It wasn't a gentle kiss. It was hungry, pent-up passion, the kind of kiss a man gave a woman when he'd gone without for too damn long. Valerie tasted the fierce need in the way he moved his mouth over hers, in the commanding way he laid his hands on her, even in the way he breathed.

He rocked against her, his cock already stone-hard. It shocked her to her toes to realize he wanted her this much. No man who had a steady woman—like that blonde in the bar—or who was getting sex on a regular basis, could be this ravenous.

A part of her was giddy with this knowledge. But her elation fled under the rampant assault of his mouth on her senses.

His hands were everywhere, roaming her body, lifting up her nightgown, baring her skin to the night and to anyone else who might be wandering the ranch property.

"Mason." She pulled her lips from his. "We're on the back porch."

"No one's around." He bent, lifted the blanket and draped it over her, shielding her. "I need to touch you."

"We could go inside."

His lips lifted in a dangerous smile that made her quiver. "I don't want to go inside. I want you here. Do you know how pretty you are in the moonlight?"

She'd never hear that from a man in the city. She tucked her bottom lip between her teeth, mesmerized by his face, the lines snaking out from the corners of his eyes because he never wore sunglasses. She reached up, traced the lines on his face, the ones that spoke of working while the elements beat down on you.

He took her wrists in his hands and tucked them down at her sides, then captured her lips again with a slow slide of his mouth against hers that made her forget she was on the back porch, made her forget everything but being in this place with this man. She tingled all over, was singly aware of every brush of his lips, every flick of his tongue against hers.

He cupped his hand at her neck, then let it slide down to her collarbone, burning a path toward her breasts.

"You aren't wearing much."

"I took a bath. Threw on this nightgown."

He leaned back, scanned her body. "Sexy."

Her nipples were tight points awaiting his touch. He slid his thumb over them and she damned her gown for being in the way. She gasped, wanting more, needing to feel his hand against the taut, aching buds. This tease of his thumbs rolling over her made her legs shake, made her wet and needy and ready to pull the gown off so he could cup her breasts. But he laid his hand between her breasts, then snaked his fingers down over her belly. It quivered in response. He tugged on the hem of the gown and bunched it in his fist.

"I want to take a lot of time with you, Valerie, but I don't have much patience."

"I don't need it."

He tightened his hold on the fabric, lifted it over her hips to bare her lower body to the cool night air.

"You naked under this?" he asked, his gaze direct, probing, hot.

"Yes."

"Damn. Part your legs."

Mason was no-nonsense about everything, including sex. He went after what he wanted, a trait that had always thrilled her, especially now when she didn't want hearts and flowers and sweet-talking. She wanted him with a primal passion that belied her usual reserved nature.

She broadened her stance, giving him access.

He wasted no time, sliding his palm across her sex. She gripped his shoulders at the first contact of his calloused hand on her flesh, his touch sparking pleasure peaks along her clit. She shuddered at the contact, arched against him, craving more.

He was relentless, not giving her time to breathe as he rubbed her flesh and slid his finger inside her. Heat and moisture pooled as her pussy gripped his finger in a tight vise.

"Look at me, Val."

She tilted her head back, her body shaking with desire as she read the tension on his face when he touched her. Mason knew her body like no one else ever could. Maybe that's why she'd never let another man touch her. Who could give her this kind of pleasure but him?

She rose up on her toes to draw closer to his touch, waves of pleasure undulating around her. She arched against him, rocking her sex against his hand, silently begging him to take her there.

"I've missed being inside you." His whispered words were harsh and filled with promise as he wrapped his arm around her back, drove his hand against her clit and shattered her.

He dipped down and took her mouth, drinking in her cries of pleasure as wave after wave crashed over her, leaving her shaky and senseless. He took her down easy, his finger still inside her, pumping slow and easy.

He'd always mastered her body like this, made her forget where she was, who she was. Who they were.

And who they weren't anymore.

He eased his finger out of her, smiled down at her, made her ache inside for more. It would be so easy to touch him, to unbuckle his belt, slide her hand in his jeans and wrap her fingers around the hot, hard heat of his cock. Even the thought of fucking him outside, sheathing him inside her, made her weak in the knees.

But she'd already lost her mind once tonight, had connected with him in a way she'd sworn never to do again. And she wanted to again, wanted him inside her so fiercely it shook her to her core.

She shouldn't want that much. She shouldn't want Mason. This was wrong. Hadn't she spent two years away from the ranch so she could get over him, so she could stand next to him without feeling the bone-melting desire for him that had always made her lose her senses?

Maybe two years hadn't been long enough.

She took a step back and his smile died.

"What's wrong?"

She smoothed her hair back, bent down and reached for the blanket to wrap it around her like a shield of armor. "We shouldn't have done this."

He arched a brow. "Why not?"

She felt awful, like she'd led him on. She hadn't meant to, hadn't meant for this to happen at all. "I think you know why not. We're divorced."

His jaw set in what she knew was irritation, he said, "Doesn't mean we can't fuck."

"Is that all we are together?" Then again, he should be pissed. At her. He had every right. God, she was confused. "And don't you have a girlfriend? What is she going to think?"

He rubbed his temple. "What the hell are you talking about? What girlfriend? I don't—"

She held up her hand. "Never mind. Maybe I'm wrong. And why don't you have a girlfriend? It's been two years, Mason. You have to let me go."

He stared at her, shook his head. "Woman, you make no sense at all." He turned and walked away, down the stairs, blending into the darkness.

Valerie stood on the porch, watching him disappear, feeling a hundred times stupid for letting this happen. For hurting him, when she should have known better.

She was always hurting him. And herself in the process.

She should have never come back, no matter how much Jolene demanded it.

Two years hadn't been enough time.

seven

"you're grumpy as a horny bull with no cows," Jolene announced the next day.

Mason decided to ignore Jolene, instead putting all his concentration on rewiring the section of fence they'd set out to work on today.

"Are you deliberately ignoring me?" she asked.

"Trying to."

She bent beside him, clipped off the end of the wire that Mason had just wound tight around the top of the post, then stood, moving down the line next to him. "It's Val, isn't it?"

"Leave it alone, Jo."

"Oh, right. She gets you all riled up and I have to deal with the aftereffects. So I don't think I'll leave it alone. What did she do now to piss you off?"

Got him hard, came apart under his hand, then said the whole thing was a mistake. She made him half-crazy, confused the hell out of him. He had no idea what Valerie wanted, didn't know why he'd bothered to step up on the porch last night. He should have ignored her, walked by without saying a word. But she'd looked so damn lost sitting up there by herself. And he was just fucking stupid enough to want to comfort her.

He should have known that comfort would lead to sex. Or almost sex. She'd gotten off, anyway. Being with her only led to complications. Complications he didn't need.

"She didn't do anything. Just let it go."

"She doesn't really know what she wants, Mason. And she still loves you."

He choked out a laugh. "I don't think so."

"Don't you? Bet she's confused as hell, running hot and cold, isn't she?"

He didn't answer.

"Thought so. Let me talk to her."

He shifted his gaze up to Jolene. "I don't think that's a good idea. You know she doesn't like to talk about the two of us, especially not to anyone else."

Sunlight shadowed Jolene's features, but Mason could well imagine the giant grin on her face. "And pissing off my sister gives me a particular pleasure. Since she doesn't live on the ranch anymore, I've missed our tussles. Don't deny me that."

He shrugged. "What you do with your sister is up to you. Don't do it on my account. I can take care of my relationship with Valerie on my own."

"Yeah. You're doing a bang-up job so far."

He sighed, tipped his hat up and leaned one arm against the fence post. "What the hell do you think I should do? You're right. She runs hot and cold. One minute she says what she wants, and the next she wants something different. She left for a reason, Jo. She didn't want to stay."

Jolene laid her gloved hand on top of Mason's. "She left because she was scared."

"I know what she's scared of. I can't change how she feels. Neither can you. Leave it alone. You might think you can bully her, but she'll just dig in her heels and run again."

Jolene sighed, turned away and leaned against the fence. "You're probably right. But it frustrates the hell out of me when I know she still loves you."

"I don't know about that. I used to think she did. Now I'm not so sure. And either way, you can't force her to stop being afraid. She's either going to get over it, or she isn't."

"You can live with that?"

"I can't decide it for her. Those choices need to be hers." He picked up his tools. "Come on, there's a section of old fence that needs to be cut off and relaid a quarter mile south. Let's ride."

Ride, work and not think about Valerie. That's what Mason needed to do today. He'd done too damn much thinking about her already and it was taking time away from his job. A ranch didn't run itself.

valerie busied herself going over the ranch paperwork that Jolene had insisted she and Brea catch up on. Tedious, mile-high financial and inventory reports, but Jolene said they both needed to understand the ranch's net worth and current inventory before they got together to make any decisions about the future ownership.

Since he had no heirs, Uncle Ronald's portion of the ranch ownership automatically went to all three sisters, as agreed upon when Ronald and Valerie's father had generated joint ownership in the Bar M. So Uncle Ronald's will would have no bearing on the ownership of the ranch.

"And I thought technical reports were hideously boring," Brea said, pushing the chair back in the office and yawning.

Valerie nodded. "I'm sure Jo is doing this to punish us for leaving the ranch in her hands."

"In her more than capable hands, from the looks of these reports. The growth in the Bar M the past ten years has been nothing short of phenomenal. She and Mason have done an amazing job."

Yes, they had. Valerie remembered Mason talking about plans for the ranch. She'd only half paid attention. The Bar M had been her parents' ranch. After they died, she wasn't much interested in what happened to it. Now she saw what a mistake that thinking had been. Her parents would be sad to know she hadn't taken an active part in making the Bar M grow, in nourishing their dream.

But Jolene had. And so had Mason. They'd kept her parents' homestead flourishing and profitable. "Jo and Mason have done wonders for the ranch."

Brea sniffed. "I don't know about you, Val, but I don't feel like we deserve any part of it. I've been so busy with my life in Tulsa, I didn't pay much attention to what they were doing out here. And to look over these reports now . . . wow."

"Yeah. Wow, indeed. While you and I selfishly went about our lives, Jolene and Mason have been busting their asses making something out of the Bar M. Mom and Dad would have been proud."

"Of them."

"Yes. Of them." Valerie was ashamed of her fear and her cowardice. And yet she still couldn't see herself staying here, being a rancher's wife. Being Mason's wife. Throwing her heart full-fledged into a relationship, knowing that at any moment it could be taken away. Loving someone was dangerous.

Just then Jolene burst through the door of the office, her hands, shirt and jeans covered in blood. "Valerie. Come now."

Valerie flew out of the chair. "Are you hurt?" she asked as she caught up to Jolene, grabbed her arm and swung her around.

"It's not me. Come on."

"Hang on a second." Valerie dashed upstairs to grab her medical bag, slipped into her boots and practically flew down the stairs. Jolene was waiting impatiently at the door. Without a word, they ran out the door.

"What happened?

"Knife slipped. Got him in the leg."

"Who?" Valerie asked as they jumped into the Jeep.

"Mason."

Valerie went cold; her heart stuttered and her throat went dry. "Mason? How bad?"

"I don't know. There's a lot of blood. He wanted to hop on his horse and come back here. But there's blood pouring everywhere and I wouldn't let him."

Jolene drove fast, zooming down the road, then off-road as she sailed into the pasture. Valerie held on to the door handle as the Jeep went flying over hard rock and bumps in the field. She saw Mason's horse tethered along the fence line. He was on the ground, still conscious, thankfully. Before Jolene came to a complete stop, Valerie flew out of the Jeep; she dug her heels in and pushed off into a dead run, her heart pounding.

"Jesus, Valerie, you're white as a sheet," Mason said.

"Shut up." She dropped her bag beside her, slipped on latex gloves and grabbed a scissors.

"Hey. Don't cut those."

"Shut up," she said again, forcing herself to focus on the task at hand. Right now Mason was a patient. That's all she'd allow herself to think about.

"Jo, go get some of the hands. We're going to need help getting him into the Jeep when we're done here."

"Got it."

"I don't need—"

"Shut up, Mason."

"You're a mean doctor."

She ignored that, too, and cut away his jeans from the bottom up and over his knee, then gently pulled away the material. The blood was fresh, the gash on the top of his thigh deep. Dear God, it was so close to his femoral artery. A few more inches . . .

"It's not bad," he said. "I was just a dumbass and stabbed myself when the clippers slipped."

"It is bad. You need stitches. You're damn lucky you didn't nick an artery or we wouldn't be having this conversation."

"Just throw a few stitches into me so I can get back to work."

She jerked her gaze up to his face. "Are you out of your mind? You're done for the day."

His jaw set, he leveled a mutinous glare in her direction. "I'm not a pussy. It's hardly a scratch."

Jolene came back with Walker and Gage.

"Trying to commit suicide, I heard," Walker said with a smirk as he came up to them.

"Fuck you," Mason said. "You trying to take over my job?"

"You dyin' today?" Walker asked.

"Not likely."

"Then I guess I'll have to wait until you pull some other dumbass move."

Gage squatted down next to Valerie. "She scissored right through your Wranglers."

"I know."

"That's a hangin' offense, cutting through a man's Wranglers," Gage said with a smirk on his face.

Valerie finished pressure dressing the wound, taped it, then glared up at all three grinning men. "I can't believe all you're worried about is his jeans."

"Hey, work clothes are hard to break in," Gage said, standing. He held out a hand for Mason. "Think you can get up or do you need Walker and me to carry you?"

"Assholes." He jerked on Gage's hand and stood.

"Hey!" Valerie pivoted to shoot daggers of venom at Gage. "Take it easy. I don't want that bandage falling off and him bleeding again. I just got it stopped. Now, let's see if you morons can gently get him into the Jeep."

"Yes, ma'am," Walker said, sliding around Mason's side. "Come on, honey. Let me carry you."

"You try picking me up and you can pick up your last paycheck when we get back to the house."

Valerie rolled her eyes as Gage and Walker snickered the entire way to the Jeep. Men so didn't take injuries seriously.

"Take him upstairs to my room," she instructed when they reached the house.

"My place is fine," Mason said.

"I have more medical supplies in my room," she replied.

Gage and Walker took him upstairs. She ran ahead of them and placed a sheet over her bed.

"Lay him down there. And get his pants off while I get my supplies ready."

She went into the bathroom and grabbed some towels, ran a washcloth under hot water. When she came out, Mason was alone. On her bed. Wearing just a sleeveless T-shirt and his boxers.

"Where did everyone go?"

"The guys snickered about you ordering me stripped down and what kind of wicked intentions you might have for me, so they said they'd give us privacy. And Jolene and Brea said they didn't care to see me in my underwear. So I guess it's just you and your patient, Doc."

She rolled her eyes. "Whatever." She eased the bandage off, cleaned the wound area with hot water, then antiseptic. Mason always had been tough and didn't even wince when she poured the antiseptic in the wound, or when she numbed it with the needle. He just watched her with that unfathomable gaze of his that never failed to make a room heat up a good ten degrees or so.

She pulled off her jacket and long-sleeved shirt, leaving her in only her tank top, and went to work.

*   *   *

mason was enjoying the view. sure, he'd done something stupid today, but at least the end result was turning out pretty enjoyable.

"Hey, I didn't know a striptease went with the stitching."

She lifted her head, her bewitching gaze colliding with his. "It's hot in here and I need freedom of movement."

"Whatever you say, Doc."

Her lips compressed and he knew she was trying desperately for control.

He liked her out of control, like she'd been last night. Not thinking, just reacting. The softness of her skin under his hand was enough to make him hard. Which given his current predicament was probably not a good idea. He counted cattle instead of thinking about Valerie's half naked body next to him.

"Am I hurting you?" She paused, needle in hand.

Yeah, she made his balls ache. "No. Not feeling a thing."

"This cut is deep. You're lucky it's farther down your thigh and not near your femoral artery. Out there, middle of nowhere, stabbing yourself like that. You could have bled to death in minutes if you'd hit the artery. There's not a hospital near enough we could have gotten you to."

He was pretty sure she was talking to herself and not to him, so he let her ramble. Her hands were sure as she sewed him up. Part of her hair had escaped her ponytail and fell against her cheek. It didn't seem to bother her any as she concentrated on her task. He wanted to reach out and sift strands of her hair through his fingers. He already knew the sensation—it felt like silk. He remembered how it used to slide across his thighs when her mouth had been busy on his dick.

She jerked up, stared at his now erect cock lying rigid against his boxer briefs. Her gaze slid to his face.

"Do you mind? I'm trying to work here."

He grinned. "I have to do something to pass the time."

She lifted a brow. "Mason."

He shrugged. "Can't help if it I was thinking about the last time you were . . . down there."

Her face turned a pretty shade of pink. "Goddammit, I'm sewing you up here. This isn't foreplay."

"Sorry. I'll think about horse shit instead."

Her lips quirked. "Uh . . . thanks."

She bandaged his leg after she finished sewing, then filled a syringe. "Roll on your side."

He did. She drew his boxers down over his hip to give him a shot.

"You just want to look at my ass."

"I'm giving you a shot of antibiotic to ward off infection."

She wasn't going to give. Even a little.

"Want a Band-Aid?"

"I'm not twelve, Valerie." He rolled back over, then started to sit up.

"Oh no. You stay right there." She planted her palm on his chest and applied pressure. As if she could keep him down if he really wanted up. To placate her, he stayed there.

"I'm stitched, right?"

"Yes."

"You're a good doctor, Valerie. Thanks. But I'm going to be fine."

There was something about her expression that was . . . off. He didn't know what it was.

"Just . . . hang there for a minute, okay?"

She didn't wait for his answer, just pivoted and went into the bathroom. Mason heard the water running, so he slid off the bed and walked in there.

She was leaning over the sink, the water running. She gripped the sides of the sink so hard her knuckles were white. So was her face. Their gazes met in the mirror.

There were tears in her eyes. He stepped into the bathroom, stopped just behind her.

She didn't turn around. "I told you to stay on the bed."

He wound his arms around her. "I'm fine. What's wrong?"

"Nothing."

He'd seen the tears in her eyes, felt the tension in her body. "Valerie. What's wrong?"

She shuddered, sighed, then leaned against him. "This is what's wrong, Mason. What's always been wrong."

"You caring about me. Worrying about me."

"Yes."

She was shaking.

"Honey, it was just a little cut."

She shook her head. "All that blood. It wasn't just a little cut."

He smiled over her shoulder. "If Jolene hadn't made such a big deal out of it, I'd have stopped the bleeding, slapped a bandage on it and gone back to work."

She shuddered. "It was a deep gash. It needed stitches."

"Maybe it did. It's not the first time I've gotten cut up doing chores around here. That's ranch life. We get hurt out here all the time."

She lifted her gaze to the mirror, met his. "And sometimes you die."

"Your parents didn't die on the ranch."

"I know. But people do die out here."

"People die in the city, too. Every damn day. Odds are higher there than here."

"I don't . . ."

"What?"

She shook her head. "Nothing." She tried to pry his fingers loose. This time he wasn't going to let go. He turned her around, cupped her face in his hands.

"You can't run from how you feel, Val. Sometime you're going to have to face it."

"I can't."

Her pain hurt him. He wished he could take it out of her and make it go away. But he couldn't. Instead, he drew her lips to his, brushed his mouth across hers. Her breath whispered across his with a quivering sigh.

"Mason."

"Quit fighting what we both want." What they both needed. He walked backward, leading her into the bedroom.

"Your leg . . ."

"Is fine. Not bleeding. You stitched it up good." He held on to her, leading her to the bed, sitting down with her, then lying down with her. On their bed, where they belonged together.

"You shooting for a pity fuck?" she asked as he rolled her to face him.

He laughed. "Is it working?"

Her lips lifted, color coming back to her face now. "Maybe. I'm worried about your leg."

"Then I guess you can keep close watch over it, Doc." He grabbed her butt and rocked her against the long, hard part of him that ached to be inside her.

She gasped, pressed her hands against his chest. "You rip those stitches out with . . . strenuous activity, I'm not sewing you back up."

"Duly noted." He slid his hand against her neck and laid his mouth on hers, let her know how much he wanted her, wanted this. Her pulse kicked up and he supposed that was his answer—she did want to be here with him, no matter how much she protested the opposite. The warmth of her breath released against him in a sigh and her body relaxed. Whatever war she fought internally, he supposed she'd finally given up the fight.

That was all the encouragement he needed. He let his hand slide from her neck to her collarbone to her breast. She didn't have a bra on, and her nipple peaked under her flimsy cotton shirt. Damn, it felt good to touch her, to feel the softness of her body against him again. He smoothed his palm over the hard bud to torture it a little more, and she arched into his hand, filling it with the softness of her breast. He jerked the material to the side and planted his mouth over her nipple, encouraged by the sounds she made as he sucked and licked. He'd missed those sounds of pleasure, had always loved listening to her in the dark when she writhed against him. The one thing Valerie could never deny was the sexual chemistry between them. There might be a million things wrong with their marriage, but sex hadn't been one of them. Here they could connect, and all problems were tossed. It was just the two of them, naked, him inside her, rocking her until she screamed.

He wanted that now, wanted to give her a release he knew she needed. He let go of her nipple, lifted her shirt off, and she rolled onto her back, gifting him with that serene, knowing smile that said she knew there was no going back now. She raised her arms over her head and let him remove the rest of her clothes.

Naked, she still took his breath away. He slipped off his briefs and shirt, then rolled back onto the bed, climbing between her legs to press a kiss to her inner thigh. He slipped his hands under her butt to lift her, then laid his mouth against her sex, taking in the sound of her delighted sigh.

God she was hot, her taste tart and sexy, and it made his cock so hard he could go off right there, spilling all over the sheets like a first-timer. Valerie did that to him, always did, made him hot and hard and ready in seconds. He never could resist the taste and sweet smell of her. She'd been a fire in his blood since he first became a man. She'd always been the only woman he craved like a drug he couldn't do without.

She lifted against him, her eager movements urging him to lick around her clit, flick the hard nub until she let out a soft moan, her juices melting all over his tongue and chin.

He licked her pussy, slid his tongue inside and ate all she

gave him. He could never get enough of Valerie, had always loved spending nights pleasuring her, listening to her moan, making her come. Her body responded to his touch, to his mouth, with wild abandon. Once she had given up thinking about all the reasons she shouldn't . . . or wouldn't . . . then yeah, she gave it all to him.

He slid a finger inside her, and her walls grabbed onto him while he thrust. He licked her, sucked her clit, felt her tighten inside and out.

Yeah, baby, give it to me.

She arched, her body tensed, and she shuddered, cried out with her orgasm. He held on to her, licking her, taking her down easy. He waited for her body to stop shuddering, then reached onto the floor and into his jeans pocket for the condom he'd stuck in there—just in case. Now he was damn glad he'd thought about being prepared, even if he had presumed. The last thing he wanted was to be without, especially right now. His balls throbbed and he wanted inside Valerie so badly he was about to burst.

She rolled onto her back and watched as he tore open the packet and applied the condom. "So you either carry those things on you all the time or you thought I was a sure thing."

He spread her knees apart and climbed between them. "I don't carry them with me all the time. Just . . . recently."

She cocked her head to the side. "Because . . ."

"Because all I've done is think about fucking you since you showed up here."

valerie sucked in a breath. mason's naked honesty had always gotten to her. His sexual frankness was brutal, intense, and had always excited her, especially now. Knowing he still wanted her despite everything that had happened between them stunned her.

"Mason, I—"

He slid his hand over her breasts, cupped one and lazily circled her throbbing nipple with his thumb. "How about we stop talking?"

Distracted by the sensations, she realized he was right—she should just shut up and enjoy being with him. She always overanalyzed the hell out of everything. Now wasn't the time. Not when his cock nudged her pussy, and she ached to feel him inside her.

She cupped the back of his head and drew him on top of her, absorbing the feel of his body against her. Sometimes she wondered what the hell she'd been thinking walking away from something that felt this good, especially when Mason slid his cock inside her with a powerful thrust. She gasped, and he claimed her mouth with a demanding kiss.

And she felt a hundred times stupid for ever leaving this man. No wonder women from all over wanted him. She'd oh so conveniently allowed herself to forget what it was like to be made love to by Mason. He pushed inside her, then withdrew, swept his hands underneath her butt to lift her pelvis against his, grinding against her clit and causing explosions of sensation that made her cry out and forget that they weren't in the house alone.

She lifted against him, wanting more of him inside her, more of him moving intimately against her, more of his mouth, his tongue licking against hers. His possession of her was relentless, demanding, sweeping her away until she had no thought left. She could only feel his cock sliding in and out, thrusting hard, moving her back against the mattress as if he wanted to crawl inside her. That's what she wanted, his ultimate possession of her, what she'd missed so damn much but refused to face. She raked her nails down his arms and he growled against her mouth, deepened his kiss at the same time he plunged deeper inside her.

Tears threatened, and she knew being close to him like this would open her emotions like never before. Being with Mason had always been more than sex.

It had been love and sex—a dangerous combination. With Mason, her heart wasn't safe.

But oh the things he could do to her body. He moved his mouth from her lips to her neck, licking his way down her throat. She shivered and he groaned, lifted up and drove deep, and that was all it took for her to crumble. She let out a soft cry and shattered around his cock, rocking against him with wild abandon. He moved back to her mouth and kissed her, tightening against her as he came in several hard thrusts.

They stayed glued together like that for a long while. Valerie smoothed her hands over Mason's sweat-soaked back, her legs locked around him like she never wanted to let him go.

But she would let him go. This had been a onetime thing, never to be repeated.

"I'm hungry," he said against her neck.

She laughed. "What time is it anyway?"

"No clue. But I'll bet we missed supper. Let's go check the kitchen for leftovers." He swung his legs over the bed and went into the bathroom for a minute, then came out and grabbed his jeans. She took a look at his leg as he got dressed. The wound wasn't bleeding, so their sex session hadn't affected his injury.

He zipped his jeans and grabbed his shirt. Valerie made no move to climb out of bed or get dressed.

"You coming?"

She drew her knees up to her chest. "I don't think us being seen together is a good idea."

"Why not?"

"I don't want people to know."

He sat on the bed, slid his hand up her thigh. "Val. We've spent the past few hours up here in your room. I think folks will make the connection."

She laid her head on her knees. "Damn."

"Hey, maybe I'm not a movie star, but I'm hardly ugly enough to have to put a bag over my head when you fuck me."

She laughed and raised her head to look at him. "That's not at all what I meant. It's just that people will assume we're back together."

"And we're not."

She knew it would come to this—she was going to hurt him again. "No, Mason, we're not."

"So you just want to meet me in dark corners and fuck me?"

She snorted. "Uh . . ."

His hand drifted up her thigh, and her body flushed with heat and desire.

"I think you worry way too much about what people think. But if you want to use me like a sex toy, then that's just between us and nobody else's business."

That wasn't at all the Mason she used to know. "So that's what we're down to? Just sex?"

He shrugged. "You're the one setting the ground rules, darlin'. I like a good fuck just as well as anyone else. And we're damn good in bed together."

She blew out a breath. He was right about that. "And you'd be all right with that? With it just being about the sex?"

"If you are."

Could she be? If Mason was, she supposed she could be, too. God knows there wasn't enough sex in her life, and when she got back to Dallas there'd be no time for it. Why not enjoy it with a man she had such incredible chemistry with, while she had the chance? "You're on."

"Okay, then." He stood, pulled off his shirt and unzipped his jeans, letting them fall to the floor.

"What are you doing?" she asked as he climbed onto the bed and pulled her on top of him.

"Getting started."

"I thought you were hungry."

He drew her body up so her nipple teased his bottom lip. He grinned up at her. "I am. We have two years of lost sex to catch up on. We can have food later."

eight

according to jolene, mason's injury was the big
news around the neighboring ranches for the next several days.
Though Valerie had no idea why it was such a big deal. Mason seemed
to heal fast; in fact, the next day he had been back to work riding his
horse and herding cattle, as if nothing had happened to him.

Truth be told, she probably had overreacted. So had Jolene, who
admitted being freaked out by seeing the shock of crimson spreading from his jeans. But Valerie assured her sister she'd done the right
thing by coming to get her. There was no way to know how bad
Mason had been hurt, and like a lot of ranching men, Mason would
have tried to brush her off no matter how bad the injury was.

They all thought they were impervious to serious injury.

And okay, he was fine. More than fine. Every spare moment he
had, they spent together, alone, making out or making love. Valerie
doubted they were fooling anyone—at least no one at the house.
The curious and knowing glances they got from her sisters, Lila
and the hands told her everyone was aware of what was going on

between her and Mason, but no one had said a word. And as long as no one asked, she didn't have to explain their relationship. Since there wasn't a relationship. They were having sex as long as she was on the ranch. And when it was time to leave the ranch . . .

She didn't want to think that far ahead. For now, it was fun. She'd finally given up feeling so tense around Mason and everyone else in the house, which she was certain made everyone happy as hell, since she realized what a total bitch she'd been since she arrived. Maybe getting laid had helped. She giggled, glad she was alone in the kitchen after having insisted to Lila that she was perfectly capable of putting the breakfast dishes away. Poor Lila did everything around here. Valerie had already talked to Jolene about bringing in someone to help Lila, though she suspected Lila would pitch a fit about it, claiming she could manage just fine without someone underfoot getting in her way. But Valerie had noticed that Lila didn't bend as easily as she used to; her ankles were swollen, and she rubbed her back a lot. It was time for her to start taking it easy.

Valerie had just gotten the last of the dishes put away in the cupboard when she heard the front door. She hung up the dish towel and saw Brea swoop in, her cheeks pink from the strong spring wind.

"We've got company," Brea said, pulling off her jacket and tossing it over one of the kitchen chairs.

"Really? Who?"

Valerie stepped around the corner and smiled at the older couple in the entryway. It was Bob and Margaret Stenner from one of the neighboring ranches. "Bob, Margaret, come on in."

Bob nodded and took off his cowboy hat, but he wouldn't step off the front door rug. "Don't mean to bother you, Miss Valerie, but Margaret has been complaining about this pain in her neck for about a month now."

"Excuse me?"

"You're a doctor, Valerie," Brea whispered over her shoulder.

"I know I'm a doctor," Valerie snapped back in a hushed whisper, then turned and smiled at the couple. "Um, I'm sorry about your neck, Margaret. Have you been to see Doc Parmalee?"

"Doc Parmalee retired three years ago, Miss Valerie."

"He did?" She scratched her nose. "I didn't know that. Who's the doctor in town now?"

"Isn't one," Margaret said.

"There isn't? So who treats everyone?"

"No one." Bob shook his head. "Gotta drive all the way into Tulsa now if we wanna see a doc."

Valerie was stunned. "Really? That's too far."

Margaret nodded, then winced and reached her hand up to her neck.

"Let me take a look at that, Margaret. Brea, will you take Bob and Margaret into the kitchen while I get my medical bag?"

"Sure. Come on, you two. I'll put some coffee on."

"Sounds great," Bob said. "Much obliged, Miss Brea."

While Brea got Bob and Margaret settled, Valerie went upstairs and grabbed her medical bag, then hurried downstairs and met Mason in the entryway.

"Someone else stab themselves?" he asked, looking down at her bag.

"No. Bob and Margaret Stenner are here. Margaret has a sore neck."

"Ah," he said, nodding as he followed her into the kitchen. "Hey, Bob, Margaret."

They all said hellos, and while Valerie washed her hands, Mason helped himself to the coffee Brea had made. Valerie realized that examining Margaret in the kitchen while everyone sat around sipping coffee and gaping at them just wasn't going to work. She needed to undress Margaret to get a good look at her muscles.

"What's wrong?" Margaret asked, concern lacing her voice after Valerie took a step back.

Valerie laid her hands back on Margaret's shoulders "Nothing. You and I just need some privacy so I can conduct a thorough examination."

"What about the old kitchen?" Brea suggested. "No one uses that anymore. It's got plenty of room, plus a sink to wash up. And God knows Lila keeps every room clean in this place, so you don't have to worry about whether it's a sterile enough environment."

"That's a good idea."

They relocated Margaret to the old kitchen. It was a little sparse, but after they dragged a couple chairs in, Valerie had plenty of light—and privacy—for what she needed to do.

"I can't really tell for sure without X-rays, Margaret," she said, after finishing her examination and pulling off her latex gloves. "But it feels to me like a muscle strain. It seems to be most tender back here." She gently placed two fingers at the C-spine area of Margaret's neck. "But I don't think it's spinal in any way."

Margaret pursed her lips. "Bob's snoring is driving me crazy, so I've spent a couple nights on the sofa." She tilted her head back to look at Valerie. "It's not the most comfortable piece of furniture. I bought it more for looks than comfort. That was a mistake."

Valerie laughed, pulled up a chair in front of Margaret and sat down, then took out her prescription paid, grateful she'd gotten her medical license—and malpractice insurance—in Oklahoma as well as Texas. Not that she'd intended to let her family know that. But she wanted to be able to practice medicine in this state, just in case. "I'm going to write you a prescription for some muscle relaxers. They should help. And while you're at the drugstore in town, get some earplugs. Those should help with Bob's snoring."

Margaret laughed and laid her hands over Valerie's. "Thank you, dear. Your parents would be so proud of you. You make a fine doctor for our town."

"Oh, I'm not—"

But Margaret had already taken the prescription and headed out the door.

"—staying."

Valerie sighed, put away her stuff and closed her bag. Brea popped her head in the door.

"Might as well leave that bag open."

Valerie frowned. "Why?"

"Better come look."

She came out of the kitchen and rounded the corner, then rocked back on the heels of her tennis shoes.

There were half a dozen people in the main kitchen, all sipping coffee and visiting with Lila, who was grinning and offering up cinnamon rolls while happily chatting away as if she'd invited them all.

"Who are all these people?"

Brea's lips lifted. "Your next patients. Word's out that you're the only doctor within a hundred miles, Val. Might as well hang a shingle on the front door."

before he walked in, mason waited until leonard Russell ambled his way out of the old kitchen, tipping his hat to Mason as he did. Valerie was cleaning up medical instruments and washing up the counter. He shut the door behind him and turned the lock.

"Long day?"

She turned and offered up a tired smile. "You have no idea. I must have seen forty patients today." She tossed the paper towels into the wastebasket and pulled up a chair, then collapsed into it.

He had two bottles of beer in his hand. He handed her one.

"Lila left a plate of meat loaf and mashed potatoes in the fridge for you."

She took the beer he offered. "Thank you. This is just what I need. I might be too tired to eat."

She took a couple long swallows of beer and sighed, then set the bottle on the table and smoothed her hair away from her face. She lifted her shoulders up and down.

"Muscles?"

"Yeah."

He moved behind her and started rubbing the kinks out of her shoulders, digging in when he found hard knots. Valerie let her head fall forward.

"God, that feels good."

He continued to work at her muscles, from her shoulders up to her neck, sliding his fingers into her hair. He pulled the ponytail holder out so he could spread his fingers into her scalp and massage there.

"You keep that up, I'll be your slave."

He smiled. "I like the sound of that. Never had a slave before. What would you do for me?"

"Rub my temples and I'll show you."

He came around front and slid his fingers along the side of her head, smoothing lightly along her temples.

She moaned.

His cock hardened.

"I'd forgotten how good this felt, how talented you are with your fingers."

"I like using my fingers on you."

She lifted her head, her hair falling across her face. She swept it away. "Yes, you do. I remember that, too."

His balls throbbed and he laid his hand across the hard ridge of his shaft. Her gaze drifted down, then back up again, her eyes taking on that glassy look that he knew meant desire.

Damn.

"Step closer, Mason."

"I didn't come in here for you to take care of me, Val."

"I know you didn't. Come on."

He did, and she reached for his hips. Just Valerie laying her hands on him got him hot and bothered. Hell, it didn't take much. He loved the woman, had never stopped. That hadn't been a secret to anyone, including himself. He'd wanted her from the first moment he'd met her, when he was a cocksure sixteen-year-old. He still wanted her. Every time with her was like the first time. Their lovemaking had matured, but the fire still burned hot between them.

Maybe he shouldn't want her.

If wishes were horses, as his mama always used to say. And you couldn't help who you loved. She was going to leave again, and he knew it, couldn't stop her if that's what she wanted to do. But while she was here, he was damn well going to have her.

She unzipped his jeans, slid her hand inside and cupped his balls.

"Christ, woman."

She tilted her head back and smiled at him. A devil's smile. His balls tightened.

She peeled back the denim, tugged his jeans over his hips, then his briefs, and wrapped her sweet, hot hand around his shaft. He sucked in a breath when she stroked him, sliding her hand to the base, then drawing it slow and easy to the tip.

"Tease."

The tip of her tongue slid out to coat her lips. He watched the action intently, wanting her tongue on his cock head. But Valerie was in the mood to tease, instead winding her hands around his shaft, smoothing her thumb over the crest, skimming around the pearly fluid that spilled from the slit.

"Woman, you're playing with fire."

She tilted her head back so he could watch her slide her thumb in her mouth. Then she sucked, and he damn near dropped to his knees. She popped her thumb out of her mouth. "Tell me what you want, Mason."

He cupped the back of her neck. "Suck me."

He caught the slight lift of her lips before she took his cock between them, then curled her tongue around the crest and licked him.

If a man could die that way, he'd go damn happy. Valerie's hot mouth wrapped around his cock made his balls tighten. Watching her suck him deep made him want to shoot off right then. But he had to wait, because this was a sight meant to be savored.

He wrapped his hand in her hair, wound it around and clenched hard when she brought the roof of her mouth and her tongue together, creating suction, squeezing him until he tilted his head back and groaned.

Then she hummed, and his head shot back. "Damn, darlin'. Are you trying to get me to come in your mouth?"

She smiled around his cock, and he knew then that's exactly what she wanted. And if that's what she wanted, he'd let her have it.

He leaned back, then thrust forward, fucking her mouth with gentle strokes. She grabbed his ass with both hands and pulled him tighter against her, taking his cock deep—all the way in. When she swallowed, squeezing his cock head, he nearly lost it right then, tightened his hold on her hair and began to thrust faster.

Sweat poured from his face, but he refused to swipe it away. He could only look at Valerie's sweet mouth as she gripped his ass and licked him, the sucking sounds driving him to the brink of sanity.

He was panting now, leaning back, no doubt pulling her hair, but he was past the point of reason. And she wasn't complaining, she was—goddammit—she was humming against his cock again, like she was encouraging him to come.

And oh, hell yes, he was going to. He let out a groan and jettisoned into her mouth. She dug her nails into his ass, which only sent his pleasure higher as wave after wave ripped from him. Valerie kept her mouth around him, letting go of the pressure, until he had nothing left to give, until he was spent and weak. Hell, his legs were shaking.

She pulled her mouth away, licked her lips and sat back in the chair with a satisfied smile.

Still fighting for breath, Mason jerked his pants up, then pulled her up, his fingers fumbling with the zipper of her jeans. She helped him and they managed to get her pants off. He didn't even bother with her top, just lifted her and placed her on the counter.

He felt like a teenager eager to get in a girl's pants. Hell, when *hadn't* he been eager to get inside Valerie? And after what she'd done to him, he was more than ready to return the favor.

"Lean back, darlin'."

She did, bracing herself on her hands. He pulled her legs apart, and damn if that wasn't the sexiest thing seeing her half-naked, her legs spread on the counter. It made his dick harden all over again seeing her like that. He grabbed a chair and pulled it over, then sat and drew her butt to the edge of the counter, heard her soft gasp as he laid his hands on her thighs and moved his head in between them.

"Mason."

She had the softest whisper, and he heard need in her voice. She wasn't anxious anymore, or wary of the two of them being together. He knew Valerie—she wasn't going to accept forever between them. It was just "right now," and he was going to have to be satisfied with that, but he aimed to convince her that forever wasn't such a bad idea.

He kissed her inner thigh, that sweet, sensitive part of her that was so tender, and smelled so damn good. He felt her tremble, and moved his mouth over her sex, licking along the crease of her pussy, just letting his tongue rest there. He liked feeling her body tremble against him, liked knowing he could coax that kind of reaction from her. And when he began to move his tongue against her—up and down—lazily licking her, she moaned and reached out to tangle her fingers in his hair, directing his movements. He liked that she told him, even without words, what she wanted. If there was one thing

Valerie wasn't, it was shy. Once he got her to admit the two of them were great in bed—or in the kitchen—she dove into sex like she'd been starved for it.

Hell, *he'd* been starved for it. She rocked her pussy against him like his tongue was the magic key to heaven. And he was damn well going to take her there. He slid his tongue inside her, then rolled it over her clit.

"Mason. Oh, God, Mason." She cried out as she came, held tight to his head as she shuddered out her orgasm. Goddamn, the woman made him crazy the way she responded. He didn't give her time to come down off that high. He grabbed a condom and pulled her down, bending her over the counter.

He shunted her legs apart and slid inside her with one easy thrust. Valerie arched her back, pushed against him and growled as he drove deep, her passion as hot and intense as his. He gripped her hips, grinding against her, feeling his cock swell as her pussy tightened around him.

"Goddamn, Val," he muttered, leaning back to watch his cock slide into her.

Her only reply was to buck back against him, bending over even more so he could power in deeper.

And he did, fucking her harder, faster, until he had her pinned between his body and the counter. He wrapped his arm around her waist so her belly wouldn't hit the stainless steel counter, and then he pumped harder, hitting her deep.

She dug her nails into his arm and he felt her pussy tighten around him. He buried his face against her nape.

"You gonna come again for me?"

"Yes. Oh, Mason, yes."

He stilled, wanting to feel her pulse around him while she climaxed. She squeezed his cock in a tight vise and that was all it took. He rocked against her a couple times, then let go, his orgasm hitting him so hard it felt like he was splitting in two.

They stayed there like that for a while, catching their breath, Mason still inside her and his arm wrapped around her. She still had a death grip on it.

"I might need more of your doctoring."

"Why?" she asked.

"Your fingernails are embedded in my skin."

"Oh. Sorry." She laughed and smoothed her hands over his arm. "It's your fault."

They disengaged and cleaned up, got dressed and grabbed their long-forgotten beers. Mason leaned against the counter while Valerie sat in the chair and gathered her hair into a ponytail.

"Hope your muscles are a little more relaxed now," he said, finishing off his beer.

"I probably won't be able to walk out of here."

He smiled at that.

"I feel good, Mason. Thank you."

He didn't know what to say to that, so instead, said, "What's good is what you did for the folks in the community today."

Valerie sighed. "I can't believe there's no doctor in town and hasn't been for years. And from what I understand, these people normally won't take the trip into Tulsa, which means they're not being seen on a regular basis. That's not good."

"No, it's not."

"Especially our older folks. They need regular care."

"Yes, they do. Since Doc Parmalee retired, and no one has stepped in to take his place, if someone gets sick, they either have to take the trip into Tulsa, or go without. Most go without."

"Why?"

"Because it's too far. People got used to a local doctor. Someone they could see in town. And Doc Parmalee made house calls. Tulsa is a big, foreign city to a lot of people out here. They don't trust the doctors there."

"That's ridiculous. They can get quality care in the city."

"They want a small town doctor. Hard to get a doctor to set down roots in a place like this."

"Well I don't see why not." She crossed her arms.

Mason gave her a pointed look, and her eyes widened. She shook her head.

"Oh, no. Oh, hell no."

nine

valerie avoided mason all the next day. whenever he came into a room, she made up a valid excuse to leave. She even went so far as to hide, like she was right now. Mason had come in for supper. She was going to feign being busy with patient . . . stuff, so she hid behind the thick wood column. As soon as he passed, she was going to hightail it into what everyone now called the medical office. They'd moved a sturdy folding bed in there so her patients could lie down, and Valerie had ordered instruments and medical supplies she needed for them. Or *the* patients. Not her patients. She wasn't staying. This wasn't a regular thing. It was temporary. She was temporary.

"What the hell are you doing?"

She nearly jumped out of her boots as Jolene caught her in the hall. She whipped around, pushing Jolene into the office and closing the door.

"Don't ever do that to me again."

Jolene held her hands up. "I'm not the one skulking around my own house."

"I'm not skulking. I'm . . . avoiding."

Jolene crossed her arms. "I know what you're doing. You're avoiding Mason. Why?"

"I just don't want to talk to him right now."

"Lovers' quarrel?"

"No."

"Then what is it?"

It was petty and stupid, but ever since Mason had planted the suggestion that she would make a good country doctor, Valerie had done her best to avoid him. First he had to remind her how great the two of them were together. And now this? It was all so . . . comfortable, convenient. It made sense in her head and in her heart. And she wasn't going to have any of it. She was just addled by great sex and being in the comfort of her own home, around her family. His suggestion was ludicrous, and avoiding him was logical. She would not have him talk her into staying when that wasn't at all what she wanted.

"Nothing I want you to know about."

Jolene slid her butt onto a chair. "Come on, Val. Spill it."

She skirted past Jolene and went to wash instruments. "I'm not going to talk about this with you."

"I'm not leaving until you do."

"Fine. Then I'll leave." She pulled open the door and nearly shrieked as Lila was there, hand poised as if to knock.

Was everyone out to scare her to death today?

"Sorry, didn't mean to bother you. You seeing Jolene as a patient?"

Jolene snorted behind her.

"Um, no. We were just talking," Valerie said.

"Good. Supper's on the table."

"I'm not hungry."

Lila grabbed her by the wrist. "You've avoided having meals with your family for too long now. Enough is enough. You will eat with us tonight."

Valerie knew her stubborn refusal to see Mason was only going to last so long, at least where Lila was concerned. "Yes, ma'am."

Valerie walked in behind Lila, refusing to even look at Mason. But she knew he was there, sitting at the table. Jolene sauntered in behind her and took one of the two remaining chairs, which left Valerie stuck in the middle between Jolene and Mason since the rest of the seats were occupied.

Jolene leaned toward her, looking entirely too smug.

"Oh, man, I hate to get all childish and little sister on you, Val. But . . . neener neener."

"Bitch," she whispered back.

Brea cocked a brow from across the table. "Now isn't this reminiscent of us as kids. You two bickering at each other."

Jolene reached for a roll. "And you clear across the table, avoiding."

Brea lifted her chin, but didn't offer up a retort.

"Brea, that outfit you're wearing is spectacular, by the way."

Valerie felt bad that she hadn't made enough of a fuss over how awesome her sister looked after Jolene had taken her into the city for a makeover. Her hair was cut shorter, her bangs swept to the side, and gone were the hideous outfits she'd been wearing, replaced instead by jeans and shirts that hugged her curvy figure.

Brea blushed and skirted her glance down the table, then back at Valerie. "Thanks."

Valerie followed Brea's gaze. She had stolen a glance at Gage, who cast a very smoldering look in Brea's direction, which only made Brea's cheeks pinken further.

Interesting. Very interesting. She'd like to know what that was all about. Maybe she'd ask Brea later.

Right now she intended to concentrate on getting through supper as fast as possible so she could get away from Mason. She stole glances in his direction during the meal, and even though every time she looked, his gaze wasn't directed at her, she couldn't help but feel he was watching her. Judging her. Expecting her to . . . what?

"So Valerie," Brea said. "You've been busy."

"Uh huh."

"Treating a lot of people from the community," Lila said, beaming from her spot at the end of the table. "She's a fine doctor."

"Thank you." She scooped up a few peas on her fork and slid them into her mouth.

And then it started, and moved around the table. One comment after another.

"The town needs a good doctor."

"It's been three years since Doc Parmalee retired. Poor folks around here don't have decent medical care."

"Most won't take the trip into Tulsa. Injuries, illnesses, even well baby care. It's a shame, really."

"Hard to get a doctor to want to live in a small community like this unless they're from the area."

With every word Valerie sank farther into her chair, hoping she'd become invisible.

"Valerie, what do you think about all this?"

She lifted her gaze to Lila. "About what?"

"About the sad state of our community having no doctor."

She grabbed her glass of milk and took several gulps. "I think it sucks."

"You could fix that, you know."

Her shoulders tightened at Mason's words. She snapped her gaze to his. "I'm not the solution to the problem."

Mason didn't seem at all bothered by her glare; instead he slung his arm over the back of his chair and stretched out his legs. "You could be, if you just thought about it. What it would mean to you, to your family and to your community."

"You'd make an incredible doctor for the people of this area, Valerie," Lila said with a giant smile.

"It's what Mom and Dad would have wanted for you," Jolene said, nodding.

Valerie shot up out of her chair, pushing it back with her legs. "No. Absolutely not. Look. I have a life. A carefully orchestrated plan that's about to see pay dirt. I worked my butt off in school to get to this point. Besides, I have a brand-new job. I'm committed. In Dallas. I've agreed to a partnership with a great group of doctors. I'm going to make incredible money."

Even as she said it, the words sounded hollow, narcissistic, selfish. Her stomach hurt.

But dammit, she wouldn't be deterred.

"I'm not a ranch doctor. I'm not a small town doctor. I know what I want to do with my life, where I'm going." She looked at Mason. "It's not here."

It's not with you.

Mason just continued to give her that smile, the one that made her want to march over to his chair, kick it out from under him and then pummel him until her frustration with him—with this entire situation—went away.

"Everything you need is here, Valerie," he said.

Emotion welled up and she didn't know whether she wanted to crumple in his arms or punch his lights out. Her voice wavered as she stuttered out the words. "I can't do this, Mason. I can't be who you want me to be. I can't lo . . ."

She'd almost said that she couldn't love him, but stopped before she embarrassed herself further in front of everyone.

"I just can't." She turned to Lila. "Excuse me, Lila." She turned and left the room, hightailing it two steps at a time up the stairs. She shut the door to her room and sat on the bed, her heart pounding so hard she felt light-headed. She bent over, folded her hands together and willed the shakes away.

Coming home had been an epic mistake. She'd known it, and yet she'd stupidly done it anyway. She had known something bad would happen. It always did whenever she came home. This place was filled with nothing but bad memories and failures. Her parents' death, the failure of her marriage, and now her inability to help the people of her community.

She hadn't been able to save her parents or her marriage. Now she couldn't save the people of her town.

But dammit, she'd enjoyed tending to the people, enjoyed seeing the smile on the craggy faces of the elderly folks, enjoyed wiping off toddlers' sticky fingers, enjoyed listening to the fetal heartbeats and excited faces of expectant parents. The thought of any of them not getting appropriate medical care . . .

She wrapped her arms around her middle, as if the very act could squeeze the ache away.

It wasn't her responsibility. None of it. She didn't have the capacity to love all those people.

She'd loved her parents so much, and that love hadn't been able to keep them with her. She'd loved Mason, too.

She still loved Mason. And oh, God, it hurt to love him. She could never be what he wanted her to be. She refused to stay here and he'd never be happy in Dallas. She couldn't live in this house, in this town, with its choking memories of love and loss.

And the people of the town? They'd just have to find a doctor willing to settle in the middle of nowhere and tend to them. It wasn't going to be her.

She had to get out of here. The ranch ran just fine without her input, and would continue to do so. Jolene and Mason had it all under control, and she'd stayed here long enough.

Too long.

She went to the closet and dragged out her suitcases, then started packing.

"What are you doing?"

Valerie figured it wouldn't take long for Jolene to barge her way in and stick her nose in Valerie's business. "I'm leaving."

Jolene took a seat on Valerie's bed. Brea was right behind her and took a seat, too. "Why?" Brea asked.

She paused and lifted her gaze to her sisters. "Because I can't be who and what everyone expects me to be here. I can't be a ranch owner, a doctor . . ."

"And Mason's wife?" Jolene asked.

A few seconds ticked off before she answered. She didn't want to talk about this, but she knew Jo wouldn't leave it alone. "Yes."

"You were always the strongest of all of us, Val. You held it together when Mom and Dad died, took care of Brea and me, held us when we cried at night. We'd have never made it through those dark years without our big sister."

Valerie fought back tears remembering what it was like back then. Three young girls who'd had their lives shattered in the blink of an eye. "We relied on each other. You two helped me through it, too."

Brea shook her head. "No, Valerie. Jo is right. It was you who was the strong one, the one who made us get up every day and put one foot in front of the other. You were the one who told us life moves on for the survivors even when those we love die."

She couldn't remember saying that.

"And now here you are, running like a coward instead of facing the truth."

Valerie snapped her gaze to Jolene. "This isn't the same thing. And I'm not running. It's time for me to go. I have things to do in Dallas to prepare for my new job."

"You promised to stay here a month."

Valerie shrugged. "I just . . . can't."

"Because of Mason," Brea said. "Because you still love him and you can't face it."

She slammed the lid on her suitcase and glared at Brea. "No. Not because of Mason. I don't love him. We're over."

Jolene laughed. "Please. It's so obvious to everyone here how you feel about him. And how he feels about you. But at least he isn't running away instead of facing his feelings."

This was pointless. Arguing with her sisters had never gotten any of them anywhere. She zipped up her second suitcase and reached for her purse, then hauled both suitcases down the stairs, Brea and Jolene on her heels.

Mason was in the hall near the front door.

Damn.

He cocked a brow. "Leaving?"

She swallowed past the dry prairie in her throat. "Yes. I have . . . things to do in Dallas."

"Uh huh." He grabbed her bags. "I'll go put these in the car for you."

Jolene let out a disgusted sound. "I can't believe this. He's just going to let you go."

Valerie turned to her sister. "He knows not to push me."

Brea shook her head. "He knows what a stubborn pain in the ass you are."

Jolene stepped in front of her, and Valerie wasn't sure she'd ever seen her sister look that angry.

"Look, Valerie. You're my big sister and I love you. But this time you are wrong. Dead wrong. You'll regret running away and not facing your feelings about Mason, about being here at the ranch again, and how you really feel about treating the people of our community."

Valerie lifted her chin. "I know how I feel about all those things, and none of them have anything to do with my leaving."

Jolene grabbed her and hugged her, then whispered in her ear, "Physician, heal thyself." She kissed her on the cheek, then walked away.

Brea hugged her, pulled away, sadness evident in her downturned lips. "Don't go, Val. This is a mistake. You can't run away from everyone and everything you love. They'll all still be there no matter how far you go." Brea fisted her hand and held it to her heart. "Right there. You can't escape it."

Valerie's eyes filled with tears and she shook her head. "I have to."

Brea stepped out of her way, and Valerie hurried to her car, half expecting to see Mason waiting for her. She dreaded the inevitable confrontation.

He wasn't there. Her bags were in the trunk, but Mason was nowhere to be found.

She ignored the knot of disappointment tightening in her chest. This was what she wanted and she was grateful he wasn't making it difficult for her to leave. She slid into the driver's seat and headed down the long drive, watching the horses and cattle grazing in the pastures. She swiped away the tears that rolled down her cheeks, ignored the agonized pain ripping through her at the thought of leaving all this behind.

It hadn't been this hard leaving two years ago. Why now? How had she become so ingrained in this place again in such a short time?

She shook her head. It didn't matter. She was making the right decision. The ranch held nothing but pain for her. She and Mason would never work. She wasn't a country doctor. She was supposed to live in the city. That's where her life, her future, was.

A truck pulled into the entrance to the ranch just as she reached the end. Whoever it was climbed out and waved his hands wildly over his head. Valerie jerked to a stop and he ran over to her.

It was Red Mitchell, one of the ranch owners who lived nearby.

"Dr. Valerie, I'm so glad I caught you before you drove off."

He was panting, his face beet red like always, mostly due to him being about a hundred fifty pounds overweight.

"What's wrong, Red?"

"It's Mama. She's fallen on the floor and I can't wake her up."

"I'll follow you."

He tottered over to his truck and climbed in. Valerie drove behind him the few miles down the road to his ranch. As soon as they pulled up in front of his one-story house, Valerie threw the car in park, hopped out and went to the trunk to retrieve her medical bag.

"She's in her bedroom, on the floor," Red said, panting and struggling to keep up. "Straight down the hall, last room on the right."

Valerie didn't bother waiting for him, just ran through the front door and found Red's mother, Eugenia, on the floor of her bedroom. She dropped to her knees, put on latex gloves, then tapped Eugenia a few times, called her name, but no response. She was still unconscious, her skin pale and sweaty.

She got out her stethoscope and blood pressure monitor. BP was low, heart rate too fast.

By then Red was in the doorway, breathing heavy.

"Red, sit down on that chair before you pass out, too."

Red fell into a nearby rocker.

"Has she been sick?" She felt Eugenia's pulse.

"She's diabetic. Doesn't follow her diet too good."

Shit. That had to be it. "What did she eat today?"

"Don't know. I was out plowin' most of the day, but Mama said she was feelin' poorly so she wasn't all that hungry."

Valerie dug into her bag and pulled out the glucose test kit. It told her immediately what she already knew—insulin shock. She grabbed glucose wafers, lifted Eugenia's head and slipped a wafer into the side of the woman's mouth. "Her glucose is off. Some sugar should bring her around shortly. Help me get her back into bed."

By the time they had Eugenia settled in her bed, she was regaining consciousness. Valerie breathed a sigh of relief. Once she had Red's mother stabilized and made sure Eugenia had had something appropriate to eat and drink, she and Red stepped out on the porch.

"You need to take her into Tulsa to see a specialist, make sure she follows the doctor's instructions carefully."

Red looked down at his feet. "That's all fine, Dr. Valerie, but we ain't got no insurance. And them city doctors is expensive. I get Mama's insulin and all like I'm supposed to, but we can't go see those doctors in the city all the time. Besides, who's going to do my chores? It takes up a whole day to run Mama to the city."

At Valerie's pointed look, he swept his gaze to the floor again. "Okay. I'll save up some money and take her soon as I'm able."

Son of a bitch. She patted Red's arm. "You do that." But then he wouldn't look at her, just the rickety wood floor of the porch. *Well, hell.* "Red, she's going to be fine. Make sure she eats right and takes her insulin."

He lifted his head and nodded. "I will. I promise. Thanks for comin' out here in a hurry, Dr. Valerie. I don't know what we would have done without you."

Feeling the idiot tears welling again, Valerie made a hasty retreat, climbed in her car and headed down the road again. When she reached the end of the road, she had a choice to make. Left turn was toward the main highway. Right turn was back to the ranch.

She chewed her fingernail and thought long and hard about which way to go. Decision time.

And for the first time in her life, she didn't know what choice to make.

Or maybe she did. Maybe she'd always known where she really belonged, and that choice scared her more than any she'd ever made before.

ten

mason gunned the engine on the jeep, pushing it way past the speed limit for a two-lane country road in pitch-black darkness.

Red had phoned him at his house to pass along his thanks again to Valerie, saying what a great coincidence it had been to run into her at the end of the road, and how she'd saved his mother's life.

That had been ten minutes ago. Which meant she would be getting to the end of the county line road soon. And he might just have a shot at reaching her.

Which was probably a really stupid idea, given that she'd made it damn clear she wanted to hightail it out of there. And he'd almost let her.

Almost.

But maybe her pit stop at Red's had been a sign that she shouldn't go. And maybe she'd see it that way, too.

Or maybe she wouldn't. Either way, he was going to give it one last shot and try to convince her to stay. Because he hadn't yet told her that he still loved her, that he still needed her, that he still wanted her. And all those things needed to be said. Then if she still walked away, he'd at least know he'd given it all he had.

And maybe he'd finally be able to put it to rest this time.

Maybe.

He hit the brights as the Jeep bounced over the rough bumps in the unpaved dirt road, though he knew this road like he knew his own name, had traveled it by bike, horse and car since he'd arrived here at sixteen. He knew where the intersection was, could find it blind.

There was a car stopped there, its lights cutting through the thin layer of fog creeping up from the surrounding pasture. Mason slowed, waited for the car to make a turn.

It didn't. So he turned left and pulled up alongside, already knowing who it would be. No one traveled this road at night because there was no place to go to on it.

He waited.

She got out of the car. So did he, moving around the front of the Jeep. He hooked his thumbs in his belt loops and hitched a breath, prepared to spill his guts—and his heart—to the woman he'd loved his entire life.

But he never got the chance, because she launched herself against him, wrapped her arms around him, lifted herself up on him and knocked him against the front of the Jeep when the force of her body connected with his. Her mouth sought his, and every word he was going to say was gone in the night fog and the spring wind as Valerie slid her tongue into his mouth.

The heat of her body wrapped itself around his, her kiss telling him everything he needed to know.

She was here to stay. He grabbed hold of her butt and lifted her, and her legs wrapped around him tight while they kissed each other, their mouths exploring, her questing fingers knocking off his hat to tangle in his hair. He did the same, pulling her ponytail holder out so his fingers could dive into her hair. He just wanted to hold on, wanted to inhale the scent of her shampoo, the soapy sweet smell of her skin, and hope like hell this wasn't a dream.

Breathless, she finally pulled away from the kiss, her expression somber.

"Mason."

"Yeah."

"I love you with all my heart. I'm an idiot. I always have been. I don't deserve you, but God, I love you so much. And if you'll have me, I'd love to be your wife again. For good and forever this time."

Mason had never welled up tears for anything in his life.

Until now. And if that made him less than a man, then he could live with it. Because nothing on this earth could make him cry except this woman.

Love did that to a man.

it was dark and foggy and windy, and maybe it was the wind that stung Mason's eyes. And maybe it wasn't, because Valerie could swear she saw moisture in them. But she'd never in a million years say anything to him about that. Her heart swelled with more emotion than she'd ever carried inside herself, and she'd just laid her heart in the hands of the only person living who had the power to break it.

"Valerie."

"Yes."

"I've loved you since the minute I met you. And when you're ornery and obstinate and stubborn and refuse to see things my way, I'm still going to love you. I will love you for every moment on this earth we have together. And I would be honored to make you my wife, forever."

She hadn't let the walls down in such a long time, but with Mason she knew she could. Finally, she could. She buried her head against his chest and sobbed, a mixture of relief that he still loved her, and sadness for what she'd almost let go again.

"I'm so sorry. Mason, I'm so sorry." And once she let it out, she couldn't seem to stop, mumbling and sniffling and crying and apologizing. And through it all, Mason held her tight and stroked her back and kissed her hair, until she had nothing left but hiccups and a stuffy nose.

He dried her eyes with his handkerchief and handed it to her so she could blow her nose.

"I look a wreck," she said, wiping her nose.

"Yeah, you do."

She laughed and punched his arm.

"And you're still the most beautiful woman I've ever laid eyes on. You always will be."

She didn't think she could cry anymore, but fresh tears pooled. "Stop saying nice things to me. It'll make me cry more."

"You want me to call you a selfish bitch?"

She choked out a laugh. "That's a good start."

"Come on. Let's get these vehicles back to the ranch and tell everyone the good news."

"And then you can take me to your place and make love to me."

He held her at arm's length. "Or better yet, I'll take you upstairs to our room, to that bed I hate because my feet hang off. I know you love that house."

"We'll make modifications. We'll build an addition. And get a king-sized bed. Or we'll build our own place. A new one that's just ours."

He laughed. "That's good enough. Maybe a few extra rooms, too."

She looped her arms around his neck. "For all those kids we're going to have."

"We'd better get home in a hurry so we can get started first."

She gasped. "I'm scandalized. You would knock me up without benefit of marriage?"

"In a heartbeat, Doc."

"Then I guess it's off to the courthouse for us, stat."

"Let's stop off at the bedroom first before we break the news to your family."

She moved against him, feeling the hard ridge of his erection. Heat swelled between her legs, her nipples aching and tight. "The hell with stopping off at the bedroom. How about right here?"

He arched a brow and jerked her closer, his hands roaming her ass. "Out here, in front of nature and cattle and who knows who might drive by?"

She lifted onto her toes and tightened her hold around his neck. "If I'm going to be a rancher's wife, I'd better get used to dropping trou . . . wherever. This seems as good a spot as any."

The look he gave her melted her to the spot. "You make my dick hard, Valerie."

She shot him a wicked grin. "Why, I'd love to do it against the Jeep. I thought you'd never ask."

He flipped her around so fast her head spun. In seconds, her jeans were unzipped and around her ankles and his hand cupped her sex. She let out a low moan at how fast he'd worked her into a frenzy of passion and need.

"Now, Mason."

She heard his zipper and the rustle of his clothing, and then he was inside her, unsheathed, hot and thick and thrusting until she screamed. It was so damn good she didn't care who heard her.

"Yes. Fuck me."

He wound his arm around her and found her clit and she was there in seconds, the emotion and sexual energy combining to get her off in record time.

"Mason, I'm coming."

And he was right there with her, pumping inside her, then groaning as he came.

Her legs were shaking as he withdrew and helped her pull her jeans back up. She turned around and suddenly they were both laughing. Mason dragged her into his arms and kissed her so deeply the fires of passion burst inside her again.

"I think we'd better get home in a hurry," he said, his cock hard and insistent against her.

"I think you might be right."

He turned her away from him. "I'll lead. You follow."

She moved to her car. "Don't drive slow. I need you."

The smile he gave her as he slipped on his cowboy hat and climbed into his Jeep was one she'd never forget. And for as long as she lived, she'd know she'd made the right decision.

She turned the car right and headed home, where she belonged.

branded

Brea

WHAT KIND OF HOUSE?	CAR?
Mansion	Miata
Apartment	Mini Cooper
Shack	Lexus
House	*Navigator*

WHERE TO LIVE?	NUMBER OF KIDS
Paris	5
San Francisco	3
Tulsa?	*1*
The Ranch?	2

GUY	OCCUPATION
Caleb	Artist
Steven	Teacher
Gage	*Writer*
Jeff	Millionaire

one

brea stared at her notebook where she'd scribbled her most recent M.A.S.H. entry. Her one and only M.A.S.H. entry written as an adult.

Silly game. Childish game. A game of fantasy, of wishes, of what-ifs. Not at all grounded in reality. Not her reality, anyway.

She stared out the window at Gage Reilly, watching him work in the corral with one of the young horses. His jeans fit snug to his mighty fine ass, his boots kicking up clouds of dust as he walked circles around the horse. Brea held her breath as only Gage's skills as a trainer and one length of rope kept him from being trampled by one very angry, very wild horse.

How different their two worlds were.

Gage's reality was daily tussles with magnificent creatures, primal and wild and free as the land they lived on.

Brea's reality was quiet, books, and her fantasies. And she liked it that way. Most times, anyway. Her life in Tulsa was peaceful. She had her job as a freelance programmer/analyst and she loved it. It was challenging to her mind, and she made her own hours, which gave her plenty of time to read, and she enjoyed that most of all. Getting lost in a book, in the characters, in the romance of it all . . . now that was heaven.

But lately she had to admit she had a desire for something a little more satisfying than what she'd found between the pages of the books she read. She attributed that to being on the ranch again, instead of spending all her time in her apartment in Tulsa. Her life there was work, living in her apartment and occasional trips to the gym and the grocery store. At the gym she worked with Sheila, her trainer, and since the hot and sweaty muscle-bound guys there totally turned her off, she paid about as much attention to them as they paid to her. Men more interested in staring at their own muscles than in looking at a woman just didn't interest her.

But here on the ranch? Now that was a different story altogether. There were real men on the ranch, with muscles built from hard work, not gym work. They spent the day surviving the elements, whether it was blazing heat, whipping wind or frigid cold, flexing muscles the old-fashioned way. And Brea had about as much chance of corralling one of them as she did of roping a man in the frozen foods section at Walmart. Especially when she was stuck in the middle of her two amazing sisters.

Valerie was a doctor. Talented, beautiful, an icon of fashion, a perfectly long, lean body and amazing green eyes, and everything that came out of her mouth was laced with wit and intellect. Jolene, their baby sister, was a knockout with blond hair, a stunning heart-shaped face, hazel eyes and a body most women would kill for. Jolene was outgoing and ballsy and afraid of nothing.

And then there was Brea. Plain old Brea. Mousy brown hair, nondescript brown eyes, dumpy figure, a little too curvy in all the wrong places, and no personality to speak of, which made her choice of career just perfect since she didn't have to interact with . . . anyone. Computers were her friends, her books were her lifeline. And she liked it just fine. So she wasn't beautiful, savvy and smart like Valerie or gorgeous, sexy and outgoing like Jolene. And despite Jolene dragging her into one of Tulsa's premier salons for a haircut, color and manicure/pedicure, and forcing her to buy some new clothes that Jolene insisted fit her body better, inside she was the same old Brea. Just with better hair and clothes that fit.

A haircut and painting her toenails fire-engine red weren't going to change who she was. Nor were these tight jeans and new cowboy boots.

She'd long ago realized—after a couple of disastrous attempts at what couldn't even be called relationships, which included some awful tries at sex that left both her and her partners unsatisfied—she was a dismal failure with men. Her life was better suited to fantasy.

And God knows there was plenty of fantasy fodder here on the ranch, though she had to admit there was only one man who'd caught her eye since she'd come back to the Bar M.

She let her gaze drift out the window again. Gage was still wrangling the filly, who wasn't going to give up her wild nature easily. Brea was mesmerized by the way Gage approached the horse, and found herself leaning over the chair to press closer to the window so she could get a better look.

But the corral wasn't fully visible from the window, and she was leaning over the arm of the chair, her nose practically smashed against the window. This was ridiculous. She owned this ranch. Okay, she partially owned it, but it was still perfectly feasible for her to go out there to . . . check things out.

She stood, smoothed her hands down over her sleeveless shirt, looked over her jeans and boots, and wished for the voluminous skirts and tops she'd always worn. Damn that Jolene for hiding her old clothes after she'd taken her shopping. There was nothing wrong with what she'd worn before. These damn jeans clung to her body, outlining every flaw—too wide hips, too thick thighs and a less than cinched waistline. And a little bit of excess baggage in the booty department. She worked her body to death at the gym, and she was firm, but she was never going to have a *Playboy* centerfold body like Jolene's.

Dammit. She was just going to have to live with the body she had. Besides, she was only going outside to check out the horses, not to ogle Gage Reilly. He wouldn't even notice her anyway. Most men didn't.

The sun beat down on the center of the corral area, and she was grateful for the shade of a couple elm trees on one side as she made her way to the fence. She spied Grizz—one of the older hands—and waved.

"What you up to today, Miss Brea?" he asked as he came up to her.

"Just decided to get out of the house and enjoy this nice spring day. I saw Gage working with the horses so thought I'd take a look."

Grizz nodded, turned and spit tobacco juice onto the ground. "Young man's doing a fine job trainin'. Go have yourself a look-see."

She slid her fingers in the front pockets of her jeans and nodded. "Thanks. I think I will."

It was just Gage and the filly, a beautiful dark mahogany young-ster with a lot of spirit. She raised her muzzle and snuffled in protest as he approached.

Brea climbed up onto the top rung of the fence to sit and watch, mesmerized by the dance between man and beast. Gage gave the filly no quarter, nor did he torture her or demand submission. The filly was near as big as any of their full-grown horses, but she hadn't been ridden yet. This was her test. And Gage's full-time job.

It was as if every step Gage took was carefully orchestrated, as if he knew where the filly was going to go, and he anticipated it and knew where he'd go, too. The filly didn't like Gage in her personal space, but Gage didn't back off, didn't show fear, only gentle dominance, making soft clicking sounds with his tongue and teeth to let the horse know he was there and he wasn't going to back off no matter how much the filly stomped her hooves or threw her head back in the air.

It took a while, but Gage never gave up, never once seemed frustrated or angry or ready to quit. The horse would charge, and Gage would quiet her, in his own way setting the ground rules. He was the boss and the filly was just going to have to deal with it.

When the filly finally settled, Gage came up to her, pressed his shoulder against the horse and moved her in the direction he wanted her to go. And so it went, all the way through laying a blanket, then a saddle on the horse.

Gage must have known Brea was there, yet he didn't once take his attention off the horse. Not until he had a saddle cinched around the filly's belly. Then he tied the reins to the fence post near the water trough so the horse could have a break, get a drink and get used to having a saddle on her.

Gage wiped dust off his hands, reached down into the cooler on the other side of the fence and grabbed a couple bottles of water and headed in her direction.

He smiled as he approached, and Brea's body quivered. Okay, so they might have exchanged a few glances since she'd been there, but she assumed he was being polite. *He* was being polite. She was lusting. Who wouldn't? He walked like he owned the world around him, a sexy saunter that screamed he knew who he was and he damned well didn't care what anyone thought. She'd kill for that kind of confidence. The closer he got, the harder she gripped the rail she sat on, poised to flee.

He unscrewed the cap on one of the bottles of water and handed it to her.

"You look hot."

Her jaw dropped. "Huh?"

"It's hot out here today. Thought you might want a drink."

"Oh. Yeah." He didn't mean she looked hot, he meant he thought she was thirsty. Duh. She took the bottle and sipped, watched him guzzle down half of his, watched his throat work, stared at his mouth.

Unfortunately she was still staring at his mouth long after he finished taking a drink. He cast a knowing smile at her, and she blinked herself back into reality.

Damn, Brea. She felt the rush of heat to her cheeks. She really needed a life. Or an orgasm. Anything to stop her from acting like a nervous geeky twelve-year-old in front of a guy.

Especially this guy.

He tilted his hat back to stare up at her, and she fought for something intelligent to say. Unfortunately, her brain, though usually filled with all sorts of tidbits of interesting things, decided at this moment to refrain from sending any intellectual signals to her mouth. Nothing came out. How could it, when he was staring at her with ocean blue eyes that just screamed sex? The man was walking testosterone, from his sexy gait to his tight ass, flat abs and those Popeye muscles bulging from the short sleeves of his T-shirt.

"You like horses?" he finally asked, no doubt thinking she was an idiot, since all she'd managed to utter so far was "huh", "oh" and "yeah." Just freaking brilliant, Brea.

"Uh . . . yes, I do. I like watching you train them. You have a way with them."

He half turned to survey the filly. "Stormy is pretty easy. She's got a lot of passion in her, but she's not as wound up as some I've trained."

"Is that right? She seems pretty spirited."

He turned back to her, eyed her up and down, from her boots to the top of her head. She dissolved in a puddle of desire right there.

"I like them spirited. It's no fun if it's not a challenge."

Oh, honey, are you ever barking up the wrong cowgirl. "What if she's shy and a little skittish?"

She couldn't believe she'd just said that. It could even be considered flirting. Brea did not flirt.

Gage laid his hands on either side of her thighs. Great, the body part she least wanted to draw attention to.

"I have a lot of patience for shy and skittish, Brea. And you know," he said, moving his hands a little closer so his thumbs brushed against the denim of her jeans and made her breath hitch, "the shy ones can sometimes surprise you."

She shuddered out a breath. "Is that right?"

"Yeah."

"How so?" She found it difficult to swallow.

He cocked his head to the side and gave her a lopsided smile. "They can end up full of fire and passion. They just need the right kind of . . . training." His fingers whispered down the side of her legs, the touch so light she wasn't even sure if it was real or if she'd imagined it.

But her body didn't think it had imagined it. It was full-on ready to jump on him and fuck his brains out. Her breasts were tight, her panties were wet, and her pussy quivered.

And Gage's nostrils flared like a bull sensing a female in heat. Was it even remotely possible he was . . . interested in her?

He tipped his finger to his hat. "Have to get back to work now. You have a good day, Brea."

"Yeah. See you, Gage."

Apparently she had a vivid imagination. He turned his back on her and headed back to work. She enjoyed the view of his ass in those tight jeans. And sighed.

She watched him work with Stormy awhile longer, then decided she'd rather hang herself than torture herself further. She headed back toward the house and ran into Jolene along the way.

"Ogling some hot cowboy?"

Brea shrugged. "Maybe."

"Looks like he likes you."

Brea rolled her eyes. "Please. How would you know?"

"He practically had his hands on you. I thought maybe he was going to throw you down on the dirt in the middle of the corral and have his way with you."

Brea ignored the visions pummeling her of Gage doing just that. Instead, she snorted. "Yeah, right. We were just talking horses."

"Don't bullshit a bullshitter, Brea. You're hot for him, he's hot for you. I can see where this is headed."

She pushed through the front door, sighing in blessed relief at how much cooler it was in there. "How can it be forty degrees at night and blistering hot during the day?"

"You grew up here, Brea," Jolene said, tossing her work gloves on the hallway table. "You know what spring is like here. Or lack of spring. It's either cold or hot. Today it's hot. And you're avoiding talking about Gage."

She followed Jolene into the kitchen. "I'm not avoiding at all. He's not interested. Neither am I."

Jo reached into the fridge for a beer. "Now I know you're lying. Your tongue was dragging the ground."

"You're so full of it, Jolene. Why don't you go chase your own man and quit browbeating me and Valerie."

Jo kicked a chair back and took a seat. "In case you didn't notice, my browbeating of Valerie resulted in her and Mason getting back together. Where they belonged in the first place."

She had a point. But God her sister was pushy.

"And second, it just so happens I have my eye on a man."

"Walker Morgan."

Jolene tipped her beer in Brea's direction and smiled. "You got it."

"And does Walker have his eye on you?"

Jolene laughed. "Of course he does. He's just being . . . wary."

Brea pulled out a chair. "Wary? Why?"

Jo shrugged. "Don't exactly know yet. But I aim to figure it out. I want that man naked and on top of me."

Brea laughed. "The poor guy. He doesn't stand a chance, does he?"

"Nope." Jolene took a long swallow of beer, then set the bottle down on the table. "I've had my eye on him for a while. I let things simmer between us for a bit. Soon, though, it'll be time to set the temperature to boiling."

Brea leaned back in the chair and crossed her arms. "I don't know how you do it."

"Do what?"

"Set your mind to something . . . or someone . . . and get it."

"Well, I haven't exactly gotten Walker yet. But I see no reason to be shy around a man. Walker's hot and sexy and just flat-out melts my butter. If he wants the same thing, why be coy about it?"

"How can you tell he wants the same thing?"

Jolene arched a brow. "Brea, don't you know anything about men?"

"Not really."

"Then I guess Jolene and I need to educate you."

Brea looked up to find Valerie leaning against the door frame, a wry smile on her face. Great. She so didn't want to discuss her lack of skills in the romance department with her sisters. Then again, maybe she did need some advice. And despite the squabbles they got into, she trusted her sisters.

"I mean it's not like I'm a virgin or anything. I'm just . . . not very good at this."

Valerie pushed off the door and came into the kitchen, grabbed two more beers out of the fridge and passed one to Brea, then pulled up two chairs—one to sit on and one to prop her feet up.

"Long day?" Jolene asked, still so damn happy to have Valerie permanently back at the ranch. And now that she and Mason had hurriedly remarried down at the courthouse and Valerie had decided to set up medical practice there, Jolene couldn't be more content. At least with one of her sisters.

"Long day on my feet. But it's over now. So what's up with Brea?"

Jolene took another long drink before setting her bottle down. "She has the major hots for Gage Reilly."

Valerie's brows rose. "Really. Good choice. Great ass."

Brea laughed. "I think so. But we're not exactly . . . compatible."

"Why do you say that?" Jolene asked. "He's hot, you're hot. He's a man, you're a woman. Sounds pretty compatible to me."

"He's more than just a man. He's way out of my league."

"And you, my younger sister, underestimate your value. You always have," Valerie said, pointing the tip of her bottle of beer toward Brea. "You're stunningly beautiful, especially now that you've cleared that bird's nest of hair away and got your eyebrows mowed. You have the sexiest brown eyes I've ever seen. And with your hair cut like that . . . you look like Mom."

Brea's heart tumbled. "Really? You think I look like Mom?"

"You've always looked like her. More so than either Valerie or me," Jolene said. "Same color hair. And you have her eyes."

Brea's eyes welled up with tears. "Mom was beautiful."

"And so are you," Valerie said.

"I don't know about that. I've always thought myself a bit plain . . . and on the chubby side."

Jolene snorted. "Please. You have a woman's body. Beautiful curves. I'd kill for long legs like yours. Don't you see how the guys around here look at you when you walk by?"

"Uh . . . no."

"Maybe you need to stop staring at the ground and lift your head up, Brea," Valerie said. "Men are looking."

"Gage is looking," Jolene added.

Her gaze whipped to Jolene. "He is?"

"Hell yes he is. Pull your head out of your ass and pay attention."

two

brea thought about everything her sisters had said. She'd thought about it well into the night as she sat downstairs in the living room reading after everyone had gone to the bar in town. She'd begged off, claiming a headache. She had some thinking to do about herself. About men.

She hadn't been paying attention. Or looking at the guys who allegedly had been looking at her. Had some of the men on this ranch been watching her? She found that so hard to believe. But maybe she shouldn't. Maybe it was time to start believing in herself.

A very hard thing to do when every time she looked in the mirror she still saw the gawky, chubby girl who just wasn't pretty. You hear that enough times, you get shot down by men enough times, you start to believe that maybe you just aren't worthy. She wasn't strong enough to build herself up. Which was why it was so much easier to imagine herself the lithe, strong, smart, capable heroines in the romance novels she read. She could put herself in their places, live their lives, fall in love with their incredibly romantic heroes who would sweep them off their feet and love them no matter what. And not once in those books did the hero tell the heroine he'd totally fall for her if she could lose ten pounds.

And even if she did find the guys approachable, would it make any difference? She'd gone the sex route before and found it decidedly lacking. Or rather, found herself decidedly lacking. She was afraid she'd set herself up by romanticizing sex the way it was in the books she read. And sex just wasn't that good in person. Not the sex she'd had, anyway.

Too restless to read, she stood and stretched, then noticed a light on at the bunkhouse. She was surprised, since she'd seen everyone pile into the trucks and take off for town. She wouldn't mind a little company. Maybe Grizz had stayed behind and she could talk him into a game of gin. He often didn't go into town with everyone.

She headed down the walk toward the bunkhouse, breathing in the night air, the smell of hay and cattle and horses. Not unpleasant smells at all to her, since they all signaled spring settling in. She knocked on the bunkhouse door, but no one answered. Maybe no one was there at all, and they'd just left the light on. She tried the door, and it was unlocked, so she opened it, thinking she'd find it empty.

Music was playing, loud, coming from one of the other rooms.

"Anyone here?" she yelled. "Door was open."

She moved in farther, shaking her head at the disarray. Cowboys definitely lived here. Scattered boots all over the floor, dishes left on the tables in the living room, beer and pop cans littering every available surface. Brea knew Grizz would get after the guys about once a week to clean the place up, and they'd do their housecleaning, but other than that, they mainly lived like pigs. It was like a dorm, and some of the cowboys who didn't have their own place or lived farther out of town were welcome to stay here.

She started picking up a few cans since she didn't have anything better to do and figured the place was empty. When the call came to load up the trucks and head into town, you either hustled or got left behind. Chances were the last one out the door hadn't turned off the stereo and lights. She'd get those on her way out. She had her arms full of beer cans and was headed into the kitchen when she heard someone whistling. She stopped and pivoted.

"Brea. What are you doing here?"

Her breath caught and she nearly dropped the armful of aluminum she carried.

It was Gage, fresh from a shower, his hair damp and curling around his neck, his body still dripping, and a towel balanced on his hips. Broad shoulders, wide, ripped chest devoid of any hair. Washboard abs, slim hips and, dammit, even his feet were sexy.

The rest of him she couldn't see under the towel he wore. Which was all he wore except for a damn sexy smile as his lips curled.

Brea's heart kicked up about twenty notches and she fought to swallow. "I knocked. Didn't think anyone was here. I'm so sorry." Her face flamed with heat. She was so not pretty when she blushed.

"Don't be. Why are you cleaning up?"

She shifted her gaze away from his taut, flat abs to the beer cans in her arms. "Oh. Uh, well I saw them lying around."

"Drop them. You're nobody's maid."

Grateful to tear herself away from his killer body, she turned and headed into the kitchen. "Don't be ridiculous. I'll just throw these away." *And then try to crawl out of here with my dignity intact. And without looking at you again.*

Because it was possible if she got another look at him she might want to pull that knot out of his towel and see the rest of him. Arousal flared in her, making her breathing difficult.

"So," he said, seemingly unconcerned that he was practically naked, "why did you come over here?"

It was probably stupid to keep her back turned to him. She spun around to face him. "I . . . I saw a light on here. I thought Grizz had stayed behind, so I was going to see if he'd like to play some gin."

He folded his arms over his chest, which only served to showcase his mighty fine guns. Damn, he had nice muscles. "Grizz decided to party it up some tonight with everyone else. Why didn't you go?"

She shrugged. "I had some reading to do."

"Reading, huh? What kind of reading?"

Her eyes drifted closed for a second then opened again. Might as well end this now. She lifted her gaze to his. "Romance novels."

"Oh yeah? I like horror myself. The bloodier the better."

What? No making fun of her reading tastes? No crack about romance novels being fluff? What the hell was the matter with this guy? "I've read some horror, too. I read a lot."

"I do, too, when I have some time and can get away from the constant noise around here. It's hard to concentrate when half the guys around here think this is a party house."

She laughed, then found herself relaxing. "I can imagine. I like a quiet place to read."

"Me, too. Sometimes I take my horse out to one of the pastures to read on the weekends."

"Oh, that's a great idea. No one can disturb you out there." She couldn't believe she was having a conversation about books with one of the sexiest cowboys on the ranch. She was probably dreaming this, but what the hell.

He moved toward her, and her muscles tensed again.

"Why didn't you go into town tonight?" she asked.

He shrugged. "Not in the mood to party."

She couldn't figure him out. Not at all. He was damn fine looking, could probably have his choice of any woman in town. They'd be all over a hot guy like Gage. And he preferred staying home alone? He was like . . . her. That made no sense at all.

"So what else do you like to do for fun besides reading, Brea?"

"Uh, um, not much, really." She took a step back, then hit the wall. She would look like an obvious coward if she moved around it, so she stayed put and watched him advance on her.

"That's all you do? Just work, and read?"

"Yes. Yeah. Pretty much."

He stopped in front of her, only an inch or so separating them. Any other guy invading her personal space like this would piss her off. With Gage, though, she wanted him closer. She wanted his body pressed full-on against her. God, he smelled so good. Like soap and something indescribable. Earthy and sexy and oh man she wanted to lick that spot on his neck where water dripped from his hair, coating his skin with droplets of moisture. She licked her lips and focused on his face instead. But then she got lost in his eyes—deep blue like an ocean, fringed with long black lashes that were almost too pretty for a man. Almost, but not quite.

Okay, Brea, stop ogling and say something intelligent.

"Um, what do you do, Gage?"

He searched her face, and he wasn't smiling now. "I train horses. I ride. I read. I like to go to town now and then. I like to go to movies sometimes. I like museums."

She cocked her head to the side. "You like museums?"

"Yeah."

"Why?"

He laughed. "You think it's odd that a cowboy would go to a museum?"

"No. Yes." She frowned, shook her head. "I don't know. Maybe. You confuse the hell out of me, Gage. I don't know what I'm saying. I should go."

"Why do you want to go, Brea? Do I make you uncomfortable?"

She swallowed. "Yes."

"Good uncomfortable or bad uncomfortable?"

His question made her pause. "Honestly? I don't know."

gage watched the stream of reactions cross brea's face. She might try to hide what she felt, but her expressions told him everything. Which was a damn good thing, because what she said confused the hell out of him. Her body said one thing, while her mouth said something else entirely.

And his body's reaction to finding her in the bunkhouse while he'd just been in the shower thinking about her—getting hard thinking about her—now that was a bonus. Hell, he'd been getting hard thinking about her since the day she'd stepped foot on the Bar M wearing her quirky skirts and sandals, trying to hide behind all that hair. He'd thought her sexy and mysterious then. When she'd gone into Tulsa with Jolene and come back looking like a goddamn fashion model, he'd just about swallowed his tongue. No matter how she dressed and how she wore her hair, Brea was beautiful. It was in her eyes—a mysterious chocolate brown that couldn't hide her thoughts or reactions.

And the flimsy towel he wore did nothing to disguise *his* reaction to her. Good thing she seemed too preoccupied to notice the nice tent the towel made in the vicinity of his dick. He liked talking to her, liked her being here with him, and he didn't want to scare her away with his raging hard-on.

The last thing he'd ever do was push a woman into doing something she didn't want to do. He liked his women willing. So if Brea was throwing off mixed signals, he'd just as soon step away. The thing was, he didn't think he'd read her wrong out at the barn today, or even the last couple weeks since she'd arrived at the ranch. She'd tossed enough glances his way that let him know she was damn well interested. That's why he always zeroed in on her eyes—the ones that always seemed to be glancing his way. A man would have to be dead or disinterested not to notice. And he sure as hell wasn't dead or disinterested.

It was just getting her to admit *her* interest that might be tough.

Then again, she might want him to take charge. And yeah, he liked being in control, so if that's what she wanted—as long as he was damn sure that's what she wanted—he was all over it.

"Tell me what I do to make you uncomfortable."

He liked the way she blushed. It was sweet, innocent, and a lot of the women he'd been with had long ago forgotten how to blush—over anything.

"I . . . You're very direct, aren't you?" She cast her gaze somewhere over his left shoulder. He tipped her chin and put it back on his face.

"Yeah, I am. I don't think there should be any misunderstanding between a man and a woman. If you're honest with each other up front, then there's no disappointment later on."

"I guess you're right about that. Most men I've known haven't been very honest."

He cocked his head to the side. "Honest about what?"

"Anything. Everything. What they want, how they feel, what they're thinking about. They've all been one great big mystery I've never been able to figure out."

And probably all jerkwads, too. "You'll find out real fast I'm not a mystery, Brea. I'll tell you anything you want to know, and I'll be honest with you."

If it had been possible for her to lean farther into the wall, she would have. "That would be refreshing."

He laid his palm next to her head, wanting so damn bad to press his body against hers, to feel her lush body, to tuck his head against her neck so he could inhale her fragrance. But he didn't want to push her into anything she wasn't ready for. This filly was skittish. He wanted to give her a taste of what she could have, but it was up to her to ask for it, to tell him she wanted what he intended to offer her. And he wanted her coming into it with her eyes wide open.

"I'll tell you right now I like you. I want to get to know you better. But I'm not looking for a relationship or romance. I'm a drifter, Brea. I move from one place to another, so I'll let you know up front that while I'm attracted to you, I'm not boyfriend or husband material."

"I see."

"I want to kiss you, touch you all over. I'd like to get you naked, lick every inch of your body and make you come in ways you could never imagine."

Her big brown eyes widened. "Oh, my."

"Does that scare you?"

"No. That's . . . really honest." But he saw her throat work as she fought to swallow. Yeah, she was scared all right.

"I'm gonna kiss you now, Brea. Okay?"

She gave a shaky nod. "Okay."

He moved in, pressed his body flush against hers. Damn, that felt nice. She was all firm, lush curves, and he couldn't resist touching her. But like a wild horse, she was jumpy and flinched at the first touch of his hand against the bare skin of her shoulder.

"Easy, honey." He kept his hand there, then let it slide slow and easy down her arm. "See? Nothing to be afraid of."

"I'm not afraid of you."

He smiled down at her. "Bullshit. I terrify you."

Her lips lifted. "Maybe a little."

"I'm not going to hurt you. I'm just going to kiss you."

Holding only her wrist with his fingers, he leaned in and brushed his mouth against hers, a slow slide of lips against lips, breathing in her breath. Oh, man, she tasted sweet, her lips so soft he wanted to press in and go deeper. But he didn't, just took it slow and easy, letting her get used to having him close to her, his mouth against hers, until she sighed and relaxed. Then he moved in, slid an arm around her waist and tugged her against him, again nice and easy, not with the violent passion he had to work hard to restrain.

He wanted this woman, wanted her bad, wanted to bury his straining, hard cock inside her. Hell, he wanted to do a lot of things with her, including get her naked and spread-eagled on his bed so he could touch and kiss her all over. He wanted the sweet mouth she kissed him with wrapped around his throbbing dick. But none of that was going to happen tonight, not when she was still wary, so he was just going to have to tamp down his needs and see to hers.

So he let her get used to the feel of his mouth on hers. Light kisses, with just the touch of his tongue against the seam of her lips. And maybe he did press his body against hers, and maybe she could feel his erection—after all, he was only wearing a towel, and he couldn't mask his hard-on—but he wanted her to know how she made him feel. And when she moaned and unglued herself from the wall to align her body with his and laid her hands on his shoulders, he took that as a positive sign.

So he did have to rein in his baser impulses, like ripping off his towel, then her clothes, and burying his cock inside her. There was plenty of time for that later. With Brea he'd have to take baby steps. While he didn't know everything about her, he could tell she had a decided lack of experience, and he didn't want to overpower her. So he settled for a few kisses, lightly holding her, and gritting his teeth against his overwhelming urges. He wanted her to feel in control, like she could take a step back at any time and just walk away and catch her breath.

Only she wasn't stepping back. She wasn't walking away. She leaned into him, wrapped her arms around his neck, deepened the kiss and slid her thigh between his legs, pressing her jean-clad pussy against him. And she made sounds that would drive a sane man crazy.

Gage had all kinds of control, but he was still a man. A damn near naked man with throbbing balls and a moaning, sexy woman in his arms kissing him like she wanted him. He liked her eager, but he was afraid his careful control was going to shatter in the next few seconds if he wasn't the one to take a step back and run like hell.

He broke the kiss, sucked in a breath of air and extricated himself from her arms around his neck. He smiled down at her and kissed her fingers. "I think that's enough for tonight."

Her eyes were glassy, her lips puffy from their kisses. She had a hazy smile that gradually receded as she frowned in confusion. "What? You're stopping? Why?"

He took a careful step back, hoping like hell his towel would stay attached to his hips. "Because I want you to think about what you really want."

She moved forward again. "I know what I want. I want you."

Now his lips curled. "A minute ago you said I terrified you."

She shook her head. "Now you don't. I'm fine, really."

He folded her hands over each other, then took another step back, creating distance between them. Whether it was for her or him he wasn't sure. "Think about it, Brea. Make sure you know exactly what you want before you decide it's me."

She heaved a shaky sigh. "Fine." She moved to push past him. She was hurt and angry. He didn't want her to misunderstand, so he grabbed her wrist, jerked her against him.

"I don't want you to get the wrong idea."

She tilted her head back. "I don't think I got the wrong idea at all. I think you made yourself perfectly clear."

"No, I don't think I did. I was patient with you tonight, Brea. I held back. This is what I want you to make sure you're ready for." He fisted his hand in her hair, brought his lips to hers and gave her what he'd wanted to give her all night—a real kiss. She gasped as he parted her lips with his and drove his tongue inside her mouth. He claimed her mouth with demand, with possession, with the understanding that if she came to him again, she'd be his for the taking. He wound his tongue around hers, then sucked, crushing his lips against hers, pushing her back against the wall and letting her feel him—all of him—until there was no mistaking exactly what he wanted. And when he'd pushed her—and himself—to the brink, he let go.

Brea's eyes shot open.

"If that's what you want, if that's what you can handle, then you let me know."

She still hadn't moved; she stared at him in shock and confusion. It took all the willpower he had to stay away from her.

"Good night, Brea."

He turned and walked back into the bathroom, his cock hard, his body on fire for her. The kiss had shaken him more than any other woman had before. She might not be experienced, but she banked a fire that, once stoked, would burn out of control.

He wanted to be the one to light that fire, stoke its embers and watch it rage.

three

brea hadn't slept all night, had spent most of it in her room pacing and touching her lips. They still burned with the power of Gage's kiss. Almost twenty-four hours later, she could still smell him on her, could still feel his arms around her, the strength of his body against her. She wrapped her arms around herself, so lost in her own thoughts she wasn't sure what time it was. She'd spent most of the day hiding up in her room—thinking.

He'd been right about her. If she'd jumped into bed with him last night, she'd have been terrified, especially after finding out he'd taken it slow and easy with her.

But that last kiss, the way he'd jerked her hair and held her tight and shown her who was in control . . . that had been anything but slow and easy. It had been fire and passion and everything she had imagined a kiss could be—should be—between a man and a woman. It was her every fantasy.

She rubbed the goose bumps on her arms, shuddering at the awesome power of the man. Could she handle that? She'd seen the control he exhibited with the horses since she'd been at the Bar M, had an inkling that Gage was a man who knew exactly who he was and what he wanted. She'd guessed that he was someone who liked to be in charge.

But she really had no idea what she was getting into, did she?

Or maybe she did. Maybe she'd gravitated toward Gage because he was exactly what she'd been looking for all along. Maybe he was what she needed, what she craved.

And maybe that's what the problem had been with the guys she'd been with before—with the sex she'd had before. It had been dull, boring, unfulfilling. There'd been no passion, at least not on her side of things. She'd always thought it was her fault, that she'd done something wrong.

But after last night, after the way she had responded to Gage . . . now she wasn't so sure.

Had it taken her this long to figure out the problem was she'd been with the wrong type of men?

A knock at her bedroom door roused her from overthinking the hell out of the past ten years of her life.

"It's open."

Valerie and Jolene came in and closed the door behind them, then made themselves comfortable on her bed.

"You're obviously not sick, because you're not in bed," Valerie observed.

Brea nodded from her spot on the cushioned windowsill, her favorite reading—and thinking—spot. "Obviously."

"So why have you spent the entire day holed up here? It's creepy, even for you, Brea," Jolene said.

She shrugged. "I've had some thinking to do."

"Thinking? Or reenacting your hot night with Gage?" Jolene laced her hands together behind her head and crossed her ankles.

Brea's spine straightened. "I don't know what you're talking about."

"Please. Everyone knows the only two people left behind on the ranch last night—besides Lila, who we all know goes to bed early—were you and Gage. Coincidence? I think not."

She refused to dignify Jolene's suspicions with an answer.

"Really?" Valerie leaned forward. "So what happened with you and Gage last night?"

The fact that Valerie was asking—and seemed surprised—meant Jolene hadn't been blabbing all about it to everyone.

"I don't want to talk about it."

"You aren't denying it. So something did happen between you."

Brea glared at Jolene. "I didn't say that."

"You didn't have to. Come on, Brea, tell us about it."

Maybe she should. She was confused about what had happened with Gage. And she had no one else to talk to. Yet she wasn't sure how to talk to her sisters about what she felt, what she wanted. What if they judged her?

"Brea, you know you can tell us anything," Valerie said. "And it will never go further than this room."

"He didn't do anything to you, did he?" Jolene asked. Her brows knit in a tight frown. "If he hurt you at all, he's history. He's fired. No, first I'll kick his ass. Then I'll boot him off the ranch."

Brea swung her legs off the window seat, worried now that Jolene would jump to conclusions. "No, he didn't hurt me at all, Jo. He was every inch the gentleman last night." Okay, maybe not a gentleman, but that's not what she wanted, anyway.

Jolene settled back against the pillows. "All right. Then maybe you should tell us what happened between you two."

"I saw a light up at the bunkhouse, thought it was Grizz since he often stays behind. I ran into Gage. We . . . talked."

"Talked," Valerie said. "That's it? You just talked?"

"Is 'talked' a code word for sex?"

Brea rolled her eyes at Jo. "No. We didn't have sex. We just talked."

Jolene crossed her arms. "Somehow I don't think you spent the day up here because you and Gage spent time in conversation. Spill it, Brea."

"Okay, we kissed a time or two."

"And that's it?" Jolene threw up her hands. "You have to hide in your room all day and night because he kissed you? Jesus Christ. Here I thought he'd thrown you down on the floor and fucked your brains out, and all he did was kiss you?"

"Jo, quit being such an ass," Valerie said before turning her attention back to Brea. "Somehow I don't think it was just a kiss. There's more, isn't there?"

Brea nodded.

"What is it?"

"I think he might be more than I can handle."

Jo frowned again. "In what way?"

Brea shrugged. "I don't know yet. I just think if he and I . . . get together . . . I might be in over my head."

"I don't understand, Brea," Valerie said, her tone much less accusatory and suspicious than Jolene's.

Brea blew out a breath. "I'm not sure how to word this. I think I might want what he's got to offer, but I'm not sure. It kind of scares me."

"I have no idea what you're talking about," Jolene said.

"I think I do." Valerie stood and pulled the desk chair over to the window seat, sat and held Brea's hands. "You mean Gage is very aggressive, sexually."

She nodded. "Yes."

"And you don't want that."

"No. I mean yes, I think I do want that. It's just that the guys I've been with before—haven't been like that."

"Oh. I get it," Jolene said. "You've got yourself an A-number-one sexual tiger on your hands, and you don't think you can handle him."

Brea nodded. "Something like that."

Valerie squeezed her hands. "When he kissed you last night, did he overpower you? Make you feel uncomfortable?"

"No. He was gentle. He took his time, didn't back me into a corner or make me feel like it was something I couldn't handle. It was sweet. Damn, it was really nice."

"Then I don't get it," Jolene said. "Why would you think he was an aggressive kind of man?"

"Because he was the one who put a stop to things. And I thought he just wasn't interested. So when I turned to leave, he told me he'd been holding back. Then he really kissed me. He showed me how things could be between us if he let go."

"Ohhh," Valerie said, nodding. "Now I get it."

"Well, yee haw, honey," Jolene said with a wide grin on her face. "There's nothing better than being with a man who knows what to do with his dick. Congratulations. So what the hell are you doing with us? Go ride that bad boy until you wear him out."

Brea laughed. "Leave it to you to just put it out there, Jolene."

Jo shrugged. "Well, why not? There's nothing wrong with a woman enjoying sex. And if you've roped yourself some hot stud, then ride him for all he's worth."

Brea turned her gaze back to Valerie, who said, "I have to agree with Jolene on this. Sounds to me like he didn't want to push you too hard too fast, but when he thought you'd misunderstood his intent, he made it very clear to you that he wanted you. There's nothing wrong with that. He isn't pushy, but he sounds damn sexy, Brea. Go for it."

"See, that's the thing. I'm not sure I can . . . measure up."

"Bullshit." Jolene swung her legs over the bed and stood. "He obviously thinks you can. And believe me, Gage doesn't whore around with every girl in town who tries to throw herself at him. I know because I've been around town and there are a lot of women who try. He's pretty picky. If he's decided it's you he wants, then I'd say he's a smart guy."

"Don't miss an opportunity to tangle with a smoking hot man, Brea," Valerie said.

"And don't think every man you have sex with has to be the one and only, forever and ever like in those books you read," Jolene added. "Go explorin', honey. Have some fun."

if having fun meant her heart in her throat, every limb shaking uncontrollably and breaking out into a decidedly un-sexy sweat, then Brea was having the time of her life. And she hadn't even seen Gage yet.

After Valerie and Jolene left, she'd taken a shower, done her hair, put on makeup, lotioned her body, then stared into her closet look-ing for something appropriate to wear.

What, exactly, did one wear to meet a hot man? Jeans and boots, she supposed. Or maybe a skirt and boots. Yeah, that was better. And the weather had stayed blissfully springlike, so she put on a sleeveless silk top and her leather jacket over that. She stared at her reflection in the mirror, surprised to see that she looked—not too bad. She might have fussed over Jolene dragging her into that salon and having her hair cut and colored and her eyebrows waxed, but it had done wonders for her appearance, something she'd never both-ered with before. Now she was glad Jolene had talked her into it, because Gage no doubt wouldn't have given her a second look if she hadn't had the makeover.

But the fact was, she was dressed, ready to go and scared to death. And sitting out on the front porch reading a book, her booklight clipped to the pages while she swatted the night bugs away from the small light.

She glanced up every now and then at the bunkhouse, knew Gage was in there. It was Saturday night and no one was around. People tended to scatter on the weekends. Valerie and Mason had driven into Tulsa; Jolene had gone into town with all the guys. Just like last night, there was no one else left on the ranch except Lila, who'd long ago gone to bed. Which meant just Gage was left.

When the bunkhouse door opened, she held her breath, her gaze shooting down to the pages in her book. The words blurred together because she wasn't really reading. She watched him out of the corner of her eye. He was leaning against the door, just looking at her. She tried to focus on the book, but she couldn't concentrate when she knew Gage was watching her.

This was ridiculous. He'd told her if she knew what she wanted, she'd have to come to him. What was stopping her?

Fear. Absolute, choking, petrifying fear. What if he was just kidding? What if he didn't really mean it?

She laid the book in her lap and stared down at the cover with the couple clutching each other. That kiss between her and Gage meant something. He wasn't toying with her. And his words couldn't have been any clearer.

She tensed as she heard boots on the wood steps of the front porch, then lifted her gaze to see Gage there, partially shrouded by the darkness and his cowboy hat. Was he angry that she hadn't come to him?

"Real life is more fun than what you're going to find between the pages of those books, Brea."

She sucked in a shuddering breath at the way he looked in dark jeans, a black button-down shirt and his cowboy boots and hat. And couldn't muster up a damn thing to say to him.

"Change your mind about you and me?"

She lifted her chin. "No. I was just"—she fumbled for the book and flipped through the pages, trying to find her bookmark and failing miserably—"engrossed in this chapter."

"You're hiding in that chapter." He stepped onto the porch and leaned against the rail, crossing one ankle over the other. His legs were long, his thighs muscular, and she remembered exactly how every inch of his exposed skin had looked last night when he'd been wearing only a towel. She'd memorized that moment in the bunkhouse, certain it would never be repeated.

"I'm not hiding. Books are just a nice escape."

His lips quirked. "Had such a busy day you need that, huh?"

She narrowed her gaze. He knew damn well she hadn't been anywhere outside today.

He moved in front of her, squatted down, and oh God he smelled so good. He must have just taken a shower. She resisted taking a deep breath just to get a whiff of his soap and his scent.

"Brea, I like to read, too, but there's nothing like experiencing life firsthand. Real life. Maybe you should try that instead of living yours buried in a book."

She bristled, not at all liking the way this was going. Okay, so she hadn't run down to the bunkhouse to be with him. She was . . . weighing her options. Because she had so many options to weigh. "I live my life just fine."

"Do you? When was the last time you went out dancing, or rode a horse with a guy, or had hot sex under the stars?"

The last time she'd been dancing had been with her sisters. The last time she'd ridden a horse had been with Grizz, who was old enough to be her father, and she'd never had *hot* sex, period, let alone under the stars. She remained mute.

Gage grinned. "I thought so." He stood and held out his hand. "Come on."

She laid the book down and slid her hand into his. "Where are we going?"

He took a sidelong glance at her from her waist to her feet. "You can ride in that skirt, can't you?"

"Yes."

"Good." He held on to her hand and led her down the walk toward the barn.

Once inside, Gage turned on the light. Two horses were already saddled, a dappled gray mare and a brown and white paint that she already knew was Gage's horse.

"It's nice out. Thought we'd take a ride."

"Where to?" she asked.

"I know this place."

He let the sentence end there. And wasn't this what she wanted? An adventure outside the books she read? This was real life, with a real man. She could either turn tail and run for the house, hide in her room with her books, or take a chance and have a real experience.

"Okay."

He cinched the saddle on his horse. "You sure? You didn't come to me willingly."

She did the same to her own horse, then turned to him. "I just did."

His lips lifted. "So you did." He moved over to her and stood behind the right stirrup. "Let me help you."

She shivered as he cupped his hands around her waist, then held on to her while she laid her foot in the stirrup. With ease, he lifted her onto the saddle. Even though she'd been doing this since she was a child and she could ride a horse blindfolded, without moonlight and stars, his chivalry was romantic.

"Thanks," she said as she sat her horse.

"Don't thank me. I just wanted to look up your skirt."

She blushed crimson, but couldn't help the thrill of delight that a man like Gage found her attractive.

He climbed onto his horse, then led them out of the barn and shut the doors behind him. There was a full moon tonight, which meant they needed nothing else to light their way. They traveled side by side at first, since there was plenty of room on the dusty, unpaved road. Brea enjoyed the silence, the breathtaking night, inhaling air and just being next to a man like Gage.

"When was the last time you rode?" he asked, finally breaking the silence between them.

She shifted her gaze to him, noticing how easy he was in the saddle, as if he'd been riding a long time. If you spent any time on a ranch, especially around horses, you knew who were greenhorns or pretenders and who were true ranch folk, comfortable with the country lifestyle. Gage rode easy, his body one with the saddle and the horse. He had a good command of the animal, held the reins lightly in one hand as if he knew exactly what his horse was going to do.

"It's been a few years. Probably three or four."

He nodded. "You ride easy, like you haven't forgotten."

She smiled. "My daddy put us all on horses as soon as we could sit upright. First we rode with him, then as soon as our mom wasn't hysterical about us falling off, we rode alone."

"Good idea. You like riding?"

"I used to love it."

"Used to?"

"When I lived here I rode all the time. You could almost never get me to climb into any of the vehicles if I could ride instead."

"You liked it here."

She studied the landscape, the way the gray light of the moon washed across the scrub of the prairie. It was stark, serene, as if she and Gage were the only creatures here. Besides the cattle that she heard mooing off in the distance, of course.

"Yeah, I did."

"So what made you move to Tulsa?"

She shrugged. "I wanted something . . . more."

"Like?"

"A few years ago I knew exactly what I'd been searching for. Excitement. City life. Something I'd never had that I thought I wanted. I'd gone to college in a small town, had grown up here, in a place that had what I thought was nothing. Tulsa isn't exactly a major city, but it's still a city. It had museums and movie theaters and malls and fancy restaurants."

"And all those are things you wanted and couldn't have out here in the middle of nowhere."

She laughed. "Yeah."

"So you like big city life."

"I spend most of my time in my apartment."

"Why?"

She shrugged. "I don't know. I used to love being outside."

He stopped his horse. She halted, looked over her shoulder at him. "What?"

"Something happen to spook you?"

"Here? No."

"I don't mean here. I mean there. In the city."

"I don't know what you're talking about."

He inched his horse up to hers, then halted again. "You stopped going out. What does that mean? You stopped going on dates or you stopped leaving your apartment?"

"I'm not agoraphobic, Gage. I go to the gym and the grocery store and the office supply store. I'm out all the time. It's just not the same as being here."

"You didn't answer my question."

And men thought women were obtuse? "What question?"

"When was the last time you had a date?"

She stiffened. "What difference does that make?"

"Just answer the question."

"I'll tell if you will."

He laughed. "Okay. I took Cheryl Daniels to the drive-in two months ago."

She arched a brow. "Two months ago? Kind of a long time for someone like you, isn't it?"

He tilted his head to the side. "Someone like me?"

"Yeah. Good-looking men like you don't typically go without a woman."

"I'd like to think I'm not typical. Now your turn."

No, he definitely wasn't typical at all. She inhaled and spit it out. "Two years."

He frowned. "Why?"

Brea looked away, patted her horse's neck. "I don't want to talk about this."

Gage drew closer, took her reins in his hands. "Who hurt you?"

She slid her gaze to his. "I don't know what you're talking about."

"Some guy did a number on you."

She hadn't even realized they were moving again, or that Gage had control of not only his horse, but hers, too. And she wasn't going to reply to his comment.

They rode for about forty-five minutes and Brea was pleased that she wasn't sore from the ride, even if she hadn't been on a horse in a long time. But she was in shape and she exercised regularly, so maybe that accounted for her ability to climb aboard and acclimate again so quickly.

She remembered this part of the ranch, though she hadn't traveled this way for years. They arrived at the pond where her dad used to take them to fish. There was a small cabin just up the bank from the pond. It was just a one-room shack, really, but Brea recalled it had a fireplace and a bed and a sofa.

Gage stopped, got off his horse and came around to hers.

"I do know how to dismount, you know," she said, looking down at him.

He gave her one those now-familiar half smiles she found incredibly disarming. "It's more fun this way." He held his arms out and she slid into them, letting him draw her to the ground. He held on to her for a few seconds, his fingers burning into the skin of her waist, before he stepped back and tethered the horses to a tree near the water.

He retrieved a blanket from the saddlebag, then pulled out a sack containing . . . something.

"Come on over here," he said.

She thought they'd go inside, but she walked down the bank and saw him spreading the blanket out on the hill.

"What are you doing?"

He took a six-pack and a bag of chips out of the bag.

"It's warm tonight. Thought we'd stretch out on the blanket, look at the stars and have a snack."

She skirted her gaze to the chips and beer. "That's the snack?"

"Yeah."

She laughed, then sat on the blanket.

Gage stretched out on the blanket, popped open two cans of beer and handed one to her. He laid the bag of chips between them.

This had to be the strangest date she'd ever been on. No, strange wasn't even the right word for it. Unique was the appropriate word choice.

"I like coming out here because the stars feel like they're bearing right down on you," Gage said, tilting his head back and looking up at the sky.

"You come out here often?"

"Yeah. Usually in the summer, on the weekends. I'll stay in the cabin overnight, get an early start on fishing."

Brea smiled. "My dad used to bring us girls out here when we were little. He taught us to fish in that pond."

Gage turned his gaze to her. "Is that right?"

"Yes." She sipped her beer. "I remember countless mornings Dad dragged us out of bed before dawn, fishing poles and tackle already loaded in the back of the pickup. We'd spend hours out here watching the sun come up. Dad said it was how we learned patience."

Gage laughed. "It's a good way to teach kids to be still."

She nodded. "He didn't much appreciate us jabbering away and scaring the fish. And teaching three impatient, wiggly, talkative little girls to shut up and be still was no easy feat."

"Your dad sounds like he was a great man."

"He was."

"What about your mom?"

She grinned. "She'd pack up scrambled egg sandwiches to take along for breakfast, and cold fried chicken for lunch, but wouldn't come with us. She said it was our time with our father. I think she said that so she could have half a day of peace and quiet to read."

"So you got your love of reading from your mama?"

"I guess so. She was always busy doing something around the ranch. But whenever she managed to sit down she always had a book in her hand."

"Must have been hard to lose them both."

She stared out across the water, the memories of her parents still sweet, still painful. "It devastated us. It left a gaping hole in all three of us. Especially Valerie, who had to suddenly become mother to us all while she was barely a teenager."

"Your uncle, I assume, was no great shakes as a parent."

She snorted and grabbed a handful of chips. "He was legally our guardian, but he didn't know the first thing about raising children. The man didn't have a warm bone in his entire body."

"Yeah, I got that impression having worked for him. Must have been hard on all of you."

"We had Lila, and she was full of love and hugs. But it wasn't the same. No one can replace your mother."

She munched on chips and wished she hadn't revealed so much. It made her heart hurt to relive the anguish of losing her parents. And now she'd laid a melancholy downer on her time with Gage. Great. Just great.

"I'm sorry," she said, wrapping her fingers around the can of beer.

He reached over and cupped her neck, drawing her attention to his face. "Sorry for what?"

"For dragging sadness and death and such a depressing conversation into our night together."

"Hey, I'm the one who brought the topic up. If I didn't want to know how you felt about it all, I wouldn't have asked."

"Still, I could have just been vague."

"Why? I'm here with you because I want to know about you. I want to know how you feel, who you are. And that means where you came from, what events shaped you."

Who was this guy? Cowboys weren't . . . deep. Not the ones she'd always known, anyway. Even the city guys she'd dated couldn't care less about who she was or where she'd come from.

It was clear Gage was some kind of alien life form and not a regular guy.

"So now it's your turn. Tell me about yourself."

"Not much to tell, really. I was born in Denver, raised there."

She cocked her head to the side. "A city boy?"

He nodded. "Yup. A city boy."

"I wouldn't have imagined it. So where did your love of horses come from?"

"I had a friend who had a ranch, and I spent summers there starting when I was twelve. It was either that or trips to Europe with my parents, and I wasn't interested."

Her jaw went slack. "Your parents went to Europe every summer?"

"Yeah."

"You must come from a wealthy family."

"You could say that."

She realized she didn't know Gage at all, and what she thought she knew about him was dead wrong. "So you stayed with your friend on the ranch instead of summering with your parents? Why?"

He shrugged. "I liked the horses there, liked working with them. Gave me a chance to do something physical that meant something, rather than loafing and skiing. I'm not much of a skier."

"Bet that's blasphemy to those who come from Colorado."

He laughed. "Yeah, my family wasn't too happy that I didn't take to skiing. Or their jet-setting lifestyle."

"So how did you end up here?"

"After a couple years in college I realized that the family business just wasn't for me. I dropped out and got a job on a ranch. Been working with horses ever since."

"And your family?"

His smile disappeared. "My father died about five years ago."

She laid her hand on his arm. "I'm so sorry, Gage."

"I wasn't very close to him. My mom remarried a couple years ago."

"I see. Did you go to the wedding?"

"No."

"Why not?"

"Because that family really isn't my family anymore. I never really belonged there."

"How can you say that? It's your mother."

"True, but I had a younger brother, too, and he's everything . . . I'm not. He's a great skier, went to college, continued on the family business."

"So? I'm sure they don't love you any less because you chose a different path."

He snorted. "You don't know my family."

She squeezed his arm. "You can't mean that."

"Hey, I'm fine with it. I chose who and what I wanted to be, and they disagreed with my choice. I'm free of all their expectations now."

Brea sighed, wondering how it felt to have that kind of pressure on you to be someone you knew in your heart you couldn't be. It made her feel very lucky that she had her sisters. They might fight and argue, and she might have left, but she knew she could always come home, that no matter what separated them, they would always love one another.

"Family should love you no matter what," she said.

"That's the way it's supposed to work. In some families it doesn't. And when it doesn't, you're better off without."

"I'm sorry for that, Gage."

He smoothed his hand over her hair. "Don't be sorry for me. I like my life. I'm free to go where I want, do what I want and be whoever I want to be. No one has any expectations of me and I like it like that."

She stared at him, and it finally dawned on her why he'd said he was unable to commit to a relationship. And that's why he drifted from place to place—because he didn't want anyone to tie him down like his family had tried to do. Now she understood and she admired even more his ability to be his own man.

"What?"

She shook her head. "Nothing. You're just . . . different."

His lips curled. "Is that a bad thing?"

"No. Trust me, it's not a bad thing."

"Good. Then come lay down next to me and look at the stars."

She situated herself on her back next to him and stared at the clear night sky. "I haven't done this since I was a kid."

"You should do it more often."

She probably should. She'd forgotten how awe-inspiring the night sky was, especially out here in the country where no city lights dimmed the darkness and the awesome cosmos could shine down on them in all its glory. Gage was right. She hadn't appreciated this as a child. Whenever she looked up in the city, street and building lights masked the stars. Out here, nothing did. She lifted her arm and traced the Big and Little Dipper with her fingertip, then scanned the constellations to locate her favorite star systems.

She was so lost in stargazing that it was awhile before she realized Gage had stopped speaking. She turned her head and found him on his side, his head propped in his hand, staring at her.

"You're supposed to be looking at the stars, not me."

"I did look at the stars. Now I'm looking at you."

"Well, stop it."

He traced her cheek with one finger, and chills popped out on her skin.

"You don't like when men pay attention to you."

"That's not true."

He shifted, scooting over toward her. He raised up and loomed over her, planting one hand on each side of her ribcage. "Is that right? So me leaning over you like this doesn't bother you?"

Oh, it bothered her plenty. But not in the way he thought. "No."

He moved again, this time straddling her, his crotch aligned with hers. He held his weight off her with the powerful muscles of his arms and thighs. But his body on top of her was so intimate she could barely breathe. Her skirt had ridden up her thighs, and if he shifted just a little more, he could be rubbing all that delicious denim against her panties. She got wet just thinking about it.

"How about this? Does this bother you?"

She was finding it hard to breathe. Sexual arousal got in the way of all her synapses firing correctly. "No."

"Just 'no'? That's all you have to say?"

Her heart pounded, her breasts felt full and achy. She wanted Gage to touch them, to lift her top and fit his mouth around the throbbing buds. Did he really want to have a conversation with her now? Couldn't he read her breathy signals?

"What's wrong, Brea?" He leaned forward, captured her wrists in his hands and moved her arms to her sides. "This bother you?"

"No." She'd squeaked the word out, all she was capable of now. Her entire body, including her tongue, felt swollen, thick with desire and need.

"Is there something you want?"

Why was he torturing her like this? Couldn't he tell? Her bra was flimsy, and so was the top. She was sure her hard nipples were poking through, her arousal evident for him to see.

Gage had a firm hold on her wrists, but she knew he'd let go of her if she asked. And for some reason him holding her like this, his weight on her, was so damn exciting. She felt his erection, knew he was affected, too, and that stimulated her even more. Unable to resist her body's primal instincts, she lifted her hips, searching for that intimate male-to-female contact.

"I like that, Brea. Do it again."

Why was it so easy for him to say exactly what was on his mind, and so difficult for her to put voice to her own needs? She lifted, rocking her pelvis against him.

He leaned toward her, his breath washing over her face. "That makes my dick hard."

He spread his body over hers, and now she could really feel his cock, hot and hard, pressing insistently against her. He nudged her legs apart so his shaft wedged between her legs, right at the sweet spot of her pussy. She let out a moan and he surged against her.

"Like that?"

"Yes."

"Want more?"

"Yes."

"Then tell me what you see happening between us tonight, Brea."

four

dear god. gage wanted her to spell it out for him? Wasn't it obvious? They were body-to-body, though still fully clothed. He could rectify that easily enough. Or they could do it without taking their clothes off. At this point she didn't much care. She just wanted to feel him inside her. She tried to shift, to spread her legs, to give him a subtle—or maybe not so subtle—message, but he had her effectively pinned to the ground.

He shook his head, his blue eyes boring into her. "Not with your body, honey. Tell me what you want. Say it."

"Isn't it obvious?"

"To my dick? Yeah. But I think you need a few lessons in self-esteem."

She rolled her eyes. "Really. And what made you decide there's anything wrong with my self-esteem?"

He let go of her wrists and brushed his hand over her hair. "Your eyes have a wounded look. When you're around men, you draw your shoulders toward your chest and almost shrink inside yourself. And you avert your gaze and look at the ground like you consider yourself unworthy of a man's attention."

She gaped at him like he'd grown two heads. "How long have you been watching me?"

"Since the first day you got here."

"You make it a point to study women's body language and eyes?"

"No. Just yours. And I can tell a woman who's been hurt by men before. You have."

She opened her mouth to object, but he pressed his finger over her lips. "Don't bother to deny it, Brea."

Okay, so she wouldn't. And fine, so he'd read her signals all too clear. It was a little disconcerting to discover she was so transparent. Or maybe she wasn't and Gage was just more adept at reading women—at reading her—than any other man she'd met. "Why do you care?"

He smiled down at her. "Because a woman deserves to be cherished. She deserves to be treated like she's the most special creature a man has ever met. And if you haven't been, then it's damn time someone gave you the power you deserve."

She snorted. "Women don't have the power."

"Oh, that's where you're wrong, darlin'. Ain't no woman alive who doesn't have power over a man."

"How do you figure that?"

He rolled to the side and fisted her skirt with one hand, drawing it up her thighs.

With his free hand, he slid his palm over her sex. Heat lightning shot between her legs and she melted right there.

"Because you have this," he said, pressing his palm lightly against her pussy. "And a man will fall to his knees and do whatever you want just so he can have it."

He slid his fingers under the fabric of her panties, his touch a bare whisper over her flesh. She shuddered at the contact, was so close to orgasm already it was embarrassing. She gripped his shoulders and arched her pelvis against his hand.

"Now. Tell me what you want, Brea, and I'll give it to you."

She wanted his hand right there, doing exactly what he was doing. She wanted his mouth covering her sex, licking her until she screamed. She wanted him to rip away her panties to shove his cock inside her. She wanted him to fuck her hard. And then even harder. But she couldn't form the words, could only fight to retain control before she tunneled off into oblivion.

"No. Don't think them. Tell me. I want to know exactly what you're thinking about."

She swallowed—God, her throat was parched—and took a deep breath, nervous as hell about uttering these words to a man for the first time.

"I want you to make me come, Gage."

His lips lifted in that smile that made her turn to melted butter. "Good. How do you want me to make you come?"

"First with your hand. Then with your mouth. And then I want you to—"

"Go ahead. You can say anything you want to me. Do you know when you tell me what you want it gets me hot?"

"I want you to rip my panties off and fuck me."

Now it was his turn to suck in a deep breath. "Oh hell yeah. I like the sound of that." He slid his hand back and forth, using light and easy motions, coating his fingers with her moisture. "You want me to fuck you easy or hard?"

She dug her nails into his arm, hardly aware of her own sanity as his fingers danced magic across her clit. "Hard. Really hard."

"Make you scream kind of hard?"

Her belly did flip-flops hearing him say it. She tightened her grip on his shoulders. "Yes."

"Then let's get to it."

Molten heat burned her, took her ever closer to the edge as he slid his finger inside her and pumped while he used the heel of his hand to glide against her clit.

"You're a beautiful woman, Brea, your body is made for sex. I can feel you clench around my fingers. You're wet and hot and you're body's crying out to come."

And then he kissed her, that same blistering kind of kiss he'd given her the night before, the one that made her believe he could take possession of a woman and she'd beg him for more. She whimpered against his mouth as he continued to do magical things with his hand and fingers, never once letting up. That and his sinfully sexy words were all it took to send her crashing into a climax. She cried out and arched her butt off the blanket to drive herself closer to his hand as waves of pleasure catapulted through her.

Gage covered her lips with his, absorbing her cries, swirling his thumb around her clit while she rode an orgasm that could only be described as the best she'd ever had. And still, his finger lingered inside her. Her pussy continued to spasm around his finger until the pulses grew light and easy, just like her breathing. Clarity returned bit by bit. He drew his lips from hers, smiled down at her. She lost herself in the incredible beauty of his mesmerizing eyes.

"Now that was sweet, Brea. Nice to see you all warmed up for my mouth. You ready for it?"

And just like that, heat and desire and need swelled inside her. She wasn't used to this. "But what about you?"

"There's plenty of time for me. This is all about you right now. Just lay back and enjoy my mouth on you."

She shivered, though the night was still plenty warm. She couldn't believe she'd just come, cried out, bucking in Gage's arms here in the outdoors. And now he was lazily drawing her skirt up over her hips, kissing her thighs, raking his fingers down her legs and back up again, then teasing her by kissing her belly.

She leaned up on her elbows, wanting to watch everything he did. The man was too beautiful for words. What was he doing with someone like her? There were girls in town built like centerfolds or models who'd be more than willing to give a hot guy like Gage a ride.

"Brea."

"Yes?"

"What are you thinking about?"

"Nothing." She couldn't tell him.

"I want you thinking about the fact that I'm about to go down on you. How good that's going to feel. And nothing else. Got it?"

She swallowed. "Got it."

"Good." He gave her a lazy half smile, then teased his tongue over her panties, his hot breath ruffling the silk against her sensitive tissues. She started to lift so he could take her panties off, but he pressed her hips back down to the blanket.

And then he put his mouth over her sex. She felt his wet tongue right through her panties, the warm melting sensation of her own response, her body drifting in some sort of state between relaxed and tense, where all she felt was his mouth, his tongue and the incredible sensations he evoked. Soon she was nothing but liquid limbs, spreading her legs to give him more access. He tucked his fingers under her panties, teasing her flesh by running his fingertips over her pussy lips while he sucked on her clit. The sensations were maddening. She wanted to feel his mouth on her without the silk barrier, yet she couldn't deny the sensuous torture ramped her up inch by delicious inch.

And then he pulled her panties aside and covered her sex with his mouth, his tongue drawing lazy circles around her clit—teasing, but not yet hitting the sweet spot. She arched against him, craving the contact. He only hummed against her, which further tightened her need. He had to hold her down because she wanted to lift against his mouth, to slide against his tongue, anything to draw closer to the heat and wetness of his mouth.

She was close again, so embarrassingly close to orgasm after just experiencing one of monumental proportions. Maybe it was the man, or the location, or a combination of both. And maybe it was the masterful way he seemed to know her body, to know exactly where to lick her, to move his fingers, to give her the sensory experience that would take her right to the edge and hold her there as if she were suspended in space, hovering, waiting for the moment when he pressed his tongue flat against her engorged, throbbing clit at the same time he slid two fingers inside her pussy.

She was watching him, and feeling it all at the same time, and it was all too much. His fingers buried deep inside her, pumping away, his tongue pressed hard against her clit, drawing circles around the taut bud as if he knew exactly what it would do to her.

She shattered, reaching down to hold his face right there, rocking against him with wild abandon as she cried out, this orgasm even more intense than the first. She felt like she'd never come before, as if this was the very first time she'd had an orgasm. She felt it in her muscles, in her bones, in her nerve endings, shooting out from her toes all the way to the ends of her hair, leaving her shaking all over.

And then Gage was there, his face hovering over hers. He kissed her, and she tasted the tart sweetness of her own come on his mouth. She'd never done that before—never knew it would excite her to taste herself on a man's lips. She held his head between her hands and licked his lips, loving that he groaned, that the muscles of his body tightened against her. She felt the rough slide of his denim-clad shaft rubbing against her and wanted him inside her so badly she could hardly stand to wait any longer.

She let go of his face and he pushed to his feet.

She swallowed hard as he stared down at her with the kind of look that screamed predator. And she was the prey.

She kind of liked that.

She waited in breathless anticipation for what was coming next.

* * *

control was a big thing in gage's life, in his work, and especially with women. But God help him, if Brea continued to smile up at him like a hungry wolf who wanted to eat him alive, he was going to lose it.

Shy? Yeah, he knew that about her. But he hadn't expected her to be so responsive. He thought he was going to have to coax it out of her.

He'd been wrong. She was a natural at sex, once given the right stimulus.

And he was stimulated as hell, his cock and balls throbbing for release after touching and tasting her. Lying on the ground like that she was an invitation he couldn't resist.

But the wind had picked up and a chill cut the air around them. The last thing he wanted was an interruption.

He grabbed her hands. "Come on, darlin'. It's getting cold out here."

He pulled her to her feet and she tilted her head back to stare at him. "Are we leaving?"

Disappointment shadowed her eyes and made him smile. He squeezed her hand. "Are we finished yet?"

"Well, uh, I didn't think so." Her gaze skirted south, right where the bulge in his jeans hadn't even begun to subside.

"You're right. We haven't. We just need to change locations. Thought we'd go inside the cabin where it's warmer."

"Oh. Good idea."

They went inside, and Gage held on to her hand, leading her toward the sofa. He turned on the lamp on the table.

"Um, wouldn't you rather leave the lights off?" she asked.

He turned to her. "No. I want to see you. All of you."

"Oh." Her gaze drifted toward the double windows leading outside. He tipped her chin and forced her attention back to him.

"Brea. No one is around but you and me. If you and I are going to do this, you have to trust me. If you don't want to, say so now and we'll head back."

"I want this."

No hesitation. That was all he needed to know. He moved in, wound his arms around her waist and drew her close.

And she tensed. All that relaxation he'd felt in her body earlier had disappeared.

He loosened his hold on her and took a step back. "What's wrong?"

She tilted her head back and smiled, but there was fear in her eyes. "Nothing. I'm ready. Let's get to it."

She'd made it sound more like a pending execution than love-making. She was girding up for battle, for something unpleasant. Not quite the scenario he'd pictured.

"Bullshit." He took a step back and sat on the sofa. "Come on. Sit down and let's talk."

Brea frowned. "Talk? About what?"

He laid his palm on the sofa cushion. "Sit down, Brea."

She did, looking like someone who'd just been called into the principal's office for doing something bad. She stared down at her boots, not at him. He looked at her for a few seconds, trying to figure out the problem. Outside, she'd been eager, responsive, had melted under him. But a minute ago she'd acted like a scared virgin. Huh.

"You have had sex before, right?"

Her gaze shot to his. "Of course. Tons of times."

He avoided laughing, instead arching his brow. "Tons? Define 'tons.'"

She was really cute when she blushed. "A lot."

"How old were you when you had sex for the first time, Brea?"

"Do we really have to go there, Gage?"

"I think it's important, yeah."

"How old were you?" she asked.

"Fourteen."

She rolled her eyes. "Why am I not surprised?"

He shrugged. "You asked."

"So you've probably had thousands of women."

He snorted. "When I was a horndog teenager, I got around, yeah. But when I got older I got more selective."

"So what you're saying is that you're not such a manwhore now?"

He laughed. "Yeah, you could say that."

"And I should be complimented that you chose me."

This wasn't about him and he knew it. The bite in her tone was about something else. And Brea was smart. She was doing a good job turning the topic to him. "We weren't talking about my sex life, though. We were talking about yours. And I think you either haven't had much experience, or what you had wasn't good."

She lifted her chin. "I think you presume to know way too much about me. And based on what, exactly?"

Defensive, too. "The fact that as soon as we got in here and you knew we were going to fuck, you tensed up."

"I did not."

"Yeah, babe, you did. Did you have some bad experiences with sex you want to talk about?"

"No."

"Talking about them might help."

"I meant no, I didn't have any bad experiences. Jesus, did you take some psychology classes or what?"

He grinned and swept his hand over her hair." I just read people pretty well. Or at least I can read you. And something's bothering you. I want to know what it is."

"Shouldn't you be trying to get into my pants like most guys would do instead of worrying about how I feel?"

"Is that what you think guys do? That all they think about is getting pussy? That we don't give a shit about the woman?"

She glanced away, shrugged.

"You must have had some pretty lousy experiences with men."

"Or maybe I'm just not very good at this."

And like a lightning bolt, the problem zapped him. "You think you're no good at sex."

She met his gaze with wide eyes. "I didn't say that."

"No, but some guy said it to you, didn't he?"

She didn't answer, just clamped her lips shut.

"What an asshole."

She crossed her arms and lifted her chin, defiance written all over her face. "It wasn't just one guy. That's how I know it's true."

"Jesus, Brea. How long ago was this?"

She shrugged. "I don't remember. A few years ago."

"So you had a couple losers who couldn't take the time to show a young girl what sex was all about and you believed them when they said it was your fault?"

She clasped her hands so tightly together her knuckles whitened. "It wasn't their fault I couldn't . . ."

"Come? They couldn't get you off, or get you excited and they said it was your fault. And you believed them."

"What was I supposed to believe?"

"That they were lazy assholes, for starters." He shifted to face her. "Honey, sex happens between two people. That means it takes both parties to make fireworks happen. If it didn't happen for you, it wasn't your fault, it was theirs."

She frowned like she didn't believe him. Of course she didn't believe him. He'd like five minutes in a locked room with the guys who'd done a number on her self-esteem.

"I'll bet they didn't think to warm you up or do you first, thought only of themselves and finished in record time. And then when you didn't get off, they claimed there had to be something wrong with you, right?"

"Maybe."

"There's nothing wrong with you, Brea." He swept his thumb over her cheek, needing her to believe in herself. "Outside you showed how passionate you are, how responsive you are."

"But you were . . ."

"Go ahead."

"You were doing me. And you know what you're doing."

He laughed. "And you think we can't make magic *together* when we fuck? That I can't make you come that way?"

"No."

He arched a brow. "Babe, I believe you've just issued a challenge. I accept."

five

brea stared at gage.

What challenge? She hadn't challenged him to anything.

"What are you talking about?"

"You know exactly what I'm talking about," he said. "You think you're defective or something. That's a mental block, not real. You think you can't come during sex. I aim to prove you wrong."

"Oh. Uh, that's totally unnecessary. I'm sure we can have fine sex together. Don't worry about it."

"Fine? Did you just say 'fine'?"

There was a wicked gleam in his eye as he leaned toward her. She backed away, scooting farther down the sofa.

"Oh, no you don't. There's no escaping now. You've challenged me."

A little thrill shot up her spine. Gage was certifiable, but she couldn't help laughing as he grabbed her and pulled her onto his lap. Dammit, she liked being with him. He was a lot smarter than she'd thought he'd be, and that was her own prejudice about cowboys in general being dumb. He read, he could carry on an intellectual conversation, he made her laugh, and he even seemed to care about whether she had a good time with sex.

She still didn't think men like him actually existed.

And he was bound to be disappointed in her before the night was over. But she intended to enjoy him while she had him.

Especially if he continued to stare at her like he was hungry. And not for food.

He shifted, sliding her underneath him, his body covering hers. In one swift move, he became the predator. She liked the feel of him on top of her, the feeling that he wanted her. Especially when something hard and insistent brushed against her thigh.

She shuddered at the quick flash of need that roared through her, priming her for him. Gage was way too much man for her. She already knew this, had prepared herself for his disappointment. She should have said no, should have walked away at the first sign of interest, but she couldn't seem to resist the sizzling pull of attraction she had for him.

Once. That's all she wanted with him, just one time. Then she'd have a real fantasy to think about during all those long nights when she was alone in her room reading.

He pressed his lips to hers, and this time there was nothing easy about it. He took, he demanded, and all she could do was hold on, try to catch her breath as he ravaged her senses with his mouth. He slid his tongue between her teeth, forcing her to open for him so he could wrap his tongue around hers, lick against her, at the same time rocking his body against hers in the most primal way imaginable. Brea held on to his arms, feeling the rock-solid strength of him, the corded muscles of his arms, the sheer power of his thighs as he molded his body along hers. And when he nestled between her legs and thrust his cock against her sex, her body wept for joy, climbing a pinnacle of need and desire that she'd never climbed before.

She poised, waiting for him to draw her skirt up, pull her panties aside and shove his cock inside her, but all he did was continue to kiss her senseless, over and over again until she had no idea how much time had gone by. Every inch of her body was nothing but raw nerve endings. He slipped his hand under her butt, and just his hand resting there while she was fully clothed made her ache to be naked, to feel him touch her all over.

And still he kissed her, finally pulling his mouth from hers to travel down her jaw. When he dragged his tongue along her throat, she tilted her head back and moaned, her body covered in goose bumps despite the warmth in the cabin.

This was torture.

He lifted up on his hands to stare down at her. "I'm going to make you come for me tonight, Brea. And not just once."

She shuddered. But she still didn't believe him, knew she was going to disappoint him. Yet her body was on fire and they both still had all their clothes on.

Holding himself above her, he surged against her, against her sex, his denim-clad cock the sweetest torment.

"Don't doubt me."

His harsh whisper thrilled her.

She still doubted. With his hand, yes, his mouth, oh hell yes. But inside her, it wouldn't happen. It never had. She wasn't capable.

He reached for her top, lifted it over her belly. She raised her arms and he smiled at her.

"Not yet."

Instead, he bent down and pressed a kiss to her belly. Her abdomen quivered at the touch of his warm lips to her flesh. She remembered what it felt like to have his mouth down there, wanted to feel him there again. And again. She'd never released like that before.

Maybe Gage was right. The cursory licks and sucks the other guys had given her in the oral sex department had barely warmed her up. Gage had given her oral pleasure like he had really enjoyed it. She had given herself up to the mastery of his exquisite mouth and tongue until he rocketed her right over the edge.

But shouldn't she be doing something for him, too? She started to lift, sliding her hand between them to reach for his cock.

Gage lifted his head. "What are you doing?"

"You've been doing everything for me. I should—"

He removed her hand. "Just relax and let me kiss you. And dammit, quit worrying about what you think *you* should be doing. The only thing you should concentrate on is enjoying what's happening between us."

She flopped back onto the sofa and Gage raised her shirt, taking his maddening time kissing her belly, her rib cage, burning her with his mouth across her skin. He lifted the shirt over her head and rose up on his knees to stare down at her, tipping his finger across the valley of her breasts. She shivered, though she wasn't sure if it was from the contact or the way he looked at her.

"Pretty bra."

She smiled. "Thanks." Okay, so maybe she had dressed just for him, right down to her lacy underwear.

"It's coming off." He reached for the front clasp, and with two fingers and one flick, the clasp parted.

"You're pretty good at that."

"Years of practice in the front of dark pickup trucks. I learned to do it by feel."

She laughed, until he spread the cups apart and bared her breasts. With the light on, she caught the sensual gleam in his eyes as he traced his fingers over each breast.

Her nipples puckered, hardened, the buds aching for the touch of his finger. And when he swept his finger over the tip of one distended nipple, she arched up toward the lightning-like pleasure of that sensation, craving more.

He swept his tongue over her nipple, covered the bud with his mouth, sucking and licking until she went liquid underneath his tender assault. He alternated from one breast to the other until she shook from the effects of his mouth on her. Every lick, every suck, every touch of his fingers shot straight to her pussy. And as with his kissing, he seemed in no hurry to get to the promised land, content to lavish praise on her breasts and nipples as if he had all the time in the world.

She felt worshipped, like he truly believed her body was something special. She'd never felt this way with a man before.

He swept his hand under her back and partially lifted her, only long enough to pull her bra off. Then he lowered her to the sofa again. He climbed off and moved to her feet, where he removed her boots and socks, rubbed her feet, kissed her toes until she shivered, having never had anyone pay attention to that particular body part before.

"You have pretty feet," he said, standing next to the sofa and rubbing the arch of one foot.

Her gaze traveled the length of him, surprised to see the unmistakable bulge straining against his jeans.

"Yeah, you make me hard, Brea. I've been hard all night." He lowered her foot and rubbed it against his erection.

She swallowed, her throat gone drought-dry as she felt the thickness of him, wanting him inside her more than she wanted to draw her next breath.

He lowered her foot to the sofa, then reached for her skirt, sliding it over her hips and down her thighs. She realized all she wore now were her panties, while he was still fully clothed.

But he was about to rectify that, because he lifted his shirt over his head, and she was rewarded with a wide expanse of tanned chest, muscles everywhere as he turned to lay their clothing on a nearby chair. His back was smooth, tapering down to a narrow waist, and dear God what a fine ass he had. When he turned, he had his hand on his belt buckle and a half smile on his face.

Mesmerized, Brea held her breath while Gage undid the buckle of his belt then drew the zipper of his jeans down. She inhaled on a shaky sigh when he pushed off his boots and let his jeans fall to the floor, his cock riding against his belly in his tight boxer briefs.

She couldn't resist. She sat up and palmed the heat and thickness of him.

"Shit," he said, fisting a handful of her hair and bending down to plant his mouth over hers in a hard, passionate kiss that devastated her senses. She rubbed her palm against his cock, feeling bolder than she'd ever felt in her life. But Gage turned her on more than any man had before.

She reached for the waistband of his briefs to drag them down his hips and thighs. His cock sprang into her waiting hands. She wound her fingers around his shaft, sizing him up, imagining how he would feel inside her.

He pulled away. "Damn, woman, you make me crazy."

He bent down in front of the sofa and ran his hands over her breasts. "You are so beautiful. And oh man I like you touching me. But you do too much of that and this is going to be all over before it even starts. And the only place I'm going to come first is inside you. Plenty of time to play later."

Later. Like they were going to do this again. She liked the sound of that, but she didn't want to pack too much hope into what was going to happen between them.

Gage licked across one nipple and spread the wet fire of his tongue along her neck before taking her mouth again in a blistering-hot kiss. At the same time, his fingers blazed a trail down her belly to slide inside her panties and cup her sex. He teased her clit, her pussy, firing her up hotter than a dry August on the plains. She arched against his hand, coaxing his fingers inside her, begging him to fill her with more. And more.

"You ready for my dick inside you, Brea?"

She gripped his arm, held his fingers inside her, wanted him even deeper. "Yes. Yes, I want it."

He rose and went over to his jeans, pulled a foil packet from his pocket.

A condom.

Finally.

He laid the condom aside and leaned over to press a kiss to her belly before reaching for her panties. He smiled up at her, then ripped her panties into shreds.

Shock filled her, followed by the slow melt of liquid heat that spread through her.

"I believe that was one of your requests."

"Yes," she said between heavy breaths. "It was."

He tore open the condom packet, skillfully slipped it on, then shifted her to face him, her legs dangling over the sofa. He kneeled in front of her and pulled her to the edge of the cushion, slid one hand underneath her, and used the other to smooth over her sex.

"I can smell you," he said, staring down at her sex before lifting his gaze to hers. He moved in, nestling his cock against the entrance to her pussy. "Sweet and hot and ready."

He slid between her pussy lips, the glide easy because he was right—she was ready for him. With one thrust he was in.

Her body pulsed around him, squeezing his shaft until pleasure burst inside her. Gage stilled, looked down at her, and Brea just . . . felt. The stirrings of excitement only grew as he pulled back and pushed inside her inch by delicious inch.

She waited for him to pound against her, to start fucking her with relentless thrusts.

But he didn't. Only sweet, easy movements that teased her clit every time he brushed up against her, ratcheting up the tension until she reached for his arms and dug her nails into his skin.

"Yeah," he said, his gaze glued to her face. "Your pussy squeezes me tight every time I slide deep inside you."

Oh, God, his voice was dark, soft, made her tingle all over. He smoothed his hand over her breasts, her ribs, snaking down over her belly until it rested against her sex.

"Widen your legs, Brea," he said, his thumb dipping down to circle around her clit. "Let me have this."

Panting, she did, and he swirled his thumb over the most sensitive part of her. She swallowed, then gasped as he moved inside her at the same time he applied pressure to the engorged bud. She lifted against his questing fingers, rocked her pelvis against him, and began to meet his thrust as pleasure burst through her.

She gripped his arms and pulled herself toward the source of that pleasure. Gage was relentless, never breaking rhythm as he brought her closer to what she'd never experienced before. His cock seemed to swell inside her, stretching her, sliding against her walls and making her nerve endings sing. She wanted to savor every second, and yet she knew she was close, so close to having this magic. She wanted it more than anything.

She doubted at first, but now she was beginning to believe, especially as Gage applied more pressure, deepened his thrusts so he ground against her whenever his body met hers. He murmured encouraging words to her that thrilled her, aroused her, and took her right to the edge, all the while watching her with his dark gaze that she couldn't look away from.

And he held on, waited, seemingly in no hurry to get to the finish line himself, as if they had hours to do this. She felt no pressure to release, and it made getting there so much easier.

With his free hand he gripped her butt and lifted her, brought her closer to him and rolled his hips against her.

With a cry she splintered, her orgasm such a huge surprise she shuddered, her body pulsating around Gage's cock. The sensations were like nothing she'd ever felt before, so much deeper, more intense, like the sweetest pleasure both inside and out. She threw her head back and let go as sensation poured out of her in a never-ending maelstrom of hot pulses.

Gage gathered her to him and ground against her, groaning as he pumped furiously with his own release, which sent her catapulting even farther into the abyss of pleasure.

It had never been like this—never. And she knew she was going to want it again and again and again.

Tiny throbs of pleasure continued to spark inside her long after. Gage still held her against him, stroking her and kissing her neck. She was out of breath and still shocked that it had happened.

She wrapped her arms around his neck, kissed his shoulder and was certain she never wanted to let go of this moment.

Finally, he withdrew and went into the bathroom, coming back with a washcloth to clean her up. He pulled her onto the sofa with him and they reclined there side by side, facing each other, not saying a word.

She didn't have anything to say, felt giddy and warm and . . . satisfied.

Gage smoothed his hand over her hair. "So now you tell those other guys to shove it."

She laughed. "I suppose so."

"Feel better?"

"I do."

He dragged his thumb over her nipple. It hardened.

"There's not a damn thing wrong with you, Brea. You're hot, you're sexy, and you can come just fine. But there was a lot wrong with those guys."

Her heart swelled with emotions she knew she needed to bury deep. This was just sex. Really good sex, but just sex and nothing more. "Thank you. I see that now."

He kissed her, and her toes curled. "Don't thank me. Sex is always a joint effort. I got just as much out of it as you did."

And then he did something totally unexpected. He pulled her against him and just held her, stroking her back and kissing her softly. He held her like that for the longest time, talking to her about mundane things, as if he was in no hurry, as if this wasn't just about the sex.

Brea would have to guard her heart around Gage. He was truly someone . . . unexpected.

Finally, they dressed and started back to the ranch. Once in the barn, Brea helped Gage remove the saddles from the horses and return everything to the tack room. It was still early enough that everyone else hadn't returned from town yet, which was good. She wasn't in the mood to answer questions from her nosy sisters. She wanted time to settle in her room and think about the incredible night she'd shared with Gage.

"I guess I should head on back to the house." She figured he'd want to get back to the bunkhouse before people started returning.

"Wait," he said, turning the light off in the barn. "I'll walk you back."

Surprised, she waited, and was even more shocked when he slid his hand in hers as they walked the path back to the main house. He took her right to the front door, turned her in his arms and gave her a kiss that melted her to the wood porch.

"I had a great time tonight, Brea," he said as he pulled away from her.

"Me, too."

"Good night." He stepped off the porch and headed to the bunkhouse.

Brea sighed and went inside, nearly floating up the stairs to her room. She took off her clothes, climbed into bed and shut off the light, staring out the window at the stars overhead and thinking about lying on that blanket with Gage.

It had been an incredible night. One they probably wouldn't repeat. She felt a wistful ache all over at that thought. But at least she'd had this one night. It had changed her, had shown her that those guys before Gage were totally and completely full of shit.

Gage had shown her that.

And he was right. There wasn't a damn thing wrong with her.

six

gage wiped the sweat from his face and handed the reins of the unruly stallion he'd been training over to Grizz, who grinned and spit a wad of tobacco juice out of the side of his mouth.

"That one's gonna try to take a bite out of your ass," Grizz said.

Gage looked back at the stallion. "Many have tried. He'll come around to my way of thinking soon enough."

Grizz just laughed and whistled for a couple extra hands to help him with the stubborn horse. Gage hopped over the rail and went to the cooler for a bottle of water. While bent down, he saw Brea coming out of the house with her sister Valerie. They were assisting John Dowring, one of the old-timers who had come to Valerie for medical care and needed some help getting back into his truck.

Once John had taken off, Valerie went back inside. Brea lingered for a few minutes, her gaze skirting over to the corral. Gage stood, smiled at her, and she grinned at him before heading back up the stairs and into the house.

She walked with her head held higher and a lightness to her step since they'd had their time together a couple nights ago. Unfortunately, since then, they hadn't had any time alone together. Walker had brought in a new herd of horses that had kept Gage busy from sunup to sundown, and he hadn't had time to do much more than just ogle Brea from afar whenever he caught a glimpse of her.

Which didn't mean he wasn't thinking about her. He had been ever since he dropped her off at her front door that night.

Brea wasn't at all like the women he was used to. They were all pretty forward, and much more experienced. While he liked that just fine, there was something about Brea that was different. Her shyness around men was cute, her lack of experience endearing, but it was more than that. She was fresh and sweet and soft and had an innocence about her most of the girls he knew had lost around age sixteen or so.

But the other night he had a feeling he'd woken the sleeping tigress. And he wanted to explore that further. A lot further. Which meant getting some alone time with her, which wasn't going to be easy on this ranch with all these people breathing down their necks.

Brea stepped outside again, this time with Jolene, who as usual was going someplace in a hurry. That woman could eat up a stretch of dirt with her long strides faster than a cheetah on the hunt. Brea raced to keep up with her sister, and Gage enjoyed the view of her quick-stepping it down the path toward the barn. He especially liked the back view of her fine ass in tight jeans.

He also noticed that despite nearly running to keep up with Jolene, Brea took a second to glance his way as they passed the corral. He tipped his hat and winked and even from across the fence he saw her cheeks turn pink.

"You're wading in dangerous territory, my man."

Walker had come up and laid his forearms across the top bar of the corral fence.

"Yeah? How do you figure?"

"Brea is one of the owners of the Bar M now."

"So?"

"So her, Jolene and Valerie are our bosses."

Walker always was a little too worried about that kind of thing. "Again, so?"

"You mess around with Brea and piss her off, your job is history."

Gage shrugged and grabbed the rope hanging from the hook on the outside of the fence post. He climbed over the fence, then looked at Walker. "Wouldn't be the first job I was fired from. I can always get another. Besides, it's not in me to stay in one place too long anyway."

Walker frowned. "Being fired over fucking a woman is a shitty reason to lose a job."

Gage laughed. "You got that wrong, Walker. Being fired over fucking a woman is the *best* reason to lose a job."

"good gravy, brea. pay attention."

Brea turned her focus on Jolene and a couple of the other hands. How she had gotten roped into working the calves in the pen today was beyond her. She supposed she'd spent entirely too much time holed up in the house working on her computer. She knew she couldn't hide from Jolene—or chores—forever. She had been helping Valerie, until Jolene dragged her outside and said since she was part owner she could damn well earn her share.

Not that she had considered herself an owner of the Bar M. She intended to put her time in because Jolene had insisted, but she had a life—and a job—in Tulsa. While it was true that she had a computer and could do her job pretty much anywhere there was an Internet connection, it didn't mean she intended to do it on the ranch. This wasn't home for her anymore. It was Jolene's place. Okay, and now that Valerie had settled in with Mason again, she supposed the two sisters could split ownership of the ranch.

Brea's life was computers and programming and books. Not horses and cattle.

Though one horseman sure had caught her interest.

She helped push the cattle down the chute and looked across the yard at Gage, who over the past few days had managed to sweet-talk one unruly stallion into doing what Gage wanted him to do. No small feat, considering the stallion had strongly objected to the bridle and bit and then the saddle.

But Gage had an infinite amount of patience and had worked diligently with the horse until the stallion had finally acquiesced and given up the fight. And all without a whip or any damage to the horse's beautiful spirit, which still showed through when the stallion tossed his nose up in the air.

The way Gage broke a horse—or trained it—was one of the things she liked most about him. He always let the horse keep its dignity, but Gage made it clear he was the one in control.

"You know, Brea," Jolene said, huffing and puffing as she managed cattle that didn't want to be led where Jolene wanted them to go, "if you'd quit drooling over Gage and pay attention to what we're doing here, we might be able to finish this job before midnight."

She snapped back to Jolene. "What?" Realizing the cattle were trying to mutiny and head in the other direction, she wrested control back and started moving them again. "Sorry."

"Uh huh." Jolene closed the chute gate and leaned on it. "If you're going to be useless, I'll just call someone else over."

Brea followed Jolene toward the opposite end of the corral. "I'm here, aren't I?"

Jolene glared at her. "Physically, yeah. Mentally, not so sure. I think your mind is across the way, undressing Gage."

Brea looked over at Bobby, who was standing on the other side of the corral. Bobby grinned at her and Brea blushed a hundred shades of crimson before turning a livid look on her younger sister. "I was doing no such thing."

"Please," Jolene said. "Lust is written all over your face." She nodded at Bobby. "Let's take a lunch break and we'll get back to this in half an hour. Tell the others."

"Yes, ma'am," Bobby said before heading off. Jolene and Brea went into the house and grabbed sandwiches that Lila had made for them. Brea poured two glasses of lemonade and they pulled up chairs at the kitchen table. They ate in silence, Brea realizing she'd worked up an appetite. Typically she picked at food, but since she'd been on the ranch she'd done more physical work and it made her hungry. Getting outside and back to doing what she used to do before she'd moved into the city was . . . fun. Even if it wasn't what she was going to spend the rest of her life doing, it was nice to get back to her roots again.

And also nice to watch Gage.

"You're doing it again."

Brea lifted her head to stare at her sister. "Doing what?"

"Getting that dreamy, moony, sickly sweet look on your face. It's disgusting."

Brea rolled her eyes. "I am not."

Jolene pushed her empty plate to the side and picked up her glass of lemonade. "I'm serious. You must have it bad for Gage."

She refused to answer.

"Did you fuck him yet?"

"Jolene!"

Her sister didn't look apologetic in the least, instead tapped her fingers on the table. "Well?"

"I'm not going to discuss my sex life with you."

Jolene smirked. "That means you have one. Good for you. Just don't drag him off behind the barn to blow him while I need him working."

Brea rolled her eyes. "You're such a tart."

Jolene waggled her eyebrows. "Don't I know it. Now if only I could get Walker to see just how much of a tart I am."

Thankful to turn the topic away from her and Gage, Brea leaned forward. "What about Walker?"

"I've got the major hots for him and he's running scared."

"Why? He doesn't seem the wimpy type to me." Walker was gorgeous. Tall, lean, one hell of a hot cowboy, filled with testosterone and 100 percent male.

"Yeah, you wouldn't think so. But he won't give me the time of day."

"Maybe he's not interested in you."

Jo gave her a sideways look of disbelief. "Please. If he wasn't interested, I wouldn't bother. I know when a guy's interested. Trust me, he is."

"Then what's the problem?"

"I'm his boss. He seems to think that's an issue."

"Oh." Brea leaned back in the chair. "Well, you do basically run this ranch. I can see why he'd think that might cause a conflict."

"Too bad. I want him. He wants me, I know he does. We're going to tussle."

"Just because you say so?"

Jolene grinned. "I always get what I want."

"Must be nice to be that confident."

"You should try it."

Brea laughed. "I'm not you, Jo."

"You don't have to be me. You just set your sights on what you want and go after it. And don't let anything or anyone get in your way. Life's too short, Brea. Get what you want while the gettin's good."

brea spent the rest of the day thinking about what Jolene had said, and realized she'd been patient long enough waiting for Gage. She wanted him again and was bold enough to at least admit that to herself.

But she wasn't Jolene, didn't have the self-confidence her little sister had.

Still, maybe it was time to stop assuming Gage would come after her.

When she was finished with the calves, she hung out near the barn and watched Gage train the horses. When he was done and climbed outside the fence, she took a deep breath and headed in his direction. She'd made it halfway before he spotted her, wiping the back of his neck with a rag as he watched her approach.

His lips lifted in that smile that made her toes curl in her boots. "Afternoon, Miss Brea."

"Gage."

"Saw you working the cattle today."

"Jolene made me."

He laughed. "It's your ranch, too."

"So she keeps telling me."

Silence. *Say what you came to say, Brea. He isn't going to make the next move.*

"I want to see you tonight, Gage."

One brow arched. "Is that right?"

If he shot her down, she was going to run to her room and hide in the closet until she died. "That's right."

"Where?"

"In my room. Late."

He propped one arm on the top of the fence and leaned closer. "You want me to sneak into your room tonight?"

"Yes, I do."

His lips quirked. "I'll be there."

She shuddered her next breath, her nipples tingling at the thought. "I'll be waiting."

Before she embarrassed herself by kissing him right there in front of God only knew who was watching, she pivoted and walked away, feeling his gaze on her the entire way back to the house.

She liked knowing he watched her.

Now could she be brave enough to let Gage into her room to-night, right under the noses of her family?

She was going to have to be, because she'd just invited him.

gage kept an eye on the goings-on at the house. He'd come in and had supper with everyone earlier. Jolene gave him a knowing smile—Brea must have told her the two of them had something going on. Fortunately Valerie had eyes only for Mason, so he didn't think he'd have to be too concerned about the two of them. They had remarried at the justice of the peace a couple weeks ago, and were practically honeymooning again, so absorbed in each other they didn't notice anything going on around them. Walker just shook his head.

Gage knew Lila went to bed early. Valerie and Mason had left in the truck earlier. Jolene took off out of the house and headed toward the barn, then rode off and hadn't come back, no doubt seeing to the cattle farther out on the property, because Walker had gone with her.

That left Brea alone in the house except for Lila.

Gage left the bunkhouse, the other hands occupied with a game of Texas Hold Em. They didn't even notice him leaving. He went up to the house, careful to come in through the back door instead of the front. No one locked doors on the property. No reason to, first because they were remote and knew everyone within a hundred miles, and second because everyone who lived on the ranch was plenty handy with a shotgun in case of intruders.

Gage wasn't intruding. He'd been invited, which had surprised and pleased him. Brea had finally been bold enough to be the one to do the inviting. Besides being busy as hell the past week, he'd also purposely held off instigating anything with her. He wanted her to realize she was worthy of having a man in her life. If she wanted him, she was going to have to come to him this time.

He climbed the stairs, inching his way quietly on the toes of his boots. He sure as hell hoped Lila was a sound sleeper, though he knew her room was on the first floor and on the east side of the house, far away from where the sisters slept.

Brea's room was down the hall, at the end. No light shined there. He hoped she hadn't chickened out and headed into town. He reached her door and turned the knob, easing the door open.

Soft candlelight bathed the room.

He moved in and shut the door behind him, making sure to lock it. As he turned to face the bed, his breath stuttered.

Brea sat on the bed, one leg curled behind her. Her hair caught the flickering candlelight and looked like waving flames in the semidarkness. She wore a silky dark slip that molded to every one of her lush curves.

Gage swallowed, his throat gone dry at the sight of her perched in the middle of the bed, her wary gaze following him as he made his way fully into the room.

She looked like a sex goddess, her hair falling over one eye, her lips glossy and full and slightly parted in invitation. Did she have any idea what that did to his cock?

He stopped at the foot of the bed, content just to look at her. Brea tilted her head back to capture his gaze.

"Say something," she whispered.

"You're beautiful."

Her lashes dipped down, hiding her eyes.

"Look at me, Brea."

She did.

"You're beautiful. I wish I had a picture of you sitting on the bed the way you are right now. You take my breath away."

"No, I don't."

"I don't say anything I don't mean."

"Thank you."

"This is nice. The candles, the room, you." She had some snacks on the bedside table, some cheese, and a bottle of wine chilling. He sat on the edge of the bed and reached for the bottle.

"Would you like me to open this?"

She nodded and he grabbed the corkscrew.

"I wasn't sure you even liked wine. It might be too fussy for you."

He pulled the cork out and reached for the glasses. "I like it just fine." He handed her a glass and took a sip of the wine. "It's good."

She held the glass and peeked at him through the fringe of her lashes, the action making her look even sexier than she already did. His cock tightened and swelled.

Down, boy. The night was just starting. He was going to let Brea play this out her way, since she'd done the inviting.

"How's the horse training coming?"

"Good. Making some headway. He's stubborn, but he's starting to see things my way."

Brea's lips quirked. "You can be very convincing when you want something."

"No point in beating around the bush. Just lay it out there and make your wishes known."

"I suppose so. Waffling would be a sign of weakness and would cause unnecessary delays."

"Yeah. Besides, if you're straight up about what you expect, there are no surprises later on. And then you both get what you want."

"The horse wants to be wild and free, doesn't it?"

"The horse wants food and water, shelter and affection. I can provide that."

"If he does what you want him to do."

"He gets what he wants, I get what I want. It's a win/win."

She laid her glass on the table. "You meet in the middle."

He put his glass down, too. "Yes. That's the way it's supposed to be. Power shouldn't be one-sided. My aim isn't to break him, just show him a different way than what he's been used to."

She shifted, planting her palms on either side of his legs to draw closer to him. Gage inhaled her sweet fragrance of soap and shampoo.

"I like your way. It's honest."

He slid his hand into her hair, sifting through the silken softness of it. "I'll always be honest. It's the only way I know how to be."

"Then I'll try to be the same way." She climbed onto his lap, straddling him, aligning the heat of her sex against the throbbing hardness of him. "I honestly want you to kiss me."

His lips were on hers as soon as she finished the sentence, his body taut with the need tightening inside him since the last time he'd had her in his arms. It had been too long, and he craved the touch of her, her taste against his lips, on his tongue, the way her scent floated along his senses, more intoxicating than any bottle of wine. He leaned against the headboard and took Brea with him, her legs sliding along his, her breasts pressed to his chest. He got to touch her this way, run his hands along the flimsy little thing she wore, feeling it and her soft curves as she squirmed against him. He let his hands roam down to her sweet ass, squeezing her, pressing in so her body rubbed his cock. Damn, it felt so good having her against him.

She broke the kiss, sat up and began to unbutton his shirt.

Oh, yeah. He let her have at it, figuring she could do whatever the hell she wanted with him. She slipped each button out, tugging her bottom lip with her teeth in concentration. He wanted to reach for those tiny little straps on her shoulders and tug them down so he could see her breasts, but he got the idea she wanted to be in charge, so he left his hands at his sides and let her open his shirt.

Her hands were cool as she spread her palms over his chest, smoothing them over his nipples until they hardened. She bent down and ran her tongue over his nipples, sucked them. Damn, that felt good all the way to his balls. He swept his hand over her hair.

"I like that."

She looked up at him and smiled, then licked her tongue over his ribs, stretching out over his legs to snake down his body as her tongue moved in fluid motion over his skin.

He liked her exploring his body, would give her free rein to do anything she damn well pleased as long as her hands and mouth stayed on him. Bold Brea was something new. He was enjoying this side of her and wanted to encourage more of it.

She scooted farther down, her tongue mapping his ribs and abs, sizzling across his body until she got to his jeans. She stopped only long enough to unzip his pants and tug them down with relentless determination, freeing his cock. Before he could take a breath, she had his shaft in both hands, her now-warm fingers wrapped around him, stroking up and down. He sucked in a breath and watched her as she stared at his cock like she was enraptured. He sure as hell was, fisting the sheets as she played with him as if what she did had no effect. Hell, it took all the self-control he had not to come all over her hands. She might think she was a novice, but her touch made him crazy.

Brea glanced up at him. "Is this okay?"

"Darlin', if it was any more okay this would be over already."

She stilled. "You want me to stop?"

"Oh, hell no. I like your hands on me. A little too much. It feels really good."

She smiled, and he saw the power brighten in her eyes. That's what he'd wanted to see.

"Brea, you can do whatever you want, whatever feels right to you."

She looked from his face back to his cock, then bent over him again. "I want to taste you."

Son of a bitch. He gritted his teeth as she took his cock head between her sweet lips, her tongue darting out to sweep over him. The combination of hot and wet was nearly his undoing. He jerked, and she hummed in satisfaction, gripping the base of his cock to feed it into her mouth inch by sweet inch. And he had a front-row seat for the most beautiful sight he'd ever seen—watching her swallow him.

She might not be practiced at blow jobs, but what she lacked in technique she sure as hell made up for in eagerness and genuine desire to please. And that was more exciting than what any woman had done to him before. That she seemed to genuinely enjoy doing what she was doing jacked up his pleasure even more. He raised up, fisting his hand in her hair to control her movements.

She moaned, seeming to like when he took over.

Yeah, he figured she would. His balls tightened as he moved her mouth over his cock, pushing her a little farther than might be comfortable. But she took him, all the way to the back of her throat, as he taught her what he liked, how deep he liked it, until he couldn't take it anymore.

He lifted her mouth away and dragged her across his chest. "You keep doing that and I'm going to come in your mouth."

Her lips were wet, swollen, her eyes glittering with desire. "I want you to, Gage. Let me."

Christ, she was going to kill him. He kissed her hard, his tongue diving in to possess, to sweep and tangle with hers before letting go. "Then do it."

She slid down his body again and engulfed his cock in her mouth, grabbing the base with her hand. She swept her other hand over his balls and gave them a gentle squeeze.

He lifted against her, fucking her mouth, his balls tightening as he felt the rush he wouldn't be able to control now. "Yeah, like that. Take it deep until I come."

He widened his legs and she cradled his balls in her hands, took his cock as deep as she could and pressed down hard with her lips, sucking as she moved her mouth in the rhythm he set.

"I'm going to come, Brea."

She moaned her appreciation and that was all it took. He came in torrents, trying to withhold shouting but unable to hold back the loud groan as he pulled on her hair and rolled his hips to feed more of his cock into her greedy mouth. Brea held on to him, her nails digging into his thighs as he thrust between her lips until he was empty and damn well panting.

And still she lingered there, licking his cock, kissing it, stroking his thighs.

He pulled her up his body, kissed her. "Thank you, darlin'."

"No, thank *you*. That was very enjoyable."

He laughed, petted her hair, not sure what to make of this woman who seemed innocent about sex one minute and a tigress the next. "I'm liking this change in you."

She shrugged. "You're a good teacher. You make me want to be open."

He arched a brow. "Is that right?"

She tilted her head back to gaze at him. "That's right."

And that made him want to do a lot of things with her. Everything. "How open?"

There was an eagerness in her eyes, a light he hadn't seen before.

"Anything. Everything. Teach me. I've missed so much."

Damn. His cock stirred to life just thinking about the things he could do with her.

He rolled her onto her back and held her there, smoothing his hands down the satiny shift that pressed against her curves, highlighting her erect nipples. He covered one with his mouth, capturing both the fabric and the bud between his lips. Brea moaned and arched against him, tangling her fingers in his hair as he sucked her nipple.

But it wasn't enough. He wanted her hot flesh in his mouth and under his hands. He lifted the slip up, his hands roaming under to slide with just a hint of a tease over her sex, taking the fabric with him as he moved his hand over her ribs and breasts, giving her light touches and caresses only.

He removed her slip and cast it aside, then looked his fill of her naked body, lush and goddess-like under the flickering candlelight. He laid his palm between her breasts and felt the fast thump of her heartbeat, liked that just his light touch could rev her up like this.

"Darlin', I could lick you up like barbecue sauce dripping off ribs."

She laughed. "That's quite the compliment."

He rolled his tongue over her nipple, took it between his lips and sucked until she let out a whispered moan. When he raised up, her eyes were glassy with desire. "It's my highest compliment. You are definitely edible." He moved to the other nipple to do the same thing until she writhed under his mouth and hands. Then he moved down her body, breathing in the scent of her skin, the way her scent—soap and shampoo—mixed with the heady natural aroma of aroused female.

Nothing smelled sweeter. He liked that she didn't douse herself in perfume. He always thought woman who did were trying to hide something. Brea smelled like . . . Brea: clean, natural, like she'd just stepped out of the shower. Something about a woman's natural scent got to him and made his dick hard.

Brea made his dick hard. He liked the feel of her body moving under his hands, the way she squirmed as he kissed her belly and moved even lower, spreading her legs with his shoulders as he sank between them. He kissed the top of her sex, slid his fingers along her pussy lips. She was wet, ready for him, and he slid his tongue along her folds, wanting to capture every drop of what she gave him.

Because she was hot for him. She was wet for him. And she was going to come for him.

seven

brea tightened her hold on the sheets, lifting her butt to draw closer to Gage's lips and tongue. He was magic with his mouth, took her from languid foreplay to ready-to-come in minutes. He got her hot and ready so fast it was almost embarrassing how well he knew her body already. All she could do was sink into every touch, every lick, and hang on for the ride, hoping she didn't fall too soon.

He dragged her right to the edge several times, only to back away, lick her inner thighs and tap her lightly with his fingers until the sensation subsided. Then he'd take her there all over again until she was right . . . there . . . only to pull away. It was maddening. She lifted her head when he did it again.

"Gage?"

He smiled up at her. "Yeah, darlin'?"

"What are you doing?"

He slid his tongue up the length of her, making her shudder. "What does it look like I'm doing?"

Her only answer was to tangle her fingers in his hair and hold him steady so he'd continue doing exactly what he was doing. He captured her clit between his lips and flattened his tongue over the sensitive bud. She threw her head back, lifted her hips to drive her pussy against his mouth, and came, rocking against his face as waves of pleasure swept over her. She couldn't let go until the tremors subsided. Gage held on to her and went with her the entire time until she was too sensitive to endure the flicks of his tongue on her clit.

Panting, she fell back against the mattress, her limbs boneless. She waited for him to move up beside her, to spread her legs and fuck her. But he didn't. Instead, he continued to kiss her sex, to caress her legs, until she lifted her head and looked down at him.

"Gage?"

"Yeah."

"Come up here with me."

"Not yet. I'm not finished with you."

He swept his tongue across her sex, and she trembled at the renewed sensation sparking across her nerve endings. She'd just come, and yet she felt the hot stirrings of arousal begin again. What was he doing to her? How could he drag her from languishing after release to pent-up desire with one swipe of his tongue? Yet her body was tense and anticipating the next lick, the next touch.

And when he lifted her legs and bent her knees to her chest, exposing her intimately to his gaze, she cringed.

"Gage."

"Relax, Brea. You told me everything. I want all of you. Even here."

He swept his tongue along her folds, all warm and wet and probing until her inhibitions fled. And when his tongue traveled south and drifted over her anus, she shuddered, utterly shocked at the pleasure she felt there. She had no idea it would feel so . . . good. Gage rolled his tongue back and forth until she couldn't think straight, could only imagine what would come next.

"You have lube?"

She pointed to the drawer at the side of the bed. He left her for only a moment, then came back, spreading her. He licked her pussy again, surrounding her clit, warming her, exciting her. And then his finger circled her back-door entrance, lubed up and slick. He didn't enter her with the digit, just teased her, excited the nerve endings there until she was turned on and curious and overwhelmed with the sensations he created.

"Gage." She moaned his name on a long, low whisper, not sure what she even wanted other than to voice the pleasure he gave her.

He kept his mouth on her sex and slid his finger inside her anus, pushing past the tight barrier, sucking her clit while he inserted his finger all the way into her. His knuckles bumped her buttocks as he pulled out and pushed in, licking and sucking her as he did.

It was a wild, primal sensation, a sweet burning pain that brought her insane pleasure at the same time. As he eased in and out of her anus and licked her pussy, he drove her closer and closer to the edge again.

And yet, somehow, she wanted more.

"Gage, there's a dildo in the drawer. I want that in my pussy."

She'd never been so daring before. The thought of doing that— of him doing that—shocked her, and yet excited her in ways she had only previously imagined when she was alone, touching herself, wishing for this to happen but thinking it never would. And now it was. She wanted to be filled when she came, to feel contractions in every part of her.

He pulled the dildo from the drawer and lubed it. "This what you want?"

She lifted up on her elbows to watch, unable to believe this was really happening. "Yes."

Gage smiled up at her as if he was more than happy to grant her wish. He eased the dildo inside her pussy, stretching her. It felt so good, especially when he put his mouth on her clit and laved the tight bud with his tongue. She tilted her head back. "Oh yes. That's exactly what I want."

And then he slid his finger inside her anus again, exactly what she'd imagined—being filled both ways. It was like being double fucked, something she'd never experienced, and the lightning-like pulses shot her into the stratosphere. The sensations she felt coming from his mouth, the dildo, his fingers—it was all too much. Her orgasm rained down on her like a torrent and she couldn't hold back. And she felt it everywhere, in every part of her, pulsing and squeezing and zinging out from her clit, her pussy and her anus. She bucked off the bed and cried out, not caring who heard her, because it was just too damn good to hold back. Gage held tight to her, his mouth and his hands all over her as she rode the wave until she fell back on the bed, exhausted and utterly satisfied.

He removed the dildo and left her for a few seconds to wash up, then came back and slid next to her on the bed, pulling her against him, his face aligned with hers. She swept her palm against the stubble of beard across his jaw. He was so rugged, so damn sexy her heart did leaps whenever she saw him outside. But here in bed he saw to her every need like the lover she'd always dreamed of. He demanded her release in ways she could never have imagined, yes, but because he had such faith in her sexuality, she found it so easy to give in with him.

She was never going to be able to thank him enough for giving her such a precious gift.

Brea was afraid more than just her body was becoming entangled with Gage. And she knew that wasn't at all what he was interested in.

Keep it light, Brea. Keep it fun. Don't fall in love. She already knew Gage was only in it for the fun and the sex. There was nothing wrong with that. If she pushed for anything more, he'd walk away. And she was having way too much fun discovering great sex to lose him.

He caressed her back, using his fingertips to walk along her spine. "You have a very serious look on your face for a woman who just screamed the rooftop down when she came."

She giggled. "I'm thinking we're not quite finished yet." She reached between them and wrapped her fingers around his cock. It was hard and hot and he thrust against her hand. "You have to be more than ready."

"I'm patient. I don't mind waiting while you come a few times."

Another thing she admired so much about him, and what made him so different from the men she'd been with before. He saw to her needs first instead of his own.

"Now it's time for you and me to come together."

He grinned. "I like how bold you've become. A few days ago you wouldn't have said that."

She pressed her lips to his. "I have you to thank for my newfound confidence. Now, let's get this inside me."

He laughed. "Greedy tart."

She squeezed his cock, sliding her hand up and down the shaft. "Tease."

Gage flipped her onto her back and kissed her, and she forgot all about talking as he heated her up with his mouth and tongue until she was senseless and craving him inside her. He rolled them onto their sides and lifted her leg over his hip, then quickly grabbed a condom and put it on in record time, before turning back to her and sliding inside her.

She melted around him, surging forward to push more of his cock inside her.

"You feel better than the dildo," she said, smoothing her hand down his arm.

"Good to know you like a lifelike dick inside you." His cock twitched inside her and it was so much better than anything plastic or silicone could ever be for her.

"Oh, I definitely like the real thing a lot better. But what you did . . . oh my God, Gage, it felt so good. I've never . . ."

He slid his hand down her back, his finger dipping between the globes of her buttocks. "Never, huh?"

"No."

"Good. I like giving you a first."

He fucked her with gentle, easy strokes, continuing to tease between her ass cheeks with his fingers, driving her to the brink of madness. Brea had no idea she was so sensitive there, that someone touching her anus could ratchet up her pleasure so much. But the more he touched her there, using just his fingertip to tease the hole, the more she knew what she wanted. Something she'd never experienced before. Something she wanted Gage to do.

"Gage."

"Yeah, darlin'?"

"I want you to fuck me there."

He stilled, his cock jerking inside her. "Are you sure?"

She kissed him, rimming his lower lip with her tongue. "Yes."

His nostrils flared as he inhaled deeply, then thrust forward, his cock seeming to swell thicker with every movement.

Then he withdrew and grabbed the lube and dildo. "Roll over onto your side and slide this dildo in your pussy."

She did, inserting the phallus into her, unable to resist stroking it in and out.

"I like watching you do that," Gage said, crawling back onto the bed behind her. "If I was the kind of guy who liked to share, it would be fun seeing you get fucked by some other guy. Or seeing you suck another guy's dick while I fucked you."

Visions filled her head of Gage fucking her and some nameless, faceless other man shoving his cock in her mouth. Or Gage fucking her ass while another man thrust his cock in her pussy. She shuddered and shoved the dildo in faster.

"Don't come yet, darlin'," Gage said, pouring lube on his cock and settling in behind her. "Not until I fuck you."

She stilled, panting in excitement and a little fear as he spread her ass cheeks and coated her anus with lube.

"Anytime you want to stop, just tell me."

She nodded, but she was past the point of stopping. She wanted this.

He teased his cock head against the entrance to her anus, and her nerve endings went wild, her pussy contracting with spasms of pleasure. She held tight to the dildo, pumping it light and easy so she wouldn't come yet.

And then he pushed the head of his cock inside her, and it hurt. It burned, and yet at the same time, the feeling was pure pleasure. He eased all the way in, and Brea had never felt anything like it before. She had a cock in her pussy and one in her ass, and all she could do was fantasize about having two men. She'd never want that in reality, but what she was doing now with Gage was the ultimate fantasy, and it was more than enough.

"Fuck yourself," he said as he began to move behind her, sliding his cock ever so slowly inside her ass. "Feel both cocks fucking you."

She pulled the dildo partway out and slid it back in, dragging it past the part of her that screamed with nerve endings. Everything felt tighter now that Gage was buried in her ass, and she arched her back and laid her head against his shoulder as he began to move in earnest. And so did she, pumping the dildo in rhythm to the movements of his cock.

"Fuck, that's tight," he said, his voice laced with a hard edge. He dug his fingers into her hip and pulled her against him, and Brea was lost in the sensation. She slid her other hand down to rub her clit, unable to stand the need rising inside her.

"I need to come, Gage," she said through panting breaths as she strummed her clit and shoved the dildo furiously into her pussy. "Fuck me harder."

"Oh, yeah. I'm going to shoot come hard into you, Brea. You ready for it?"

"Yes. Fuck me. Yes."

She was so lost now, the stirrings of orgasm taking her over, that when he held tight to her hips and tunneled deep, she went over, crying out in wild abandon as her orgasm shattered her.

She felt it in every part of her, stronger than the last one, squeezing everything she had inside her. She bucked back toward Gage and he yelled out and shuddered against her, burying his face in her neck as he came.

She was sweaty and exhausted and couldn't have moved if she tried. Gage withdrew and somehow managed to get them both into her bathroom and into the shower, where he washed her off and then towel-dried her before carrying her to bed and sliding in behind her.

He kissed her neck and shoulders and threw an arm around her. Brea smiled, realizing that they hadn't said much the entire time after. But he'd smiled at her in a way that she understood all too well.

No words were necessary. She let herself drift off.

A few hours later, Gage woke her with a kiss and a whisper.

"I'm going to sneak out of here. Don't want to be found here in the morning."

She smiled and snuggled deeper into the pillows. "I don't think anyone would mind that we're sleeping together."

"I mind. I have too much respect for you to have people snickering about us. Besides, what we do is our business, no one else's, okay?"

She yawned. "Okay."

"See you tomorrow."

He pressed a kiss to her lips and she heard the soft snick of her bedroom door as he let himself out.

She was smiling as she fell back to sleep.

eight

gage had worked late today so everyone had gone ahead without him. He could barely find a spot in the parking lot. And when he walked in, the scene rocked him back on his boots.

The bar in town was packed. Even for a typical Friday night, it was full up and people were crowded in like cattle in a chute. It was the busy season and new hands had hired on. Gage scooted inside and looked around to see who was there that he knew.

Hell, everyone was there. Mason and Walker nodded as he walked by the pool tables; several other hands were playing poker, and a couple were hitting on women.

Gage moved through the bar, surveying the strangers that mingled with the people he'd known since he'd been at the Bar M. For the first time in a lot of years, there were people he called his friends.

And didn't that set off warning bells.

He wasn't the type to set down roots. He liked people well enough to get by, but he didn't get close to them. Drifting from one job to another suited him just fine. Staying in one place too long meant you'd get attached. And getting attached only spelled trouble. He'd long ago vowed never to get serious about anything, whether it be a place or a thing or especially a woman.

People might say they loved you, but Gage had personal experience in that department. Love was for fools, just a word people threw around when they wanted something from you. If you kept your distance and didn't get close to people, you didn't get hurt.

Gage was going to make sure never to fall into that trap. Love was nothing but trouble. Freedom was everything.

Speaking of trouble, he spotted Brea moving through the crowd. She sashayed over to her sisters, who were leaning against the bar talking to Sandy, the bartender. Brea wore a pair of tight jeans that molded to her ass, a green tank top that brought out the fiery red in her hair, and earrings that glittered despite the smoke in the bar. Damn, she looked good enough to eat.

The past few days they'd spent almost all their time together. She'd started helping him with horse training, claiming she was interested in what he did. He figured Jolene had given up on Brea paying attention to any ranch duties since she always seemed to want to be close to the corral where Gage was training.

Even tonight she'd wanted to linger behind and wait for him, but he wasn't sure he'd even get done in time to make it to the bar, so he told her to go with her sisters, and she'd reluctantly agreed. She hadn't wanted to leave him.

Not that he minded that. When she wasn't around, he missed her and wondered what she was doing and where she was. Which was bad. Really bad. He never thought about women other than when he was with them. Out of sight, out of mind.

Except with Brea. Out of sight, *on* his mind. And that sent the warning bell clanging even louder.

Brea tilted her head back and laughed at something Sandy said. Brea had a beautiful laugh, and now that she'd come out of her shell, everything about her seemed to sparkle with life and laughter. He thought she'd been beautiful before, but now she sizzled.

And apparently others had started to notice Brea, too. While Valerie and Jolene headed out to the dance floor, Brea was left alone with Sandy. When Sandy went to fill a drink order down the bar, two guys moved up on either side of Brea, both leaning in to speak to her.

She looked kind of surprised, but she smiled at both of them and didn't seem uncomfortable. One of the guys signaled Sandy with a twirl of his fingers for another round for all three of them. Brea sat on the bar stool and accepted the beer one of them handed her.

The guy on the left, tall and lanky with a smile meant to charm the ladies, pulled up a seat next to Brea and leaned in, his body language loud and clear as he leaned his arm on the bar so it would brush Brea's shoulders. The other one, with long shaggy blond hair, tipped his hat back and stuck out his chest, straddled his bar stool and crowded Brea.

She didn't seem all that crowded, though. She was laughing.

Gage's hand balled into a fist and he thought of a hundred different ways he'd like to castrate the two cowboys.

"Looks like a couple of greenhorns are trying to muscle in on your woman," Mason said as he and Walker moved up on either side of him.

"Yeah," Walker said, laying a hand on Gage's shoulder. "And you don't seem too happy about that. So what are you going to do about it?"

His woman. They saw Brea as his woman. Was he that obvious? Maybe it was the clenched fist or the tight set of his jaw. Things between him and Brea had gone further than he'd thought they would. It was time to pull on the reins, hard.

He relaxed and shrugged. "She's not my woman."

Mason coughed and muttered, "Bullshit."

Walker laughed and slapped him on the back. "You trying to convince us, or yourself?"

He leaned back against a thick column and crossed his arms. "Brea can do whatever she wants with whoever she wants. We just had some fun together, that's all."

"Uh huh. Keep talkin', Gage. In the meantime, those cowboys are rustlin' your filly."

He wouldn't look. He didn't. Not until Walker and Mason tired of giving him a hard time and went back to the pool table. Then his gaze shot back to the bar stool where Brea . . . had been sitting. She wasn't there anymore.

Neither were the two guys.

Goddammit. Where was she?

"Were you planning on hiding from me tonight?"

He whirled around to find Brea standing behind him. He smiled down at her. "I'd never hide from you. You looked busy."

"Oh, those guys?" She rolled her eyes. "They swooped in and hit on me like they'd been living in the desert and hadn't seen a woman in years. They were kind of obvious."

"Is that right."

"Yes." She hooked her arm in his. "I wasn't interested."

"Why not?"

She stilled, then tilted her head back, a look of surprise on her face. "Duh, cowboy. Because I already have the man I want."

Gage's gut clenched. "Uh, Brea, I think we should talk."

She frowned. "About what?"

"About you and me. But not here. Let's go outside."

"Okay."

He led her outside, where it was quieter, but part of the crowd had spilled outside to smoke and talk, which meant they still didn't have enough privacy. "How about we sit in my truck?"

They slid into the front seat, and Brea snuggled across the bench to sit next to him. She laid her hand on his thigh. "This is nice. Want to make out like teenagers?"

Dammit, he loved her sense of humor, the way she'd broken out of her shell and how comfortable she was in her own skin now. He loved everything about her. Which was why he was going to have to hurt her. Otherwise, he might start thinking he'd like to stick around, keep his job on the Bar M just so he could be near her. He might start thinking he was falling in love with her. And Gage was never going to fall in love.

"Darlin', we've had a lot of fun together . . ."

Her smile died and she removed her hand from his lap. "Why do I think there's a 'but' about to follow those words?"

"Brea, I made no secret of the fact that I'm not the kind of guy to settle down."

She shifted to face him, but he saw it as her inching away from him. "I don't recall asking you to marry me, Gage."

"I know you didn't. But I know where this is going between you and me. And I can't go there with you. I can't be the kind of guy you need."

She slid farther away, her face showing her pain. He hated doing this to her, but better now than later. "Really. And what kind of guy is it that you think I need?"

He moved toward her, lifted her chin so she'd be forced to look at him, so she'd read the truth in his eyes. "Someone who'll love you like you deserve to be loved. Someone who'll be there for you every day, who won't leave you."

"You're leaving."

He shrugged. "Sooner or later, yeah. I don't put down roots. I like to keep my life fluid."

Her eyes filled with tears and she blinked a few times. He knew she was trying to keep from crying, which only twisted his insides more. He wanted to pull her against him and hold her, kiss her, tell her he didn't mean anything he just said. He wanted to take a chance for the first time in his life, and tell her how he really felt.

But he couldn't.

"So you're ending things with me now so I don't get hurt later."

"Something like that."

"How utterly noble of you, Gage, sparing my feelings like this. I mean, I'm sure women fall in love with you all the time, so you must be used to this."

"Brea . . ."

She held up her hand. "Please, don't bother trying to placate me. I'm so glad you told me before I did something stupid, like tell you how grateful I am for everything you've done for me, for making me feel like the woman I always wanted to be but never thought I could be. How, thanks to you, I don't feel like a wallflower anymore, and that's why those men approached me tonight. It was because you showed me I'm attractive and worthy of being desired. It's just too bad you're too much of a coward to see this out, because it could have been really damn good between us."

"Brea, that's not what—"

"Spare me whatever practiced speech I'm sure you've used before, Gage." She lifted tearful eyes to his. "I'm not going to fall apart and hide in my room. You're not crushing me. You've already shown me I'm worth more than that. So you did a great job coaxing this butterfly out of her cocoon, and some other guy will be the lucky recipient of all your work."

She popped open the door and slid out, slammed it shut and graced him with a smile that made him want to beg her forgiveness.

"I hope you find whatever it is you're looking for out there, Gage. But I have to tell you, I think what you're looking for is right here. And I think what you really need is me."

She turned and walked away, her head held high.

And he realized as he watched her open the door and head back into the bar that the dumbest thing he'd ever done in his life was let her go.

nine

"you *what?*" brea laid her coffee cup down on the kitchen table before she dropped it.

"I fired Gage," Jolene said, so matter-of-fact about the whole thing Brea couldn't believe she'd even said it.

"How could you do that? Why?"

Brea sat with Jolene and Valerie at the kitchen table having breakfast, three days after Gage had told her it was over between them. She'd tried to keep it to herself, but she'd finally confided in her sisters, which had obviously been a colossal mistake.

"Because he hurt my sister, and that's just not allowed." Jolene scooped up a forkful of eggs and waved them at Brea. "Besides, I thought you'd be relieved that he's gone. Now you don't have to walk around here on eggshells afraid that you'll run into him. He's a bastard, and now he's gone."

Brea shoved back her chair, so furious her entire body was flushed with heat. "You had no right to do that! What happened between Gage and me was personal."

Nonplussed, Jolene continued to chew while she regarded Brea. "I had every right to do it. He worked for me and I didn't appreciate what he did to you."

"Last time I looked, all three of us owned this ranch equally. You don't get to make independent decisions," Brea argued.

"Last time I looked, you weren't the least bit interested in ranch business, and you stated clearly your intent to head back to Tulsa."

"I've changed my mind. I want my third. And my first decision is going to be to hire Gage back. Now, where is he?"

"Really?" Valerie grinned. "You're staying?"

"We'll talk about that later," Brea said, turning to Jolene. "Where is he?"

Jolene shrugged. "Hell if I know. I fired him last night, and he packed and left right away."

Brea fell into her chair, her chest aching. "Did he say anything about where he was going?"

"Nope."

"Goddammit, Jolene. I will never forgive you for this." Brea pushed away from the table with her plate half-full and headed to the sink. After wiping her plate clean and loading it in the dishwasher, she turned to Valerie. "And why aren't you weighing in on this?"

Valerie raised her hands. "I want no part of this squabble. This is between you and Jo."

"Wuss," Jolene said with a mouthful of food.

"You got that right," Valerie agreed, then glanced up at the clock. "I've got patients coming in soon, so I'll let you two fight it out." She cleared her plate, then stepped in front of Brea, putting her hands on Brea's arms. "If you love this guy, if your feelings for him are true, then don't let anything—or anyone—stand in your way."

"I heard that," Jolene said.

"You own this ranch as much as Jo does. Fight for what you want," Valerie said.

Brea nodded. "I intend to."

"So, you love him?" Jolene asked, pivoting around in her chair to face Brea.

"Yes. I think so. I don't know. We didn't really have a chance to find out, since you fired him," she said, accentuating the last three words.

Jolene shrugged. "I thought he hurt you. I was trying to help."

Brea blew out a sigh. "I know. Thank you for that, but I really can take care of myself."

"Did you mean it when you said you'd stay?"

Brea rubbed her finger over an eyebrow. "I don't know. Maybe. It sounded right when I said it. Being here has felt . . . good." She smiled down at Jolene. "So we'll see."

Jo's lips quirked. "The cowboy make you feel that way?"

"Yes."

"Then go rope his sexy ass and bring him back. And then we'll see if I feel like hiring him back or not."

brea was out of breath by the time she'd searched every merchant in town asking around about Gage. Disappointment had washed over her when her first queries turned up nothing. No one had seen him. But on her last stop, at the motel on the outskirts of town, she found out from Amanda, one of the girls she'd gone to high school with, that Gage had stayed there last night. Amanda had put Gage in touch with one of the nearby ranches that was looking to hire on some hands for the coming year, and she said Gage was going to head out there today and look into the job.

Brea thanked Amanda and drove the thirty miles to the Knotty Oak ranch, where she wound down the long gravel drive until she saw the great three-story house at the end of a circular drive. The Knotty Oak was a huge horse ranch. Gage would probably love it here.

She mustered up her courage and went to the front door and

knocked. The door was opened by one of the Davidson teenagers, a young girl who went in search of her mother, Rhonda.

Rhonda came to the door smiling. "Hi, Brea. I'm so sorry Heather didn't let you in. Teenagers have no manners."

Brea laughed. "It's no problem. I'm intruding and I know you must be busy."

"Not at all."

They exchanged pleasantries and ranch conversation, and Brea knew she'd have to bring up the reason for her visit. "I was wondering if you had any new hands come on today."

"You mean Gage Reilly from your ranch?" Rhonda asked with an amused smile on her face.

"Uh, yes. How did you know?"

"He was here early this morning to talk to Carl. He's got amazing experience as a trainer and Carl wanted to hire him on the spot, but then Gage changed his mind."

Brea's breath caught. "He did?"

Rhonda nodded. "Said he had some unfinished business at the Bar M, apologized for taking up our time and left."

Brea's heart leapt into her throat. "Unfinished business?"

The corners of Rhonda's mouth crinkled. "Yes. Something about a woman."

"Oh. Oh! Um, thank you." She hugged Rhonda and practically ran back to her SUV, climbed in and tore down the driveway to the main road, her heart pounding the entire way back to the ranch.

Something about a woman. Unfinished business.

By the time she arrived back at the Bar M, she was a nervous wreck, not knowing what she would say to Gage when she saw him, or if he'd even be there. It could be he'd just changed his mind about the job at the Knotty Oak and made something up. But he wouldn't tell them it was about a woman, would he?

She'd been honest with Gage that night in the parking lot at the bar, though probably not as honest as she could have been, because she was in shock. He'd hit her with his casual brush-off unexpectedly; though he'd told her he didn't get involved and never planned to stay on the ranch, she hadn't been ready for the end just yet. Not when things between them had been going so well.

Maybe that's why she'd blurted out what she had about the two of them being so good together, and why she'd called him a coward. Because it had been honest. He was running away from something that had potential, and she didn't care if that wasn't his style. She'd spent her entire life hiding, so she knew what the hell she was talking about.

She pulled up the drive and saw Gage and Jolene standing together in the front yard, facing each other. Jolene had her hands on her hips and Gage's arms were crossed.

Valerie was sitting on the front porch, watching both of them.

Uh oh. Standoff. That didn't look good.

She parked and got out of the SUV, trying to act nonchalant, though her palms were so sweaty she was afraid her keys would slide right out of her hands.

Gage looked over at her and couldn't quite meet her eyes.

"What's going on?" she asked as she came to a stop in front of them.

Jolene pointed. "He's what's going on. He has the nerve to tell me he's not going to accept being fired by just one of the owners of the Bar M, as if what I have to say means nothing."

Brea's gaze shot to Valerie, who just smiled but said nothing, so she turned to Gage. "Is that right?"

"That's right. She fired me because I'm sleeping with you, not because there was anything wrong with my horse training." Gage turned to Jolene. "Isn't that right?"

Jolene shrugged. "Doesn't matter why I fired you. I run this ranch and whoever gets their ass booted from it stays that way."

"Not necessarily."

They both turned to Brea.

"Excuse me?" Jolene said.

"If I'm going to take over as one-third owner of this ranch, I expect to be involved in major decisions. I would think firing a hand with exceptional horse training skills like Gage should require a vote by all three of us. Especially if he was fired just because he was sleeping with me, and not for anything he was doing at work. Don't you think, Valerie?"

Valerie tried to hide her smirk and failed. "Oh, absolutely."

Jolene whirled on Valerie. "Bitch."

"I owed you one," Valerie said to Jolene. "We're even now. I vote Gage stays. Now I'm going inside to find my husband. Welcome back, Gage."

"I vote he stays, too," Brea said. "You're outvoted, Jo."

Jolene opened her mouth, closed it and threw up her hands. "I give up." She marched over to Brea and shook her finger. "If he breaks your fucking heart, you're on your own."

"Duly noted." She reached for Jolene's hand. "And I love you."

Jolene sighed, and threw her arms around Brea. "I love you, too."

Jolene walked away, but stopped in front of Gage and said, "If you ever hurt my sister again, I won't fire you. I'll just shoot you."

Gage tipped his hat at Jolene. "Yes, ma'am."

Jolene shook her head and went into the house, leaving Brea and Gage alone.

They both took steps toward each other at the same time. Brea slid her fingertips into the pockets of her jeans. "I went all over town looking for you today."

He tipped his hat back so she could see his face. "You did?"

"Found out you'd gone to the Knotty Oak, so I went there and talked to Rhonda. She told me Carl offered you a job as a trainer."

"Yeah, he did. I changed my mind."

She tilted her head back to look at him. "Why?"

"Unfinished business elsewhere."

"Where?"

He took his hat off and wrapped one arm around her to tug her against him. "Here."

His mouth came down on hers and their lips met in a heat of passion and need that made Brea whimper. She wound her arms around Gage and pressed her body tight against his, running her palms across his back, unable to believe he'd come back to her.

"I thought about what you said the other night," Gage said after he broke the kiss. "You were right. You are the best thing that's ever happened to me."

She looked away for a second. "You've given me some amazing gifts, one of the biggest being this ranch and my love for it again. I can't imagine leaving it for city life. I've been running my whole life, Gage, so I understand what that's like. It's time I set down some roots." She cupped his face with the palm of her hand and lifted up on her toes to kiss him.

"And maybe it's time I think about doing the same thing."

"You can't run from things that are unpleasant, or who you are, or were. You can only stay and face the past, and make sure in the future you don't make the same mistakes. I let myself be overshadowed by the death of my parents, by my talented older sister and my beautiful and confident younger sister. And somewhere in there, I just lost myself."

He tightened his hold on her. "You have no idea what kind of gifts you have. Your love of books, your intelligence, your wit and your laughter, and your amazing capacity to love someone. Do you know how special that is?"

"I do now, thanks to you. You made me see that I did have value. And so do you. Even if you decide not to stay here, Gage, I still want the time you are here to be with me. I won't ever hold you here if it's not what you want."

He held her close and kissed her hair. "I don't think I've ever wanted anything more. And it scares the hell out of me."

"Then we'll be scared together. It's uncharted territory for both of us. But somewhere along the way you branded me as yours, and I'm not going to let you slip through my fingers so easily."

He picked her up and walked to his truck, opened the door and deposited her inside, then climbed in.

"Where are we going?"

"For a ride. I need to be alone with you and there are too damn many people around."

He drove down the road, staying on Bar M land until he got to the clearing where they'd gone the first night they'd been alone together.

"I like this place," she said, starting to scoot over toward the door.

Gage reached for her wrist and tugged her against him. "Uh uh. Here."

"In the truck?" Her body sizzled with instant heat. "I've never done it in a truck before."

Gage pushed the seat all the way back. "Then we get to pop another one of your cherries, don't we?" He undid his belt buckle and slid the zipper of his jeans down, reaching into his pants to take out his cock. It was already erect. She loved that he could get hard so easily for her.

Brea licked her lips. "Already thinking about this, were you?" she said, inching closer and wrapping her hands around his cock.

"Kissing you makes me hard. All I can think about once you put your mouth on me is being inside you."

Her nipples tightened and her pussy swelled with arousal. Only Gage could get her hot and wet this fast. She kicked off her boots, unzipped her jeans and slid them off, leaving them on the floor. "I've never had a quickie either. Well, not an intentional one, anyway," she said as she bent over and licked at his cock head.

"Christ, Brea." He fisted her hair and lifted her mouth up and down on his cock. While she sucked him, he moved his hands across her back and caressed her hip, then slid his hand between her legs, parting the fabric of her panties to touch her pussy.

"You're wet," he said as he tucked two fingers inside her and began to pump in time to the rhythm she set sucking his cock. She whimpered against him, her tongue swirling over the heated head. She was already so close to coming with his fingers fucking her that she squirmed against him, straining to feel his fingers deeper inside her.

"Enough," he said, pulling her lips away from him. He reached into his jeans for a condom, put it on and pulled her astride him.

Brea inched down over his cock while Gage held on to her hips and guided her. The intense pleasure as he filled her was so strong, so delicious, she curled her nails into his shoulders as she seated herself fully on him.

"Oh yeah, that pussy is mine," he said, lifting his hips against her. "Now fuck me. Fuck me hard and make us both come."

He'd given her the control. She set the tempo, rising and falling soft and easy against him to begin, loving the feel of him expanding inside her, rubbing every part of her so, so good. But as the crescendo built, so did her need to feel Gage deeper, to have him thrust harder, and she told him exactly what she wanted, which he gladly gave to her, until words were no longer possible. Then she leaned forward and ground against him. He kissed her, his tongue plunging into her mouth at the same time his cock plunged up inside her.

And when she came, it was with her tongue wrapped around his, her thighs snugged against his, and her arms wrapped around his neck so that no space separated their bodies. She rode out her orgasm rocking against him, feeling him shudder and tremble and hearing his loud groans as he exploded so hard the truck rocked like an earthquake had hit it.

He took her down easy with light kisses, until she laid her forehead against his and just tried for normal breathing.

"I love you, Brea."

She stilled, not sure if she'd even heard what he said because he'd said it so softly. She lifted her head and searched his face, afraid to say or do anything, sure she was mistaken.

His eyes were clear, blue as the ocean, and filled with an emotion she'd never seen before.

"I said I love you. And I've never said that to a woman before."

"I love you, too, Gage. And I've never said that to a man before. Because I've never loved anyone before."

He brushed his lips across hers, and it was so different this time, as if something monumental had passed between them. A trust, a new beginning.

"I don't know if I'll ever be any good at this, but I'll give you the best I've got," he said, smoothing his hand down her back. "And I will never intentionally hurt you. I might fumble this a few times because I don't know what I'm doing, but I'd really like to try to make a life with you."

And that was all she could have ever asked for, because it was real, and it was better than anything she'd ever read in any book.

brazen

Jolene

WHAT KIND OF HOUSE?	CAR?
Mansion	Tractor
Apartment	*Truck*
Shack	SUV
House	ATV

WHERE TO LIVE?	NUMBER OF KIDS
On the ranch	2
On the ranch	0
On the ranch	3
On the ranch	*4*

GUY	OCCUPATION
Walker	Rancher
Walker	Rancher
Walker	*Rancher*
Walker	Rancher

one

when the prairie was on fire, a smart man would
run like hell in the opposite direction.

Nobody had ever accused Walker Morgan of being smart.

And Jolene McMasters was one hot prairie fire.

He should walk away, but she was a wildfire out of control, and
he was having a damn hard time resisting the heat.

He rode in his truck behind her, watching her lean over in her
open Jeep, igniting fires along the side of the roadway on Bar M
land. It was a no-wind day, which was pretty damn rare in Oklahoma in the spring. Perfect time to burn away the tall dead winter
grass around the acreage. And it figured Jolene would just have to be
in the front of the line, in control of the whole deal.

Of course she did own the ranch, and for the most part had been
running it herself for the past few years, since her uncle had gotten
too sick to see to the day-to-day things. Her sisters, Valerie and
Brea, had both lived out of town and hadn't wanted any part of the

Bar M until they'd recently come home, and even now seemed content to let their baby sister take the lead.

Right where Jolene liked to be—at the lead. She hopped out of the Jeep and raised her hand so the convoy of trucks behind her stopped. They'd circled around behind the fires they'd set so they could monitor the progress of each fire and keep them from getting out of control.

Jolene shielded her eyes and face from the whipping flames and climbed onto the bed, and then the roof of one of the trucks. She had such a catlike grace as she moved, comfortable in her own skin, unafraid as she widened her stance and balanced on top of the truck to scan the track of the fire.

"Walker, climb on up here and tell me what you think."

He swung up onto the bed and climbed onto the roof to stand next to her. "Looks steady," he said as he surveyed miles of charred black land with thin rows of flame. "It's under control as long as the wind doesn't pick up."

Jolene nodded. "Good enough."

Walker jumped down and held out his hands. Jolene slid into his arms, over the rail of the truck bed and onto the ground, grabbing her gloves as she headed toward the water truck.

"Joey, take the truck to the west end. I don't like the direction or how fast that fire is moving. We don't want to burn up that grove of trees on the western end of the property, so be sure it doesn't get that far."

Joey, one of the hands, tipped his hat, climbed into one of the water trucks and took off. At ten thousand acres, the Bar M was one of the largest ranches in their part of Oklahoma. Which meant it was a huge responsibility, and Walker thought Jolene did a fine job handling it all for someone as young as she was. In fact, the harder she had to work, the happier she seemed to be.

Walker admired her for that. She never whined or complained, and one would think a girl in her mid-twenties would rather be in the city dancing and drinking in the clubs or dating a different guy every weekend instead of standing in the middle of a scorched field sucking in ash and smoke.

But Jolene was grinning and swilling down bottles of water like she was having the time of her life, her face smeared with black ash and soot, her perfect lips cracking a wide smile. He wanted to go over to her, grab her pigtails, drag her sweet body against his and kiss her until the ache he had for her went away.

But he already knew kissing her would only make his dick hard, and then he'd want a hell of lot more than kissing.

She'd want more than kissing.

Jolene had already made it clear what she wanted, and what she wanted was him. He was the one backing away, saying no, which wasn't something he was accustomed to doing. When a sexy blonde with a heart-shaped face, a mouth that was created for one thing only and curves that won't quit wanted you, you didn't say no. Yet that was what he found himself doing.

Ronald McMasters had hired him five years ago, and he'd taken the job and started working for Mason. And then he'd met Jolene, barely twenty-one at the time. Even then she'd been a beauty, with womanly curves and a face that would stop a man in his tracks. Now she had come into her full womanly beauty, and she was devastating, a devilish temptress in blue jeans and cowgirl boots.

He wanted her like he'd never wanted a woman before. And she was 100 percent off limits.

She was the boss and he was a ranch hand. He'd already gone down that road once and vowed he'd never do it again. He was determined not to break that vow, even if Jolene McMasters was the hottest thing on the Oklahoma prairie.

He was still going to tell her no, and no again, until she got the message loud and clear.

*   *   *

the fires were out, all the grass they'd wanted
burned was scorched to the ground, and Jolene and the guys were
now enjoying the fruits of their labor—beer and barbecue in the
backyard of the main house. No way was Lila going to let any of
them inside, since they were all covered in soot and ash from head
to toe. But there was plenty of food and cold beer to drink. They'd
been at this before dawn, and the sun had just set. Jolene had known
the hands would be hungry when they got back, so she'd made advance arrangements to have this feast prepared.

There was nothing she liked better than seeing a bright orange
glow lining up across the horizon before the sun even came up. The
day had been perfect, the winds had been calm and they'd only had
to chase a couple fires threading out of control.

She craved a shower and her scrubber so she could get the grit
out of her skin and the smell of smoke out of her hair and nostrils.
But right now she wanted to celebrate with her guys—they'd worked
their asses off today.

And while they all hooted and hollered and told stories about
their heroics of the day, Jolene took a seat on the ground under one
of the many shade trees. Away from the crowd and nobody needing
anything from her, she could watch Walker Morgan to her heart's
content. And her heart was pretty damned contented to watch him
a lot.

Like her, he was covered in dust from his face to his shirt and
jeans and pretty much everywhere else. His hair was black as the
charred fields, and his eyes as gray as the ash that coated their
clothes.

He was doing his damndest to ignore her, but Jolene knew better. He noticed her all right. She could tell when a man watched
her, and she'd felt his gaze on her today. Since Mason was off on the
other side of the fire, and Walker was usually Mason's right-hand
man, he'd been right there by her side the entire time. She didn't
know if he enjoyed that or if it irritated the hell out of him.

Walker had been at the ranch for five years now, and he was as tight-lipped about himself as any man she'd known. Maybe that was part of the attraction—she liked a mystery. There were a lot of things about Walker she didn't know, but she intended to find out. If she could just find time to be alone with him, and get him to admit that he was interested in being with her. Because she knew damn well he wanted her. She was pretty adept at reading a man, and she caught the sidelong glances he sent her way when he thought she wasn't looking. Jolene was always looking.

And in those looks she saw a hunger that equaled her own. What she didn't understand was why he turned and headed in the opposite direction whenever they had an opportunity to be alone.

If there was one thing Jolene was, it was determined. She wasn't going to let Walker keep running. She'd made up her mind a long time ago that Walker was who she wanted in her bed, and she wasn't going to give up until she had him there.

She glanced over at her sisters, admittedly a bit jealous at their smiles of contentment. She was happy for Valerie and Mason, who had a second chance at happiness, and for Brea and Gage, who'd found kindred spirits in each other. It was just seeing her two older sisters happy and in love made Jolene crave something she had never really wanted before.

She liked sex just fine, enjoyed a roll in the hay as much as any other woman her age did. But the sudden craving for permanence was new, as was the need to have a man claim her as his and the need to claim him in return. It was something she had never considered before, probably because she'd been too busy running the Bar M and arguing with her uncle Ronald. She'd never had the time to think about settling down, about falling in love, about who she'd eventually end up with. She figured there'd be time for all that later.

But now, seeing her sisters with men at their sides made her look at the men in her life differently.

She'd have to get around to settling down one of these days.

She thought about that silly M.A.S.H. game she'd played with her sisters last month, and realized she'd only listed one man's name, not four. And that name had been Walker's. Probably because no other man was on her radar at the time.

Hell, no other man had ever been on her radar like Walker had been, no doubt due to the fact that he wouldn't even give her the time of day.

She was hardly hideous in the looks department, so what was it about her that made him not want to occupy space with her? They worked together just fine, but when it came down to socializing, he was nowhere to be found.

Like now. She'd been so deep in thought she'd lost sight of Walker. As she glanced through the crowd, she couldn't find him. She stood, threw her empty plate into the nearby trash can and grabbed another beer, then spotted Mason and Valerie and headed their way.

"Lila outdid herself on these ribs," Mason said as Jolene stopped in front of them.

"And you need a shower in the worst way, Jo." Valerie brushed her thumb over Jolene's cheek and showed her the blackened evidence.

"Yeah, I know," Jolene said, scrubbing her cheeks with her fingertips.

Valerie laughed. "Now you've made it worse."

"I don't care. I know I'm a mess."

"And yet, still as beautiful as Cinderella after cleaning the chimney," Valerie said with an affected sigh.

"Bite me, Val. Have either of you seen Walker?"

Mason's lips twitched, and he motioned with his head over his left shoulder. "I think he said he was going to the bunkhouse."

"Okay, thanks."

The party would be going on as long as there was beer left, and there was plenty of beer, so she didn't think any of the cowboys would be moseying on to the bunkhouse anytime soon.

She knocked on the bunkhouse door and waited. No answer, so

she knocked again, and when he didn't answer, she crossed her arms and tapped her feet.

She rapped again, harder this time. "Walker, open the door."

Still no response. Irritation drove her to pound on the door. He was avoiding her and that pissed her off. "Open the damn door and be a man. I know you're in there, Walker."

"Actually, I'm not."

She yelped and whipped around.

"Dammit, Walker, you scared the shit out of me."

His lips curled as he unlocked the door and pushed it open. "It's your own fault for having a hissy fit on the doorstep."

She followed him inside and shut the door. "I was not having a hissy fit. I never have hissy fits."

"If you say so." He went to the fridge and grabbed a beer without bothering to offer her one.

"There's plenty of beer over at the main house."

He popped the top off the can and bypassed her to lean against the counter. "I know that. I just didn't feel like socializing. I'm going to finish this beer, then I'm going to take a shower." He pointed the beer can at her. "You could use one, too."

She knew what she looked like, and it probably wasn't her finest moment. It was hard to attract the man you're hot for when you were covered in black ash, but he'd seen her looking a lot worse. She had him alone for the first time in ages and she intended to take advantage of that. "I could shower here," she said, grabbing the beer from his hand and taking a long swallow before handing it back to him.

"Why would you do that when you have a shower at your house?"

Was he truly that dense? She moved in, trapping him between her and the counter. She laid her hands on the tile counter, only a fraction of an inch separating her body from his, and inhaled the scent of smoke, and male. He frowned at her, but didn't push her away. That was a good start.

She raised up on the toes of her boots, her lips next to his ear.

Her breasts brushed his chest and she heard his harsh intake of breath. *Bingo.*

"Maybe we could share the shower. I could wash your back and you could wash mine."

She leaned back to gaze at his face. A flicker of heat sparked in his stormy eyes. They narrowed, his brow arched just a fraction of an inch as if he were considering the idea, and just the way he looked at her made her hot all over. Despite dirt, ash and whatever else was coating them, Jolene still wanted to get him naked and explore every part of his body. With her tongue.

And when he grabbed the front of her shirt in his fist and hauled her up against him, she bit back a gasp, her heart pounding. His knuckles brushed her breasts and her nipples tightened.

Yes, this was what she'd wanted from him for far too long. His body was steely muscle, and as he pulled her against him, she felt the hard evidence of his desire brush against her hip. She melted right then, everything that was female in her responding to all that was male about Walker. She automatically slid her hand down his body to reach for him . . .

Right before he flipped her around so her back was to his chest and rudely pushed her toward the front door.

"I've got no patience for your games tonight, Jolene. Go home and take a shower. A cold one."

He shoved her out onto the porch and closed the door behind her.

She flipped right around and turned the handle, chagrined to discover he'd locked the door.

Son of a bitch.

She stared at the door for a full minute, debating whether to knock. But she did have a little pride.

The bastard. She owned everything on this land, including the goddamned bunkhouse. If he thought he could keep her out of the building, he was wrong.

But her indignant march back to the house cooled off her anger.

What was she going to do? Open the door, walk into the shower and force herself on his cock?

As appealing as that idea was, she was going to have to go about this a different way, be more subtle.

She was going to bring Walker Morgan to her. Because he wanted her, she'd felt it during the brief few seconds he'd held her against him. Oh, had she ever felt the evidence of his desire for her. Why he turned her out when it was evident they both wanted the same thing remained another one of those mysteries she was dying to uncover.

But she was going to have him. It was just going to take a little longer than she thought.

walker let the water spray over his head and slide down his body. The shower felt good, but it did nothing to cool the heat raging inside him.

His gaze drifted down to his dick, which stood erect and throbbing as it had been ever since Jolene assaulted him in the kitchen, her sweet body pressed up against his.

She could be in the shower with him right now, her full lips surrounding his cock, sucking him, squeezing him and bringing him the relief he needed so damn bad his balls ached. But oh no, he had to have scruples.

Or fear, which was probably more likely.

But he liked this job and intended to keep it, and screwing the boss was a sure ticket to the unemployment line. So as long as he worked at the Bar M, Jolene was going to be off limits, and he'd just have to get sex elsewhere.

Or do it himself, which he wasn't in the mood for right now, not when his mind was on a woman with the face of an angel, eyes that changed color from blue to green to brown and everything mixed together, tits he was dying to touch and suck, legs he wanted wrapped around his waist, and a mouth begging to be kissed.

He groaned and fisted his cock in his hands, unable to resist the visual of fucking Jolene up against the wall of the shower, pushing into her with force until she screamed and he came in huge gushes inside her. He tightened his hold around his shaft and palmed the wall of the shower, gritting his teeth as he pumped harder, just like he'd thrust inside Jolene's sweet pussy while she wrapped her leg around his hip and cried out, her pussy squeezing him when she came.

"Fuck," he said, as streams of come shot out with his orgasm, leaving him weak, hot and not at all relieved.

He finished his shower and grabbed a towel, realizing he wasn't going to be satisfied until he got laid, and got Jolene off his mind. The best way to do that was to get some other woman in his bed.

Too bad there was no other woman he wanted but her.

two

"why aren't you over there making walker's life miserable?" Mason asked as he held up two fingers to Sandy, the bartender.

It was Saturday night, and everyone had come to town to hit the bar to drink and play a little pool or dance.

Jolene had come to put her plan into action. Said plan was none of her brother-in-law's business. She leaned against the bar and took a long swallow of her bottle of beer. "I have no idea what you're talking about."

"Sure you do. Walker's been on your radar for a while now. Figured you'd have hog-tied him and dragged him off to your bed."

"Mason." Valerie shoved an elbow into her husband's ribs and wedged in between him and Jolene. "Men are such crude pigs."

"I know," Jolene said with a grin. "Aren't they great?"

Valerie shook her head. "Only you would appreciate Mason's perverted sense of humor."

Beers in hand, Mason kissed Valerie on the lips and wandered back toward the pool tables. "He's right, though," Valerie said. "It's pretty obvious to anyone who knows you that you've got your eye on Walker. So why haven't the two of you hooked up?"

"He's avoiding me."

"Avoiding you? Why?" Brea asked, sliding next to Valerie. "Because I can't imagine any red-hot-blooded cowboy turning you down."

Jolene laughed. "Well, thanks, but I don't know why. We've been dancing around each other for a long damn time. And I know he's interested, but he just can't seem to pull the trigger. It's like I've got the plague or something."

"Hmm." Valerie frowned. "Maybe he's been hurt by a woman in the past."

"Please. I'm not asking him to marry me. I just want sex."

Brea snorted. "Then there's no reason he'd turn you down, unless he's playing for the other side."

"He's definitely not gay. He's been out with plenty of women since I've known him. Besides, I can get him hot, hard and ready to ride without even touching him."

"Been that close, have you?" Valerie asked.

"Close enough to know he likes women."

"Then I don't get it," Brea said. "There's got to be some reason he's not stripping you down and licking you all over, then fucking you until you can't walk straight."

Jolene just stared at Brea as if that hadn't really been her sister talking. She turned to Valerie, who was doing the same thing.

"Well," Jolene said. "Rockin' hot sex and the love of a good man sure brought you out of your shell, didn't they?"

Brea didn't even blush, just waggled her eyebrows.

"And all this time Gage was right under my nose . . ."

"Don't even think about it," Brea said, glaring at Jolene. "You won't have a hair left on that pretty head of yours."

"Oooh, territorial, too." Jolene turned and winked at Valerie. "I think our sister is in love."

"I think so, too," Valerie said. "You must have caught yourself a good one."

Brea giggled. "He's everything I ever dreamed of and more."

"Better than those books you always have your nose stuck in?" Jolene asked.

"Much better. He's real, solid, with flaws and everything. And God, I love him."

"Well, hell." Jolene wrapped her arms around Brea and hugged her. "You know how damn happy I am for you. So why are you hanging out with us?"

"He's playing pool. He doesn't need to spend every second of his time with me."

"Uh huh. And so is Mason. And they've been ignoring us long enough. Come on, little sister. It's time to wrangle our men into swinging us around on the dance floor." Valerie turned to Jolene. "If I were you I'd do the same with Walker."

Jolene laid her beer bottle down. "Oh, I've got my own game plan in mind where Walker is concerned."

Valerie shook her head. "Poor guy."

Valerie and Brea headed off to recapture their men. Jolene sat at the bar for a while, nursing her beer and contemplating her course of action. Walker was playing pool and acting like she didn't exist. But she knew better. She saw him take a few glances at her when he thought she wasn't looking.

She was always paying attention to Walker.

What she hadn't been paying attention to was her own surroundings, and the tall hunk of gorgeous cowboy leaning against the bar next to her. Until she turned around and found him smiling down at her.

Well, he was certainly pretty, with striking brown eyes, dark lashes, a rugged, unshaven jaw and muscles just about every-damn-where. She didn't recognize him, and since she knew every regular hand who worked at all the neighboring ranches, she figured him for one of the new temporary hires all the ranches had brought in for spring.

"Am I stepping in somebody else's territory if I ask you to dance, honey?"

And didn't that just fall right into her plan? She offered up her sweetest smile. "Nobody's claimed me yet, cowboy, so I'm all yours."

He held out his hand. "Then every guy in this place must be blind, because you're sure the prettiest woman in here."

Just what she liked—a man utterly full of shit.

"I'm Luke," he said as he turned around and led her by the hand.

"Jolene."

She followed him out to the dance floor, which was crowded as hell, but fortunately, it was time for a slow dance. Which meant cowboy Luke jerked her into his arms and became an immediate octopus, his hands all over her as they twirled slow and easy around the floor.

Jolene made sure to give him her undivided attention—or at least 95 percent of her attention. The other 5 percent was spent on Walker, who glanced up toward the bar and tracked his gaze to the dance floor, giving Jolene and her dance partner a decided scowl.

And wasn't it perfect that Luke chose just the moment Walker was watching them to slide his hand down her back and grab a nice handful of both her ass cheeks.

Judging from the murderous glare on his face, if Walker had a six-shooter in his hand, Luke would be a dead man about now.

Yeee haw!

who the hell was the son of a bitch with his hands all over Jolene?

Gage elbowed Mason. "You know that guy?"

Mason frowned. "What guy?"

"I'm pretty sure he means the one with his hands on Jolene's ass. Out on the dance floor," Valerie said.

"Oh." Mason searched the dance floor. "Don't recognize him." Mason turned to his wife. "He is kind of grabby, though. Want me to kill him?"

"Maybe Walker should do that instead," Valerie suggested with a sly smile.

Walker shrugged and grabbed his pool cue. "She's not my woman. No reason for me to get involved. If she wants some strange guy's hands roaming all over her, that's her business."

Though he couldn't concentrate on his shot and he blew it, scratching and losing the game. Shit. That's what he got for paying more attention to Jolene's ass than playing pool.

He let the next set of guys play and grabbed his beer, deciding not to look at the dance floor. But despite his resolve, his gaze drifted in that direction every few seconds, and for some reason he could easily spot Jolene in the thick crowd of dancers. Maybe it was her hair, loose tonight instead of in her usual pigtails, blond and wavy and trailing down her back, making him wish he could slide his hand down the length of it to see if it felt as soft as it looked.

Or maybe it was the turquoise halter top with silver studs that bared her back and the tiny tattoo barely visible above the waist of her jeans. He didn't know what kind of tattoo it was, only that it was colorful and small enough that a man would have to be . . .

Fuck. Getting a hard-on in the middle of a crowded bar would be the worst thing that could ever happen to him.

"You know, if you don't want another guy touching her, you should go in there and stake your claim."

Walker shrugged and sipped his beer, determined not to let anyone know, especially Mason, of his attraction to Jolene. "There's nothing to claim. Nothing going on between us."

Mason laid a hand on his shoulder. "I'm not blind, idiot. You two have been dancing around each other for a couple years now. And Jolene doesn't exactly make a secret of the fact that she'd like to wrangle you into her bed."

Shit. He turned to Mason. "She tell you that?"

"Me? Oh, hell no. We don't talk about sex. But she tells her sister things, and Valerie tells me."

"I've never touched Jolene."

Mason laughed. "I'm not stopping you."

"She's the boss. And you don't dip into the well where you work."

"Hey, that's up to you. All I'm saying is that the two of you are distracted because of this attraction. The last thing I want to do is talk about your sex life, man. Handle it how you see fit."

"Thanks, I will." And standing around watching Jolene dirty dance with some stranger was more torture than he cared to deal with. "I'm heading back to the ranch."

jolene caught walker's exit out of the corner of her eye and sighed.

Damn man.

Okay, so this plan had crashed and burned.

She turned her attention to Luke-of-the-wandering-hands, tilted her head back and smiled sweetly at him. "Honey, you have about two seconds to get your hands off my ass, or you'll be wearing your balls as earrings."

Time for Plan B.

around two in the morning, as jolene was check-ing cattle in one of the pastures, she still hadn't quite come up with what Plan B was going to be. Walker was proving to be more stubborn than she'd anticipated. She figured he'd see Luke-of-the-wandering-hands pawing her on the dance floor, his possessive caveman instincts would kick in and he'd stomp over, jerk her away from Luke and kiss her senseless right on the spot.

Ha! And she'd had the nerve to accuse Brea of living in fantasyland with her books. Obviously it was Jolene who needed a good hard dose of reality, because she'd been way off base with that flight of imagination. Walker had looked all right, and then done . . . nothing.

Maybe he wasn't as interested in her as she'd originally thought. Or maybe he was, but figured she wasn't worth fighting over.

Dammit. Why were men so hard to figure out? If he wanted her, what was so difficult about saying so, and then doing something about it? She was always straightforward about what she wanted. Was that a bad thing?

Her horse spooked as another rider approached. She pulled up on the reins and calmed Paradise down, then turned in the direction of the approaching rider. Who the hell was out this time of night, especially this far from the main houses?

She was surprised to see Walker coming up alongside her. And he was angry.

"What the hell are you doing riding out here by yourself this late?"

She arched a brow. "Not that it's any of your business, but I couldn't sleep so thought I'd take a ride."

"This is one hell of a ride. What if you'd gotten bucked off and hurt?"

She patted Paradise. "My horse never bucks."

"She would if a snake slithered in front of her. Come on, Jolene, you were born and raised out here. You know it's not safe to ride alone at night, even on your own property."

She lifted her chin. "Exactly. My own property. I can do whatever the hell I want, when I want. Besides, why do you even care, Walker?"

He went silent then, the brim of his hat and the dark of the moonless night hiding his expression. "You shouldn't ride alone."

"You said that already. And you're riding alone."

"I saw your horse was gone and came out to find you. It's late. Thought something might have happened to you."

"Awww, didn't know you cared."

"I figure someone has to look out for you since you suck at taking care of yourself."

"I've been taking care of myself for a long time. I'm a big girl and I know exactly what I'm doing."

"Is that why you let some guy you don't know put his hands all over you at the bar last night?"

So he did notice. And from the sound of his voice and the narrowing of his eyes, he wasn't at all happy about it. Perfect. "I haven't needed a father in years. In case you haven't noticed, I'm a grown woman capable of making my own decisions."

He inched his horse next to hers and grabbed the reins away from her. "I'm well aware you're a woman. So was the drifter with his hands on your ass earlier."

"You got a problem with that?"

His jaw was set so tight Jolene was amazed she couldn't hear his teeth grinding together. But underneath the spitting anger was something else—something elemental that went beyond him trying to protect her. It fairly sizzled between them and he was damn blind if he didn't recognize the sexual attraction between them.

He dropped her reins and skirted his horse away. "You should be careful not to ride alone, Jolene. You never know who could be out here in the middle of the night."

"Afraid I'll get ravished by some strange man on a horse?" She cast a pointed look in his direction.

He didn't take the bait. "Let's head back. It's a long ride and it's already late."

Like a cold drenching rain to put out the fire that had torched between them, the spark was doused. Jolene pursed her lips, wondering what the hell she was going to have to do to get Walker to give up and take what she was so obviously offering. Maybe she should have been riding naked. Too bad it was a little chilly tonight. Plus, riding naked on the back of a horse just screamed chafing in all the wrong places, so she'd have to give up on that idea.

Instead, she rode in silence next to him and pondered that Plan B.

three

for some reason, and walker knew exactly what that reason was, he found himself working side by side with Jolene for the next several days.

Subtle wasn't part of Jolene's makeup. Then again that was one of the things he admired about her. She was straight-out-forward about her needs, desires and wants.

Sometimes he wished she would hide those desires a little better, especially relating to him, because it was getting harder to resist her.

"Harder" being the right damn word.

What man wouldn't want a woman who could run a ranch at the age of twenty-six, who could manage roughneck cowboys with a steely-eyed look and a cock of her hip, who could reduce the strongest man to a blubbering baby with her honeyed voice, who could get two dozen cowboys dragging their tongue in the dry dirt and willing to follow her anywhere as long as she'd cast a smile their way.

And the worst thing was, he really didn't think she had any clue what effect she had on the men who worked for her. More than half of them wanted her, and she was oblivious to it all.

All of them except him. For some reason she wanted him, and damned if he knew why, since he'd done his best to completely ignore her. She could crook her finger at any one of half a dozen guys who worked for her and they'd be more than happy to give her anything she wanted.

Instead she had him glued to her side. Today they'd split up the hands to move cattle to richer pastures. It had been raining on and off the past few days, and this morning the sky had dawned clear and dusky, so Jolene figured they should move the cattle before another storm came in. They'd trekked off at dawn, six of them in one team, driving cattle from barren pasture into another rich and green with verdant grass.

Walker had to admit, he liked to watch her work, the way she directed the hands left, then right, hollering like a woman who knew exactly what she wanted and when.

Some men were intimidated by a woman in charge. Walker wasn't. He just wanted to get her naked and show her what it was like to have someone else take charge. Or maybe see what she was like in bed, if she wanted to take charge then. Because he liked control, too, and the clash of two dominant forces between the sheets could be like two bolts of lightning slamming together.

Damn. His dick twitched at the mental visuals of what it would be like, and that wasn't what he needed to be thinking about, because no way in hell was he ever going to get Jolene naked. Or have sex with her.

But it would be good. He knew it would. Right now she took off like hell for leather after an errant cow, whipping the reins from side to side, using her spurs to dig into her horse and race that cow down. She cornered it, turned her horse around and forced the cow back to the herd.

She didn't sit on her ass and let someone else do the work. She dug in and did it herself.

Yeah, he'd sure like to see what she could do in bed.

Too bad he'd never find out.

They'd wrangled most of the cattle to the new pasture. Jolene sent the rest of the crew back to the ranch, then told Walker they'd double back to pick up any strays. With that many cattle, sometimes a few lagged behind or broke off from the herd, so double-checking was necessary.

Today was one of those odd spring days that dawned scorching and stayed that way. Coupled with the rain they'd had lately, it was downright hellish. Walker was hot and drenched under his clothes, and his horse had steam rising off his coat. The sooner they got back to the ranch the happier he'd be.

Despite sweat running down her back and drenching her shirt, Jolene didn't seem to be bothered by the sun beating down on them. She rode easy, surveying either side of the land for wayward cattle. Walker contented himself with watching her backside in the saddle since they were on a narrow stretch of road, which meant they had to ride single file.

She sat erect in the saddle, her back straight, her hand holding the reins resting on her right thigh. Her shoulders shifted back, her head held high, her hat shading her face. Hell, she looked like she was showing the damn horse underneath her, not dragging like she should be. They'd all been up since before dawn and riding hard.

The woman had stamina. And there went his thoughts again, wondering how much stamina she'd show in the sack.

Shit. It might be hot as the infernal blazes of hell today, and his ass might be dragging, but he wasn't too tired to think about sex. And his cock wasn't exhausted. It was twitching and raring to go.

"There." Jolene pointed off to the left, down the hill. "I saw one."

Walker surveyed the area, a hill-swept valley dense with trees and a creek winding through. "I don't see it."

She lifted on the reins and hitched her horse to the left. "Follow me."

She took off at a fast gallop toward the cow, Walker right on her flank. He spotted it—a calf—just as Jolene pointed for Walker to go around to the right. He did, cutting off the calf's attempt at a mad escape. The creek prevented the calf from getting too far, though this area was muddy from previously rising waters due to the excess rain they'd gotten over the past few days, so their progress was slowed as they had to rein in the horses and step through the thick mud.

The mud also impeded the calf's progress. Too much, apparently, because the calf was half sunk in a mud hole. Walker jumped off his horse and tethered it to a tree, and waded in toward the stranded calf. Jolene approached from the other side of the mud bank, both of them pondering the now bawling calf.

"Well, now what?" Jolene asked, loud enough to be heard over the calf that had realized the error of its ways and was crying for its mama.

"We sure as hell can't drag it out of there on our own. That calf is too heavy, and the mud weighs it down even more."

Jolene nodded. "I'll get Paradise and some rope line. We'll have to pull her out."

While Jolene fetched the rope, Walker waded into the mud hole and promptly sank up to his thighs. Great. Just fucking great. He lobbed over to the flailing cow just as Jolene came back with the rope.

Her lips twitched as she looked down on him. "I hear mud baths are good for the skin."

Mud oozed into Walker's boots. "You're funny. Now get your ass in here and help me."

"I don't think so. You're already in it up to your . . ." She tilted her head and inspected his body, her scrutiny lingering far too long for his liking. "Ass. I think you've got a handle on it."

She tossed the rope at him. He caught it and looped it around the calf while Jolene tied it to the saddle horn on her horse. She climbed on and began walking her horse backward while Walker got the tail end of the cow and began to push. The cow, terrified, resisted.

"Come on, you dumbass, we're trying to help you here." Walker pushed, Jolene pulled, and finally the cow's brain engaged and she cooperated, heading for the sloping bank of the mud hole. Then she was scraping her hooves on the sides, kicking up mud into Walker's face as she mooed and scrambled for solid ground.

The cow made it, and Walker slipped, falling face-first into the mud. He came up sputtering and spitting out the foul, thick liquid, wiping his eyes to find Jolene standing at the foot of the mud bank, laughing her ass off.

"Think this is funny, do you?"

"Freakin' hysterical," she said, whipping off her hat and wiping the sweat from her brow.

Her inattention gave him just enough time to grab the ankle of her boot and pull, which sent her sliding down the already slick embankment. All he had to do was step out of the way and let her enjoy the ride.

She was lucky, because she went in feet-first, but the slope was steep and he'd pulled her right on her ass with enough force to send her under. He stood there watching, his arms folded together when she came up spitting curses at him.

"You son of a bitch!"

He smiled as she wiped mud from her eyes and glared at him.

"What the hell did you think you were doing?"

"I hear a mud bath is good for the skin," he said, crossing his arms to smirk at her.

She rolled her eyes, turned and started crawling up the side of the mud bank. Without traction or footing, she slid right back down, her nails scraping the wet side of the bank.

"Goddammit, Walker, help me out here."

"Yes ma'am." She started the crawl up again, and this time he shoved his shoulder in her butt and boosted her up. She fell onto the grass and rolled onto her back. Walker followed, digging the toes of his boots into the soft side of the slope as he pulled himself out of the mud.

"You're a mess," he said, realizing he was an equal disaster as mud squished out of the top of his boots.

"No shit," she said, yanking off her boots and tossing them aside. She pulled off her socks, then stood and went for the zipper of her pants.

Walker stood, too, and gaped as Jolene fumbled with muddy fingers for the buttons on her shirt. "What the hell are you doing?"

She stared at him like he was the dumbest cowboy on the planet. "Stripping, moron. What does it look like I'm doing?"

She bent over and retrieved her boots and socks, then headed toward the creek.

Walker followed behind her. "Are you serious? The creek has got to be icy cold."

"I don't care," she said as she peeled off her shirt, then the sleeveless tank she had on under that. She started to shove her pants down next as she turned around to face him. "I am not taking that long ride back with twenty pounds of mud stuck to me."

"Your clothes will still be muddy."

She shucked her jeans to the ground and stepped out of them, leaving her wearing only a bra and panties. And damn if her body wasn't even more perfect than what he'd imagined. Long legs, curved waist and breasts nearly spilling out of the cups of her bra. His mouth watered.

She grabbed the clothes and started rinsing them in the creek.

"No, my clothes will be wet," she said. "But in this heat they'll dry fast. And I need a goddamned bath. This mud stinks."

She rinsed her clothes and boots and laid them on a large rock in the sun. Then she turned to Walker and unhooked her bra, letting it fall to the ground.

Walker tried to swallow, but he had no spit left.

And when Jolene dropped her panties, she might have been covered in mud, but she was still naked.

And he didn't think he'd ever seen a woman more beautiful than her.

She turned around and walked into the creek. And there on the base of her back was that tattoo, some kind of tribal symbol full of the same variations of colors that glittered in her eyes.

"Coming, Walker?"

He could. Easily. Just watching her strip had made him hard as a rock. Her body, face and hair covered in mud, she should have been one wreck of a sight. Instead, she was sexy as hell. And that body? Jesus Christ, what man could resist it? All curves, beautiful breasts with light pink nipples, a triangle of dark blond hair covering her pussy and the tightest, most perfectly formed ass he'd ever seen.

She disappeared under the water and came up right away, shaking her hair loose, droplets flying everywhere.

"It's not too bad once you get in it," she said. "Temps have been warm enough and it's hot today. Come on in."

Walker unbuttoned his shirt and pulled it off. "This isn't appropriate."

She cocked her head to the side, bobbing up and down in the water, her breasts hidden, but the sweet swell just visible. "What isn't appropriate?"

"Us getting naked together."

She laughed. "I don't recall propositioning you."

He bent down at the water's edge and rinsed his shirt, then pulled off his boots and washed out the mud.

"Walker. Strip down and get in the water."

Tempting. Too damn tempting. "Is that an order?"

"Maybe."

"I don't think I'll follow that order."

She rolled her eyes. "I promise not to touch you. You know, in case you're afraid of me."

"I'm not afraid of you, Jolene."

"Could have fooled me the way you've been acting lately. But I'm not the big bad wolf, Walker. I won't attack you. You don't have anything to be afraid of."

Afraid? She thought he was afraid of her? That did it. Months of repression had taken its toll. Between denying what he wanted and her impromptu and obvious striptease of a few minutes ago, Walker had taken all he was going to take from Jolene. He pulled off his T-shirt and unbuttoned his pants, then slid the zipper down.

Jolene didn't take her gaze from him, instead watched him strip. And he didn't bother to hide his erection as he let his jeans fall to the ground and pulled off his boxers. It jutted out high and hard as he padded to the cold water and dove in headfirst.

The water felt damn good. He surfaced a couple feet from Jolene, found his footing on the bank and waded over to her. She was resting on a rock, submerged from the waist down, her breasts out of the water and glistening under the sun.

He didn't bother to say anything to her, just sloshed through the water and swept her into his arms.

He pulled her off the rock and jerked her against him. Her lips parted with her gasp. Then she smiled and wrapped her legs around his waist, trapping his cock between them.

"It's about goddamned time, Walker."

"Shut up, Jolene." He pressed his lips to hers and kissed her, hard.

four

jolene resisted a whoop of joy. wrapped around Walker, both of them naked, lips pressed together, was everything she'd dreamed of. And more. He was rock-hard—everywhere, his body a solid wall of muscle as he effortlessly carried her out of the creek and onto the grass.

He held on to her as if she weighed nothing, dropping to his knees and then down on the grass, bringing her on top of him.

Talk about sensory overload. Splayed over his body, her synapses were firing reactions to her breasts mashed against his chest. Her nipples tingled as they brushed the crisp chest hairs there, and she rocked her pussy against him, wanting him inside her right now.

But oh, there was so much to experience—his tongue doing devilish things to hers, his hands roaming over her back and then cupping the globes of her butt. And when he surged against her, letting her know that the cold water of the creek hadn't affected his hard-on in the least, she trembled with need, warmer than if he'd thrown a blanket over her.

He was all man, everything she'd imagined him to be. And he wasn't turning away from her this time. He held on to her hips and ground his erection against her, his mouth bruising her in its intensity. Exactly what she wanted from him. She tangled her hands in his hair and gave as good as she got, twining her tongue around his to suck, greedy for more.

Walker rolled her over onto the grass, then pulled away and stood. They were in the shade, and she shivered at the loss of his body contact.

She leaned up on her elbows, wondering if he was going to once again walk away from her. Surely not, not when they'd come this far already.

But she had nothing to worry about. He came back a few seconds later with a blanket he'd gotten from the saddlebag. He spread it out on the grass.

"Inch over. This is softer than the grass. I don't want to have to worry about ants crawling up your pussy."

"The only thing I want crawling up my pussy is you," she said as she scooted over.

He shook his head. "You are something, Jolene McMasters."

"I'll take that as a compliment. Now, get down here and fuck me."

He lay down beside her, his gaze roaming over her body. He trailed one finger along her nose, down to her jaw and neck, then over her collarbone snaking the trail between her breasts, eliciting chills that made her nipples pucker. "You're in too much of a hurry. There's territory here I need to explore."

She pushed him onto his back and sat on him, straddling him. She laid her palms flat on his shoulders, and saw his lips curl. Yeah, he was trying not to laugh, because if he really wanted to get up, he could. She was a strong woman but no match for someone like Walker.

In this, though, she intended to have her own way.

"Look, Walker. We've had years of foreplay, and that's plenty for me. I'm hot, I'm wet and I want you inside me. We can play later."

He shifted, sliding his hands behind his head. "You're the boss, then. Take it for a ride."

She rolled against him, tilted her head back and moaned as her pussy slid along his cock. "God, that feels good." She scraped her nails down his arms. "I don't suppose you have condoms on you, do you?"

He reached underneath the blanket and pulled out two. Jolene arched a brow. "Haven't been planning this, have you?"

"You've launched a heavy assault on me. I figured you might wear me down eventually and I should probably be prepared just in case you tied me up and had your way with me."

She laughed, grabbed a packet and tore it open, then shifted down his body so she could wrap her hand around his cock. It was hot and steely hard like the rest of him. She wanted time to explore all of his body, but she couldn't right now. Later, when the fever burning inside her had been doused, she'd taste and touch him all over.

But oh he felt so good in her hand, she couldn't resist sliding up and down his shaft, measuring him, feeling him lift his hips and surge against her.

"You gonna put that condom on, woman, or are we gonna play?"

As she lifted her hand around the top of his cock, she slid her thumb over the crest, swirling it through the pearly liquid that escaped there. "I'd like to suck your cock until you come in my mouth." She rolled the condom over him. "But that'll have to wait until later, because I want this inside me."

He grabbed her hips and dragged her up, tangling his fingers in her hair to draw her face toward his. "You're a vicious tease, Jolene."

She laughed. "You have no idea."

He pulled her head down to his and kissed her, and her pulse jumped at the contact of his mouth on hers. Damn, he had nice lips—soft—the only soft part on him. He kissed her with that hard intent, his tongue plunging inside to lick at hers. She slid her pussy along his belly, igniting sparks of arousal that flamed ever higher when she reached between them to fold her fingers around his cock and felt it jerk in her hands. He groaned against her lips.

Jolene lifted upright and positioned his cock at the entrance to her pussy. "All this kissing is nice, Walker, but if you don't fuck me right now I'm going to explode just rubbing myself against you."

He dug his fingers into her hips. "Is that a bad thing? I want to watch you come."

She slid down his cock, trembling as he entered her, hot and thick and stretching her as she fit herself onto him. "You will."

When she was fully seated on him, she began to move forward, then back, using his body to hold on to, to lift herself only to ease back down. Shocks of pleasure sizzled through her from the inside out as she rode him, enhanced by the wicked storm of desire reflected in his eyes.

"Lean forward, darlin'."

She did, and he reached up and slid his thumbs across her nipples. She gasped as the sensation shot straight to her clit. She sat fully on him, grinding against him to capture more of that sinful pleasure.

"Harder," she said, continuing to rock against him as he rolled each nipple between his fingers, increasing the pleasure. She repaid him by squeezing his cock inside her.

"Damn," he whispered, pulling her down to kiss her again.

Jolene was drowning in sensation. His mouth, his hands, moving over her back to grab her hips and lift her up and down his cock. He dragged her against his pelvis, rolling his hips to give her the greatest pleasure.

She felt him everywhere, from his tongue to his hands to the way he eased up into her slow and easy, then pumped fast and hard until she was squirming, coming, crying out against his lips, digging her nails into his chest as she rose up and rode him like her life depended on it.

He gripped her, holding her down on him as he groaned and thrust into her. Pulsing with climax, Jolene rode the wave of her orgasm while he shuddered underneath her.

This was what she'd been waiting for. And it had been so worth the wait. Walker was everything she had imagined he would be, her match in every way. He loved sex as much as she did, and he went for it with a gusto that equaled her own.

Spent, she fell on top of him, laid her head on his shoulder, listening to his rapid breaths and feeling his heart pound against her.

Walker stroked her back, just holding her, seeming in no hurry to jump up and get away from her.

She hadn't expect this tenderness, the way he wrapped his arms around her, kissed the top of her head and seemed so content to just . . . be with her. It was so incongruous with the man who'd spent all this time running like hell in the opposite direction.

She was glad he'd stopped running, because she wanted nothing more than to be with him. Maybe she'd convinced him that enjoying each other was worth it.

She lifted her head and smiled down at him. "That wasn't too painful, was it?"

His look was wary. Maybe she hadn't convinced him after all. "It didn't hurt."

She laughed and pushed off him, then grabbed her clothes. "They're damp, but they'll do." She started to get dressed, deciding that she was just going to ignore the often grumpy Walker Morgan.

After all, she'd convinced him once that sex was a good idea. She could convince him again.

But after tethering the squalling calf and starting the long trek toward home, Jolene bristled at Walker's dead silence.

They'd just made love. To her, it had been pretty damn monumental.

Walker looked unhappy, uncomfortable, and she was pretty sure it wasn't because his boxers were wet and twisted.

Halfway home she'd had enough of the grimacing and silent treatment.

"What crawled up your ass, Walker?" she asked as they rode side by side. She had to raise her voice to be heard over the nonstop wailing of the calf.

He turned his head to face her. "Nothing's up my ass."

"You look like you just lost your best friend. Having sex with me that awful?"

His jaw clamped shut and he didn't say anything for a few minutes. Finally, "I just don't think that was a good idea."

Irritation made her eyebrow twitch. She gripped the reins tighter. "It felt like a really good idea when we were doing it. And I didn't hear you complaining."

"You're my boss. I work for you. It's not a good idea to mix business with pleasure."

She rolled her eyes. "Oh, please. That's a load of crap and you know it."

"Maybe to you, it is. To me, it isn't. There's a line that shouldn't be crossed, and we crossed it."

She pulled the reins and halted her horse. "Do you really think I'm going to give you any special favors just because we had sex?"

He had been ahead of her, but he turned his horse around and came back to face her. "That's not what I'm talking about."

She leaned against the saddle horn and tipped her hat back on her head. "Then explain what you are talking about."

"It's . . . complicated."

"I'm not a dumbass. I think I can reason it out. Toss me a few crumbs, Walker."

"It's nothing. Forget it." He turned his horse around and started moving again, staying far enough ahead of her that she couldn't hitch Paradise into a gallop without forcing the poor tethered calf into running to keep up.

Asshole. He'd turned a nice time between them into something unpleasant.

Why did sex have to be so complicated?

walker rode far enough ahead of jolene that she wouldn't be able to catch up, but not too far ahead. He still had sight of her, and still heard the calf, though he paid no attention to the noise. His thoughts centered on Jolene.

What kind of a sissy-assed weakling was he, anyway? He had no willpower. He should have said no. Sure, she'd been naked and all, but he was a grown man. He'd seen plenty of naked women before. Didn't mean he had to go jump on every one he saw. He was hardly a horny teenager who had to fuck a woman just because she offered it up. Not that he was God's gift to women, but he got his share of offers from eligible women in town. He could have turned Jolene down.

Instead, he'd let her climb on and he'd enjoyed one hell of a ride. And even worse, he'd held her after. Like he . . . cared.

Shit.

It wasn't going to happen again. He liked this job, had fought hard to get it when no one else would hire him after what had happened at the last ranch. The last thing he needed was another scandal.

He was so dumb. And even dumber was that even now his body still craved her. He'd only scratched the surface of his desire for Jolene. There hadn't been enough time, it hadn't been the right place. There was so much more he wanted to do with her.

Too bad. What he wanted and what he was going to get were worlds apart.

five

one week. one whole friggin' week, and walker had done his best to avoid her.

Jolene paced the kitchen. It was well before dawn, and she'd already had four cups of coffee. She was as agitated as an unbroken horse and ready to do some damage.

"You're going to wear a hole in the floor stomping your boots like that."

Valerie yawned and padded into the kitchen on bare feet, still in her pajamas. Her hair was a mess—great sex, no doubt—and she had pink cheeks.

Jolene was profoundly jealous. Valerie was sleeping with someone. Jolene was sleeping alone, through no fault of her own.

Valerie grabbed a cup of coffee, pulled up a chair, yawned loudly and stared at Jolene through half-opened eyelids.

"Do you have to look so damn content?"

Valerie cocked her head to the side. "What's got you in a lather this early?"

"Walker."

"Ah. And what's he done this time? Or not done?"

Jolene leaned against the kitchen counter and palmed the hot mug of coffee. "I don't understand men."

Valerie lifted her mug in salute. "Welcome to the club, honey. They're as mysterious to us as, I'm sure, we are to them."

Jolene's only response was to grumble and take a long swallow of coffee.

"So what's the specific problem?" Valerie asked.

"We had sex."

Valerie laughed. "That doesn't sound like a problem."

"He's avoided me for a week."

"Yeah, that is a problem. I'm sorry, honey."

"Oh, it's not that he dumped me. He liked it. I liked it. He wants to do it again. I know he does."

Valerie sipped her coffee and studied Jolene, then shook her head and smiled. "You are nothing if not humble, little sister."

"That's not what I mean. I know he didn't dump me because he didn't feel anything or the sex was lousy. I know he isn't seeing anyone else. I mean I was there. I know what went down. It was good for both of us. We connected. So I just don't get what his problem is."

"Men are notorious noncommunicators."

Jolene sighed. "Tell me about it."

"But you don't strike me as someone who backs down, Jo. If you want him, and you say you're pretty sure he wants you, then go after him."

"Normally, I would. But honest, Valerie, I'm getting tired of the chase. I've already done it. I've been doing it. I think it's time he came to me."

Valerie shrugged. "Up to you. But don't be surprised if he doesn't. There's something holding him back."

"I know." Jolene studied her coffee, looking for answers in the black brew and knowing she wouldn't find them there. "I wish he'd open up and tell me what it is, but he's pretty tight-lipped about it."

"Then you're either going to have to wait for him, or go after him."

"I went after him the first time." Jolene lifted the pot and watched the steaming brew slide into her cup. "The ball's in his court now."

walker was beyond stupid. this was a huge mistake. He was going to get fired, just like last time. Only last time he hadn't deserved it.

This time, he would.

But he couldn't help himself. Jolene was like a drug in his system and he was addicted.

He'd ignored her for over a week now, made sure he volunteered to work on whatever Mason was working on. Since Mason was the foreman, he and Jolene generally split up and didn't work together. Which meant if Walker worked with Mason, he'd be far away from Jolene. And Walker figured lack of proximity would help.

It didn't.

He also figured she'd chase after him like she usually did.

She hadn't.

It had been more than a week, and he'd barely seen her.

That bothered him. It actually pissed him off that she hadn't come after him when he'd done everything he could to ignore her, to create distance between them. What kind of an asshole did that make him?

A huge one.

And now he stood at the back porch door to the main house at one in the morning, knowing that back door was unlocked, knowing the place was dark, knowing Jolene was in there.

And knowing he was going to sneak into her room.

He was a hundred kinds of crazy for doing this, but he turned the knob and he stepped into the mudroom, quiet as could be as he tiptoed past the kitchen and into the hall. He looked up the stairs.

Last chance to change his mind, to come to his senses and realize this was a really bad idea.

Instead, he held on to the banister and headed upstairs, just waiting for the steps to creak.

They didn't. He got to the top of the stairs, turned left and headed toward the door to Jolene's room.

He turned the knob, quiet as he could, inched open the door, slid inside and closed it behind him.

And heard the unmistakable click of a round being slid into the chamber of a revolver. Hard metal pressed against his side.

Shit.

"You are so damn lucky I'm a light sleeper and I see well in the dark, Walker Morgan. And that I don't shoot without knowing who or what I'm shooting at."

Jolene pulled the gun away from his back and set it on the nightstand. Leave it to her to be armed in her bedroom. She turned on the bedside lamp and sat on the edge of her bed, her long legs peeking out of a white T-shirt that sported some kind of pink cartoon bear on it.

Annie Oakley in a teddy bear shirt. Didn't that just figure? As usual, Jolene was unpredictable. All sweet and innocent looking in her kiddie T-shirt, all soft desirable woman underneath, and a hard-ass with a gun to boot.

No wonder he wanted her so much he was willing to risk his job.

"What the hell are you doing sneaking into my room in the middle of the night?"

Relaxing now that he wasn't going to be shot, he leaned against the wall. "If I need to explain it to you, then maybe I should leave."

She pushed onto her bed and leaned against the pillows, stretching out her legs. "You think you can ignore me for a week, then come up to my room and fuck me just like that?"

"I was ignoring you, I admit that. I didn't think you and I getting together was such a good idea." He shoved off the wall and headed toward the bed, stopping when he reached the side of the mattress where Jolene's long legs were so temptingly displayed. He sat on the edge of the bed and smoothed his hands over those legs. They felt like silk under his calloused fingers. He watched her eyes go dark, her nipples peaking hard under her thin T-shirt.

"And now you've changed your mind."

"No, I still don't think it's a good idea." He pulled off his hat and let it sail across the room and onto a nearby chair, then leaned over her, placing his palms on either side of her hips. "But I just don't think I care all that much anymore."

"Really. And why's that?"

"Because I want you. And I'm tired of denying myself what I want."

His face was inches from hers. God, she was beautiful, her hair a cascade of blond waterfall over her shoulders, her eyes so many different colors he could get lost in them. And her mouth—he leaned in and brushed his lips across hers. Last time he'd been in a hurry, had taken and demanded instead of explored. All he'd thought about since then was all the things he'd missed.

She sighed against his mouth, and he smiled against her lips. She tasted like cookies and milk, and he swept his tongue along her bottom lip to capture more of her flavor before sliding it inside to lick against her tongue.

Jolene moaned and scooted over, and Walker climbed onto the bed, then pulled her onto his lap, his hand sliding over the bare skin of her butt as he did. She didn't have anything on under that T-shirt, a fact that made his dick go rock-hard in a fraction of a second. He pulled her tight against his chest and slid his hand up the back of her shirt, scoping out those sweet mounds of her ass, so firm and yet her skin was so soft. He felt bad that his hands were so rough, and yet everywhere he touched her she moaned, so she must like his hands.

And he liked the feel of her skin, like gliding his fingers across butter.

He deepened the kiss and held Jolene as he moved on the bed, then laid her in the center of the mattress. He climbed over her, lifting up her shirt and bending down to press a kiss to her belly, ignoring her sex for now even though the scent of her filled the room. He wanted to bury his face in her pussy and lick her until she screamed.

She tangled her fingers in his hair, raised her hips against his chest, and his cock pressed hard and insistent against his jeans.

His cock was going to have to wait. This was playtime.

He took her T-shirt off. Bare, she made his breath hitch. He'd seen enough of her that first time to know she was beautiful and built. But now he could look his fill with her underneath him, could take his time to smooth his hand over the soft column of her throat, the valley between her breasts, admire the pretty pink nipples that seemed to pucker and harden to tight points just from him looking at them.

He bent down and laved his tongue over one. Jolene arched her back and dug her fingers in his hair, pulling at him as he took the nipple in his mouth and sucked, hard, while he used his hand to roll over the other nipple, to tease and torment it.

"Oh. Oh, God, Walker, I really like that."

Her voice was a yielding whisper, nothing like the hard barking orders she gave out on the trail. He enjoyed her soft like this, her body squirming under his mouth and hands as he moved down her rib cage, teasing her belly button by diving into it with his tongue. Her hands followed his trek south by staying in his hair, holding onto him like he was a lifeline and she was drowning.

He wanted her drowning. He wanted her coming. He wanted to taste her.

He slid off the bed and kneeled on the floor, and dragged Jolene to the edge of the mattress, her pussy dangling right at the edge, sweet and wet.

"You have a pretty pussy, darlin'," he said, gliding his thumb over the moist puffy lips, then sliding one finger inside. Her walls gripped around his finger as he pulled partway out, then tucked back in again, fucking her slow and easy. "You're wet. Have you been thinkin' about me?"

"All I do is think about you, Walker," she murmured, her eyes closed as her fingers danced in his hair. "I touch myself thinking about you doing this."

His cock twitched, his balls tightening high and hard. He wanted to plunge inside her, kiss her while he fucked her hard. But not yet. Not when he could feel her hot and wet surrounding his finger, not when he could breathe in the scent of her, not when he could taste her.

He leaned in and swiped his tongue around her clit, and she let out a low moan.

"Yes. Like that," she said, once again drawing his head down with her hand. "I like that a lot."

And he liked that she talked to him, that she was right there with him while he lapped at her clit, took the bud in his mouth and sucked it, all the while continuing to slide his finger in and out of her pussy.

"Walker, I'm going to come. Lick me right there, I'm going to come."

She lifted and he gave her what she wanted. She bucked against him, sliding her sex all over his face as she writhed in orgasm. Oh, man, he liked feeling her and tasting her when she came, liked feeling her body move as spasms gripped his finger over and over again, until she fell back against the bed and panted.

He removed his finger and crawled onto the bed, popping his finger into his mouth to taste her.

Jolene grabbed his head and brought his mouth to hers for a deep kiss that rocked him to the soles of his feet. She licked at his lips, tasting herself, and didn't that just make his balls tight as stone.

When she let go, her eyes were glassy with spent passion, her skin flushed warm and pink. "Now get your clothes off so I can touch you."

And not a minute too soon, either. He was as eager as a teenager fumbling with his clothes and about to have his first bout of sex with one hot, experienced woman. He stripped, pulled a couple condoms from his pocket and laid them on the nightstand. Jolene arched a brow, smiled and made room for him as he crawled onto the bed. As soon as he was flat on his back, she rolled over onto him.

"My turn," she said, pressing her lips to his and kissing him with her sweet lips until his cock was a raging beast ready to slide up into her and fuck her into oblivion. But when he reached for her, she pushed him back.

"Oh no. You are not going to deny me this time. I want your cock in my mouth."

Heat shot straight to his shaft. "Well I'm sure as hell not going to tell you no, honey. Suck that dick all you want."

She laughed, moved down his body and positioned herself on her belly. With a wicked gleam in her eye, she focused on his cock. Now, what guy wouldn't get his balls tied in knots to have a beautiful woman like Jolene lick her lips so close to his dick?

And when she put her hands on him, it was a slice of sweet heaven on earth. Whenever he jacked off, he did it to get a release, and his hands were calloused and rough. Hers, even though she worked hard for a living, too, were softer and smaller, and he could sure as hell tell the difference as she wrapped both around his shaft. And because she was a tough girl and not timid, she put some pressure on him, which he liked, swirling one hand over the other as she moved up and down.

He could lie back, watch her do that for hours, and die a happy man. But when she pushed forward and took the head of his cock between her lips, he gripped the sheets in both hands and tightened his jaw, because son of a bitch she had one hot, wet mouth. She let go of her hold on him, then it was all her mouth doing the work, as she got up on her knees and went down on him full tilt, taking him from top to bottom all the way to the back of her throat.

"Fuck," he bit out as she took him hard and over and over again, sucking him deep, then releasing him only long enough to slide her pretty pink tongue over the crest and the underside of his shaft. Then she'd slide that tongue all the way down and flick it over his balls until he thought he'd die.

He tangled his fingers in her hair while she wound her tongue around his balls, licking and sucking them just the way he liked it, taking them into her mouth and rolling her tongue over them there, too. By the time she had his cock back in her mouth again, he was out of breath and ready to come.

And she knew it, too, because she smiled at him, held on to his shaft and began to stroke him. He jerked her hair, holding her in position while he pumped between her lips, his balls tightening with the pressure of her mouth around his cock.

"I'm going to come in your mouth, Jolene. Right . . . now."

He groaned, then flexed his hips up as he jettisoned a stream of hot come into her waiting mouth. She squeezed and stroked every drop from him as he rocked against her, shuddering as the impact of his climax tore through him with blazing heat. And Jolene stayed with him the entire time, taking everything he had to give, continuing to lick and suck every drop.

"Damn," he managed when he could speak again. He reached for her, pulled her up against him, then rolled them side to side, facing each other so he could see her, kiss her, taste what she'd done to him.

She slipped her hand between them, holding his cock gently to stroke him again while they kissed. He reached for her breasts and slid his thumbs over the buds, feeling them harden, listening to her moan and whimper as he cupped her, then kissed and licked them.

His cock was hard again in record time, no surprise considering the woman he was with. He reached for a condom and put it on, then spread her legs and slid inside, burying himself deep. Jolene wrapped her legs around his back and lifted against him.

There were no words this time, and it seemed so right to kiss her, to slide his hand underneath her to lift her, to need to be closer to her as he fucked her, as he felt the sensations intensify inside. Her pussy gripped him tight and hard, and he wanted her to come again, rolled his hips to grind against her clit, listening to the sounds she made. He knew when she was close, and he'd draw back a little, extending their pleasure until she was clawing his back, growling at him with the need to release.

And when he couldn't stand it anymore, when perspiration poured down his face, when their bodies were both wet with pleasure and sweat, he thrust and ground against her, watching her eyes widen as she came. And then he came, too, wishing he didn't have the burden of a condom so he could spill inside her, to fill her with his come and feel her hot and wet surrounding him.

He'd never been this . . . intimate with a woman before. With Jolene, it seemed natural. She gave as good as she got. She was something new and fresh and exciting, as wild and free in the bedroom as she was out on the prairie.

There was a reason he'd sought her out when he shouldn't have, that he couldn't stop thinking about her, that he needed to be close to her.

He was falling in love with her, and damned if that wasn't the worst thing in the world that could happen.

six

jolene pulled into the parking lot at dirk's, realizing that even though she was alone, she wore a giant grin on her face. Okay, so she was in heaven. Work was going well, and Walker was the best lover she'd ever had. They'd been together almost every night for the past few weeks, and she had no complaints. What more could she ask for than a dynamic lover, a valuable ranch hand and someone who was fun to be around?

Though she'd noticed he wasn't into public displays of affection, and she got the distinct impression he intended to keep their relationship just between the two of them. Which was fine with her—for now. But she certainly had no intention of hiding it forever, especially since she realized things were getting serious between them. Or kind of serious. Oh hell, she didn't know for sure. The sex was great, and she loved being with him. Mason thought highly of Walker and wanted to make him assistant ranch foreman. He had the skills and experience and had been at the ranch long enough. He'd earned it.

Jolene was beginning to see a future with Walker. What she didn't know was what kind of future Walker saw, because everything with him seemed to be all about right now. Though they enjoyed each other's company, they hadn't talked about the future. They didn't talk about much of anything, including Walker's past. He knew everything about her, had asked her to fill in the blanks about her family and her past and anything he didn't know. He liked her to talk about herself. But when she asked him about his past, he always managed to change the subject.

If things were going to go any further between them, that would have to change. She wasn't going to fall in love with someone she didn't know.

Or maybe she was already in love with him. She'd never been in love before, so how was she going to recognize it when it happened?

She opened the front door of the bar and country music blasted her in the face.

God, she loved this place. Grin still plastered on, she went inside, spotted Brea and Gage and headed over to their table.

"Where's Val and Mason?" she asked.

"Home having hot sex while they have the place to themselves, probably," Brea said, waggling her eyebrows.

"Decided to stay in tonight?"

"Yeah. Valerie said she needed to inventory medical supplies, so Mason said he'd stay to help her."

"Which means they're having sex instead of doing inventory," Gage said. "Or at least that's what I'd be doing."

"Yeah, but you're perverted." Brea elbowed him in the ribs.

"And that's why you love me." Gage grabbed her and kissed her.

Jolene rolled her eyes. "Maybe you two should have stayed home and had sex, too. I'm going to the bar."

She leaned against the bar and waved to Sandy, who was working at the other end. She didn't have to bother to order. Sandy would just bring her favorite beer when she had a free minute. Jolene flipped around, putting her back against the bar, and scanned the room. Mainly she was looking for Walker. They hadn't made plans for tonight, but she'd told him she was coming to Dirk's. He'd nodded and said he might be here, too.

They didn't make plans, they didn't have dates, they didn't go out together.

And that was beginning to irritate her. They were going to have to talk about having this secret relationship. Jolene didn't want it to be a secret any longer. Walker was going to have to talk to her about why it was necessary to have all their meetings be clandestine.

She spotted him playing poker with some of the guys from the ranch, and waited for him to make eye contact. When he did, she smiled, but he looked away immediately.

Okay, maybe he hadn't seen her.

"Hey, girl, you're looking good tonight."

Jolene turned around and grinned at Sandy. "So are you."

Sandy was a beauty. A stunning, tall, built-like-a-brick-shithouse raven-haired beauty, one of the main attractions for men at Dirk's. At thirty, she owned the bar that she'd inherited from her dad, ran it single-handedly and had a shotgun under the bar that she used to handle anyone who got out of hand, though plenty of the guys acted as unpaid bouncers if some out-of-towners got out of control and didn't understand the rules.

Sandy was another mystery that most people questioned, just not to her. She'd never been married, claimed she'd been in love several times, and that once you got your heart stomped on twice by the same man, you weren't up to having it happen again. And when she gave you the evil look, you knew not to ask questions. So no one did. She never went home with anyone, though many of the guys tried. She just seemed happy to run the bar.

"Looking for some fun tonight, or just killing time?" Sandy asked.

Jolene shrugged, dying to tell Sandy about Walker. But she figured she and Walker needed to come to an understanding before she started blabbing about their relationship.

So she shrugged and grabbed a handful of peanuts. "Keeping my options open, as usual."

"Have fun, honey."

Jolene grabbed her beer. "I intend to."

She swung around and tried to act nonchalant this time, determined not to zero in on Walker right away. But despite her best intentions to remain oblivious to him, her gaze kept drifting in his direction.

He kept his focus on his cards, not on her. In fact, after she'd looked right at him for a full five minutes, she realized he looked up from his cards only to place a bet or respond to something one of the other players said.

He knew she was there, dammit. And he knew where. Yet he ignored her.

Poker face? Maybe. It was important to concentrate when playing poker, and flirting with her across the bar wasn't a good idea when a game was going on. But he could at least acknowledge her presence. This was exactly like he acted on the ranch during the day.

So she waited until he finished his game, left the table and came to the bar to get another beer. And even at that he headed to the opposite end of the bar.

Son of a bitch. Was he blind and in need of glasses so that he could see her?

Enough was enough. She headed down the bar and tapped him on the shoulder.

"I thought maybe you didn't see me."

He turned around, beer in hand, actually looking to see who was around them before he acknowledged her. "I saw you."

That was it? "I saw you"? "Are you planning on ignoring me tonight? I thought we had a date."

He scratched the side of his nose. "I don't recall making a date with you."

"I told you I was going to be here."

"And I said I was coming, too. That doesn't make it a date."

Unbelievable. She pushed aside the ache of rejection in the pit of her stomach and replaced it with a good healthy dose of anger. She laid her beer on the bar. "You know what, Walker? You're absolutely right. We had no plans for tonight. Or any night for that matter. Have a good time."

She walked away, tears blinding her and impeding her progress across the dance floor. She bumped into several people, but she was determined not to stop until she pushed through the front door and out into the parking lot. She dug her keys out of her pocket and opened the truck, slid in and started the engine, tears streaming down her face now.

As she put the truck into gear, she caught sight of Walker coming toward her. She jammed her foot on the gas and burned rubber peeling out of the parking lot, gravel shooting from her back tires as she did.

No way would she let him see how much he'd hurt her in there.

She'd never allow any man to crush her heart.

Though she was afraid it had already happened.

walker stood at the edge of the parking lot and watched the taillights on Jolene's truck disappear down the road.

Asshole. Motherfucking, heartless asshole. His gut had clenched when he saw the tears well up in her eyes, the way her lips turned down, her bottom lip trembling as she tried so hard not to cry in front of him there in the bar.

He'd hurt her. What kind of a son of a bitch did that to a woman he cared about? He was so damn worried about keeping his job that he didn't pay attention to how he was treating Jolene. He hadn't noticed what he was doing . . . or what he was doing to her.

He pulled his hat off and jammed his fingers through his hair, trying to figure out how he was going to fix this. He could climb into his truck and follow her back to the ranch. Talk to her.

But she was angry, and right now talking to her wasn't a good idea.

He'd give her a day—or two—to cool down. Then they'd talk. Besides, if he disappeared right after Jolene, people would notice. They'd talk. And that's what he'd been trying to avoid. Better to let it go right now.

He turned and headed back into the bar, the word "coward" screaming in his head.

Yeah, yeah. He already knew that.

seven

jolene hadn't had any time to dwell on her misery about Walker, because ranch business took front and center. There was cattle to move and calves to process, and those duties required all of them to get busy from dawn to well after night fell, leaving everyone in a state of exhaustion at the end of each day. It had worked out perfectly, because she'd needed to drive herself from sunup to dark to keep thoughts of Walker from entering her mind.

Fortunately Walker had stayed busy with Mason and she hadn't seen him, which helped. And the weather had been prominent on her mind, keeping Walker out of it.

Even worse were the ugly clouds that had begun to form yesterday morning. Jolene knew Oklahoma weather. Mason had checked the forecast and it wasn't good. They were about to enter a rain pattern that was due to last several days, on top of already rain-soaked land and swollen creeks, which meant they needed to get all the cattle moved to the higher pastures. A steady bout of rain would fill all the creeks on the property to overflowing, and the runoff on the hills would be even worse. She wasn't about to lose any of the cattle to flooding.

The first drops had fallen midday the day before, followed by torrential downpours that hadn't quit. The already saturated ground wasn't soaking anything up; runoff had already begun and the ponds filled up fast. They'd ridden out to check the water levels, and decided it was inevitable the creeks were going to overflow. They'd moved as much cattle as they could already.

Now, late afternoon on the second day of nonstop monsoon-like weather, Jolene, Mason and Walker huddled inside the barn and talked strategy.

"Head count looks good. Other than a hundred or so grazing in the outermost portions of the property, we've got most of them moved," Mason said.

Jolene wrinkled her nose. "Problem is we don't know where the remaining ones are. We're going to have to split up in groups, take the vehicles and scan the acreage until we find them, make sure they're safe and not stuck in lower ground where they might drown."

Mason nodded. "Grizz and I will take the south. You and Walker can head east. I've got Gage and Joey tracking north, which leaves Bobby and Ray to the west. Four teams should be able to cover the property and be back before nightfall."

Jolene was going to object to the pairings. The last thing she wanted was to be anywhere alone with Walker. But she had no other reason to object. She could do her job, even if it was with Walker. Right now her relationship with him was the least of her worries. "Pack up survival and overnight gear in your trucks just in case the creek rises and any of you get stuck," she said, mentally plotting the routes they'd take.

Jolene dashed across to the main house, where Lila had already packed up food and drinks for all four crews. Loaded down with waterproof packs, she met everyone back at the barn. Walker had the Jeep backed up to the barn entrance. She tossed her gear in the back, handed off the food and drink packs to the other crews, then climbed into the passenger side of the Jeep and started pulling off her rain gear as Walker pulled away and headed east.

Tension filled the Jeep as soon as they took off. Jolene inhaled and exhaled, forcing her shoulders down. It wasn't going to help the cattle if all she thought about was her anger at the man sitting next to her. She had to focus, and not on Walker.

The rain came down so hard it was difficult to see more than a foot in front of the vehicle, but Walker maneuvered the wet, muddy road with ease. Jolene held on with both hands as they traversed sunken, mud-and-water-filled holes while circumventing rushing water by climbing up and over hills. She'd done this plenty of times before, the unpaved road washing away whenever it rained, creating an off-road course that was nothing short of a wild roller-coaster ride. Her main concern was her cattle and making sure they survived the storm.

While Walker drove, Jolene watched out of all the windows, looking for stray cattle.

"See anything?" he asked after they'd been driving for about half an hour.

The sound of his voice made her stomach knot up. She shook it off and focused out the window. "Nothing yet."

"That's good. They might have made it up to higher ground already."

"Let's hope so." But she knew better. Cattle not with the herd were the stupid ones. They weren't smart enough to head to higher ground and didn't know enough to get out of the way of rushing water.

Jolene loved the stupid ones, damn her soft heart. Someone had to look out for them.

They'd just ridden down into a valley when she spotted them, a large herd of brown blotches in the distance.

"There," she said to Walker, pointing. "At two o'clock."

"Got it." He turned the wheel and headed off road and toward the wayward cows. Once again Jolene had to hold on as they flew over rough terrain, mud splattering the windshield as Walker zeroed in on their cattle.

Walker knew what to do and where to go. Herding cattle was the same no matter if you were on horseback or in a vehicle. The cattle were on low ground, and the creek was rising. They were at risk of being caught amid the rising waters with no way of escaping if Jolene and Walker didn't get them to the higher elevations where they'd be safe.

She threw on her rain gear and rolled down the window, hooping and hollering at the cattle as Walker scared the holy bejeebers out of them with the careening Jeep. At first curious to stare at the approaching vehicle, they ran like hell up the hill—well, as fast as cattle run, anyway—especially when Walker laid on the horn.

"It's working," she said, finally rolling up the window and shaking off the dripping water. She grabbed a towel from the backseat and dried her face and hair, keeping her gaze trained on the cattle, who were more than happy to stay as far away from the Jeep as possible.

"Looks like they're going to be just fine, but we should hang out here to make sure they don't drift back down."

She nodded. "Good idea. I counted eight of them here, so that's a good number of them accounted for." She got on the walkie-talkie and reported their find to the other teams. Mason said they'd found some of the herd, and Gage had found others. All were headed to higher ground.

"Sounds like all are accounted for," Walker said as Jolene slipped the walkie-talkie back into the waterproof bag.

"Yeah. That's a relief, especially since this storm doesn't appear to be letting up anytime soon."

To prove her point, a loud crack of thunder shook the ground under them, followed by an arc of lightning that zipped across the sky, low and threatening. The downpour renewed its efforts.

"Cattle seem to be staying put," Walker said. "I don't like the way the rain is coming down. We should head back."

"Okay."

Walker turned around and headed the way they'd come. It was a good thing he knew the ranch property as well as Jolene did, because the road was completely washed away, leaving rivers of mud in its wake.

And what she feared they'd find when they got to low ground had come true.

Walker stopped the Jeep several feet back from the rushing water where the road had once been. A wall of water at least fifteen feet wide and who knew how deep made passing impossible. Jolene knew as well as Walker that you didn't drive through fast-moving water like that. Not only was the depth unknown and your car could stall, but the raging water could carry a vehicle off or sink it in minutes. And out here in the middle of nowhere, drowning just wasn't on her list of things to do today.

"You know of any other way back?" he asked.

She shook her head. "No. We could head north a bit, but that part of the road is on low ground, too, and the creek runs nearby. We're likely to run into the same thing."

"So we're flooded, and the creek is overflowing, cutting the road off between us and the way back to the main house."

She chewed her bottom lip and pondered various routes back, but all had to cut near the rain-swollen creek, which had obviously broken its banks. "I'm afraid so."

He put the car in reverse, backed up and turned around. "I guess we'll head to the cottage then. It is on higher ground and should be safe."

"Okay."

It looked like they were going to ride it out there, because there was no way they were going to make it back home until the water receded enough to chance driving the Jeep through it.

By the time Walker pulled up in front of the cottage, the rain was torrential. Jolene leaned over the seat and grabbed the food pack, tossed on her rain gear, and ran like hell to the front door, her boots sinking into the ground as she dodged the deeper water holes gouged by the pounding storm.

Walker had already pushed the door open.

"I'm going to secure the Jeep. Be right back," he said.

She nodded, went inside and tossed off her wet gear, then went in search of firewood to heat the place up. The cottage was just a one-room cabin with a bed, kitchenette and a small living room, perfect for anyone who wanted to fish or hunt on the farther side of the property and get an early start, but there was no heat or air-conditioning. And the storm had preceded a cold front. Despite it being spring, with the moisture and cooler air, as well as the stone façade surrounding the building, it was chilly in there. By nightfall it was going to be really cold.

She found the firewood, opened the damper and tossed a few logs into the fireplace, then lit a few pieces of piled up paper to get the fire started. Once that was set up, she took the food pack and laid it on the counter, washed the dusty dishes and laid them out on the rack to dry, and started a pot of coffee on the tiny stove. Next she pulled Walker's and her backpacks near the bathroom—thank God there was a bathroom in the cabin. It was tiny, but there was a toilet and a shower . . . and plumbing, so they at least had hot water.

She tossed up a mental prayer of thanks to Mason for arguing with her uncle Ronald about upgrading the fishing and hunting cottages on the property to include putting in plumbing. Ronald, being the stingy bastard that he was, never wanted to put money into improvements to the ranch. It had taken two years of her and Mason arguing him into a corner before he relented and agreed to the upgrades.

Jolene leaned against the doorway to the bathroom and toed off her boots, then peeled off her soaking wet socks and tossed them on the bathroom floor. She turned on the shower and stripped off her clothes, then stepped under the hot water.

It felt good to warm her chilled body under the steam and heat. She grabbed the bottle of liquid soap, shampooed her hair and rinsed off in a hurry, figuring Walker would want a shower, too, and she didn't want to use up all the warm water in the tiny tank.

When she yanked open the shower curtain to grab a towel, Walker was there.

"Do you mind?"

He smiled. "No."

"Shut the damn door, Walker. It's cold in here."

He did. Behind him.

"Dammit. I meant get out."

Instead, he kicked off his boots and started to undress. Rolling her eyes, Jolene decided to ignore him. She grabbed a towel and pulled the shower door closed so she could dry off.

"Seems ridiculous for you to be shy now, Jolene. I've seen you naked."

And he wasn't going to again. She wrapped the towel around her and tucked the end in between her breasts, then stepped out. "Shower's all yours."

Without bothering to make eye contact, she opened the door to the bathroom and shut it behind her. Within a minute she heard the shower running. It was only then that she exhaled, dropped the towel and rummaged through her bag for dry clothes. She threw on sweatpants and a tank top in a hurry and grabbed a brush to run through her wet hair, then picked up her wet clothes and hung them up to dry.

Coffee was ready, so she poured herself a cup and curled up on the sofa in front of the fireplace. The rain was still coming down hard, thunder rumbling the house with its intensity and lightning putting on a show outside the window. If you put aside the epic danger of flooding and the possibility of spring tornadoes, Mother Nature could sure gift them with beauty in her storms. Which was why she had never understood Valerie and Brea's desire to flee the ranch for life in the city.

Where else could you sit back and see a light show like this? Or lay in your bed at night and feel the earth move under you, have every one of your senses explode with the smell of a spring rain, the sight of grayish green clouds that signaled a storm on the way, the feel of soft growing grass under your feet, or the sound of a newly born calf crying for its mother?

She wouldn't give all that up for all the malls, traffic and city lights in the universe. This was home, had always been and always would be. And she'd never wanted to be anywhere else.

"You look lost in thought."

Thunder cracked so loud outside she hadn't heard Walker come out of the bathroom. Barefoot and shirtless, he wore only jeans, and he'd left them unbuttoned.

Her pulse kicked up a notch and she damned her libido for wanting him even though she was angry with him, even though he'd hurt her.

She sighed.

He went into the kitchen and poured a cup of coffee, then came and took a seat on the cushioned chair across from the sofa. The light from the fire danced against the skin of his chest, making him look like a golden god. Incongruous to that was the darkness on him—his raven hair and goatee, along with his storm-filled eyes that seemed to be able to read her mind, made him look like the devil himself.

His hair was still damp, and it curled a little at the ends. Jolene wanted to touch it, to slide her fingers down the damp locks, to tuck her face between his neck and shoulder and curl herself up against him.

But she wouldn't, couldn't. There was no comfort in Walker's arms. Not the kind she wanted from a man.

It stunned her at that moment to realize she wanted more. She hadn't even known it until it crept up on her during the time she'd spent with Walker. She wanted more. Not just sex, but a real relationship with a man who wanted her, who wanted to be with her outside of the bedroom.

She sighed, because Walker wasn't that man. And she was in love with him. And that just sucked.

"Are you going to give me the silent treatment?"

"What do you want me to say, Walker?"

"You could yell at me for the shitty way I treated you at the bar."

"I could, but what would be the point?"

He lowered his gaze to his coffee, then lifted it to her again. "I'm sorry. I was an ass. I felt bad as soon as you left."

"That was a little too late."

"I know."

"So why did you?"

"I have a problem with you and me being seen publicly as a couple."

That wasn't at all what she'd expected to hear, even if it was the truth. "Why?"

He stretched his legs out, crossing his ankles. "Because you're my boss."

"So?"

"People will talk, Jolene."

Was he serious? "Talk about what?"

"About what I'm doing with the owner of the Bar M. And why."

"And you care?"

"Yeah. I do. I don't want folks to get the wrong idea about us. About me. And about you."

She laughed. "I could care less what people think about me. And you've got it wrong about the folks around here. They're not like that. People mind their own business."

"Some might. A lot don't. Either way, I'm just not comfortable flaunting you and me in front of everyone."

"So that's why you've been meeting me in secret, why you didn't want to . . . at the bar the other night."

He stood and went to the window. "Yeah."

Huh. She got up and went over to him, laid her cheek against his back. His skin was warm and she threaded her arms around him, laying her palm against his chest. "Walker, I'm sorry. I don't know what to do about it. I want to be with you."

He turned around and pulled her against him. "I want to be with you, too. But you have to understand how this makes me feel."

She did, sort of. Men and ego and testosterone and wanting to be equals and all that. She got it. It was unnecessary, but she understood. "I do. I don't agree and I don't think my position and yours make a damn bit of difference in our personal lives. I can keep it separate, and you can keep it separate, and how it appears to others doesn't matter. But I understand how you feel."

He swept his knuckles across her cheek. "I hated hurting you the other night. I'm sorry."

The sincerity in his tone, the direct way he looked at her, as if he was willing to take whatever punishment she gave him, melted her heart. She slid her hand into his hair and pressed her body into his. "Forgiven. Kiss me."

He pulled her against him, his body tense as he pressed his length along hers and lowered his lips to hers.

She'd missed him, missed the brush of his mouth against hers, the taste of him, the way he always seemed so urgent when she was in his arms. It was like he was desperate to touch her, to kiss her. She liked being wanted like that.

His hands roamed over her back, lifting her thin cotton top so he could put his hands on her skin. The fire had warmed the chill in the room, but she was heating from the inside out. His touch seared her, scorched her, made her melt inside and her toes curl. She inched closer against him and splayed her hands across the naked skin of his back. He was on fire, too, his skin warm to the touch. She slipped her fingers into the waistband of his jeans and he groaned against her lips, put his hand on her butt to draw her against the hard ridge of his erection.

She reached between them, needing to feel him in her hand. She slid his zipper down and pushed on his jeans and they fell to the floor. He stepped back, kicked his jeans away, his erection jutting up and making her ache to feel him pounding inside her.

She pulled off her tank top and tossed it on top of his jeans, then pushed her sweats to the floor, too. They stood in front of the window staring at each other.

Lightning shot across the sky, casting light across Walker's face, showing the strain on his features as he looked down at her.

He kneeled in front of her and slid his hands up her thighs, then cupped her buttocks to draw her closer. She took a couple steps, holding onto the back of the sofa for support.

Walker tilted his head back and looked up at her. "Spread your legs."

She widened her stance, surprised to feel her legs shaking. Anticipation? Nervousness? She wasn't sure. She shouldn't be nervous. This wasn't the first time they'd been together, so it had to be excitement, waiting for his touch, his mouth on her. She'd missed these moments with him. After waiting for him for so long, she couldn't get enough of him.

She tilted her pelvis out and he smiled as he leaned in and flicked his tongue over her, barely touching her clit. She trembled, watching as he circled the bud, then pressed his tongue against her sex. She gasped at the contact, so hot, so perfect.

Jolene held tight to the sofa as Walker buried his face against her, licking the length of her, making her quiver as shocks of pleasure shot throughout her pussy and clit. He knew just what she liked, just where to put his tongue. He could take her from zero to oh-God-I'm-coming so damn fast he made her head spin and her legs go out from under her. Standing became an issue as the strokes of his tongue relentlessly lashed her pussy. She was close . . . so close . . .

And then her orgasm hit, hot and wet, a waterfall of lush pleasure. Lightning arced outside and the power of it shuddered through her as she climaxed with wild abandon. No one was around for miles and this time she didn't have to hold back. She could scream out her pleasure as Walker held tight to her and licked every drop from her.

Walker stood and pulled her against him, his hot shaft sliding between her legs and reawakening her desire as he kissed her, his hands tunneling into her hair to hold her head while he plundered her mouth with the same savage intensity as the storm's frenzy outside.

He flipped her around and pushed her toward the window. "Bend over."

She did, smiling as she planted her hands on the waist-high windowsill.

He pressed a kiss to the small of her back, then ran his tongue over the spot where her tattoo was.

"I like this."

She shivered, heard him tear the condom packet, and then he was behind her, his cock easing inside her. She tilted her head back and settled into the sweet sensation of Walker filling her, her body breaking out in goose bumps all over as if this was a monumental thing.

Every time with him was a monumental thing. It had never been like this with anyone else.

He pulled out, then thrust in again, this time a little harder. The hairs on the back of her neck stood up as lightning lit the room. She felt as charged as the electricity surging around them, and backed up against Walker's shaft, impaling herself on the rigid steel that gave her such pleasure.

She gripped the windowsill. "More. Harder."

He powered inside her again, holding onto her hips as he thrust and withdrew again and again, dragging his cockhead along her sensitive tissues. More goose bumps broke out along her skin as she was both chilled and heated from the force of Walker's lovemaking. Oh, the things the man could do to her.

He bent over, his lips caressing her ear as he whispered to her, "Your pussy is like hot silk, Jolene, squeezing me every time I fuck hard inside you. You like it like that?"

"Yes," she said, panting as he rolled his hips against her ass, wrapping his arm around her and lifting her upright. Now he was powering up and into her while his hands roamed over her breasts, teasing her nipples until sensation shot right to her core, only adding to the delicious shots of pleasure that threatened to topple her in a heap.

Outside, the storm raged on, just like the one battering at her from inside her body, beating at her to come, to scream, to reach the edge and go flying over. But she held back, waiting for Walker. She wasn't going without him.

But as each thrust of his cock brought her closer, she wanted more. She reached down and worked her fingers across her swollen clit.

"Oh, yeah," Walker said behind her, taking her breast in his hand and sliding his thumb over one nipple. "Make yourself come, Jolene. I wanna feel you go off when I'm inside you."

She slid her fingers along the bud, each time feeling her pussy tighten around Walker's cock.

"I'm close, Walker. Come with me."

"I will. You come and I'll shoot right inside you." He had both breasts in his hands now, using his thumb and forefinger to roll over her nipples. The combination of pleasure and delicious pain was more than she could take. She quickened the movements of her hand over her clit, and shattered, coming as hard as the torrential downpour outside.

"Walker" was all she could manage as her orgasm blinded her. She gripped his arms and held on while he thrust her off her feet, impaling her on his cock as he came shuddering against her, bending her over and wrapping his arms around her while they both rode out their climaxes.

Panting and sweating, Walker lifted her into his arms and carried her into the bathroom. After they cleaned up, they found their clothes, dressed and snuggled together on the sofa.

The rain had begun to let up, now only a shadow of the fierce storm it had been earlier.

Jolene snuggled against Walker's chest and listened to the sound of his heartbeat, realizing how comfortable she could be with him. It wasn't even necessary that they talk. Just being with him was enough. And when she wasn't with him, she wanted to be.

Like recently. Just a few days apart and she'd missed him. Despite her hurt and anger, she'd still craved his touch, being near him. She'd even missed working side by side with him.

And yes, the sex was phenomenal, but it had become more than that.

Much more.

Because she felt him deep in her heart, a place she'd never let a man in before.

She didn't exactly know what she was going to do about that, because of all the men she'd ever known before, Walker had the most potential to hurt her.

The question was, could she take the chance of allowing that to happen?

A part of her still wondered about him, if he was being completely honest with her about his reasons for treating her the way he did, for not wanting anyone to know about the two of them. Walker didn't seem to be the kind of guy to worry over his job, or to be concerned about who held what station, or whether she was the boss and he was a hand. Those kinds of dynamics didn't matter in ranching, to her, to anyone for that matter.

There had to be something else he wasn't telling her.

But what?

Some deep, dark secret? If it was, he didn't trust her enough to tell her about it.

Could she give her heart completely to someone who didn't trust her with his?

eight

"maybe the problem is that walker only sees you as the big boss, the owner of the Bar M, a coworker. Maybe he doesn't see you as a woman."

Jolene cocked her head to the side and stared at Valerie. "Huh?"

Brea nodded, studying her. "I see what she's saying. Look at you, Jo."

Jolene looked down at her jeans, her workboots, and held out her arms. Plain blue work shirt, same thing she wore every damn day. "What's wrong with what I'm wearing?"

Valerie sighed and shook her head. They were sitting in Jolene's bedroom talking about the annual town picnic tomorrow, and Jolene had filled them in about her concerns with Walker.

"The problem is you look like every other cowboy Walker works with."

Jolene rolled her eyes. "So?"

"So he can't separate the work you from the woman you because they're one and the same." Valerie pointed to her. "That's all he sees. Ever."

"Trust me. Walker knows what's underneath these clothes. He's seen me naked. We've had sex."

"Too much information, little sister," Brea said, holding her hand out, palm facing Jolene. "Don't need to hear about your sex life."

"Then I don't get it. How does what I wear have anything to do with Walker's problem?"

Valerie opened the door to Jolene's closet. In it were blue jeans, work shirts and some tank tops, and a few skirts and dresses she rarely wore.

Jolene put her hands on her hips. "So?"

"So maybe he'd stop thinking of you as the boss of the Bar M—*his* boss—if you'd stop looking like it all the damn time." Valerie closed the closet door. "What were you planning to wear to the picnic?"

Jolene shrugged. "Jeans and a tank top. My boots."

Valerie rolled her eyes. "See? That's exactly what I'm talking about. Tomorrow is a perfect time to let your hair down, literally. Get a manicure and pedicure. Wear sandals. A dress."

"I get pedicures in town on occasion. Manicures are wasted on me since I work with my hands all day. And a dress?" Jolene wrinkled her nose. "Can't win the potato sack race in a dress."

"Then don't enter the potato sack race this year. Gah, Jolene, how old are you anyway?"

"Hey, I like that race." So did all the kids. And she loved running it with the kids, dammit.

Brea laughed. "This year maybe you could win a man instead."

Jolene sighed and flopped onto her bed, twining her fingers together and pulling her hands behind her head. "You might have a point. He's never seen me in anything but jeans and boots. It might be fun to . . . dress up for him."

But did she even know how to wear a dress? She only did that for special occasions. It wasn't required for ranchers, and that included her.

Brea's eyes twinkled and her grin was a mile wide. "Trust me, there's nothing a man likes more than a woman wearing a dress. The things you can do in a dress . . . the things a man can do to you when you're wearing a dress . . ."

Jolene shot Brea a look. "Now who's giving too much information?"

Brea shrugged and continued to smile like the getting-sex-all-the-damn-time, contented, happy woman she was.

Jolene stared into her closet, wrinkling her nose as she scanned the skimpy choice of skirts and dresses she had available. "Okay. So who's got a picnic-type dress to loan me?"

"Oh no," Valerie said, hopping to her feet. "We're going into town today. You're getting a manicure and a pedicure, and a spray tan to cover up the farmer's tan lines you've got. And then we're going shopping."

"I've got too many things to do today."

"You can afford to take a day off. Tell Mason to assign whatever it is you have to do to someone else," Brea said, sliding off the bed and dragging Jolene with her. "You're spending the day with your sisters."

by noon the next day, jolene was sitting in the SUV with Mason, Valerie, Gage and Brea, her heart lodged firmly in her throat.

Her body was tan—all over. That was an experience she didn't care to repeat anytime soon. Standing near naked in a booth while someone sprayed you with cold . . . stuff. The things women did in the name of beauty were beyond her. But she had to admit the end result was excellent.

She'd loved the manicure and pedicure, though, had enjoyed sitting in the salon and relaxing with her sisters, being pampered while someone buffed and polished her nails. She now sported a pretty pink color on her fingernails and toenails, and even had a white flower painted on each of her big toes. Very cute.

And with a begrudging nod to her sisters, she had to admit the dress was comfortable enough. The last color in the world she ever thought she'd wear was pink.

Yet here she was, decked out with pink toenails and pink fingernails. A pale pink dress with yellow flowers hugged her upper body from the bust to her waist, then billowed out past her hips so it swirled around her when she twirled. And okay, she might have twirled when she saw herself in the mirror. And Valerie insisted she buy sandals that had a little bit of a heel on them, even though Jolene figured she'd fall on her ass as soon as she tried to walk in them. But they looked cute with the dress, so what the hell. If she fell, she'd be the first to laugh at herself.

Her sisters were equally as beautiful. Valerie wore a red sundress that crisscrossed in the back and showed off her slender figure, and Brea looked stunning in a copper-colored dress that made her auburn hair sparkle like it was on fire. Gage couldn't take his eyes off her. It was a good thing Jolene had sat in the back with them to keep her eye on them, or the way the two of them were gaping at each other there might have been some action going on back there.

They'd made potato salad and pies for the town picnic. Okay, Lila had done most of the pie baking, but she'd allowed Valerie, Brea and Jolene to take over the kitchen to make potato salad.

Jolene liked having her sisters back. She loved Lila, couldn't have survived all those years after her mom died without Lila's loving support. She was as close to a mother as Jolene could remember having.

But there was something about having her sisters around, sharing secrets, getting close to them again, that made her heart clench. She hadn't realized until they came back how much she'd missed them. How much she needed them. How lonely and empty her life had been without them.

Tears sprang up and she blinked in rapid succession. Valerie would kill her if she smeared the makeup she'd insisted Jolene wear.

"Are you crying?" Brea reached over and slid her hand in Jolene's.

"No."

Valerie turned around and looked over the front seat. "Jolene. There are tears in your eyes. What's wrong?"

Dammit. She looked to Valerie, then Brea. "I was just thinking how awesome it is to have both of you here. I hadn't realized how much I needed you both until you came back."

There was a dead silence for several seconds, then a lot of sniffling.

"Well, goddamn," Mason said, shaking his head. "Pass around the Kleenex box."

"No one told me it was going to get all hormonal in here," Gage said. "I'd have taken the truck."

Brea elbowed him and laughed, then sniffed and grabbed a tissue. "Shut up." She leaned over and put her arm around Jolene. "I missed you. And Valerie. I didn't realize how much I needed the two of you, either, until I came back to the ranch."

Valerie dabbed her eyes. "Ditto. I love both of you and can't imagine my life anywhere but with my family."

"I'm going to pull over and let all three of you out to walk the rest of the way if you don't knock it off," Mason said, shaking his head.

Gage made a mocking sniffle. "Now I might cry, too."

Jolene laughed then. "Okay, sorry. Waterworks over."

They pulled onto one of the side streets and found a place to park near the main street. It was still early, but the lines of traffic were already starting to get longer as people from all the neighboring ranches and surrounding towns filed in. Food, carnival rides and games abounded as the main street in town was closed off for the annual picnic. Booths were set up from various vendors offering food and craft items, rides had been brought in for the daring and those with strong stomachs, and there'd be entertainment on one of the stages set up at the end of the street. Clowns wandered in and out of the throng, making up balloon animals for the kids.

"I'm heading for the beer tent," Mason said as soon as they reached the main street.

"I'm with you," Gage said.

Valerie rolled her eyes. "I'll meet you there as soon as we drop off the food."

Jolene laughed. "I'll take it. You go on ahead."

"You sure?"

She nodded and grabbed the bags containing the pies and potato salad. The food table was only a block away, so she got there in no time at all, dropped off the food and stopped to talk to one of the neighboring ranch owners' wives who was in charge of setting out the food.

Melinda Carson was well into her sixties, and still fit and trim from all the time she spent working the ranch. No doubt her three grandchildren under the age of five and running circles around her accounted for burning a lot of calories, too.

"Is Bob here?"

Melinda nodded. "Beer tent."

Jolene laughed. "I think that's where all the guys are hiding."

"At least until the band fires up. Hopefully the men will have enough beer in them by then to want to take us out for a twirl to the music."

"Mmm, let's hope so." She'd like to dance with Walker tonight. In front of the whole town. Make their relationship public, finally.

She finished her conversation with Melinda and started down the street to the beer tent, waylaid a few times by vendors hawking their wares. Jolene was a sucker for crafts, couldn't resist looking at the jewelry, artwork, pottery and everything else on display. By the time she found the beer tent, nearly an hour had passed and the place was packed. After the big rain, the heat had rolled in, leaving the weather less humid and hot as blazes. No wonder the beer tent was such a popular place.

Jolene found her family and sat at the table. Mason passed a beer to her.

"Did you get lost?"

She shook her head. "Vendor booths."

"Oooh, find anything good?" Brea asked.

"Lots. Too many things. I'm going back later to gawk."

"I'll go with you."

"Me, too. I can never resist the pottery booth. It's my weakness," Valerie said.

Jolene sipped her beer, visited with her sisters and couldn't help but look around for Walker. He'd promised her he'd be here. She wondered if he'd ignore her like the last time they'd been together in public. She hoped not. It would be the final straw if he did. She wouldn't go through that again.

The band started up, so everyone headed outside to listen to the music, a few couples getting out in front of the grandstand to start dancing. Gage and Brea and Valerie and Mason got up to dance, while Jolene watched them twirl around, laughing at the guys' attempts at two-stepping.

"Care to dance?"

Her head shot up, expecting to see Walker standing there. It was Larry, one of the cowboys from a neighboring ranch.

She was about to say no, but since she hadn't yet spotted Walker, she figured dancing was better than looking like a wallflower, so she smiled up at Larry and offered her hand. "Sure."

walker headed into the beer tent to search out Jolene, but didn't see her in there.

The whole town seemed to be crowded into the narrow main street, making it feel even hotter and more humid than the midafternoon heat bearing down on the cement walkway as he made his way out of the tent and toward where the band played. People crowded the street in front of the band, couples dancing and twirling to a fast country rock beat. He scanned the people, looking for Jolene, but didn't see her, so he moved off and searched the tables set in front of the dance floor, thinking he'd find her there, but he didn't.

The song ended so he stopped while people moved past him. Only then did he spot Mason and Gage along with Valerie and Brea, talking and laughing with another couple. It took him a few seconds to register the gorgeous blonde in the pink dress, her arm linked with a tall cowboy he didn't recognize.

That gorgeous blonde was Jolene.

He couldn't recall ever seeing her dressed like that. He sucked in a breath, gut-punched as she turned around and lifted her head, smiling up at the cowboy.

Her hair spilled over her shoulders like soft waving wheat. She was tan from her face to her legs. And wow, those legs, peeking out under that pretty pink dress, all the way down to her slender ankles and painted toenails. The dress billowed in the slight breeze as she turned to greet another tall, dark and irritating cowboy Walker didn't know, who swept her onto the dance floor as the band started up again.

Wasn't *she* popular? Put the owner of the Bar M in a dress and suddenly every prick within a hundred miles notices she's a woman. He'd damn well noticed long before she put on a party dress. He'd noticed her in jeans, work boots and a long-sleeved shirt, with her hair hanging in a braid down her back, covered up with a cowboy hat. He'd noticed her covered up to her neck in dirt and smelling like cow shit. He'd noticed her when she was cussing like any of the men, when she was sweating and stank and when she was unpleasant. Not cleaned up and beautiful like she was now, looking like the sweetest thing this side of the Red River. Sure, she looked gorgeous today, but to him, she looked just as beautiful knee-deep in mud, too.

Where the hell were those guys when she was straining to hold a screaming calf, when she was branding and tagging and roping and doing all the things he admired so much about her? Those guys weren't around. They hadn't noticed Jolene then.

But Walker had. Though he had to admit she sure cleaned up good. And whether in blue jeans or a pretty pink dress, that was *his* woman those guys were passing around on the dance floor.

And he didn't like it one damn bit. The problem was, he couldn't do anything about it. Not without letting the whole town know how he felt about her. And that would stir up a hornets' nest he wasn't interested in messing with. It had taken years for him to even be able to show his face in town without the accusatory stares. He wasn't going down that road again with Jolene, no matter how much he loved her.

Today just wasn't a good day to go public. Too many people around who knew his history.

But he'd be letting Jolene down. Again. He didn't want to hurt her, but if she found out the truth about him, if word got out that he was seeing her, she'd be hurt anyway.

No-win situation.

Shit.

He stopped off at the beer tent and bought a bottle, then headed down to the park to think.

an hour had passed and jolene's head was spinning. She'd danced so much with guys from the neighboring ranches, her feet were killing her, and she had no idea why she was suddenly so popular.

"Put you in a dress and suddenly all the men from a hundred miles figure out you have breasts and legs," Brea said with a wry smile.

"Uh huh. How come they couldn't figure out I was a woman before?"

Valerie slid into the chair on the other side of Jolene. "Some are dumber than others. And some like their women to actually look like women."

Jolene took a long swallow of her bottled water. "And some noticed I was a woman no matter what I was wearing."

"Walker, you mean," Valerie said.

"Yes. Who I haven't seen yet."

"Saw him headed west about a half hour ago," Mason said, carefully balancing a plate overloaded with barbecued ribs, potato salad and corn on the cob.

Jolene turned to Mason. "He was here?"

"Yeah. I spotted him watching everyone dance. Then he took off. Not sure why he didn't come over when he saw us."

Jolene had a pretty good idea. She scooted her chair back and stood. "I'll be back."

West, Mason had said. The park was west of the main street. Other than that, there wasn't anything but more streets with businesses, then the residential areas, a school and the church. She decided to try the park.

Normally on a hot Saturday afternoon the park would be filled with parents toting their kids to the playground and having picnics under the dense canopy of trees. Rusty redwood tables were haphazardly spread throughout the lush green hills there. It was at one of the empty tables she found Walker, staring out at a small lake where geese paddled along the still waters.

He turned and smiled as she approached and sat next to him. "Kind of quiet here," she said.

He nodded and stared off at the lake. "I like it quiet."

"Why didn't you come and find me?"

"I did find you. You were busy."

She snorted. "Yeah, put a dress on me and suddenly half the guys in the county start noticing. Dickheads."

He turned his head her way. "Looked to me like you were enjoying it."

"Just passing the time until you got here. What I enjoy is a man who noticed me before I put on a dress." She reached for his hand, twined her fingers with his.

"You look beautiful."

It was funny, but lots of guys had told her that today. It hadn't meant a thing to her until she'd heard it from Walker. Butterflies danced happily around in her stomach. "Thank you."

He leaned over and brushed his lips across hers, a kiss demanding nothing, but giving her so much.

She squeezed his hand. "Let's go dance."

He pulled on her hand. "I think I'll sit this one out."

She settled herself back on the bench. "Walker, how long is this going to go on?"

He tipped his hat back and leaned against the tabletop of the bench, stretching out his legs. "You'd be better off not being seen with me today, Jolene."

"So you keep telling me. What you don't tell me is why. I'd like to know what you think is so terrible about yourself that might sully my so-called pristine image."

"Your image is fine. I don't want to tarnish it."

"Spit it out, Walker. We've been dancing around this too long. It's time to spill."

He blew out a breath. "Before I started working for the Bar M, I was a hand at the Double S Ranch."

"Sam Woodman's ranch?"

Walker nodded.

"That's one of the biggest ranches in all the counties around here. They hire on hands that never want to leave. Why did you?"

"I didn't. I was fired."

"Because . . .?"

"Celia Woodman decided she was in love with me. And she wouldn't take no for an answer."

Jolene crossed her arms. "Celia Woodman is a slut."

"She was sixteen years old at the time."

"Ah." Things were starting to fall into place, but Jolene kept her mouth shut so Walker could talk.

"I didn't want to have anything to do with her, and I told her that, nicely at first, then firmly. Then I point-blank had to tell her to back the hell off."

"But she didn't."

"She didn't. One night she climbed into my bed naked, in the middle of the night, woke me up out of a sound sleep. Scared the shit out of me, too. She said she was in love with me and wanted me to be her first."

Jolene snorted. "She'd probably had her first when she was twelve."

"Well, I don't know about that. All I know is that I scrambled out of bed and climbed into my jeans in a hurry. Then I told her to get dressed and get out. But she wouldn't. She held tight to the sheet, mustered up some tears, said she loved me and wanted to marry me."

Jolene shook her head, angry as hell at how Walker had been manipulated by that scheming bitch.

"I told her I liked her just fine, but I was too old for her and I wasn't going to have sex with her. So she started to cry. And cry even harder, and louder. And then her father walked in."

"Oh, shit."

"Yeah. And Celia's entire personality changed. She started wailing, said I'd been after her for months, that I seduced her. Woodman fired me on the spot, said I was trying to seduce his daughter so I could sleep my way into a better position at the ranch."

"That conniving little heifer. And Sam Woodman is a blind moron when it comes to Celia. He always has been."

"No matter how much I tried to tell the truth, no one believed me. Word got out and everyone took Woodman's side. By then Celia was telling everyone how I tried to take her innocence and how her daddy protected her from a moneygrubbing opportunist. No ranch would hire me on until Mason did."

Jolene shifted to face Walker, sliding her fingers along the nape of his neck. "None of this is your fault. How could you possibly defend yourself against a devious slut like Celia and a blind-to-her-faults father like Sam Woodman?"

Walker shrugged. "Wasn't much I could do about it. It was their word against mine. And no one was inclined to take my word as truth."

"I do. I believe you. You're not the type to seduce a young girl. And believe *me*, I know Celia. She has never been innocent. Which is why she has the reputation she has now, five years later. So apparently she hasn't managed to snag some unsuspecting cowboy into marrying her."

"It doesn't matter. I still have the reputation. And I won't ruin yours by having you associate with me. People will think I'm with you to get my hands on Bar M land."

Jolene laughed. "Do you think I care what people think? If they're that small-minded, then they're no friends of mine." She stood and held out her hand. "Come on."

He looked up at her, his gaze narrowing. "Jolene."

"Don't argue with me. We're going to dance. I want to show you off. It's time we stopped hiding."

"I'm fine with seeing you in private."

"I'm not. I'm in love with you, Walker. And it's high time people knew it."

nine

jolene clamped her lips shut as soon as she'd said the words. But now they were out there, and she couldn't take them back.

Walker stared up at her, his head cocked to the side as if he were trying to understand her, as if she were speaking a foreign language.

"Yes. I said it. I love you. No big deal." She tugged on his hand. "Now let's go dance."

He stood, but instead of following her onto the walk, he pulled her against him, wrapped his arms around her, threaded his hand through her hair, and kissed her deeply, soundly, and with more depth and feeling than she'd ever been kissed by him before. Her toes curled in the ridiculous kitten heels her sisters had insisted she buy. She wanted to lift one foot up like she'd seen in movies when the girl was being kissed by the man of her dreams. She wanted to swoon.

He pulled away, his eyes darkening to a stormy gray. "I love you, too, Jolene. Which is why I don't want to hurt you."

Oh, God. He loved her. She melted into the grass, just sank against him, never wanting to move again. "You couldn't possibly hurt me unless you left me. Now let's go dance and ignore everyone."

He didn't look convinced, but took her hand and they walked toward the main street. Despite the magnitude of the crowd, they managed to find Valerie and Brea and the guys, and grabbed something to eat and drink. When the band started up again after their break, Jolene stood.

"Ready to go kick up your heels?"

Walker arched a brow. "I'm game if you are."

She grabbed his hand and pulled him into the middle of the crowd, laughing as she realized that he was a damn good dancer. He two-stepped her around the outside of the circle of dancers and then managed to pick up one of the line dances easily enough. Her guy had some serious rhythm, which didn't surprise her at all considering his rhythm in the bedroom.

And when the band played a slow song, being in Walker's arms and swaying to the music was her every dream come true. She laid her head on his shoulder and realized her life couldn't get any more perfect than this moment.

Except Celia Woodman was on the dance floor with some random cowboy and shooting daggers her way. Jolene just smiled at her.

Too bad, honey. This cowboy's mine, all mine. She tilted her head back and slid her hand behind Walker's head, pulling his lips to hers for a kiss.

Celia could take that and choke on it. The bitch deserved so much more for the hell she'd put Walker through.

But it wasn't just Celia staring daggers at Jolene and Walker. Sam Woodman stood at the edge of the crowd, his arms crossed and a murderous expression on his face, all directed at Walker. A few of his buddies stood next to him, all neighboring ranch owners, their gazes riveted on Jolene's man.

So it appeared Sam Woodman still held a grudge. Unfortunately, Walker seemed to notice it, too.

He looked down at her. "Sorry. I warned you about this."

"I'm not a sixteen-year-old brainless twit, either. I'm a grown woman who knows exactly what she wants and what she's doing. I want you, Walker. Ignore them."

"They could make this hard on you."

She laughed. "They can't do anything to me. I'll see who I want to see. And their evil stares don't hurt me. They shouldn't hurt you, either."

He spun her around until she was dizzy and laughing. "They don't have any kind of impact on me, honey. But I'll be damned if I let anyone hurt you."

"I can take care of myself, Walker. I've been doing it a long time. But it's nice to know you have my back."

He pulled her against him and whispered in her ear. "I'd do anything to keep you safe, Jolene."

walker wished he felt at ease about things. sure, he'd talked things over with Jolene, and she understood and believed him. He didn't know why it had taken him so long to come clean with her. Maybe because he'd handled the whole thing with Celia so badly all those years ago. He should have gone to her father when she'd first started sniffing around, to make it clear he wasn't trying to climb up the ladder by climbing on Woodman's daughter. But Walker hadn't wanted to do anything to jeopardize his job, and he figured telling the boss his young daughter was hitting on him would be handing himself his own termination notice.

In the end he'd gotten fired anyway. He could have saved himself a lot of trouble if he had quit, but dammit, he hadn't wanted some . . . child . . . to bully him out of a job he liked.

And now, years later, his mistakes still haunted him. The Woodmans still haunted him. He didn't trust Sam Woodman to be content just to glare at him. The man still believed his daughter was innocent and that Walker had been the one to corrupt her. And he never believed Walker had paid for that supposed crime.

Fine with him, as long as Woodman kept his animosity directed at Walker and left Jolene out of it.

Walker searched the beer tent and spotted Jolene crowded around a table with her sisters. Gossiping, no doubt. She was pointing at Celia Woodman, and Valerie and Brea's eyes widened. Obviously Jolene was filling in her sisters on what Walker had told her, which he didn't mind at all. There was strength in numbers, and if Celia decided to do something stupid and Walker wasn't around to protect Jolene, Valerie and Brea would back her up.

"You have a lot of nerve showing your face in this town."

Walker turned around to face Sam Woodman. Sam was a formidable presence despite being forty years or so older than Walker. He was built like an oak tree, with ruddy skin and salt-and-pepper hair that peeked out of his very expensive Stetson. "Sam."

"You should have left this state five years ago. I could have had you arrested for statutory rape."

"I never touched Celia."

"So you say. My daughter says otherwise."

"Your daughter lied."

Sam's cheeks puffed out. "You think you bested me by getting a job at the Bar M. And now you've taken up with young Jolene, no doubt doing the same thing to her that you tried to do to my Celia. You're trying to grab hold of prime ranch land by seducing Jolene. But I won't let you do it, Walker. I won't let you ruin another young girl."

"Jolene is old enough to make her own choices, and I think you need to mind your own goddamn business, Woodman. Stay out of my life. And leave Jolene alone. That's the only warning you're going to get from me."

Woodman grabbed his arm. "Don't threaten me, Walker. You get out of this town and get out now, or I'll make Jolene and all the McMasters pay for hiring you. I wield considerable influence in the cattle industry. And I have enough pull to make it hard for her to do her business around here."

"Don't make threats you can't back up, Woodman. And don't ever threaten the McMasters family again."

Walker jerked his arm free and stormed away before he did something stupid like punch Woodman in the face. He took a few deep breaths to calm his anger, then found Jolene and the others, determined to enjoy the rest of the night.

But he was worried. Sam Woodman was right about one thing— he did wield a lot of power in the cattle ranching industry. He could make it difficult for Jolene and the ranch. That's the one thing Walker had feared the most, and the last thing he wanted to happen. Jolene wasn't going to suffer because of him.

jolene waited for walker to bring the truck down to the entrance at Main Street since he'd told her he'd parked a long way off. Normally she'd have walked with him, but these damn heels were killing her feet, so she gave in and let him bring the truck around.

Brea, Valerie and the guys had already gone home, and the streets were practically empty. The only people left were the cleanup crews pulling tablecloths off and picking up trash, plus the band, who were loading up their gear in the back of their van.

Jolene grinned that they'd all closed the party down. She'd had a great time, finally able to take Walker out publicly. They'd danced and mingled, and no one at all seemed to care, just as she'd thought.

No one but Sam and Celia Woodman, and Jolene didn't give a damn what they thought, anyway.

"Young lady, we need to have a talk."

She turned around. Speak of the devil. "Evening, Sam."

"Miss Jolene." He tipped his finger to his hat. "I feel I need to warn you about Walker Morgan."

She sighed. "Sam, I know all about Walker and Celia. There's nothing you need to tell me."

Sam's chin lifted. "He lied to you. He tried to rape my daughter when she was barely sixteen years old and a virgin."

Jolene crossed her arms. "If that's the case, why didn't you press charges?"

"Celia didn't want to. A public trial would have damaged her reputation more than his."

Jolene resisted the snort that wanted to escape. Celia had a reputation all right. A reputation for fucking every human male with a willing penis, and it had been going on a long damn time, since before Walker. But if Sam was determined to turn a blind eye to the fact that his daughter was a whoring tramp, Jolene wasn't going to say a word. "Look, Sam, I think you need to let this go."

"I think you need to smarten up."

"Is that a threat?"

"It might be. I don't want Walker Morgan in any county in this state, and I don't want him thinking he can gain a ranch by sleeping with ranch owners or their daughters. I thought you were smarter."

"I'm plenty smart enough to know when I have a good man at my side. Walker's a good man. Let this go, Sam."

"I will not. You're the one making the mistake. And if I have to make business . . . difficult . . . for you to get you to see the light, then that's what I'll do."

She'd tried to be nice and conversational with him, but now he was threatening more than the man she loved. He was threatening her way of life. "You don't want to take me on, Sam. Not like this. You'll lose."

Walker pulled up and got out of the truck, came to her side. "Is there a problem?"

Jolene leaned against him. "Nothing I can't handle."

"Think about what I said, Jolene. Good night." Sam tipped his hat again and walked away.

Jolene pivoted and got into the truck. Walker slid into the other side. She forced her breathing down to normal, but it was difficult when all she wanted to do was rant about what a sanctimonious bastard Sam Woodman was. And so incredibly blind to his daughter's faults, it was pathetic.

"What was that about?"

"Nothing."

"Jolene."

"Oh, fine. He said he could make things difficult for the ranch and for me if I didn't dump you."

Walker gripped the steering wheel, his knuckles whitening. "That son of a bitch. I'll kill him."

"No, you won't. And you won't treat me like I'm some simple-minded idiot who can't take care of herself. Because you know better."

He shifted his glance to her for a second, and she read the fury on his face. "I dragged you into this. I told you it was going to get ugly."

"And I told you that I loved you and I could take it. So you need to quit worrying about me."

He slid his knuckles across her cheek. "I can't quit worrying about you. I love you. And I won't let Sam Woodman hurt your family. Not because of me."

all that night jolene thought about what walker had said. There was something in the way he'd said those words on the drive back to the ranch that had a sense of foreboding. And he hadn't come into the house with her, hadn't stayed with her last night. Jolene tossed and turned, worried about Walker, unable to sleep, finally dragging herself from bed as dawn lifted over the horizon, orange rays slipping through the opening in her drapes. Giving up on sleep, she crept downstairs and turned on the coffeepot.

She'd done nothing but ponder the dilemma of Walker and that asshole Sam Woodman. The fact that he had threatened her and the ranch was ludicrous. She had just as much power in the community as he did, so his threats were worthless.

"You look like you just lost your best friend."

"You're up early, Mason."

He went over to the coffeepot, pulled down two cups from the cupboard and poured coffee, then grabbed a chair and handed her a cup.

"Want to check the new calves this morning."

"I'll get dressed and go with you."

"Don't bother. Won't take me long. So what's wrong?"

"Nothing." She took a couple sips of coffee, hoping it would banish the dark thoughts.

"I've known you too long to buy that. Tell me what's going on. Is it Walker?"

"Indirectly. Sam Woodman."

"He's a dick."

She laughed. "Yeah, he is."

"What did he do?"

She told him the story of Walker's past.

"I heard about that."

"But you hired Walker anyway."

"I knew Celia was a liar. Some of the guys on the ranch had already been trading stories about her for a couple years. That girl had been a wild child for a long time. So I didn't believe her story of being innocent and seduced. She was always the aggressor. Walker was just in the wrong place at the wrong time."

"Good for you. I'm glad you hired him."

"So is that all?"

"No. Woodman isn't happy about Walker and me. He's threatening to interfere with the Bar M's business if I don't stop seeing Walker."

Mason smirked and leaned back in the chair. "Is that right? And he thinks he has the power to do that?"

"He seems to think so."

"He's wrong. I think I'll make a visit to some of our friends today, and we'll put a stop to Woodman's extortion. I imagine most won't take kindly to those sorts of threats against you."

"I was planning on doing that myself, but if you feel the need, be my guest."

"I'd be more than happy to. The man's been interfering in all our businesses for way too long, and trying to get himself to the top rung of the local Cattlemen's Association. I don't trust him and I'd like to see him taken down a peg."

"Then go for it. I think he's a snake, and anyone who tries to take us down is in for a rude awakening."

"You said it, sister."

Valerie leaned against the door, her arms folded, anger knitting her brows together despite her half-asleep state. She went to the coffeepot and grabbed a cupful, then pulled up a chair. "I heard some of it as I was coming in. Fill me in on the rest."

"Me, too," Brea said with a yawn as she padded into the kitchen and went straight for the coffee. "Someone messing with our baby sister?"

Mason got up and gave a kiss to Valerie. Then he turned to Jolene. "I'll go get my day started, so I can make those visits we talked about. You fill in your sisters."

"Okay. And Mason? Thanks."

He nodded. "That's what family is all about. We fight the battles together."

Jolene grinned, warmed to her toes to have the people she loved around her.

Valerie squeezed her hand. "Okay, so what has that asshole Woodman done now?"

by the next day it was clear that woodman didn't have a leg to stand on. No one in the ranch community was going to support him other than a couple of his close friends, and they didn't have the power to wield. Woodman might have one of the bigger ranches in the territory, but the Bar M nearly equaled his in size. Couple that with ten other ranchers and their buying power, and Woodman was outnumbered. He could blow smoke as much as he wanted, but he was on his way out the door.

Mason had also talked to a few hands at neighboring ranches who had amassed some very compromising photographs of one Celia Woodman, all taken with Celia's knowledge and permission. Mason didn't want to play that trump card unless it was necessary, but he personally went to talk to Woodman and let him know just what he had in his possession and that if Woodman didn't back down and shut the hell up, those pictures might start making the rounds. Mason made it clear that Woodman had started this game, but the Bar M family was going to finish it.

Jolene threw her arms around Mason and kissed him on the cheek.

"I don't care for anyone who thinks blackmail's an option," Mason said. "I hated playing that card with the pictures, but you should have seen Woodman's face. And Celia's, because she was listening in around the corner."

Valerie grinned and slid her arm around Mason. "My hero."

Mason shrugged. "He's messing with one of my best hands. In fact, I'm going to make him assistant foreman, if I can find him."

Jolene frowned. Come to think of it, she hadn't seen Walker all day yesterday, or yet today. She assumed Mason had kept him busy. "I thought maybe you had things for him to do."

Mason shook his head. "Haven't seen him since the party in town."

Dread drilled holes in her stomach. "I'll go check the bunkhouse. Maybe he's sick."

She hurried down to the bunkhouse and knocked on the door. The rest of the hands were all at work, so she expected it to be empty. She opened the door and went in search of Walker, hoping she wouldn't find him slumped unconscious somewhere.

He wasn't there. All his things were there, but his truck was gone. That dread turned to panic and she ran back to the house.

"He's gone."

Mason frowned. "What do you mean he's gone?"

"I mean he's gone. His truck isn't there either."

"You talking about Walker?"

Jolene pivoted to face Lila. "Yes. Do you know where he is?"

"No, honey, I don't. But I have an envelope. He left it for you yesterday. It slipped my mind and I forgot to give it to you."

Jolene took the envelope and tore it open, hurriedly reading Walker's note.

Jolene,

I'm sorry, but it isn't going to work this way. Everyone will talk and assume the worst about you because of me. I can't let that happen.

I love you,
Walker

She stared at the note, tears filling her eyes.

"He left. He just left. He was in such a hurry he didn't even bother to pack. I can't believe he did this."

She crumpled up the note and tossed it in the nearby trash can. "That son of a bitch. After everything we've done for him, all we went through. He went yellow belly and snuck out like a scared dog. He couldn't stick it out for me."

Valerie put her arm around her. "Honey, I'm sure he loves you."

Jolene's gaze shot to her sister's. "Does he? When you love someone, you endure. Even when things are bad you put up with it, because the good times are worth it. As soon as it got bad, he took off. That's not love. His words are empty. They mean nothing."

Valerie squeezed her shoulders, but Jolene shrugged her hands off. "I need to be alone."

She pushed through the front door and went to the barn, saddled up Paradise and rode her hard, probably harder than she should have, but she wasn't thinking straight. She only knew she needed the wind in her face and had to get away from everyone who would feel sorry for her.

She'd made such a stupid mistake, had chosen the wrong man. She'd thought Walker was strong, that he would stand by her side through thick and thin, through the worst of it. But as soon as the wind blew rough, he'd crumbled.

He wasn't the man for her. She was a lousy judge of character.

She knew nothing about love. She'd spent years brazenly going after the wrong man.

ten

it was almost dark by the time jolene finished brushing and feeding Paradise. She'd ridden out to the west pasture and worked cattle with Joey and the other guys, losing herself in mindless tasks that were so familiar she didn't have to think about them, anything to keep her mind off Walker.

It had worked. She was exhausted, filthy and ready to take a shower and go to bed, where hopefully she could fall immediately to sleep.

She came in through the back door and into the kitchen, knowing she'd missed supper, but she didn't care. She wasn't hungry anyway. She grabbed a can of pop, opened it and drank it down, letting the icy cold liquid cool her parched throat. She hung her hat on a hook and swept her hair out of her grit-covered face, then headed out of the kitchen into the hall.

Walker was standing there. Her heart slammed against her chest, every nerve ending in her body zinging to life, along with a mix of emotions, from elation to utter fury.

"What are you doing here?"

"I need to talk to you."

She walked past him and up the stairs. "I'm going to take a shower."

"I'm not leaving, Jolene. I'll be standing right here when you get back."

"Stand away. After I take my shower, I'm going to bed."

As she headed up the stairs, she refused to look back to see if he was still standing there. She shut the door to her room, leaning against it to catch her breath.

Why had he come back? What did he want? His note said he had to leave, so what was there left to say? She'd been aching ever since he left. He had no right to play with her heart this way.

Screw him. She was angry and she didn't want to talk to him. She stripped off her clothes and took a long, hot shower, scrubbing the day's dirt off her body and out of her hair. When she finished, she dried her hair and slid on shorts and a tank top, then crawled onto the bed and stared out her window at the night sky.

The door opened, and Valerie walked in and flipped on the light.

Jolene blinked and covered her eyes. "Do you mind?"

"You're acting like a child. Go downstairs and talk to him."

She crossed her arms. "I don't have anything to say to him."

"Too bad. He has something to say to you. Now get your ass down there or I'm sending him up."

She blew out a breath of disgust. "Fine."

Walker was still in the same spot she'd left him, standing in the hall. Only he wasn't alone. Lila, Valerie, Mason, Brea and Gage were there with him. Jolene balanced on the last step of the stairs, not sure she wanted to go any farther.

"Jolene, I need to talk to you."

"You had plenty of time to talk to me yesterday. Instead, you left."

"I know, but I left for a reason. That's what I came back to talk to you about."

"Okay, so talk."

"I didn't want anyone on the ranch here, on any ranch around, or in town, thinking I only wanted you because I wanted the Bar M."

"No one thinks that."

"Some people do. And I didn't want that getting in the way of what was really between us."

"So you left. Once again you couldn't face the gossip about us, so you ran."

He scratched his nose and had the nerve to smile. "No, it's not like that."

"Then tell me what it is like, because it sure looks to me like you were a coward and don't care enough about me to stand up to the gossips."

Again, that smirk. She curled her hands into fists, ready to take him down as she moved off the steps.

"I left because I wanted to do things right by you. It's not right to ask a woman to marry you until you have your own land."

She stopped. "What?"

"I didn't want anyone to think I was after you for a piece of the McMasters land. So I bought my own."

She tilted her head to the side and frowned, her mind filled with talk of land and . . . Did he say marriage? "What are you talking about?"

He moved toward her, took her hand and led her into the family room, put her in one of the chairs and knelt next to her. She noticed that everyone else followed, took a seat and leaned forward like they were all watching a climactic scene in a movie.

"Walker, you don't have your own land."

"I do now. I bought the Reynolds property."

"Doodie and Rachelle Reynolds, the property that juts down along ours?"

"Yeah." He smiled and smoothed his thumb over her hand. "They've been wanting to retire and move to Florida to be near their son and their daughter-in-law and the grandkids and have been talking for a while about unloading the land."

Jolene's gaze shot to Mason. "Why didn't I know about this? I've wanted that land forever. It's perfect for us. We could have bought it."

Mason just shrugged, and smiled.

"If you marry me, it's the same damn thing as it being McMasters land," Walker said. "It'll be our land. Where we can build our own place."

"Our . . . Did you just ask me to marry you?"

"Twice, actually, but you don't seem to be following me."

She shuddered, unable to believe all this. "You bought land. For us."

"Yes."

"How?"

"Nothing to spend my money on, until now. I've been saving for a long time and I had plenty. We can't all live in this house. It's getting too crowded. Besides, you're loud. I want a place far away from everyone else so we can have some privacy."

Mason snorted, Gage laughed out loud, and Valerie and Brea snickered. Lila just coughed.

"Walker!" Jolene blushed to the roots of her hair.

"So does that mean you say yes?"

"Yes. Hell yes, I'll marry you. Now, if you all don't mind, I'd like to continue this conversation in private." She stood, grabbed Walker's hand and headed out the front door, grinning at the sounds of claps, laughs and hollers from her family.

After shutting the door behind them, Walker pulled her into his arms and kissed her until any residual anger she might have felt melted. But she wasn't angry anymore, not after knowing why he'd left. It was the sweetest surprise. Unnecessary, but she understood why he'd done it. And she liked the thought of having their own place, quiet and far removed from the craziness that was her family, yet still close enough if she needed them. When they pulled apart, she slid her palm against the rough beard of his jaw.

"You did all that. For me."

"For us. To shut up the gossips."

"Oh, I don't think there will be any gossiping."

At his questioning look, she filled him in on what had transpired with Woodman.

He laughed. "I'll have to thank Mason for that."

"We're family. We take care of each other. And you're part of this family now. Now, let's take a ride and see our new land."

They climbed into the truck and took a ride to where the Mc-Masters property ended and the Reynolds property began. It was just a fence line, but to Jolene, it represented something signifi-cant—a new beginning.

"Our land," she said as they climbed out of the truck and sat on the hood, looking out over the fields.

"A new start." Walker turned to her, bracketing her waist. "How about we toast that new start by climbing the fence and making love in the field on our new land?"

She laughed. "Since the Reynolds' house is about three miles from here, I'd say that's a fine idea."

Once they were over the fence, it didn't take long for clothes to go flying. They didn't even get everything off. Jolene was in a hurry to wrap her fingers around Walker's already hard cock. He pushed her up against the fence pole and lifted her onto his shaft.

She was ready for him. Even being away from him for a day was too long. Wet and pulsing with need, she accepted him inside her, quivering with anticipation. His mouth found hers, and he kissed her with the same kind of desperate longing coursing through her.

He slid his hand under her shirt, found her breasts and fondled her nipples, making her arch her back, craving more of the touch that set her on fire. She rocked against him, then reached down to rub her clit, needing that climax that would bond them together.

It was fast, furious, a coupling borne of passion and a deep love Jolene hadn't been looking for, but had found with Walker. He slipped his hands under her butt and lifted her, driving her onto his cock and pushing deeper inside her. She held on to his shoulders and rode him, grinding against him until she felt the pulses she couldn't hold back.

"I'm going to come," she said, staring into his stormy eyes, wanting him to come with her.

He did, pumping into her with hard thrusts that sent her sailing over the edge with a groan. She kissed him as they climaxed, both of them ending up trembling and shaky and laughing as they nearly fell over.

Later, they got dressed and made their way back over the fence, then lay on the truck and watched the stars overhead.

Jolene couldn't remember ever feeling so contented. A few months ago she was fighting her uncle, fighting to get her sisters here, and chasing after a man who paid no attention to her—or so she thought.

Now her family was here to stay, and so was Walker. Maybe going after what you really wanted wasn't such a bad idea.

She flipped over onto her belly and kissed Walker. "I love you. Stay with me forever."

He tapped her nose with his finger and kissed her back. "I love you, too. And I'm not goin' anywhere. Not without you."